In the Beginning

In the Beginning:

First Novels in Mystery Series

edited by

Mary Jean DeMarr

Bowling Green State University Popular Press
Bowling Green, OH 43403

Copyright © 1995 by Bowling Green State University Popular Press

Cover design and art by Dumm Art

Library of Congress Cataloging-in-Publication Data

In the beginning : first novels in mystery series / edited by Mary Jean
    DeMarr.
        p.   cm.
    ISBN 0-87972-673-3. -- ISBN 0-87972-674-1 (pbk.)
    1. Detective and mystery stories, English--History and criticism.
2. Detective and mystery stories, American--History and criticism.
3. Detective and mystery stories--Authorship. 4. Series
(Publications) 5. Openings (Rhetoric) I. DeMarr, Mary Jean, date.
PR830.D4I5   1995   94-23676
823'.087209--dc20   CIP

Contents

Preface

The appeal of mystery series is indisputable. Series of novels proliferate in several popular genres (science fiction and the Western, for two obvious examples), but mystery series can surely claim primacy—chronologically as well as in popularity. Poe's Dupin, appearing in three stories, serves as a precursor to the detectives examined in this collection, as does Doyle's later Sherlock Holmes. Other nineteenth-century writers, such as Anna Katharine Greene, created detective protagonists who continue from story to story—or novel to novel—and they established a form (or a group of forms) which continues to exercise a powerful appeal over a large reading public. In the traditional puzzle story, invented by such writers as Poe and Doyle, an artificial and unbelievable plot and flat characters combine to create an intricate intellectual challenge without any very obvious link to the reality most readers know. But from that central form, a variety of subgenres have developed, so that now readers may select a series because of interests or predilections of various sorts: for gritty realism in the hardboiled novel, for detailed accuracy of investigative work in the police procedural, for comic social commentary in many of the softboiled inheritors of the traditional mystery, to mention only a few. This collection of essays about the beginnings of mystery series, while it makes no claim to represent all subgenres, comments on a variety of twentieth-century series types.

Series appeal for a number of reasons, not least the comfortable familiarity they offer their readers. This familiarity relates to a number of aspects of the novels. Characters continue from novel to novel, sometimes growing and changing but always offering a known center of interest. Tone may be sardonic and harsh in such writers as Hammett, Chandler, and Parker, or comic or even parodic in Crispin and Babson. Readers' choices are also governed by kind of plotting, ranging from the puzzles of Christie, Carr, and Ellery Queen to the plodding police procedural work of Ed McBain or Dell Shannon and the predictably violent, even brutal, action in such varied writers as Mickey Spillane and Dick Francis. Social commentary, whether seriously or comedically presented, in writers as different as Dorothy

L. Sayers, Charlotte MacLeod, and Joan Hess, also strengthens the appeal of some series. Individual readers find those authors and series which particularly appeal to their tastes and then happily collect the books or wait eagerly for the publication of each new offering.

The idea for this collection of essays about the beginnings of a number of well-known mystery series grew from a session at the Popular Culture Association meeting in Louisville, March 18-21, 1992. The four papers in that session, "Detective Fiction: The First in a Series," generated so much interest and discussion that the idea for a collection was born. Those four original essays, now revised and included here, were Paula M. Woods on "Determining the First and Last Campion Novels," Frederick Isaac on "Rex Stout's *Fer-de-Lance*," MaryKay Mahoney on "Ngaio Marsh's Roderick Alleyn," and Mary P. Freier on "Nicholas Blake." All the contributors to this volume are active members of the Popular Culture Association's Mystery and Detective Fiction Caucus, and most were at that initiating session.

The subjects of the essays are varied and include series of disparate types set in differing times, established and classic authors in addition to less well known or highly regarded writers. Nevertheless, no attempt has been made to achieve full coverage of all important authors or to represent proportionally the various subgenres within the field of mystery series.

The essays represented here, however, do make a number of interesting cross connections and develop a variety of significant points about the relationships between the originating novels of series and the books that follow as well as about the nature of series mystery fiction in general. In fact, the essays create a kind of overview of the history of the genre, with many interesting comments on influences between and among authors examined here. Particularly useful in this regard is the brief history of the genre in Fred Isaac's essay on Rex Stout.

Important also are comments that help readers to correct misconceptions about important authors or about the nature of the genre: Marty S. Knepper's consideration of misreadings of that most important mother of the genre, Agatha Christie, and George N. Dove's analysis of the lack of realism in Ed McBain's police procedural series are noteworthy here. Change and continuity in series fiction is discussed in all of these essays, but particularly significantly in Kathleen Gregory Klein's consideration of Dorothy L.

Sayers and in William Reynolds's analysis of Colin Dexter—the opening and closing essays of this chronologically arranged collection. George N. Dove's remarks on McBain's failed attempts at the creation of a conglomerate protagonist are significant for an understanding of the police procedural as a subgenre. On the other hand, Joan Kotker indicates how P.D. James's development from the cozies with which she began to a greater realism of content parallels historical changes in the field. Several writers consider questions relating to the definition of what actually is the beginning of a particular series, grappling with problems relating to the establishment of formulas—or, less pejoratively, patterns—in crime fiction; Paula M. Woods on Marjorie Allingham, Mary P. Freier on Nicholas Blake, and Sharon Russell on Brett Halliday discuss these matters. For many series writers, the passage of time within and between novels is a matter of some significance; both George N. Dove (Ed McBain) and Lois Marchino (on the Amanda Cross novels) consider these problems. Social criticism, as exemplified by the shattering of social stereotypes, is discussed by Don Wall (on James McClure's racial themes) and Landon Burnes (on Joseph Hansen and his homosexual detective). The attentive reader will discover other cross connections between the essays and additional issues of importance discussed here.

In discussions of mysteries, the question of whether endings should be revealed creates passionate disagreement. The authors of these essays have tried to take a middle course: endings are not revealed unless discussing them is necessary in order to analyze thematic or structural aspects of the novels under discussion. But the reader should be aware that in several cases, the solutions to crime plots are given away.

As editor I must express my gratitude to Pat Browne of the Popular Press for seeing the possibilities of this topic and for her encouragement while the collection was taking shape. Two essential unsung heroes have been Mary Ann Duncan and Mona Dean, my frequent consultants, advisors, and assistants in the generation of copy and its editing. Without them, my task would have been very difficult; their help made it a pleasure.

Dorothy L. Sayers:
From First to Last

Kathleen Gregory Klein

Dorothy L. Sayers's twelve detective novels and several volumes of short stories span and define the two decades (1921-39) known as the Golden Age of Detective Fiction. With her carefully plotted and wittily written works, she joined such notable women writers as Agatha Christie, Ngaio Marsh, Margery Allingham, and Josephine Tey in shifting popular reading habits from the sensational crime story or the "infallible sleuth with his cut-and-dried clues and his cast-iron deductions" to novels of intelligence and perceptiveness (Sayers qtd. in Reynolds 10). The clearest indication of her talent in the genre is her continuing popularity. Not only were almost half a million copies of the novels reprinted between 1939 and 1943 by Victor Gollancz despite paper rationing (Hitchman 118) but, in *Murderess Ink*, published more than twenty years after her death and forty years after the appearance of the last Wimsey novel, Sayers was rated first in popularity of the women mystery writers among readers polled. And her popularity continues unabated. As Carolyn Heilbrun (an excellent scholar and writer of detective novels herself) assesses the novels: "they give pleasure and . . . beneath their glittering surface they question the society they portray" ("Biography" 13).

For readers, the great pleasure in a detective fiction series is to watch the play of the familiar—characters, settings, by-play, problems—with the new—crimes, criminals, characters, and opportunities. Sayers provides lavishly for readers on both counts, devoting her fictional output to Lord Peter Wimsey, aristocrat and detective, in all but one novel and a handful of short stories. In assessing the series, from first to last, it is possible to trace three kinds of changes: character development of the protagonist, thematic development, and structural changes that hold political implications. Most readers and critics, following the lead of Sayers herself, have focused on the first of these; and, indeed, the character of Peter is the dominant

5

strain of the series. Although initial readers of *Whose Body?* had no idea a series would follow, Lord Peter Wimsey as he appears in this first novel seems too good a character to waste on a single volume.

Looking back, not altogether innocently, on her output, Dorothy L. Sayers wrote in the essay "Gaudy Night" about her most famous creation and his development: ". . . any character that remains static except for a repertory of tricks and attitudes is bound to become a monstrous weariness to his maker in the course of nine or ten volumes" (210). As is now well known to Sayers's fans, she decided after *Strong Poison* either to kill off her detective or to alter him; choosing the latter, she proceeded:

If the story was to go on, Peter had got to become a complete human being, with a past and a future, with a consistent family and social history, with a complicated psychology and even the rudiments of a religious outlook. And all this would have to be squared somehow or other with such random attributes as I had bestowed upon him over a series of years in accordance with the requirements of various detective plots. (211)

And she did: ". . . so I laid him out firmly on the operating table and chipped away at his internal mechanism through three longish books" (211).

Critics have been quick to follow Sayers's lead in focusing their attention in the series on Peter's development as a character; and they have posed any number of questions. First, where did he come from; on whom was he modeled? How was the "silly ass about town" of *Whose Body?* brought to life? The most rigorous examination of Lord Peter's fictional antecedents has been undertaken by Barbara Reynolds (with help from Sayers herself). In 1956, Sayers responded to Reynolds's query about Philip Trent as a model for Peter Wimsey: "Yes . . . but with a touch of Bertie Wooster as well" (2). And, in a speech draft later uncovered, Sayers expands on the importance of *Trent's Last Case*, published in 1912:

I suppose everybody has at least heard of *Trent's Last Case*. It holds a very special place in the history of detective fiction. . . . It shook the little world of the mystery novel like a revolution, and nothing was ever quite the same again. Every detective writer of today owes something consciously or unconsciously, to its liberating and inspiring influences. (qtd. in Reynolds 3)

Bentley's inspiration was, according to Sayers, "liberating . . . from the infallible sleuth, with his cut-and-dried clues and his cast-iron deductions, [who] plodded mechanically along the train, always wearisome and always right . . ." (qtd. in Reynolds 10). Of course, neither Trent nor Wimsey was always right; Reynolds concludes, "Lord Peter's style and method as a detective are strikingly similar to Philip Trent's and echoes of Bentley's novel are to be found throughout the Wimsey series" (11, 15). They begin early, with the opening lines, right down to the exclamation points: "Hullo be blowed!" (*Trent's Last Case*), "Oh damn!" (*Whose Body?*). And, of course quoting lavishly, each character succeeds in marrying the initially unattainable woman that he loves.

Beginning with Sayers's comments that "Peter . . . is an eighteenth-century Whig gentleman . . ." Elaine Bander makes a case for Samuel Richardson's Sir Charles Grandison as Lord Peter's fictional model. And Nancy Tischler suggests that Lord Peter's literary parallels might include reference to Tristam Shandy (37). A.S. Byatt considers Baroness Orczy's Scarlet Pimpernell an ancestor of Lord Peter (235). Catherine Kenney puts forward Roland and Lancelot, in memory of Sayers's medieval training, and reminds us that Harriet pointedly calls Peter "Mr. Rochester" with nineteenth-century echoes (95-96). And Janet Hitchman's suggestion for Peter's model is not literary but a television character called Adam Adamant. She continues somewhat patronizingly, "And yet, and yet, with all his horrid perfections one cannot help being drawn to the man" (76). Sayers's subsequent remarks give pause to such intense speculation: "I do not, as a matter of fact, remember inventing Lord Peter at all. My impression is that I was writing a detective story, and that he walked in, complete with spats, and applied in an airy don't-care-if-I-get-it way for the job of hero" (qtd. in Hone 42).[1] But this over-simplification does not begin to encompass even the incompletely developed Peter of *Whose Body?*

In looking for ways to describe this confident character, critics have ranged from adulation to severe reservations. David Coomes has argued that Wimsey was "no Wexford, Morse or Dalgliesh; he was not given to introspective agonizing, nor did he see criminals or criminal activity in anything other than black and white terms" (8). But Heilbrun argues in favor of "the moral complexity that Wimsey insure[s]" ("Biography" 9). Nancy Tischler describes the earlier characterization of Lord Peter in some detail:

8 In the Beginning

In most of the early stories, Lord Peter is a comic figure, as pretentious as an Oscar Wilde man-about-town, as irreverent as a Noel Coward *bon vivant*. He seems far too frivolous to care about the human tragedy that is invariably antecedent to his entrance into the murder investigation, and takes an amoral interest in the puzzle of detection. Here we see, briefly, a person who views a body as comic, a murder as a conundrum, and detection as a fox hunt. . . . Lord Peter quickly changes into a moral and deeply emotional being. But it is clear that he was originally conceived as a suitable hero for a modern mock-epic—or perhaps more correctly, for a travesty in which human pain is trivialized by the detached intellect. (35)

Other critics argued for the positive change in his character that occurs through the series. Alzina Stone Dale concludes that "no one can seriously say that the Lord Peter of *Whose Body?* is the same complicated person who takes the stage in *Gaudy Night* and *Busman's Honeymoon*" (xvi). Sharing her conclusion, Ralph Hones notes: "As each new novel came out, Lord Peter's own history was augmented and embellished. He gradually become [sic] less foppish, less of a caricature, more clearly descended, more correctly endowed" (43). And Sayers's official biographer, James Brabazon, adds a specific contrast: "The description of him playing Scarlatti in *Whose Body?* is a piece of rather perfunctory character colouring. . . . But when in *Gaudy Night* he takes Harriet to hear the Bach Double Violin Concerto in a concert at Balliol, we are in a different world" (124).

Because Sayers's own assessment of *Whose Body?* is harsh—"conventional to the last degree, and no more like a novel than I to Hercules"("Gaudy Night" 208)—it is worth quoting Nancy Tischler's revisionist remarks at length:

Sayers keeps her audience at the point of barely suppressed laughter through much of the book with her mockery of the stale devices of detection and discovery.

This she blends with a subtle double vision, suggesting that the subject is not really funny, that the game is indeed deadly serious. Lord Peter admits to his friend Parker that he does enjoy the art of unraveling puzzles but not the necessary result of fixing on the criminals. He tends to enjoy the game only so long as he does not know either the villains or the victims. With sympathy and understanding come involvement and anguish; his disengaged mask drops off and his nerves explode. . . .

The novel reflects Peter's growing awareness of serious harm and of his own obligations. Though the book opens with the flippancy of an Oscar Wilde comedy, full of urbane wit, double entendres, and roguish unorthodoxy, we soon discover that Lord Peter is no decadent nihilist. Although his clothing may occasionally appear to be straight out of the mauve decade, his morality does not. His attention to superficial taste and appearance covers a deeper and finer taste and conscience. His frivolous manner masks a painful war experience and feeling heart.

The comedy disappears entirely in the climactic scene, when Lord Peter looks in the eye of the murderer and sees there his willingness to repeat his crime. This man is no harmless fox to be hunted down for sport and released in the spirit of fair play. Crime is no game.

This is the recognition one might expect from an author who would later write feelingly of Satan and of hell. She does not take evil lightly. (41)

And yet one asks if this is wishful thinking or retroactive reading. The novel's genesis is altogether more profane than sacred. In a newspaper interview, Sayers reports that the basic plot of *Whose Body?* grew out of an Oxford coffee party game in which those present developed an increasingly improbable story, each adding a new element. The naked man found in a bathtub wearing a pince-nez—the victim of this first novel—was one such elaborate plot element added, according to Hitchman, by Sayers herself.

But, just on the verge of being bored with her leading man, Sayers changes him; through major surgery she creates a new-old Peter Wimsey. Margaret Hannay follows both Sayers and other critics in attributing Peter's changes to Harriet's presence: "Lord Peter Wimsey rather cheerfully complies with these requirements [to eliminate the love interest from detective fiction] until introduced to Harriet Vane in *Strong Poison*; from that point on, he gradually develops a human face behind his monocle" (36). *Strong Poison* leads inexorably to *Gaudy Night*, the real "last" novel in Sayers's Lord Peter Wimsey canon.[2] The Peter Wimsey of *Whose Body?* is finally and completely dismissed from service.

Gaudy Night was immediately popular; the first printing of 17,000 copies was sold out before the November 4, 1935, publication date, and before the end of the year, five more printings were issued (Hone 76). Melvyn Burns calls *Gaudy Night* "a classic . . . [t]he University setting is skillfully portrayed, and the detective puzzle succeeds admirably in spite of the absence of corpses," unlike Julian

Symons who chooses his worst insult: "*Gaudy Night* is essentially a 'woman's novel' full of the most tedious pseudo-serious chat between the characters that goes on for page after page" (129). And Janet Hitchman critiques *Gaudy Night*—"her worst": "was she exercising that integrity [of the mind] to use the format of a detective novel to preach a sermon?" (97). Hitchman's horror is revealed in her exclamation point: "There is not even a corpse!" (86).

Not everyone is bothered by that absence: Coomes describes the opening of *Gaudy Night* this way: "in this book Harriet takes centre stage: she doesn't require Wimsey until page 265—to be fair, there isn't a murder in *Gaudy Night*—and, when he does appear, gone is the silly ass who, we are told, was merely the affectation of a man who had to make himself believable to the criminal classes; all along he was really a serious scholar with a stunning mind, a sensitive soul" (115). In the discussions about how this change occurs, Margaret Hannay's most interesting contribution centers around her identification of Harriet's function as a Jamesean *ficelle*, "allowing Peter to reveal both his crushing sense of responsibility for getting people hanged and his many personal weaknesses" (40). "By her skillful use of Harriet's perspective [in *Gaudy Night*] Sayers lulls the readers into thinking there is good reason for *them* not to have seen this side of Peter before. The truth is, of course, that these weaknesses did not exist before this novel, but they have been skillfully projected back into the past" (Hannay 48). Because of these revealing episodes, Sayers can say that "even in the five years or so that she had known him, Harriet had seen him strip off his protections, layer by layer, till there was uncommonly little left but the naked truth" (304), and make the reader share the feeling that Peter's emotions have been revealed rather than created in this book. The postscript added by Paul Delgardie, Peter's maternal uncle, also justifies Peter's apparent shallowness in the early novels and gives the impression that his complex personality has been revealed as the demands of the case (or the novel) required.

The developments in Peter's character have clearly fascinated both critics and fans, testifying once again to the power of a series detective in attracting and retaining readers' attention. But Sayers's novels were more than simply vehicles for Peter and detection. Gradually, critics have noted, they expanded to undertake serious subjects. In an earlier article, I summarized the shift from first to last this way: "Gradually, themes, social issues and characters demand more space than the puzzle-oriented, more traditional form would have allowed; the later novels interweave these elements with the restitution of social order which tracing the criminals can provide" (10).

The first four novels (*Whose Body?*, *Clouds of Witness*, *Unnatural Death*, *The Unpleasantness at the Bellona Club*), most of the short stories and *Five Red Herrings* represent the earlier style; *The Nine Tailors*, *Gaudy Night*, and—although not as successful— *Murder Must Advertise* represent Sayers's successes in the latter form. While from the beginning the theme of the importance of work is present, it changes configuration in the later works. Throughout the series, the criminals are doubly villainous in Sayers's eyes: first, they commit murder (or other crimes) and, secondly, they betray their work—their own proper job—in the process. The latter would have been as unacceptable to Sayers as the former. But in the later novels Sayers also restores the value of work; in the three later novels named above, "it is not simply the infallible detective's careful investigation of the physical evidence or even his esoteric and improbable knowledge about the murderer's work which makes him successful. His resolutions of the crime and the resumption of social order are a direct result of Wimsey's working knowledge and real respect for the killer's craft" (Klein 34). In this same vein, David Coomes cites P.D. James on Sayers's unifying theme of "the almost sacramental importance of man's creative activity" (9).

Continuing the exploration of thematic issues in the series, R.B. Reaves comments on the consistent attention to both punishment and crime in the series:

a chronological examination of her works reveals both a recurring treatment and an evolving attitude toward the subject. It is unlikely that Sayers began her career as a detective novelist with the preconceived design of an exhaustive and elaborate exploration of the subject. But the fact that the problem is raised in novel after novel clearly suggests that the issue interested her; as she matured as an artist her treatment of it becomes more varied and subtle (1). Sayers finally suggests that the rule of law requires of Christians, and perhaps ideally of everyone, that human sympathy, human compassion, be extended to the guilty as well as to the innocent victims of crime. (13)

The changes in Lord Peter are also connected by R.D. and Barbara Stock with other shifts in the novels:

the agents of evil, beginning with *Five Red Herrings*, have become commonplace (but not necessarily more sympathetic), while Lord Peter, beginning with *Strong Poison*, grows less flamboyant and overwrought. But though the changes in Peter commence with *Strong Poison*, they are not much developed in the intervening novels, and emerge convincingly only in *Busman's Honeymoon*. Of all these later books, *Murder Must Advertise* most superbly exemplifies this newer pattern. (19)

And Sayers herself supports these critical investigations, believing that each successive book brought her closer to her original intentions.

However, after only four of the eventual eleven novels in the Wimsey series and a collection of short stories, Sayers unexpectedly abandoned her aristocratic sleuth and his entourage for not only a new cast of characters but also a different style of writing. Brabazon suggests that experimentation and a search for variety led her: "Throughout her novel-writing career, Dorothy was forever searching for variations of style and approach, and she must have welcomed the epistolary novel as a vehicle for one of her great skills" (129). Whatever the reason, *The Documents in the Case* was an important diversion for Sayers. Catherine Kenney counts it among the most significant: it "seems the pivotal text in Sayers's development as a novelist. In it, she tries a new narrative method, the epistolary form used by Collins in *The Moonstone* and by other major English novelists from the earliest days of fiction-writing in the eighteenth century. . . [the] novel also makes a substantial leap into serious, sustained social criticism" (48).

Kenney's comparison with *The Moonstone* is an important one because in the battle for supremacy in detective fiction, Arthur Conan Doyle with his Sherlock Holmes stories and insistently linear style of narration clearly triumphed over Wilkie Collins and his more diffuse narrative form. Although the character of Wimsey is more humanized than that of Holmes, Sayers's first four novels clearly follow the narrative orientation of Conan Doyle. With *Documents*, she struck out in a new direction.

Told exclusively from first-person point of view, the narration in *The Documents in the Case* lacks both the limited omniscience and clever evasion that would have resulted from a detached narrator. In exchange, it provides several different perspectives of the same event, each clearly told with bias and some degree of ignorance. Not even the combined views of the letter writers, contradicting one another as they do, can present the reader with a full and accurate description of events. Nevertheless, they are jointly revealing. Although events may be garbled and objective truth about them undiscovered, character and personality are continually revealed by both content and style of the letters. In this form, no one letter writer controls the novel. Although this narrative restructuring did not appear again until *Gaudy Night, Documents* provides both the clue and the continuity to that series-climax novel.

And, so, we come to *Gaudy Night* itself, a novel equally hated and loved. In her early appreciation of Sayers, Carolyn Heilbrun suggests the importance of Sayers as a literary figure can be found in the stature of her more vehement critics, Q.D. Leavis, Edmund Wilson, and W.H. Auden ("Sayers" 454-55). Leavis's virulence (like that she spewed at Virginia Woolf) is clearly something other than literary critique:

Sayers displays knowingness about literature without any sensitiveness to it or any feeling for quality—i.e., she has an academic literary taste over and above having no general taste at all . . . evidently Miss Sayers' spiritual nature, like Harriet Vane's, depends for its repose, refreshment and sustenance on the academic world, the ideal conception that is of our older universities—or let us say a rationalized nostalgia for her student days. (qtd. in Coomes 117)

A.S. Byatt calls Leavis's rage both unattractive and pretentious, a refusal to understand the novel's popularity among faculty. But Byatt is no apologist for Sayers: "Dorothy Sayers has been cut down to size quite efficiently—university teachers are much more likely to sneer at Lord Peter Wimsey's sexual prowess, *noblesse oblige* and cricket than to confess to a *tendresse* for his milieu" (244). But the range of university professors represented only in the bibliography to this essay raises no affirmation to Byatt's claim. Writing of Sayers's continuing relevance, Kenney notes, "the educated, professional woman is now more the norm than the striking exception. By addressing one of the important concerns of this century—the tentative emergence of women into all areas of society—in the timeless terms of realistic human psychology, Sayers created a classic novel" (106). Such a range of social and cultural issues would have been not only unthinkable but also unworkable in the construction of Sayers's first novel.

B.J. Rahn calls Sayers the first writer to use detective fiction to address important feminist issues, to try to change rigid attitudes toward sexual roles, using "the full panoply of literary techniques" to do it (51). Of what does this feminism consist and how is it important? For Susan Leonardi, *Gaudy Night* "asserts the naturalness of a highly unnatural—that is educated, civilized, cultivated, and women-ridden world" (82). And Heilbrun describes *Gaudy Night*'s "portrayal of a female community and a moral universe" as offering women readers new opportunities (3). But she also acknowledges that in addition to comfort and love, Harriet Vane also brought Peter Wimsey "eventually (alas) willing subordination" ("Biography" 9). In Nina Auerbach's view, the success of *Gaudy Night* as a feminist text is undercut by *Busman's Honeymoon*: "these strong women [of Shrewsbury College] recede rather shamefacedly out of the action to be replaced, in *Busman's Honeymoon* (1937), by the self-congratulatory, cloying idyll of Lord Peter's marriage to Harriet Vane. As so often happens in cultural history, the war that seems to infuse women's solidarity with vigor and purpose leads in the end to renewed, more stringent confinement within home and its attendant mythology. Caught between the dominions of love and war, the vision of self-governing Shrewsbury fades away" (165). In short, *Gaudy Night* may be an anomaly, a one-off, Sayers's moment of combining all the best possibilities for detective fiction, for Oxford, for women, and—maybe—for herself.

The feminism can be found first in the community of women, "[a] women's college, one of the few places where women are not perforce regarded simply in reference to men. . ." (Kenney 165). The novel, despite its continuing references to women apparently perverted by not being mated to men and its continually wrestling with the question of Harriet Vane's marriage, works from within the community of women to validate women's communality. It rejects stereotyping, knowing one's place, making someone else—usually a man or a child—one's work, or giving up by giving in. "The Shrewsbury community also represents the reality of individual women living happily work-filled, unmated lives" (Kenney 165). Although the novel does eventually come around to marriage, after all it ends with a proposal and acceptance no matter how arcanely worded, this is no traditional union. Homing in on the ultimate feminist moment of the novels, Leonardi writes, "Harriet breaks . . . the paternal ritual by which women, like property and as property, are passed from man to man, from father to husband" (87). "Harriet chooses marriage not *over* the female community but *out* of it. It is there she has learned what her priorities must be, and she brings them to this marriage, thus subverting the institution while preserving many of its elements" (99). In *Gaudy Night*, Sayers goes well beyond the prevailing notions of companionate marriage as popularly enunciated by Marie Stopes in 1918 ("Marriage can never reach its full stature unless women possess as much intellectual freedom and freedom of opportunity within it as do their partners" (qtd. in Merck 156-57), but with the marriage done in *Busman's Honeymoon* she lets her characters revert, as Harriet will later say in "Tallboys," "to type."

What then remains still to be said about the Sayers detective fiction canon, about the Wimsey output from first to last, regarding the shift from *Whose Body?* to *Gaudy Night?* It is not sufficient in explaining the changes in the series to say merely "Sayers decided" or "Harriet's presence required"; one must also ask how the shift occurred, not as a function of character development but as an element of narrative. Turning to the theories of M.M. Bakhtin offers one way of assessing the fictional construction when considering the series as a whole. There is no question that *Whose Body?* is conservatively structured to follow the restrictive path from crime through detection to discovery; there is no room for side excursions, tangents, or distractions. Almost surgically, Sayers removes any extraneous narratives; for all her attempts to humanize the detective (following E.C. Bentley) she is conventional in her plotting (following Arthur Conan Doyle). By the time she arrives at *Gaudy Night*, Sayers has succeeded in decentering a number of the conventions; she has tried multiple narrators in *The Documents in the Case*, multiple personalities in *Murder Must Advertise*, side-by-side plots in *Nine Tailors*, and a love story in *Strong Poison*.

But only in *Gaudy Night* do the multiple discourses come together yet each holds its own position; this intertextuality—Bakhtin's dialogic—goes a long way toward explaining the extreme reactions to this novel. Here, the discourses are multiple, resulting in a heteroglossia that speaks not through one language but many, not through one discourse but several—each modified from its more conventional configuration. The discourse of detection breaks one of its cardinal rules: there is no corpse. Yet there is crime, evil, detection, and discovery. And it toys with a second: the novel begins with the "wrong" detective, returning to the series hero only in mid-case. The discourse of marriage, which Catherine Kenney identifies as "one of the central concerns of English fiction" (50), is shifted off-kilter by its well-educated, economically independent, non-virginal, emotionally resistant heroine. The discourse of Oxford is skewed by the intrusion of the outside world through both the criminal and the detectives. And the discourse of fiction is distorted by the appended postscript, which is present in only some printings of the novel.

It is this heteroglossia that I believe is responsible for the feminism that many critics have identified with *Gaudy Night*. The traditional detective novel, like *Whose Body?*, is patriarchal in form and content: its structure is linear, moving in a trajectory from beginning to end; its stance is authoritative, with a single voice of knowledge and power holding sway at the end if not throughout. Feminism rightly challenges these fictional constructs; and so does Sayers. In *Gaudy Night* the multiple plots/discourses/languages go beyond providing red herrings to assuming a structural and narrative stance of their own. The process of detection operates in each discourse with two vulnerable and power-declining detectives. The traditional Latinate discourse of Oxford becomes the improbable language of the marriage plot. Sayers loses no opportunity to undermine the conventions of each of her chosen discourses, creating the new plots and narratives necessary for feminist revisions not only of fiction but also of life.

After finishing *Gaudy Night*, Sayers apparently had enormous fun writing the dramatic script of *Busman's Honeymoon* with her friend Muriel St. Clare Byrne. Then she abandoned Wimsey, Harriet Vane, and detective fiction altogether to write religious drama and, later, translate Dante. But, meanwhile, she had reimagined detective fiction for those readers who had the wit to see it. In a traditional detective novel, the final chapter is reserved for the detective's ultimate moment: announcing the criminal and the way she/he was discovered. In her career as a detective fiction writer, Sayers also reaches her ultimate success in the last "real" novel. *Gaudy Night* is a triumph of her imagination and talent, an achievement one could not have predicted from *Whose Body?*

Notes

1. And then there is the spoof created by Sayers and C.W. Scott-Giles, inventing a history for Lord Peter—as though he were a real figure—back to Roger de Guimsey who followed William the Conqueror from Normandy into England in the campaign of 1066.

2. *Busman's Honeymoon* began as a co-authored play which Sayers later novelized; consequently its structural position in the canon is different from the other novels. Because my final point addresses textuality and narrative, I have decided to treat it here as separate from the rest of the series.

Works Cited

Auerbach, Nina. *Communities of Women*. Cambridge, MA: Harvard UP, 1978.

Bakhtin, M.M. *The Dialogic Imagination: Four Essays*. Trans. Caryl Emerson and Michael Holquist. Ed. Michael Holquist. Austin: U of Texas P, 1982.

Bander, Elaine. "The Case for *Sir Charles Grandison*." *The Sayers Review* 1.4 (1977): 8-9.

Bargainnier, Earl, ed. "Introduction." *Ten Women of Mystery*. Bowling Green, OH: Bowling Green State University Popular Press, 1981. 1-5.

Barnes, Melvyn. *Best Detective Fiction: A Guide from Godwin to the Present*. London: Bingley, 1975.

Brabazon, James. *Dorothy L. Sayers: A Biography*. New York: Scribner's, 1981.

Brunsdale, Mitzi. *Dorothy L. Sayers: Solving the Mystery of Wickedness*. New York: Berg, 1990.

Byatt, A.S. *Passions of the Mind*. New York: Random, 1992.

Coomes, David. *Dorothy L. Sayers: A Careless Rage for Life*. Batavia, IL: Lion, 1992.

Dale, Alzina Stone. Introduction. *Dorothy L. Sayers. Love All and Busman's Honeymoon*. Kent, OH: Kent State UP, 1984. xi-xxxiii.

Hannay, Margaret P. "Harriet's Influence on the Characterization of Lord Peter Wimsey." *As Her Whimsey Took Her*. Ed. Hannay. Kent, OH: Kent State UP, 1979. 36-50.

Heilbrun, Carolyn. "Dorothy L. Sayers: Biography Between the Lines." *Dorothy L. Sayers: The Centenary Celebration*. Ed. Alzina Stone Dale. New York: Walker, 1993. 1-14.

____. "Sayers, Lord Peter and God." *Lord Peter.* By Dorothy L. Sayers. New York: Avon, 1972. 454-69.

Hitchman, Janet. *Such a Strange Lady.* New York: Avon, 1975.

Hone, Ralph L. *Dorothy L. Sayers: A Literary Biography.* Kent, OH: Kent State UP, 1979.

Kenney, Catherine. *The Remarkable Case of Dorothy L. Sayers.* Kent, OH: Kent State UP, 1990.

Klein, Kathleen Gregory. "Dorothy L. Sayers." *Ten Women of Mystery.* Ed. Earl F. Bargainnier. Bowling Green, OH: Bowling Green State University Popular Press, 1981. 8-39.

Leavis, Q.D. "The Case of Miss Dorothy Sayers." *Scrutiny* 6 (Dec. 1937): 334-40.

Leonardi, Susan. *Dangerous by Degrees.* New Brunswick, NJ: Rutgers UP, 1989.

Merck, Mandy. *Perversions.* London: Virago, 1993.

Rahn, B.J. "The Marriage of True Minds." *Dorothy L. Sayers: The Centenary Celebration.* Ed. Alzina Stone Dale. New York: Walker, 1993. 51-66.

Reaves, R.B. "Crime and Punishment in the Detective Fiction of Dorothy L. Sayers." *As Her Whimsey Took Her.* Ed. Margaret P. Hannay. Kent, OH: Kent State UP, 1979. 1-13.

Reynolds, Barbara. "The Origin of Lord Peter Wimsey." *The Sayers Review* 2.1 (1978): 1-21.

Sayers, Dorothy L. *Gaudy Night.* New York: Avon, 1968.

____. "Gaudy Night." *The Art of the Mystery Story.* Ed. Howard Haycraft. New York: Simon, 1946. 208-21.

Scott-Giles, C.W. *The Wimsey Family.* New York: Avon, 1977.

Stock, R.D., and Barbara Stock. "The Agents of Evil and Justice in the Novels of Dorothy L. Sayers." *As Her Whimsey Took Her.* Ed. Margaret P. Hannay. Kent, OH: Kent State UP, 1979. 15-23.

Symons, Julian. *Mortal Consequences: A History from the Detective Story to the Crime Novel.* New York: Harper, 1972.

Tischler, Nancy M. *Dorothy L. Sayers: A Pilgrim Soul.* Atlanta: Knox, 1980.

Wynn, Dilys. *Murderess Ink: The Better Half of the Mystery.* New York: Workman, 1979.

The First Campion Novel

Paula M. Woods

Discussing the first novel in Margery Allingham's Campion series presents a somewhat different problem from those encountered with other detective series. Namely, just which novel is the first Campion novel? Albert Campion did not spring full grown into the series with *Mystery Mile* (1930), the first novel that features him as the main character, but appeared as supporting cast in an earlier book, *The Crime at Black Dudley* (1929). Is the "real" first novel the one in which he plays the major role, or is it the one in which he first appears? Perhaps the question is answered by one's first acquaintance with Campion. A reader who begins with *The Crime at Black Dudley* may see only Campion's subordinate position there even after reading later novels, while one who comes to *Black Dudley* with the series in hand views Campion as one of the novel's heroes, perhaps even the principal hero, knowing what he later becomes. This question of the Campion series' origins offers mystery readers a unique opportunity to consider what makes a mystery/adventure hero and what characteristics must be carried over from one novel to others in order to create the continuity necessary for a successful series. The question of beginnings might also take other forms to consider authorial intent and the constructed biography of the character/detective. What can be determined about Allingham's intentions for this supporting character? How and why might Campion have changed between *Black Dudley* and *Mystery Mile*? What inherent qualities does he have in his first appearance in *Black Dudley* that led Allingham to make him the focus of nearly a score of novels and a number of short stories?

A detective series needs a focus, a central character or set of characters around whom the events revolve. The argument can be made that *The Crime at Black Dudley* is not the first in the Campion series because Campion is not the principal protagonist, although he makes his first appearance at dinner in Chapter I. *Black Dudley* features George Abbershaw, a physician, as the hero/amateur detective. Abbershaw would appear to be a good candidate for a series character. He is intelligent, educated, the author of a book on pathology, which, "treated with special reference to fatal wounds and the means of ascertaining their probable causes, was a standard work," making him known and respected by Scotland Yard (*Crime* 6). These characteristics and connections certainly would seem to qualify him for detectivehood. Nevertheless, Abbershaw disappears from the Allingham canon at the end of *The Crime at Black Dudley*, full of thoughts of "his own affairs: Meggie, and his love for her, and their marriage" (*Crime* 207). With these few words Allingham writes him out of the detective business. He has his own world, which momentarily has crossed directly with the world of crime. He has solved a mystery involving a friend, Wyatt Petrie, but Allingham apparently found him not the stuff of which series detectives are made.

What are these qualities, the "stuff" necessary for a series hero? Leroy Panek views Abbershaw as the "Average Man with whom the reader can safely identify" as opposed to Campion, who is "the hero-leader of the middle of the book, the part filled with threats" (130). Richard Martin believes that Abbershaw "becomes the reader's representative within the fictional setting" (56). Can the Average Man be an adventure hero in a series? Can the hero remain the reader's representative? Or will his continued participation in mystery and adventure change him, turn him into a Super Man? John Cawelti discusses the ordinary hero, as "a figure marked, at least at the beginning of the story, by flawed abilities and attitudes presumably shared by the audience" (40). Cawelti distinguishes between adventure and mystery by emphasizing that the hero is present in adventure as opposed to the use of the puzzle, the intellectual challenge, in mystery. By his standards, the Campion series qualifies as both. But his discussion does not extend to a series hero, who in response to continuing challenges must change and develop in some fashion, perhaps only in minor details, if the series is to maintain the interest of readers.[1] Even in a supporting role Campion demonstrates through his abilities and intimate knowledge of the not-so-ordinary world of crime that he is not the ordinary man.

The Average Man, even if he possesses knowledge and expertise, is governed by the personal matters of his life and, while often able to rise above them, can never ignore them for long. His actions are governed by his dedication to family, friends, and other personal relationships. He lacks the disinterested dedication to the cause. Although Abbershaw possesses certain expertise, his personal interests take precedence over his sleuthing. His first inclination is to protect Meggie rather than to solve the mystery. When she is safe he can again turn his attention to the problem of who killed Colonel Croome. It is true that Campion develops personal interests and is at times distracted by them. In *Mystery Mile*, it is evident that he is in love with Biddy Paget, but he effects her rescue efficiently rather than in a chivalrous manner. In *Sweet Danger* (*Fear Sign*, 1933)[2] his growing affection for Amanda is evident, and he does take some risks he might not have otherwise, but in later novels, his love for her (and hers for him) is tempered with his dedication to the cause he is involved in. He does panic momentarily in *The Tiger in the Smoke* (1952) when she is in the dark house with Havoc. The telling moment, though, comes when she decides to stay with him and they send Rupert safely away with Lugg. Campion thinks: "They were partners again. She would look after him and he must look after the three [Albert, Amanda, Rupert] of them. It was not the only sort of marriage, but it was their sort" (169). Although he has a strong romantic interest, the partnership he and Amanda have forged allows him to remain dedicated to the cause. Because he begins without such personal interests in *Black Dudley* but develops them over the course of the series, they do not determine his course of action. Abbershaw, in contrast, arrives on the scene with his encumbrances already in place, obstacles to be overcome.

Allingham's reasons for choosing Campion over Abbershaw are unknown, leaving open to debate her intentions for this supporting character. In *Deadlier than the Male* Jessica Mann states the obvious when she says that "when she first invented him, Allingham had no idea how important the character of Albert Campion would be to her readers or to herself" (196). In a 1935 broadcast talk Allingham stated that Campion was something of a problem, appearing suddenly, causing her to give up writing for a week trying to lose him. She had, however, included him earlier on a character list for the novel in one of her notebooks (Martin 57), suggesting that his appearance was not entirely unpremeditated. The 1935 assertion might be taken to indicate that the Campion character began to assert himself in the course of Allingham's work on *Black Dudley*, even though he was not intended to be the principal focus of the novel.

Allingham never stated that she intended *Black Dudley* to be the beginning of a series, whether featuring Abbershaw or Campion. Nevertheless, the success of the novel prompted the managing editor of Doubleday, Malcolm Johnson, to suggest a novel featuring Campion (Martin 58). Allingham herself stated in *The Mysterious Mr. Campion* that she "promoted" Campion because she did not think anyone would ever again read *Black Dudley* and because he appealed to her as the "private joke-figure of we [sic] smarter youngsters of the period. . . . He was misunderstood, and regarded with misgiving by all but the enlightened few" (11). Abbershaw certainly does not meet these criteria: he is not a "joke-figure" and his seriousness is difficult to misunderstand. This variety of reasons for Campion's appearance and continuing presence and Abbershaw's disappearance point out the danger of positively identifying the intention of the author: was it all Allingham's idea or was it Johnson's, or perhaps some combination?

Another factor must be considered in any discussion of intentions for Campion: just what role did Allingham's husband, Philip Youngman Carter, play in the saga of Albert Campion? An unsigned "Note About the Author" appended to *Cargo of Eagles* (1968)[3] emphasizes Youngman Carter's contribution to the entire series, stating that "In their first year of marriage, Miss Allingham invented Albert Campion and, considerably assisted by her husband, wrote the first of the series of nineteen Campion books, *The Crime at Black Dudley*" (*Cargo* 176). Is this statement a justification by Youngman Carter after the fact, or does it provide documentation that Allingham intended all along to develop Campion, merely using *Black Dudley* as a means of introduction? Whatever the case, there is little doubt that her husband had a hand in Allingham's early work. Richard Martin comments on the contributions of Youngman Carter to *Mystery Mile*, saying that notes for chapters 15-21 appear in his hand. Allingham herself said that many of the ideas and jokes were his (59). Youngman Carter suggested Campion's name, after Edmund Campion, Jesuit martyr (Morpurgo xxiii), and has himself been suggested as one of the models for some of Campion's characteristics (Morpurgo xiii; Winn 59).

No matter what Allingham's intentions were for her eventual series hero when he first appeared, his personality and actions in *The Crime at Black Dudley* were those that she continued, modified, and developed over the course of the series. Campion was already in *Black Dudley* a character that could be used to advantage.[4]

In *The Crime at Black Dudley* Campion's presence in the house party is a mystery to all, everyone believing that he is someone else's friend and all dismissing him as inconsequential. All the other bright young people had been specially chosen by Petrie as "people of blameless reputation" so that suspicion for his uncle's death would fall on one of the Colonel's own guests. Petrie assumes that Campion is one of the Colonel's friends (*Crime* 204). He is, in fact, on a job, employed to infiltrate the house party, receive a package from the Colonel, and return it to London, as he later explains to Abbershaw (72-73).

He is described as "a lunatic," "quite inoffensive, just a silly ass" (*Crime* 11), but Abbershaw finds him vaguely familiar:

[he] stared covertly at the fresh-faced young man with the tow-coloured hair and the foolish, pale-blue eyes behind the tortoise shell-rimmed spectacles, and wondered where he had seen him before.

The slightly receding chin and mouth so unnecessarily full of teeth was distinctly familiar, "Albert Campion?" he repeated under his breath. "Albert Campion? Campion? Campion?" But still his memory would not serve him. (*Crime* 11)

Allingham here establishes what will come to be Campion's trademarks: the pale blond hair, the tortoise-shell-framed glasses hiding expression in his eyes, and the apparent vacuity. It is the description that continues through later novels, mercifully minus the receding chin. In *Death of a Ghost* (1934) "the general impression one received of him was that he was well bred and a trifle absent-minded" (8). *Tether's End* (*Hide My Eyes*, 1958) finds him in his early fifties, still wearing his large glasses, having "cultivated the gentle art of unobtrusiveness until even his worst enemies were apt to overlook him until it was too late" (7). In *The Tiger in the Smoke* Allingham describes him as an "elegantly unobtrusive figure . . . misleadingly vacant of face and gentle of manner, which he had been in the nineteen-twenties. The easiest of men to overlook or underestimate . . ." (7). *The Mind Readers* (1965), the last novel which Allingham finished herself, continues the trademarks: Campion is a "thin man with pale hair and eyes and a misleadingly blank expression" (46), and during the terrifying scene on the causeway with Arnold, he "look[s] like a civilized and essentially harmless person, his pale horn spectacles, larger in the lenses than is usual, making him appear owlish and rather helpless" (178). Actually, it is in this scene that he perhaps comes closest to being helpless in the entire series. In *Traitor's Purse* (1940) while Campion is suffering from amnesia, Allingham makes it clearer than she does elsewhere that his standard vacuous look is deliberate. He sees himself in the mirror as "a horrified man of thirty-five or so, tall and remarkably thin, with a lean wooden face on which there were far more lines than he had expected." Amanda comments that "You look much more intelligent than usual" (*Purse* 21). The disguise slips when he has no memory, no knowledge of his identity and his task.

In *The Crime at Black Dudley* Campion's actions as well as his appearance at first reinforce the assessment of him as a silly ass, a characterization which, Dilys Winn contends, is usually applied to those who "fulfill the role of victim, not Great Detective" (59). He gets into an early morning fight with an allegedly drunken butler and disappears only to be found in a wardrobe which is part of Black Dudley's secret passages, considerably the worse for wear, having been "questioned" by the gang holding the house party captive. Campion's explanation is typically inane, closing with "I didn't know where I was, so I just sat there reciting 'The Mistletoe Bough' to myself, and confessing my past life—such sport!" (*Crime* 70).

It is at this point that Abbershaw recognizes him as Mornington Dodd, an identification that Campion admits, "But . . . I assure you you're wrong about my magnetic personality being a disguise. There is *absolutely no fraud*. I'm like this—always like this—my best friends could tell you" (*Crime* 70-71). And he assures Abbershaw that "Mornington Dodd is one of my names. I have also been called the 'Honourable Tootles Ash'. . . . Then there was a girl who used to call me 'Cuddles.'" Finally he admits to an identity/non-identity which would continue throughout the series: "My own [name] is rather aristocratic, and I never use it in business" (*Crime* 71). His array of aliases continues in *Mystery Mile*, when Giles Paget relates a stroll down Regent Street with him, meeting "five people he knew, including a viscountess and two bishops. Each one of them stopped and greeted him as an old pal. And every single one of them called him by a different name" (34). In *Police at the Funeral* (1931) Caroline Farraday knows his real name—after all, she has been corresponding with his grandmother for forty-five years—but tells him, "I shall not expose you . . . after all, as long as that impossible brother of yours is alive the family responsibilities are being shouldered . . . I see no reason why you shouldn't call yourself what you like" (54). In *Look to the Lady* (*Gyrth Chalice Mystery*, 1931) Campion's aristocratic connections are implied. It is not only for his abilities as an adventurer/detective that he is hired, but because his background enables him to understand the importance of the chalice and ensures his confidentiality.

It is in *Mystery Mile* that his real first name, Rudolph, is revealed by Lugg, when calling Campion's brother Herbert for him (180). Ali Fergusson Barber further reveals that Campion is "Mr. Rudolph K——," on whom he seems to have a full dossier (202). Campion also alludes to his strained relationship with the family when he tells Herbert that "you can only disinherit an offspring once. One offspring—one disinheritance" (180).

In later novels Allingham reveals more about Campion's family. Evidently he and his grandmother are on good terms, but he and his mother are not (*Police* 54). *Fashion in Shrouds* (1938) provides him with a sister who has also alienated the family, first by marrying a man they did not approve of and then, after his death, by becoming a fashion designer of note. Also important are his two uncles, the Bishop of Devises, who is deceased in *Police at the Funeral* but conveniently resurrected in *Pearls Before Swine* (*Coroner's Pigin*, 1945), and Canon Avril, the wise innocent of *The Tiger in the Smoke* and *The Mind Readers*. These connections reveal Campion's aristocratic background and his need to use aliases—even the name Albert Campion.

Appearances and aliases aside, it is Campion, even in his first appearance, who knows that something besides simple murder is afoot at Black Dudley. And as the novel progresses, it becomes evident that Campion is not the vacuous, inane individual he appears to be but a professional with numerous skills: he fights, he uses a gun only when necessary, he uses sleight of hand to good effect, and he appears at opportune moments to save the day, all the while uttering such comments as "My dear old bird, don't lose your Organizing Power, Directive Ability, Self-Confidence, Driving Force, Salesmanship and Business Acumen" (*Crime* 130) and "A very pretty tale of love and war. . . . 'Featuring our Boys. Positively for One Night Only'" (*Crime* 137). Such remarks differentiate him from the other young men in the party who attempt amateurish heroics in deadly serious fashion in their effort to escape from the mansion. They plan adventurously; Campion actually executes, covering his knowledge and skills with flippancy. This contrast in styles of execution continues in *Mystery Mile* in the rescue of Biddy from Simister's gang. Giles and Marlow rush in when it is apparent she is in danger. Campion disappears to set off a smoke bomb so that the rescue will succeed and the gang will be caught by the proper authorities with a maximum of fuss, a fuss that covers the escape of the rescuers. Campion's disappearance has even Lugg fooled: "Lost 'is nerve for a spell. See it 'appen in the war" (157). It is the Campion stock-in-trade to make others, even his allies, underestimate him.

Campion likewise appears and disappears over the course of *The Crime at Black Dudley*. Ultimately he is not the one who uncovers the murderer; that honor goes to Abbershaw, and Campion's adventure remains a secondary plot. Campion functions as an independent operator, hired to bring a package from the Colonel back to London—hired by Simister, no less. But as soon as he sees the Colonel's own party, he "nearly cut the whole job right out and bunked back to town." Campion has recognized Von Faber, a person whose reputation Abbershaw with his connections to Scotland Yard knows quite well (*Crime* 73-74). Yet, because Abbershaw has no first-hand experience with the underworld, he fails to connect the reputation and the man. This difference between knowledge and recognition adds to the mystery of Albert Campion. When he disappears into the "portals of one of the most famous and exclusive clubs in the world," some time before Abbershaw deduces the identity and motive of the murderer, Campion is still a figure of mystery, his profession—con artist or crime solver—still vague. He has given Abbershaw his real name:

a name so illustrious that Abbershaw started back and stared at him in astonishment.

"Good God!" he said. "You don't mean that?"

"No," said Mr. Campion cheerfully. (*Crime* 168)

With this exit, Allingham leaves open the possible return of her mystery man. Although the serious Abbershaw is the hero of this tale, the reader knows that without Campion's antics the novel would be much less the adventure thriller that it is. B.A. Pike goes so far as to assert that with Campion's departure "the real impetus goes out of the book and the closing chapters constitute a rather disappointing coda to the main action" (10).

In *Mystery Mile* Allingham picks up Campion's character where she left him in *The Crime at Black Dudley*. Campion at first appears ineffectual, hiding behind his glasses and uttering inane and flippant remarks once again. Even the sacrifice of the unfortunate mouse Haig is handled in a fashion that makes Campion seem like a blithering idiot. The business card he gives to Marlow Lobbett continues the charade. It reads, "Coups neatly executed. Nothing sordid, vulgar or plebeian. Deserving cases preferred. Police no object" (*Mile* 22). However, Marlow's interview with him at the Bottle Street flat does reveal a certain seriousness. When Marlow asks, "Do you always talk like this?" he answers, "Almost always. . . . People get used to it in time. I can't help it, it's a sort of affliction. . . . My friends pretend they don't notice it. What did the police say to you this morning?" (26). This last remark has the desired effect of catching Marlow off guard. The conversation continues in this vein, with Campion alternating inanities with direct questions and shrewd observations. The patter of the "private-joke figure" that is so characteristic of Campion the comic figure of *Black Dudley* is both carried over into *Mystery Mile* and modified as Campion becomes the principal character who must be taken seriously. As the series develops, Allingham gradually decreases the amount of patter that Campion employs. There is still a good deal of it in the next novel, *Look to the Lady*, but when she moves from the adventure novel format into the detective novel with *Police at the Funeral*, the patter decreases markedly. Some of it returns in *Sweet Danger*, which revives the adventure format, but certainly not to the degree evident in *Black Dudley* or even *Mystery Mile*.

In *Mystery Mile* the Pagets and St. Swithin Cush also reveal something of the mystery of Campion. When St. Swithin remarks that he has faith in Campion, Biddy laughs that "Albert is a fishy character and no fit associate for a dignitary of the Church," to which he replies, "out of evil cometh good. . . . Albert is a true son of the Church. In the time of Richelieu he would no doubt have become a cardinal!" (*Mile* 33). Campion's antics have not fooled the wise old vicar. He fully recognizes that behind the mild exterior Campion is a force to be reckoned with, a mind and personality capable of ruthlessness when necessary. It is to Campion that St. Swithin entrusts his "secret" when he commits suicide.

As the novel progresses, it becomes evident that Allingham has abandoned much of Campion's flippancy, and it is obvious that the famous vacuity is merely a disguise. He does take the danger to Judge Lobbett seriously because he certainly takes Simister, a carryover from *The Crime at Black Dudley*, seriously, and he is less inclined to be flip. In *Crime* he was working for Simister, as Simister, alias Ali Fergusson Barber in *Mystery Mile*, recounts in his final confrontation with Campion (*Mile* 203) and as Abbershaw deduced in *Black Dudley* (94). Simister/Barber also reminds Campion of the "record of your curious profession" (*Mile* 205), the reputation that prevented Abbershaw from fully trusting Campion. Now working against Simister, Campion is affected by the knowledge gained in his previous employment, making him more cautious. This cautiousness born of knowledge reinforces the changes that Allingham begins to make in the character of Albert Campion.

The differences in Campion's attitude are further emphasized by the differences in those with whom he associates in the two novels. Campion's seriousness in *Black Dudley* was not so obvious because his plot was secondary to the murder plot. In this earlier book he associates with "beautiful young people" inclined toward heroics and not really aware of what they are up against as he is. Except, naturally, for the episode when Biddy is taken captive and Marlow and Giles act less than cautiously, the Lobbetts and Pagets are aware of the true danger they and Campion face and for the most part are less inclined toward derring-do. Judge Lobbett in particular takes Campion seriously and, like St. Swithin, trusts him with his life and his secret.

As the protagonist of *Mystery Mile* Campion appears less often in the guise of inanity, and it becomes apparent that his blank look is indeed a mask. In *The Crime at Black Dudley*, Campion is an important, if often annoying, figure. He is difficult to take seriously until he is contrasted with other characters such as Chris Kennedy, whose bravado caricatures the legendary British stiff upper lip and Oxbridge breeding. Then Campion's genuine caution appears behind those disguising spectacles. Whether she intended to or not, Allingham thus laid the groundwork for Campion's character in *The Crime at Black Dudley*. When he disappears into his exclusive club five chapters before the close of the novel, one wonders if he will reappear to aid in the final solution of the murder, since Abbershaw is certain that the group of thugs had not actually murdered Croome. That mystery, however, is not Campion's, but Abbershaw's.

Although the presence in *Black Dudley* of the core Campion characteristics is the clearest evidence that it is the first novel in Allingham's Campion series, there are features of *The Crime at Black Dudley* other than Albert Campion himself that Allingham carries into other novels in the series, in particular villains and eccentrics. The type of villain represented by Von Faber and hinted at in Simister— powerful, ruthless, and often charismatic—reappears in a number of the Campion novels which lean toward the thriller. But perhaps the most important of these continuing features of the series originating in *Black Dudley* is the eccentrics. Mrs. Meade, imprisoned in Black Dudley, awaiting her release by her son, is the first in a long line of odd characters, of both rural and urban origin. Allingham shows a deft hand in the creation of these types. In *Mystery Mile* she continues the rural branch with the brothers Willsmore, George and the silent 'Anry. Nearly every novel has its eccentric or eccentrics, contrasted with the urbane Campion who understands them surprisingly well. The pinnacle of eccentricity is perhaps reached in *More Work for the Undertaker* (1949) with the Palinode family and Lugg's undertaking in-laws. This collection can scarcely be matched anywhere else in mystery fiction. In fact, it might be said that the eccentrics are the norm in *More Work for the Undertaker*, and the ordinary people like Campion and the newly introduced Charlie Luke are the exception. In some instances the eccentrics, like Mrs. Meade, are able to impart information about the crime. In other instances they are active participants in the adventure, like George and 'Anry and Thos T. Knapp in *Mystery Mile* and the gypsies in *Look to the Lady*. In one case, *Flowers for the Judge* (1937), the eccentric is even the perpetrator.

There are various other details, types of imagery, for instance, which carry through the series and give it continuity, but those which have been discussed above are the most important. J. Randolph Cox has remarked that "There is a continuity that links the books more closely than is usually the case with a series-detective" (88). It becomes apparent through a careful reading of the Campion series, especially when the novels are read in sequence, that the foundation is laid in *The Crime at Black Dudley* for a series featuring Albert Campion. Allingham begins to build on that foundation in *Mystery Mile* and continues to employ features she initiated in *Black Dudley* through the last novel she completed, *The Mind Readers*. The Campion novels are proof that a series can be read and enjoyed either in or out of sequence, but a sequential reading offers a unique understanding of the process by which a series is created.

Notes

1. In the introduction to a new edition of *Fer-de-Lance* Loren Esteleman claims that Rex Stout never changed Nero Wolfe or Archie Goodwin, thus solving any problems created for readers by characters that change and develop.

2. Several of Allingham's novels have been published under variant titles. The title as it appears in Works Cited is given first, with the variants in parentheses.

3. *Cargo of Eagles* was the novel Allingham had partially finished at the time of her death. Youngman Carter finished it and completed two novels for which she had left notes: *Mr. Campion's Farthing* and *Mr. Campion's Quarry*.

4. Winn contends that Allingham grew less interested in Campion even as the characterization strengthened over the series to the point at which "he began to appear farther and farther back in her novels until in *Black Plumes* he disappeared entirely." This assertion is misleading in light of the fact that *Black Plumes* is preceded by *The Fashion in Shrouds*, in which Campion is hardly in the background and followed by *Traitor's Purse* which focuses on him as much as any of the novels do. She also believes him to be "insignificant" in *The Tiger in the Smoke* (60).

Works Cited

Allingham, Margery. *Cargo of Eagles*. New York: Manor, 1976.
_____. *The Crime at Black Dudley*. New York: Penguin, 1950.
_____. *Death of a Ghost*. New York: Manor, 1975.
_____. *The Mind Readers*. New York: Manor, 1965.
_____. *The Mysterious Mr. Campion*. London: Chatto, 1963.
_____. *Mystery Mile*. New York: Penguin, 1969.
_____. *Police at the Funeral*. New York: Manor, 1973.
_____. *Tether's End*. New York: Bantam, 1983.
_____. *The Tiger in the Smoke*. New York: Bantam, 1985.
_____. *Traitor's Purse*. New York: Bantam, 1983.
Cawelti, John G. *Adventure, Mystery, and Romance: Formula Stories as Art and Popular Culture*. Chicago: Chicago UP, 1976.

Cox, J. Randolph. "Miss Allingham's Knight." *The Armchair Detective* 15.1 (1982): 86-91.

Estleman, Loren D. Introduction. *Fer-de-Lance*. By Rex Stout. 1934. New York: Bantam, 1992. v-viii.

Martin, Richard. *Ink in Her Blood: The Life and Crime Fiction of Margery Allingham*. Ann Arbor, MI: UMI, 1988.

Mann, Jessica. *Deadlier Than the Male: Why Are Respectable English Women So Good at Murder?* New York: Macmillan, 1981.

Morpurgo, J.E., ed. *The Return of Mr. Campion*. By Margery Allingham. New York: Avon, 1989.

Panek, LeRoy Lad. *Watteau's Shepherds: The Detective Novel in Britain 1914-1940*. Bowling Green, OH: Bowling Green State University Popular Press, 1979.

Pike, B.A. *Campion's Career: A Study of the Novels of Margery Allingham*. Bowling Green, OH: Bowling Green State University Popular Press, 1987.

[Winn, Dilys]. *Murderess Ink*. Ed. Dilys Winn. New York: Workman, 1979.

Reading Agatha Christie's Miss Marple Series: The Thirteen Problems

Marty S. Knepper

In 1930 Agatha Christie's *The Murder at the Vicarage* appeared, the first novel to feature Jane Marple, spinster sleuth from St. Mary Mead. In a 1931 book, *Masters of Mystery: A Study of the Detective Story*, H. Douglas Thomson writes:

one cannot help thinking that she [Miss Marple] is not of the stuff of the great detectives. Inquisitiveness will not always come off, and intuitions arising from a more refined interest in human nature are cheap in these days. Moreover, Miss Marple can only hope to solve murder problems on her native heath. If Mrs. Christie is planning a future for Miss Marple, as is very likely, she will be bound to find this an exasperating limitation. (211)

Although Thomson accurately predicted Christie would continue the Miss Marple series, he was wrong in envisioning Miss Marple's detective potential as limited in the ways he describes. He did not know she would investigate murders in London and on a Caribbean island. He did not anticipate readers would find inquisitiveness, intuition, and an interest in human nature the perfect traits for a great detective, as Miss Marple has redefined the role. He never imagined that the Miss Marple series and Christie's other books would be translated into over 44 languages, her sales would top one billion copies, and the adaptations of her mysteries for stage, film, and television would be popular long after her death.

Having read only *Vicarage* and perhaps a half-dozen Miss Marple short stories published in 1928, Thomson can be excused his erroneous predictions. But what about contemporary critics who can read the complete Miss Marple series, twelve novels and twenty short stories? Hindsight should lead to fairly accurate vision, but, in fact, the criticism of the Miss Marple series in particular and Christie's mysteries in general is full of errors, misconceptions, partial truths, and debatable assertions and interpretations.

Why is Christie criticism, and especially Marpleian criticism, so strikingly inaccurate and unconvincing? A study of the Miss Marple novels and the commentary on them suggests several reasons for the questionable truisms that have developed about the series and Christie as a writer. An important factor is that the first book, *Vicarage*, is not typical of the series. The novel is a marvelous comedy of manners, containing the usual clever Christie whodunit plot, but is not, as many assume, a prototype for the series. Christie experiments continually as the series evolves, leading to considerable difference among the novels. Miss Marple evolves from a comic old lady next door—perpetually gardening and gossiping—to a righteous protector and avenger. The novels move beyond comedy of manners to become more serious explorations of human psychology, social change, and the nature of evil.

Examining the Miss Marple series in light of some of the most frequent misconceptions about Christie's mysteries and the Miss Marple series reveals further that many readers have underrated Christie's achievement as a writer. While Christie adheres to certain formulaic conventions in the Miss Marple series, the novels contain more innovation, variety, and literary artistry than is generally acknowledged. Borrowing a title from the British edition of the first collection of Miss Marple short stories, we might refer to these most frequent examples of dubious assertions about Christie novels as "the thirteen problems":

1) Miss Marple is a fictional portrait of Agatha Christie herself.
2) The Miss Marple books follow a predictable pattern or formula.
3) Throughout the series, Miss Marple undergoes "fluffification."
4) Miss Marple solves cases through the use of intuition.
5) St. Mary Mead is a bucolic setting, an Eden, a place of innocence.
6) Christie repeatedly employs the least-likely-person gambit.
7) Christie's novels are full of cardboard characters.
8) Christie is interested in the investigation of murders, not criminal psychology.
9) Christie is not a feminist.
10) Christie portrays and defends the lifestyle and values of Edwardian England.
11) Christie does not deal with social and intellectual issues in her mysteries.
12) Christie's prose style is pedestrian, non-literary.
13) There is little of Christie in her mystery novels.

Miss Marple is a fictional portrait of Agatha Christie herself.

In *Agatha Christie: Official Centenary Celebration*, edited by Lynn Underwood, two photographs appear toward the end of the book: one of Joan Hickson as Miss Marple (92) and one of Agatha Christie in her last years (97). The resemblance is uncanny, and both fit the fictional description of Miss Marple: a tall, elderly English gentlewoman with snowy hair. Actress Barbara Mullen, who knew Christie and played Miss Marple in 1949 and 1975 productions of *Vicarage*, has said, "She [Christie] was a very reticent lady—an acute observer of human nature, much like Miss Marple. . . . To play Miss Marple you have to study Agatha Christie. . . . I think the part is as near a self-portrait as you can get" (Haining 122).

The idea that Miss Marple is Agatha Christie is a common perception. Both are clever, like gardening, and are astute observers of human nature; as Christie aged, she naturally became more like her creation. But the 38-year-old Christie who created Miss Marple had married and divorced, given birth to a daughter, traveled around the world, and established herself as a professional writer. The Miss Marple first described in the story "The Tuesday Night Club" could not be more unlike her creator. An old unmarried lady, Miss Marple wears a black brocade dress with white Mechlin lace on the bodice, black lace mittens, and a black lace cap, and knits something soft, white, and fluffy. Miss Marple's dithery, digressive speech style causes her companions to underrate her problem-solving skills, honed during her life in a small English village. In *Vicarage*, Miss Marple is more active, less a Victorian relic. We see her gardening, watching her neighbors through binoculars, and displaying an unerring knowledge about events in St. Mary Mead. In 1930, Christie had more in common with the adventurous Miss Cram, who has discovered an interest in archaeology and archaeologists, than with Miss Marple.

If Miss Marple is not a self-portrait, how did she originate? Biographer Janet Morgan relates that the name comes from Marple Hall, an estate where Christie attended a sale (176). In her autobiography, Christie suggests two models for Miss Marple: her Auntie-Grannie from Ealing, who "always expected the worst of everyone and everything, and was, with almost frightening accuracy, usually proved right" (524) and Christie's favorite character in her *The Murder of Roger Ackroyd* (1926), Caroline Sheppard, "an acidulated spinster, full of curiosity, knowing everything, hearing everything: the complete detective service in the home" (522). Earl

Bargainnier, among others, has argued that Anna Katharine Green's Amelia Butterworth, the first elderly spinster detective, introduced in *The Leavenworth Case* (1878), is another model for Miss Marple (67). In *Reflecting on Miss Marple*, Shaw and Vanacker point out that "in the late 1920s, of every thousand persons in the population [of England and Wales] 43 were spinsters or widows" (38). In the 1920s single women, often older women, began appearing more frequently in mysteries. A memorable example is Sayers's *Unnatural Death* (1927) introducing Miss Climpson, another possible inspiration for Miss Marple. Sayers wrote to Christie in 1931, "Dear old tabbies are the only possible right kind of female detective and Miss M is lovely" (Shaw and Vanacker 35). A rarely mentioned source is Amelia Viner in Christie's 1928 novel, *The Mystery of the Blue Train*, apparently written about the same time as the first six Miss Marple stories. Miss Viner is a sharp-tongued, soft-hearted spinster who lives in St. Mary Mead in Kent (a village identical in spirit, if not exact location, to Miss Marple's St. Mary Mead). A letter from Miss Viner to her former companion makes reference to a new curate who is scandalously high, a vicar who is all Christian charity, a Dr. Harris, and an unsatisfactory maid—all characters who emerge later in *Vicarage* (183-84).

Miss Marple has a number of real and fictional antecedents. Although she has some traits in common with Christie, Miss Marple is not a mirror image of her creator. This misconception likely arose because the aging Agatha Christie resembled Miss Marple.

The Miss Marple books follow a predictable pattern or formula.

Christie's books are often chosen to exemplify the formula of the classic detective story as it developed in 1920s and 1930s Britain. Earl Bargainnier's *The Gentle Art of Murder*, for example, does a splendid job analyzing Christie as a mystery writer in the Golden Age tradition. *Vicarage*, the first novel in the Miss Marple series, contains the expected conventional elements. It presents a murder mystery to be solved (who killed the detestable Colonel Protheroe in the vicar's study?), a closed circle of suspects with various motives and secrets (his first wife, his second wife, his second wife's lover, his daughter, the curate, the vicar, the vicar's wife, a disgruntled poacher, an archaeologist), an investigation that reveals to detectives and readers both clues (the colonel's note, the large rock) and red herrings (the archaeologist's suitcase, the phone call to Mrs. Price Ridley); and a surprise solution revealed by the amateur detective (Miss Marple) who has outwitted the official police (Inspector Slack and Colonel Melchett).

While this very rudimentary formula can be seen throughout the Miss Marple series, thinking of Christie as a formula writer tends to blind readers to the great diversity among the novels in the series.

In *Vicarage* and *The Tuesday Club Murders* (1932) we meet Miss Marple on her own turf, at St. Mary Mead. St. Mary Mead is so strongly associated with Miss Marple in readers' minds that most would be surprised to discover that ten of the eleven subsequent novels in the series use other settings, at least in part. *The Moving Finger* (1942), *A Murder Is Announced* (1950), and *Sleeping Murder* (1976) are set in other small English villages. Much of the investigation in *The Body in the Library* (1942) and *At Bertram's Hotel* (1965) takes place in hotels, in Danemouth and London, respectively. *Murder with Mirrors* (1952) is set at an institute for the rehabilitation of young criminals, *A Pocket Full of Rye* (1953) in a posh London suburb, *Nemesis* (1971) on a tour of famous English homes and gardens, and *A Caribbean Mystery* (1964) on a Caribbean island.

Differences in narrative strategy and tone characterize the series as well. *Vicarage* and *Moving Finger* feature first-person narrators, not Miss Marple. In *The Mirror Crack'd* (1962) the omniscient narrator follows the thoughts and actions of a number of characters. In *Nemesis* we follow Miss Marple closely from beginning to end. In *Rye* we follow the investigation of Inspector Neele; Miss Marple doesn't make an appearance until page 78. *Vicarage* is full humor: Rev. Clement's wry narration, Slack's energy, the behavior of the gossiping quartet, Griselda's conversation. As the series develops, the comedy fades, and there is more emphasis on human psychology. Both *Nemesis* and *Sleeping Murder*, which repeatedly refer to famous literary tragedies, have a strong tragic tone.

Victims, murderers, and sidekicks vary in the Miss Marple series. Colonel Protheroe in *Vicarage* is a conventional murder mystery victim: a rich, disliked parent. Some of Christie's other victims in the series are less typical: a dancer, a Girl Guide, a nondescript wife, a retired headmistress, a maid, a hotel doorman, an elderly female companion. Money, the most common motive for murder in the classic detective story, drives the killers in *Vicarage*. But in the series, murderers kill for a myriad of other reasons: jealousy, revenge, perverted idealism, self-protection, possessiveness, and love. In *Vicarage*, Miss Marple is assisted by the Rev. Clement. Unlike other detectives saddled with the same sidekicks book after book, Miss Marple collaborates with many different people in the series: Sir Henry Clithering, Dermot Craddock, Dolly Bantry, Raymond West, Lucy Eyelesbarrow, Jason Rafiel, Megan Hunter, Inspectors Davy and Neele, "Bunch" Harmon, and Gwenda and Giles Reed.

In these ways and in her devices for surprising readers, the Miss Marple series, though it follows a formula, reflects a great deal of experimentation and variety. This is true also for Christie's entire output as a writer, which includes poems, plays, mysteries, thrillers, psychological fiction, autobiography, and children's stories. That people were always eager to read the latest "Christie for Christmas" does not mean that the books were recyclings.

Throughout the series, Miss Marple undergoes "fluffification."

In *A Talent to Deceive*, Robert Barnard writes that "over the years Miss Marple changes radically. Her publishers, in one of their blurbs, describe her as 'fluffy,' and her development is essentially a process of fluffification." She begins, Barnard says, as a Caroline Sheppard: "sharp-eyed, sharp-tongued, a vicious gossip with an incomparable information service and a desire to believe the worst." "But over the years," he continues, "the binoculars are put away, the gardening becomes genuine rather than just a convenient passion, the gentle, appealing manner becomes a real guide to her human qualities rather than a smokescreen. She becomes a wise and charming old lady. . . . She becomes sweet" (102-03). In *Agatha Christie: Mistress of Mystery*, written before the last Miss Marple novel, G.C. Ramsey states that Miss Marple changes "from a very shrewd small village pussy to a rather tolerant grandmother type looking over the world" (60). The "fluffification" theory has two problems, however: Miss Marple is not such a dislikable character in *Vicarage*, and she evolves into something very "unfluffy" by the end of the series.

In *Vicarage*, Griselda sees Miss Marple as a "nasty old cat" (18), one of a quartet of village harpies. But Miss Marple suffers from guilt by association with the likes of Mrs. Price Ridley, truly a holy terror. The vicar distinguishes Miss Marple from her cronies: she is "dangerous" (14) because her guesses are inevitably right, but she is also sensible, compassionate, humorous, and righteous. At novel's end, the Rev. Clement thinks, "Really Miss Marple is rather a dear" (223). Griselda soon comes around. In *McGillicuddy* we learn Miss Marple spends Christmases with the Clements (30).

Righteousness becomes Miss Marple's distinguishing trait by the end of the series. Although she looks fluffy, Mr. Rafiel in *Caribbean* comes to realize she is justice personified, Nemesis. In the novel of that name, Mr. Rafiel, now deceased, has a letter forwarded to Miss Marple that refers to her "natural flair for justice" and quotes from Amos: "Let justice roll down like waters / And righteousness like an everlasting stream" (22-23). *Nemesis* contains references to the classics, appropriately, since Miss Marple has become a symbol of righteous vengeance, a Fury. At one point, she says to Professor Wanstead, "I do not like evil beings who do evil things" (109). Later she tells him she has been able to smell evil at times in her life (114). At the end of this last-written Miss Marple novel, after she has nosed out evil where it lies buried, an Assistant Commissioner of Scotland Yard comments about her, "So gentle—and so ruthless" (222).

To say, as many have in different words, that Miss Marple undergoes "fluffification" does not take into account either the goodness and kindness of the early Miss Marple or the steely determination of the later Miss Marple. She changes from *Vicarage* to *Nemesis*, but she does not become a fluffy pussy.

Miss Marple solves cases through the use of intuition.

Just as Hercule Poirot is associated with logic and method as a means of crime solving, Miss Marple is described, in contrast, as a detective who relies on intuition. In *Murder She Wrote*, for example, Patricia Maida and Nicholas B. Spornick compare Jane Marple with Father Brown, both of whom rely on "unassuming presentation of self and brilliant flashes of intuition" (107).

Vicarage creates the illusion that Miss Marple operates by intuition because we are not privy to her actions and thought processes, except as she confides in the vicar. Thus her success seems to be a result of intuition. In fact, though, we know that a number of clues lead to the correct solution: a rock of the wrong size, a couple cheerful when they should be upset, an inexplicable note left for the vicar, and more. Miss Marple uses a process of observation and ratiocination, not intuition, to arrive at the truth.

The foundation of the Marple method is what Bargainnier calls "analogical reasoning" (74), her technique of comparing suspects with people she has known in St. Mary Mead and elsewhere. This method makes Miss Marple seem intuitive, if not possessed of magical powers, but it is based on close observation of human nature, not guesswork, as Miss Marple explains in *Vicarage*. When Griselda says she hopes Miss Marple will solve the Protheroe case as she solved the case of the missing gill of picked shrimps, by making an analogy with "something quite different about a sack of coals," Miss Marple says that what people call intuition and "make such a fuss about" is really like "reading a word without having to spell it out. A child can't do that because it has had so little experience. But a grown-up person knows the word because he's seen it often before" (76).

Because Miss Marple has seen human beings at close range, she has become an expert on types of human nature. When she meets new people, she works to find the proper analogy from her mental file of human types. This is not intuition. It is the kind of expert knowledge any police officer, minister, or psychologist might develop. This knowledge, combined with standard detective methods (observation, engaging suspects in conversation, ratiocination), Miss Marple uses in *Vicarage* and throughout the series.

St. Mary Mead is a bucolic setting, an Eden, a place of innocence.

In "The Guilty Vicarage," W.H. Auden states that the interest in a detective story is not the conflict of good and evil, but "the dialectic of innocence and guilt" (401). In describing the ideal setting for the detective story, Auden says it must appear to be "an innocent society in a state of grace . . . where murder, therefore, is the unheard-of act which precipitates a crisis" (403). The natural milieu for the detective story is the "Great Good Place," he continues, "for the more Eden-like it is, the greater the contradiction of murder" (404). At the end of a detective story, Auden concludes, after the evil is located and expunged, readers can enjoy the "fantasy of being restored to the Garden of Eden, to a state of innocence" (409).

Auden's 1948 essay has had a profound influence on descriptions of setting in the classic detective story. Its title, "The Guilty Vicarage," seems to be an allusion to the first Miss Marple novel, implying that this novel and the subsequent novels fit the pattern he describes. Critics have tended to follow Auden's lead by describing St. Mary Mead as a good place. While it is true the Miss Marple stories have everything to do with innocence and guilt, to describe St. Mary Mead (or any Marple locales) as innocent is laughable.

St. Mary Mead is not a "good society." "There is a great deal of wickedness in a village" is a Marpleism repeated throughout the series. In *Vicarage*, we find (besides the murdering, adulterous couple) a domestic tyrant, a thief posing as an archaeologist, a poacher, and a member of the clergy who stole Mrs. Price Ridley's pound note. Miss Marple alludes to a bigamist, a woman who stole a pin and framed another woman out of spite, a pretty ethereal girl who tried to kill her little brother, and a church organist who stole the money for the Choir Boys' Outing (76). The Marple novels and stories are full of references to village iniquities, leading Raymond to exclaim to his Aunt Jane in *Tuesday Club*: "God forbid that I ever regard village life as peaceful and uneventful. . . . Not after the horrible revelations we have heard from you! The cosmopolitan world seems a mild and peaceful place compared with St. Mary Mead" (67).

The amusing irony throughout the series is that Raymond who writes shockingly frank novels is an innocent compared to his elderly aunt. He and too many readers continue to view St. Mary Mead as an ideal rural setting, despite overwhelming evidence to the contrary. In *Caribbean*, the narrator comments that "really rural life was far from idyllic. People like Raymond were so ignorant. In the course of her duties in a country parish, Jane Marple had acquired quite a comprehensive knowledge of the facts of rural life," including "plenty of sex, natural and unnatural. Rape, incest, perversions of all kinds" (13).

If the society in a Miss Marple novel is not innocent, the murder does cause a crisis because people *innocent of the murder* are under suspicion. This is the aspect of innocence and guilt that interested Christie. In her autobiography, Christie writes that "nobody seems to care about the innocent" (529)—the victims of murder and those wrongfully suspected of the crime. The possibilities of more killings and of charging the wrong person with the murder are what create the tension in a Miss Marple story. In *Vicarage*, Miss Marple's concern is to trap the murderers and save the hapless Hawes from being scapegoated. Miss Marple's successful resolutions let us fantasize, not that society is restored to innocence, as Auden suggests, but that truth can be discovered and justice carried out, one case at a time.

Christie repeatedly employs the least-likely-person gambit.

G.C. Ramsey writes, "Agatha Christie has been accused of overusing the 'least-likely-person motif'" (36). This is a popular viewpoint, with some supporting evidence. In *McGillicuddy* Christie's murderer is an unlikely person peripheral to the plot. More often, as in *Announced*, the criminals are not minor characters, but persons who would be obvious, except that Christie has led us to discount them through fictional sleight-of-hand.

Eliot A. Singer's essay, "The Whodunit as Riddle: Block Elements in Agatha Christie," compares Christie's bamboozling strategies to those used by expert riddlers: providing too little information, too much information, contradictions, false gestalt, and generic blockers. The Miss Marple fiction uses all these techniques, making the series much more challenging and fun than it would be if Christie repeated the same least-likely-person technique, as she is described as doing. *Vicarage* provides too much information in the way of secrets (Mrs. Lestrange, Lettice, Dr. Haydock, Griselda) and hidden crimes (Dr. Stone, Hawes). A generic blocker is that we expect one person, not two, to be guilty. *Announced* and *Mirror Crack'd* use false gestalt, making us think the murderers are the intended victims. *Mirrors* uses contradiction to bamboozle us. In *Caribbean* we have too little information about the past of the murderer.

In the Miss Marple series, Christie also relies on manipulation of conventional stereotypes and narrative misdirection to fool us. For example, *Library* plays on the stereotype of the older married man fooling around with a younger, attractive woman. Several of her surprise endings depend on our stereotype of lovers as unrelated men and women of similar age. There are hundred of examples in the Marple series of Christie's use of narrative misdirection to confuse us. One common device is for the detective to speculate about the real motive but attach that motive to the wrong person. Another is for Christie to follow a important clue with an especially dramatic (and misleading) plot event.

Christie's cleverness is legendary, but one principle she held firmly in mind is that the reader should feel the solution is inevitable, not one of many choices the writer might have made. This is what Singer calls the "non-arbitrariness of most of her solutions" (159). If Christie had overused the least-likely-person gambit, as people claim she did, her mysteries would not be so baffling.

Christie's novels are full of cardboard characters.
    In *Great Writers of the English Language*, T.J. Winnifrith writes:

Her [Christie's] two main detectives, the Belgian Hercule Poirot and Miss
Marple, are almost entirely featureless, apart from a few irritating personal
eccentricities, and Christie does not seem interested in character
development, the other people in her novels, guilty and innocent alike,
being stereotypes, dancing like puppets in the hands of both detective writer
and detective alike. (qtd. in Ashley 4-5)

Other reviewers and critics have also been less than kind in assessing
Christie's ability to characterize the people in her mysteries. LeRoy
Panek states that her characters are "vapid or superficial" (38).
Robert Barnard argues that, because of the importance of the puzzle
to her mysteries, "the characters, with a few exceptions, are penny-
plain, cardboard-cut-out figures—though ones that admirably suit the
sort of book she aims to write" (46).
    In assessing Christie's skill at characterization, it is necessary, as
Barnard hints, to consider "the sort of book she aims to write." The
classic detective story, George Grella maintains in "Murder and
Manners: The Formal Detective Novel," is in the comedy of manners
mode (41). In other words, Christie resembles Henry Fielding, not
Henry James. Grella's discussion of genre is useful in helping us
appreciate the artistry in a novel like *Vicarage*, with its wonderful
characterization in the comedy of manners style. But the Miss Marple
series moves in other directions, later books displaying characteristics
of the romance, the psychological novel, the tragedy, and the
allegory, although following the classic detective fiction formula. Just
as Grella provides a useful way of viewing the early comedy of
manners fiction, other critics have provided helpful ways of seeing
the characters in the later Miss Marple fiction.
    Many of Christie's characters are "modern versions of the
humors characters of Roman, Renaissance, and Restoration
comedy," Grella argues (48). In *Vicarage*, many characters are
defined by a single trait, often a trait that is gently ridiculed: the
overly efficient and energetic Slack, the histrionic and self-important
Mrs. Price Ridley, the truculent and slovenly Mary, the guilt-ridden
Hawes. In the best comedy of manners tradition, Christie's humors
characters are entertaining and memorable.
    Like Dickens, Christie is skilled at describing characters vividly
and economically and in creating distinctive dialogue for her

characters. In *Vicarage* Miss Marple describes Inspector Slack: "such an autocratic man, isn't he? . . . he's exactly like the young lady in the boot shop who wants to sell you patent leather because she's got it in your size, and doesn't take any notice of the fact that you want brown calf" (193). In *Rye* Christie describes the most minor of characters, a new, inefficient, nervous typist at Mr. Fortescue's office, through a single detail: Miss Somers can never tell whether a kettle is boiling and routinely serves tepid tea (1). All the characters in Christie's novels have distinctive voices. In *Vicarage* no one could confuse the Rev. Clement with Mr. Hawes, though they are both clergymen. In *Announced*, speech patterns mark Dora Bunner as insecure, Hinch as brisk, the Rev. Harmon as scholarly, Julia as cynical, and Colonel Easterbrook as pompous.

In a fascinating essay, "Agatha Christie: Modern and Modernist," Nicholas and Margaret Boe Birns declare that Christie is significantly underrated by those who fail to see that she uses some of the same literary techniques as do modernist writers praised for their sophistication. "The pretense, disguise, play-acting, and outward show that are essential to the mystery genre are given a special intensity in Christie's work by her constant emphasis on and reference to the 'theatricality' of her characters' actions," the Birnses write (122). This technique not only leaves us astounded at the end of a novel when a character's mask drops and the stage managing of our assumptions is revealed, but it can lead us to speculate how many people around us appear to be uninteresting types, but are, in reality, much different from the masks they wear. It is also a technique that reveals Christie's skill delineating ironies of character. While this "theatricality" technique can be seen in *Vicarage*—in the revelation of Lawrence Redding's true nature—it becomes much more important and effective in later Miss Marple novels.

In *Mirrors*, which develops at length the metaphors of theatricality and conjuring, Dr. Serrocold is the man with the mask, the stage manager, the conjurer. While creating the illusion of being in one place for an "audience" of family and associates, he is, in fact, elsewhere, committing murder. But his major deception is using the rehabilitation institute to train young hoodlums to embezzle on a grand scale so he can finance a cooperative, self-supporting community for delinquents overseas. Dr. Serrocold is not an interesting character until his mask drops, and we see that he possesses true goodness mixed with criminal arrogance and that he is a man self-deceived by the illusions he created to fool others.

The murderers in *Announced, Mirror Crack'd, Nemesis,* and *Sleeping Murder,* like Dr. Serrocold, create images of respectability, grief, victimization, and ordinariness to hide their real selves, illusions they more than half-believe themselves. At the close of each novel, the characterization we have come to accept clashes dramatically with the picture of the murderer's character that Miss Marple, like a photographer, has developed in stages over the course of the narrative until the true identity emerges clearly.

Christie's characters are mostly in the tradition of the comedy of manners, but we discover as the novels close that some of the characters have projected illusions and that the comic surface of life is undergirded with pathos, tragedy, self-deception, and painful reality. People are not what they seem. While it is overstating the case to rate Christie with Edith Wharton and Jane Austen, she uses many of the same techniques of characterization—and she uses them with great cleverness.

Christie is interested in the investigation of crime, not criminal psychology.

John Cawelti has pointed out that the classic detective story does not succeed if "we become too concerned with the motives of the criminal" (92). Most definitions of the formula—and descriptions of Christie's novels—assume that detecting crime, not psychoanalyzing criminals, is the classic mystery's purpose.

As is the case with many of these questionable assertions, this one is more true for *Vicarage* than for subsequent Miss Marple novels. In *Vicarage,* we follow the investigation of the crime, in this case as carried out by both the official police force and the amateurs. We watch the investigators examine the scene of the crime, listen to interviews with suspects, monitor developments in the case, consider theories, try to explain confusing incidents, discover the truth, and enjoy the exposure of the guilty parties.

In this first Miss Marple novel, the psychology of the co-criminals is not very interesting when the truth is revealed. We do not know much about Lawrence Redding, except that he is not particular about affairs with married women and that he is as greedy and unscrupulous as he is charming. We can believe Mrs. Protheroe the second found life with her overbearing husband hell, can sympathize with her, can imagine why she might prefer a charming and clever young man to her husband, can see how she might rationalize the crime, and can even detect in her some little bit of guilt after the murder.

But all this is hardly an argument that Christie gives any serious attention to criminal psychology in the novel.

As the series progresses, however, Christie displays a much greater interest in the various forces that drive people to murder, creating characters of interest to psychologists and sociologists: for example, an incest perpetrator, a woman who has suffered most of her life with a hideous goiter that kept her a recluse, a woman who loves another woman, and a woman who never recovered her emotional stability after giving birth to a child with mental retardation.

A wonderful study of criminal psychology is Elvira Blake in *Bertram's*, the daughter of a daring but morally careless "super mom," Bess Sedgwick, who left Elvira in the care of surrogates so her daughter would not have to suffer the emotional messiness resulting from her unconventional, death-defying adventures. At first, it appears that Elvira is a typical rebellious teen, lying to her caretakers, conspiring with her best friend, and chasing a glamorous bad boy with a hot car. Elvira seems to be following in mom's footsteps, all the while convincing her elders she is an innocent. Elvira's cleverness at outwitting adults is amusing, perhaps reminding us of similar childhood deceptions. As the novel progresses and the truth emerges, we see that Bess Sedgwick's choice not to raise her own daughter deeply hurt Elvira. Feeling unloved, Elvira feels the world owes her money and happiness. Her minor lapses in obeying the rules are symptomatic of a personality that acknowledges no "thou shalt nots." Elvira is a damaged child, a neglected child, a child raised with rules but no principles, a dangerous child. Christie's portraits of child criminals are unforgettable, Elvira only one of several. Christie reminds us that children feel things strongly but lack a sense of proportion. This can make them dangerous to themselves and others.

Perhaps as a result of the psychological studies she was enjoying writing in the Mary Westmacott novels, the psychology of Christie's characters, especially her criminals, became increasingly more complex, more interesting, and more central to the working out of the mystery over the years. Those who judge her interest in criminal psychology in the Miss Marple series based solely on *Vicarage* will be misled.

Christie is not a feminist.

Whether or not Christie is a feminist is a matter of some debate. Complicating the issue is that her novels can be read from different angles. *Bertram's* can be seen as a cautionary tale warning mothers to stay at home and raise children or as a story about a daring, risk-taking woman whom Miss Marple admires. The Miss Marple series is not consistent, further making generalizations difficult. *Vicarage*, despite wonderful Griselda and the portrayal of women suffering at the hands of a domestic tyrant, is not promising material for feminist interpretation. *Announced*, on the other hand, makes women's lives central to the story and conveys enlightened attitudes about female poverty, the pressure on women to be beautiful, and lesbianism.

In "Women and Crime: Sexism in Allingham, Sayers, and Christie," Margot Peters and Agate Nesaule Krouse argue that "Christie offends least, but still offends" (144). I have argued in "Agatha Christie: Feminist?" that in decades more sympathetic to feminist characters and themes in fiction (the 1920s, the World War II years and shortly after, and the late 1960s and early 1970s) Christie developed feminist, characters, plots, and themes (406). More recent critics—for example, Marian Shaw and Sabine Vanacker—are making a case for Miss Marple herself as an independent, if not overtly feminist, character, a champion representing a despised class (older, single women), a force for justice whose forte is knowledge of people and the trivia of existence (34). Perhaps the fairest conclusion is that the Miss Marple series is not consistently feminist, but it often shows women and the circumstances of their lives in detail and with sympathy.

Moving Finger is an interesting case study. Earl Bargainnier finds the two romances in the novel "the most blatant examples of feminine subservience and male domination in Christie's fiction" (139), disliking Joanna's transformation from independent woman to worshiper at the shrine of Owen Griffith's medical genius and Megan's Cinderella makeover when Jerry buys her a "new look" in London.

The novels can be read to support a more feminist inter-pretation, however. Miss Marple encourages awkward, depressed Megan to risk her life in the cause of justice, her increased confidence the more significant transformation Megan undergoes. Joanna, previously enamored of misunderstood geniuses who use her and fail to appreciate her, links herself to a hard-working, dedicated man worthy of her. Further, the novel presents with much sympathy Emily Barton, a victim of a tyrannical mother all her life, and Aimée Griffith, who turned to do-gooding work only because her parents refused to pay for medical training. Even more fascinating (and feminist) is how *Moving Finger*, like Sayers's *Gaudy Night*, creates a surprise ending by manipulating readers' sexist assumptions about single women. We assume repressed women (or perhaps an effeminate man like Mr. Pye) are apt to write poison pen letters, but the ending exposes as fallacious Freudian notions about unmanly men and unwomanly women as dangerous and mentally ill. The criminal is revealed to be a respected member of the local patriarchal establishment, willing to victimize village women in order to rid himself of a wife he doesn't like so he can marry his children's governess.

M. Vipond's "Agatha Christie's Women" points out the contradictions in Christie's books: wonderful women role models in some books and traditional, limiting views of women in other books, or both views in the same book. Vipond points out, sensibly, that Christie's own life was full of such ambivalences. Why should her work not reflect these mixed feelings? Vipond concluded: "Despite the fact that she wrote in a form which demanded stereotypes and caricatures, Christie was not a generalizer. She knew more of life than that. That is why her books give a surprisingly accurate picture of the life of twentieth-century women" (123).

Christie portrays and defends the lifestyle and values of Edwardian England.

In Christie's thrillers, there is a "nostalgia for the heydey of Empire" (18), Robert Barnard writes. It is commonly held that classic detective stories, including Christie's, also represent the elitist, racist, imperialist biases of Edwardian England. Many have noted the nostalgia for the days of her late Victorian and Edwardian childhood that pervades Christie's mysteries, especially the latter ones: wistful descriptions of family celebrations with lots of food prepared by a staff of servants, village life before supermarkets and housing developments, and human relationships when sex was titillating, not a requirement.

Vicarage certainly presents St. Mary Mead as a traditional English village, mostly unaffected by the social upheavals of World War I and the 1920s: there is a clear class system, all the residents of St. Mary Mead are white (and apparently all Anglicans), and genteel households still have servants (though finding good servants is obviously becoming more difficult). The younger generation chafes at the old-fashioned values of their elders, but the older values seem the more admirable values in the end. In other books in the Marple canon, a distaste for those who have risen through trade—the Crackenthorpes and the Fortescues—seems to reveal an elitist attitude.

Yet to dismiss Christie as a political conservative is to overlook aspects of her novels that critique the values of Edwardian England and advocate living in the present, not the past. Unlike some of her contemporaries, Christie writes about the middle class, not aristocrats. In *Rye*, she makes reference to Britain plundering Africa. The many colonels and majors who served the empire are old bores, not heroes. *Rye* eloquently shows the tragedy that can result by not educating servants. Both *Announced* and *Bertram's* satirize those people, including Miss Marple herself, who will pay lavishly to live in the Edwardian past, but with all the most modern luxuries. After experiencing elegant, old-fashioned Bertram's Hotel for a time, Miss Marple says to Inspector Davy:

It seemed wonderful at first—unchanged you know—like stepping back into the past—to the past that one had loved and enjoyed.

. . . But of course it wasn't really like that. I learned (what I suppose I really knew already) that one can never go back, that one should not ever try to go back—that the essence of life is going forward. Life is a one way street, isn't it? (129)

This passage—as well as the book's exposing Bertram's as a front for criminal activities—shows that living in the past, wallowing in nostalgia, is unnatural. Life means change.

Christie's Miss Marple series shows a changing world and modern problems. Miss Marple and others may express nostalgia for the past at times, but her world is the present, and Miss Marple, while limited in her experiences of the world, believes, as a good Christian, that people are much the same everywhere and that human worth is based on factors other than class, wealth, race, gender, or education.

Christie does not deal with social and intellectual issues in her mysteries.

LeRoy Panek writes that the treatment of "moral and social issues" in Christie's mysteries is "banal" (38), which implies that she does deal with them, if not well. Others suggest that such issues have no place in detective fiction and tend to distract from the puzzle.

They praise Christie for sticking to puzzles and not drifting, as Sayers did, into social criticism and theology. For the most part, Christie concentrates on whodunit puzzles in the Miss Marple books and does not speculate about artistic and spiritual issues as she does in her Mary Westmacott novels. But the very nature of detective fiction leads writers, Christie included, into social commentary and moral issues.

Kurt Vonnegut makes this point in a "Writer's Workshop" television program. He comments that "some of the greatest social commentary is in British detective stories" (qtd. in Ashley 10). Like other detective fiction writers, Christie creates in her books a full, detailed picture of life at a certain time, in a certain place, and she shows changes in the fabric of everyday life caused by political events, philosophical and cultural shifts, and economic cycles. Furthermore, the nature of detective fiction itself, with its focus on guilt and innocence, leads naturally to the treatment of moral and ethical issues, implicitly, if not always explicitly.

Vicarage, Announced, and *Mirror Crack'd* present a social history of the changes in English village life from 1930 to the early 1960s, Anne Hart shows in *The Life and Times of Miss Jane Marple*. In the first novel we see a small village surrounded by woods and meadows. The core of the village is the church, the vicarage, a few Queen Anne and Georgian houses, the Blue Boar pub, and a few shops. A big house is just outside the village. People travel to the nearby town of Much Benham or by train to London to shop. Gossip travels through a network of servants and delivery boys. In *Announced*, set in the late 1940s, we can see the disruptions of village life caused by World War II. Strangers reside in Chipping Cleghorn. Newspapers, radio, and cinema are part of daily rituals. People have evolved a black market in goods because products are still rationed. Refugees from mainland Europe have settled in England, many working as servants. By the early 1960s, when *Mirror Crack'd* is set, the original core of the village still exists, but a substantial housing development has attracted couples caught up in installment buying. Young wives, like Cherry Baker, are well-educated, but do housework to bring in extra money to pay the bills. A film studio nearby has attracted movie people to the area. An aging Dr. Haydock prescribes mass-produced pills. Airplanes fly over St. Mary Mead. People worry about the bomb and crime. Divorces are common.

Christie began embedding important intellectual and moral themes into her Miss Marple narratives during World War II when she wrote *Sleeping Murder*, not published until 1976. The novel shows subtly but unmistakably what happens when incest infects a family. When Gwenda Reed attends a production of *The Duchess of Malfi*, a play about incest and murder, suppressed memories of a woman's murder pour forth. Like many incest victims, Gwenda begins to search the past to find an explanation for her memories. The resolution of the book reveals that Gwenda's stepmother, Helen, was murdered by her jealous, possessive brother. The bindweed in the Reeds' garden becomes for Miss Marple a metaphor for destructive love that knows no restraint; Helen's body, buried in the garden, emerges as a symbol of the secret of incest, buried and hidden from view.

As the Miss Marple series develops, Christie more openly examines the nature of both goodness and evil. She had strong feelings about the need to protect the innocent, and yet she saw that society's predators were human beings, whose motivations made fascinating studies. Just as the Miss Marple novels present a rich, detailed social history of England in the middle decades of the twentieth century, they also present to close readers a number of fascinating intellectual and moral issues to ponder.

Christie's prose style is pedestrian, non-literary.

Christie's style is criticized with as much vehemence as her characterization. Edmund Wilson writes in "Who Cares Who Killed Roger Ackroyd?" that "her writing is of a mawkishness and banality which seem to me literally impossible to read" (qtd. in Barnard 2). Panek states that Christie's novels "lack any sort of stylistic distinction" (38). Ashley, after stating Christie "does not concern herself with moral matters," claims that "her style was never notable and never influenced any great writers . . . or even other competent detective writers" (5).

Christie's style in the Miss Marple series is plain, direct, functional. In a passage from *Announced*, Belle Goedler describes her husband and Letitia Blacklock:

Randall couldn't really distinguish between what was crooked and what wasn't. His conscience wasn't sensitive. The poor dear really didn't know what was just smart—and what was dishonest. Blackie kept him straight. That's one thing about Letitia Blacklock, she's absolutely dead straight. (114)

Christie's "dead straight" style—simple sentences, common vocabulary, few slangy expressions and allusions—makes her writing eminently translatable and also accessible to children and teens as well as adults. But this is not the whole picture. Christie effectively employs metaphors (from theater and gardening especially) and allusions (for example, to *The Duchess of Malfi*). She is skilled in creating styles of speaking appropriate to the characters, a fundamental some of her more "literary" detective fiction colleagues have not grasped. She has the ability to select telling details that "limn character and era with so few (and such skilled) strokes," as Anthony Boucher described her style in a review of *Bertram's* (qtd. in Sanders and Lovallo 313). *Vicarage* shows Christie's ability to write witty dialogue. In the tea party scene, the older ladies tut-tut about handsome young artist Lawrence Redding, who is painting various women in the neighborhood:

> "He's a very good-looking young fellow."
> "But loose," said Miss Hartnell. "Bound to be. An artist! Paris! Models! The Altogether!"
> "Painting her in her bathing suit," said Mrs. Price Ridley. "Not quite nice."
> "He's painting me, too," said Griselda.
> "But not in your bathing suit, dear," said Miss Marple.
> "It might be worse," said Griselda solemnly. (16)

Christie moves a narrative along quickly and creates suspense, seldom bogging down her readers in the tedious reiterations of "the facts of the case" so common in mysteries. Perhaps Christie's greatest stylistic success is her skill in embedding linguistic clues into the text without our noticing them. An example is Dora Bunner's confusion about her friend's name in *Announced*, and all the comments about Miss Blacklock's central heating—humorous bits, we think, but really major clues.

As a stylist Christie is no James Joyce, to state the obvious. Christie's functional, rather plain style throughout the Miss Marple series is, however, appropriate for the mystery genre, and she uses this style with a good deal more sophistication than is usually conceded to her.

There is little of Christie in her mystery novels.

The first cited misconception was that Miss Marple is Agatha Christie herself. The final misconception is that Christie does not reveal herself anywhere in the Miss Marple series. In *A Talent to Deceive*, Barnard speculates that the highly publicized disappearance of Agatha Christie in 1926, at the time of her mother's death and Archie Christie's desertion, led Christie, innately shy before all this, to want "to withdraw, hide herself, cover her tracks, and . . . give away nothing of herself." This he maintains is the secret of her success as a puzzle-maker. He goes on to state, "Not only is there no sense of her own personality in the books; she is equally elusive as to her own taste and opinions" (55-56).

While we know less about Christie after reading her mysteries than we know about Sayers after reading hers, Christie is not entirely absent from her detective stories. Autobiographical and biographical sources on Christie and her Mary Westmacott novels reveal that Christie's own experiences and attitudes can be seen here and there throughout the Miss Marple series, but more in the later novels. *Vicarage*, for example, has no obvious autobiographical elements other than Miss Marple herself, modeled in part on Christie's Auntie-Grannie. Later novels reveal much more of Christie.

Rye is set in Baydon Heath, a golfing suburb of London, "almost entirely inhabited by rich city men" (11). Rex Fortescue and the other men who live there are interested in making money, golfing, and status. Their houses display no personal taste, their morals are twisty, and their unhappy mothers, wives, and daughters live lives of quiet desperation. That Christie's marriage fell apart after she and Archie moved to just such a suburb is not a coincidence. Neither is the affair between Adele and her golf partner: Archie eventually married his golf partner after he divorced Agatha. In *Bertram's*, a forgetful clergyman has amnesia, as Christie experienced it in 1926. Miss Marple wanders around London, reminiscing about the past, many of the memories Christie's own. Miss Marple has vivid memories of visiting the Army and Navy Stores as a child (47). Christie's uncle was the secretary of the Army and Navy Stores, where as a child she shopped with her grandmothers, according to Janet Morgan (16).

Other features in the Miss Marple novels that reflect Christie's own life include her characterization of children (Christie enjoyed her grandson, Mathew), happy marriages between couples of different ages (she was fourteen years older than Max Mallowan), and travel experiences (the Mallowans visited the Caribbean several times in the 1960s). Christie incorporated significant reading and theater experiences into the series, as well as happenings in the world around her that captured her imagination. The theater scene in *Sleeping Murder*, according to Charles Osborne, is based on a stirring 1944 production Christie saw of *The Duchess of Malfi*, starring John Gielgud and Peggy Ashcroft (323).

These examples show that Christie did not entirely disappear from her writing, as Barnard claims. That the type of mystery she wrote did not allow for much in the way of autobiographical revelation is unquestionable. But, as a writer, she did use her experiences as a basis for plot, characterization, and setting—overtly in the Mary Westmacott novels, and more subtly in the mysteries.

A study, then, of these "thirteen problems" surrounding the Agatha Christie mysteries—specifically, the Miss Marple series—reveals that there are many misconceptions about Christie as a writer and about the Miss Marple series. Why?

People sometimes confuse fiction and film. Margaret Rutherford is a comic genius, but not Christie's Miss Marple. The BBC series, with Joan Hickson, faithful as it tries to be, changes the plots and cannot replicate the subtleties and complexities of the novels. Media can muddy our memories of the literature.

Sexism, ageism, and elitism are evident in some judgments about Christie. Her emphasis on women characters—especially older women—does not appeal to all readers. Some, like Edmund Wilson, express outrage that Christie is so popular when more "literary" writers sell considerably less well. Some of the diatribes against Christie are thinly disguised expressions of rage at the idea of a mass culture.

Considering Christie in light of the conventions and rules of detective fiction of her day is enlightening, but it tends to cause readers to focus on how she fits the formulaic expectations. Much gets missed. Similarly, generalizing about Christie's mysteries minimizes very real and significant differences in the novels over time and differences among her various series.

Christie's shunning of interviews and publicity meant that, until the late 1970s, when her autobiography was published, people knew little about her, except what they could glean from *Come, Tell Me How You Live*. This silence led to misinformation and misinterpretation presented as fact. More recent studies of Christie tend to be more accurate and balanced, but some of the old misconceptions still get replayed.

Another factor behind the questionable judgments of Christie's work seems to be the human habit of polarized thinking. If Poirot is logical, Miss Marple must be intuitive. If Christie's novels are plot-driven, they cannot be strong in characterization. If her style seems simple, she cannot be complex in her ideas. If she's popular, she cannot be good.

The structure of fictional mysteries may confuse readers. Some characters lie and pretend, their true natures not apparent until the conclusion, after readers have shaped their views of the characters. It is easy to forget the ending revelations when skimming through a book and looking at characters again, remembering our first impressions of them.

Finally, and perhaps most importantly, we tend to look at detective fiction as a formulaic genre and to view series of detective fiction novels as having their own formula that gets played out repeatedly. People talk as if the latest Sue Grafton or Robert Parker novel will satisfy precisely because it will provide a known pleasure: our hero working with familiar companions and within familiar plotlines. Readers tend to view the Miss Marple series in this way and the first novel in the series, *The Murder at the Vicarage*, as the blueprint for the subsequent novels. While similarities and distinctive features exist among the Miss Marple novels, the books really are quite different and reflect considerable innovation on Christie's part. They also represent over forty years of social, political, and economic change in Britain. *Vicarage* is a wonderful first novel: it succeeds as a murder mystery and as a comic novel. Because of its success and because it is the first of the series, it is, for many people, the epitome of the Miss Marple book. This, as we have seen, can lead to erroneous generalizations about the series as a whole.

Although Agatha Christie is a much misunderstood writer, she is, in the final analysis, a writer worth reading and studying—not simply for her skill as a creator of devious whodunit puzzles, but for her insight into human nature and modern Britain, her hundreds of memorable characters (many women), and her sophisticated uses of point of view and other literary techniques. While Christie was a formula writer, "a sausage factory" she called herself (qtd. in Ashley 4), she was much more. The Miss Marple series shows that she deserves to be heralded for her literary achievement, not simply her sales record.

Works Cited and Consulted

Agatha Christie: Official Centenary Celebration, 1890-1990. Ed. Lynn Underwood. New York: Harper, 1990.

Ashley, Leonard R.N. "'The Sausage Machine': Names in the Detective Fiction of Dame Agatha Christie." *Literary Onomastics Studies* 11 (1984): 1-36.

Auden, W.H. "The Guilty Vicarage." *The Dyer's Hand and Other Essays.* New York: Random, 1948. Rpt. in *Detective Fiction: Crime and Compromise*. Ed. Dick Allen and David Chacko. New York: Harcourt, 1974.

Bargainnier, Earl F. *The Gentle Art of Murder: The Detective Fiction of Agatha Christie*. Bowling Green, OH: Bowling Green State University Popular Press, 1980.

Barnard, Robert. *A Talent to Deceive: An Appreciation of Agatha Christie.* New York: Dodd, 1980.

Birns, Nicholas, and Margaret Boe Birns. "Agatha Christie: Modern and Modernist." *The Cunning Craft: Original Essays on Detective Fiction and Contemporary Literary Theory.* Ed. Ronald G. Walker and June M. Frazier. Macomb, IL: Western Illinois U, 1990. 120-34.

Cawelti, John G. *Adventure, Mystery, and Romance: Formula Stories as Art and Popular Culture.* Chicago: U of Chicago P, 1976.

Christie, Agatha. *An Autobiography*. New York: Ballantine, 1977.

____. *At Bertram's Hotel*. New York: Pocket, 1968.

____. *A Caribbean Mystery*. New York: Pocket, 1973.

____. *The Murder at the Vicarage*. New York: Dell, 1970.

____. *A Murder Is Announced*. New York: Pocket, 1970.

____. *Nemesis*. New York: Pocket, 1973.

____. *A Pocket Full of Rye*. New York: Pocket, 1967.

____. *The Tuesday Club Murders*. New York: Dell, 1967,

____. *What Mrs. McGillicuddy Saw!* New York: Pocket, 1958.

Grella, George. "Murder and Manners: The Formal Detective Novel." *Dimensions of Detective Fiction.* Ed. Larry Landrum, Pat Browne, and Ray B. Browne. Bowling Green, OH: Bowling Green State University Popular Press, 1976.

Haining, Peter. *Agatha Christie: Murder in Four Acts: A Centenary Celebration of "The Queen of Crime" on Stage, Film, Radio, and TV.* London: Virgin, 1990.

Hart, Anne. *The Life and Times of Miss Jane Marple*. New York: Dodd, 1985.

Knepper, Marty S. "Agatha Christie: Feminist?" *The Armchair Detective* 16.4 (Winter 1983): 398-406.

Maida, Patricia D., and Nicholas B. Spornick. *Murder She Wrote: A Study of Agatha Christie's Detective Fiction.* Bowling Green, OH: Bowling Green State University Popular Press, 1982.

Morgan, Janet. *Agatha Christie: A Biography.* New York: Knopf, 1985.

Osborne, Charles. *The Life and Crimes of Agatha Christie.* New York: Contemporary Books, 1982.

Panek, LeRoy Lad. *Watteau's Shepherds: The Detective Novel in Britain, 1914-1940.* Bowling Green, OH: Bowling Green State University Popular Press, 1979.

Peters, Margot, and Agate Nesaule Krouse. "Women and Crime: Sexism in Allingham, Sayers, and Christie." *Southwest Review* 59.2 (Spring 1974): 144-52.

Ramsey, G.C. *Agatha Christie: Mistress of Mystery.* New York: Dodd, 1967.

Sanders, Dennis, and Len Lovallo. *The Agatha Christie Companion: The Complete Guide to Agatha Christie's Life and Work.* Rev. ed. New York: Berkley, 1989.

Shaw, Marion, and Sabine Vanacker. *Reflecting on Miss Marple.* London: Routledge, 1991.

Singer, Eliot A. "The Whodunit as Riddle: Block Elements in Agatha Christie." *Western Folklore* 43.3 (July 1984): 157-71.

Thomson, H. Douglas. *Masters of Mystery: A Study of the Detective Story.* New York: Dover, 1978.

Vipond, M. "Agatha Christie's Women." *The International Fiction Review* 8.2 (Summer 1981): 119-23.

Enter the Fat Man:
Rex Stout's *Fer-de-Lance*

Frederick Isaac

Some fictional characters seem destined to be created, to fill a gap. They fit both their time and the needs of the genre so perfectly that they are immediately seized upon by the public as emblematic of their genre. Such a character was the combination of Archie Goodwin and Nero Wolfe in their first adventure, *Fer-de-Lance* (1934).

Consider first the time of their appearance. In a variety of ways, the mid-1930s was a schizophrenic period in American popular culture. While the nation, and indeed the entire world, slogged through the Great Depression, the most important entertainment form for many Americans was the movies. And among the most popular film styles of that era, if our historians may be believed, were western sagas and high society romances. This dichotomy of the irretrievable past and the unachievable present is almost painfully striking today. On the other hand, the songs of Gene Autry, the adventures of Tom Mix, the elegance and high living of Busby Berkeley's "Gold Diggers" series, and the social challenge presented by "It Happened One Night" captured for their audiences a variety of emotions that are difficult to comprehend more than half a century later.

The paradoxes between the screen images of the great stars of the studio era and the lives of their viewers may not have been so obvious to those millions who lost themselves in the great movie palaces and small-town theaters as they are to us, sixty years later. Though it is in some ways a purely nostalgic commentary, Woody Allen's romantic comedy *The Purple Rose of Cairo* contains many of the contradictory impulses of the era. The woman whose wish to leave her current life is so strong that she wills the hero of a movie into reality may be a fantasy, but it was an important part of life in times when jobs were scarce and people felt abandoned by reality and had recourse only to their dreams.

In the realm of detective fiction, the distance between the poles was no less dramatic. On one side the popularity of the English Country House story familiar since World War I continued to grow, and some of the form's classics date from that period. In the mid-1930s Agatha Christie would write some of her best stories, including *Murder on the Orient Express* (1934) and *The ABC Murders* (1936); Dorothy L. Sayers would reach the top of her form in *The Nine Tailors* (1934) and *Gaudy Night* (1935), before abandoning Peter Wimsey and Harriet Vane altogether in 1937; and Margery Allingham would continue to develop Albert Campion and his supporting cast in *Death of a Ghost* (1934) and *Flowers for the Judge* (1936), adding Lady Amanda Fitton to the group in *The Fashion in Shrouds* (1938).

As the British writers, especially the women, reached their high point, American authors were creating their own version of the Golden Age. The pseudonymous S.S. van Dine (Willard Huntington Wright) and eponymous Ellery Queen (Frederic Dannay and Manfred B. Lee) had each created his own style of detecting, based in many ways on the British form but at the same time quite distinctive. While the insufferable and increasingly unbelievable Philo Vance's career would decline in interest until it ended in 1939, the Queen series was only in the first of three well-defined stages, the collection using the "Challenge to the Reader" as a prominent, and unique, element.

While these successful writers continued to engage many readers, the mid-1930s brought into the fold a number of other memorable and long-running characters on both sides of the Atlantic. Erle Stanley Gardner's Perry Mason began his courtroom career in Los Angeles, and John Dickson Carr's Dr. Gideon Fell first hobbled through London in 1933.[1] Ngaio Marsh's Roderick Alleyn was born along with Wolfe and Archie in 1934;[2] Cecil Day Lewis, under the pen-name of Nicholas Blake, introduced Nigel Strangeways in the following year.[3] And Michael Innes's erudite Inspector John Appleby arrived in 1936, first investigating a campus murder in the President's Lodging.[4] These new characters remain pre-eminent among the dozens of lesser novels and writers of their era. We should note several things about them before proceeding:

1) They were all men. The only significant woman sleuth in a series during the period was Leslie Ford's Grace Latham, who was always paired with John Primrose in their Washington, DC, stories. Because

she was a proper lady, however, Mrs. Latham could never become the sort of investigator Pamela North would become in Richard and Frances Lockridge's series. And of course real, active heroines were unheard of.

2) They were all wealthy. Even those without obvious means, such as Ellery Queen and his father the inspector, were well aware of propriety, and dealt with high society as knowledgeable insiders.

3) Even though they came late to the scene, they are today all considered members in full standing of the Golden Age. That phrase may therefore be seen as a formulaic identification, bonding works with similar plot structures and heroes, rather than simply identifying works written between 1920 and 1939. This is even more critical when we recall that most of these series lasted well into the post World War II era, and that even today new writers are identified with and judged by the standards of the inter-war period.

At the other end of the spectrum, the 1920s had witnessed the creation and rise of the American hard-boiled detective. First described in short stories by Dashiell Hammett, Carroll John Daly, Erle Stanley Gardner, and dozens of less well-remembered writers, the gritty business of "working a case" was presented in graphic detail for readers in magazines like *Black Mask* and *Clues*. As the first novels (the best starring Daly's Race Williams and Hammett's unnamed Continental Op) appeared in the mid- and late-1920s, it became clear that this subgenre was as popular as it was different from its more sedate British cousin. By the mid-1930s, when Jonathan Latimer and George Harmon Coxe created amateur investigators Bill Crane and Kent Murdock, the hard-boiled action-oriented hero was well established in the world of fiction readers.

There were very few attempts, in the early years, to mediate between the two forms. Among those which attempted to close the gap the most obvious might have been Leslie Ford, whose Grace Latham and Colonel John Primrose first appeared in 1932. Their partnership, which swings toward and away from romance, attempted a balance between the romantic duo (epitomized in 1933 by Hammett's Nick and Nora Charles in *The Thin Man*) and the serious whodunit pair (best identified by Richard and Frances Lockridge's Mr. and Mrs. North starting in 1940). Though Ford had a good idea, her plots were quiet and domestic in nature, distinctly on the traditional side. There certainly were no successful blends between the two worlds of detection until Rex Stout created Wolfe and Archie in 1934. Their appearance and their immediate and continuing popularity are due as much to Stout's blending of the two styles as to his extraordinary talent as a writer.

In his sensitive and exhaustive, if at times exhausting, biography of Rex Stout, John McAleer seems to know where the writer was every month if not every day of his life. But despite his fascination with the chronological details of his subject's life, McAleer is strangely silent on Stout's thinking processes throughout his long career. In particular, he passes over Stout's creation of Wolfe and Archie as characters, though he does spend several pages identifying—at almost numbing length—many of their well-known traits, noting which could be found in Stout himself, as well as delineating those coming from the writer's mother's side of the family and which others from his father's.

While this catalog has its uses, it ignores a more important question: How did Stout come to merge the two vastly different strains of detective fiction, and how did he—either intellectually or emotionally—create these two characters? The dichotomy seems quite pure on its surface, though there must have been some uncertainties on the part of an author new to the mystery form trying to merge two such different styles. More interesting still, how much of what we remember about this important series actually appears in their first adventure, *Fer-de-Lance*?

Perhaps the most critical element in the makeup of Nero Wolfe is his immovability. The few occasions in the novels and stories when he leaves his brownstone are part of his legend, though it has its roots in such avatars as the Baroness Orczy's Old Man in the Corner (who appeared only in short stories)[5] and the arthritic Dr. Gideon Fell, a near contemporary. It is in fact the first thing a reader knows about Wolfe. Sending Fritz out to find "every kind of beer procurable" (1-2) is a stunt that readers would come to find lovable about Wolfe over the years; finding it on the opening page of this, his first appearance, is startling.[6] This indicates, however, an essential point about *Fer-de-Lance*: Nero Wolfe's basic character is already formed for the ages and many of his idiosyncracies are securely in place. In Chapter 6 Archie returns from Westchester to find Wolfe in the first recorded "relapse" (62). This weekend-long occasion contains the famous mention of the Great Detective sitting at Archie's kitchen table eating half a sheep cooked twenty different ways. Another incident occurs in

Chapter 13, when Wolfe mentions to a visitor that his mother lives upstairs. (Archie tells the reader in an aside that she actually lives in Budapest. This is an out-and-out lie of the sort that Wolfe would abandon in later books, except in dire emergencies.) A third example of Wolfe's peculiarities is the almost unique instance of his sending Archie and their client, Sarah Barstow, upstairs to visit the hallowed plant rooms on the roof (133-34).

The book also contains a number of what readers would come to recognize as typical comments by Wolfe: "It would be futile for a man to labor at establishing a reputation for oddity if he were ready at the slightest provocation to revert to normal action" (44) and "I am merely a genius, not a god. A genius may discover the hidden secrets and display them; only a god can create new ones" (157).

All of this suggests that Wolfe was created whole by his creator. Meeting him, it is impossible not to believe in him, his powers of reasoning, or his whims. Archie, however, is more difficult to comprehend. Perhaps the critical realization the reader makes about him in *Fer-de-Lance* is that he is not like any previous character in the form. Since Poe's Dupin fascinated his audience-of-one, the role of the assistant has been primarily as the great detective's adoring— and ineffectual—public. Dr. Watson's active participation in the Holmes stories is at its best when Watson serves as a decoy, leading villains away from Holmes. Other "second bananas" through the years had even less to do. Hercule Poirot's friend Hastings may be near the top of this this all-too-ordinary heap. Hastings's and the others' primary value is as audience, watching their heroes doing whatever it takes to solve a case. The very best of the British Golden Age's assistants may be Charles Parker, whom Dorothy Sayers made an increasingly active though perennially unsuccessful partner with Peter Wimsey;[7] while at the other end of the spectrum is the positively cipherous S.S. van Dine, whose entire span of activity is to stand in a corner, along with the police's Sgt. Heath and District Attorney Markham, while Philo Vance waits for the murderer to make his inevitable mistake. In Willard Huntington Wright's books, the situation is aggravated because Vance, on catching the villain, takes on the added roles of judge, jury, and executioner; and unlike his opponents, Vance never slips up. The killers in these books may truly be said never to have had a chance.

On the other end is the private eye hero of the hard-boiled story, who works without either a "net" or an assistant. As developed in short fiction in the 1920s and continued to our own day, the hard-boiled protagonist is by definition active rather than contemplative, as likely to get information by fighting as by asking questions, and liable to get to the solution by luck rather than by logical analysis of his problem. When Stout created Archie, this concept was embodied in a growing number of novels but was still more often at its height in magazines.[8] Though books featuring private investigators were popular by the mid-1930s, the series featuring a hard-boiled hero in full-length novel form would not hit high gear until 1939, when Raymond Chandler's Philip Marlowe moved from the pulps with *The Big Sleep*. And though some private eyes have accepted one-time aid it is still a subject for debate whether there have ever been any successful private detective series with continuing assistants.

All of this is critical to our understanding of Archie Goodwin as a revolutionary character. While he is not permitted the deductive leaps to solutions that his eccentric-yet-traditional boss Wolfe makes, we understand very clearly and early that Archie is *smart*. Unlike other Watsons back to the original, he has a real talent for investigation. As a result, Wolfe often allows him the freedom to do what he thinks best, even in this first adventure; and when he deems it necessary, Archie makes his own decisions. At one point he tells Sarah Barstow that "I'm sorry to have to pester you, but there's no way to get the facts. Wolfe says he feels phenomena and I collect facts" (70). Though he makes mistakes, they are mistakes of action rather than inaction (in contrast with the traditional assistants) and it is clear that he is an indispensable part of the process, unlike any prior Watson. Here, and throughout the series, Archie may be seen as a heroic character in his own right, and not as the plaything of a far-superior being. Wolfe is indeed the Great Detective, but Archie is, from the very beginning, far more than merely a useful (or less) tool, and both they and we know it.

Therefore, we can see that Rex Stout's genius was two-fold. First, he created two memorable characters. The idea is worth pondering for a moment. Either of them could have sustained a legitimate series as the sole hero. Wolfe was part of an established tradition, the eccentric investigator, surrounded by a small but complete household and a stable of competent operatives led by Archie and Saul Panzer. Archie, on the other hand, can rightfully take his place as one of the first serious private eyes, combining good instincts and the ability to think.[9] But Stout had the additional genius to match them and make them work with and against each other. Neither, through the entire series, is entirely superior—they can certainly not be considered complete without each other—and at the same time they provided the unique opportunity for their creator to develop an effective creative tension through an ongoing relationship including a mutual appreciation for each other's abilities. Wolfe especially comes to rely on Archie over the years, something it is hard to imagine Holmes doing with Watson. While they are never equals—Wolfe won't permit it—they do merge into a true team in ways that no other pair has achieved.

In many ways their first novel presents the entire Wolfe-ian world. Fritz Brenner is in the kitchen catering to Wolfe's physical needs, and Theodore Horstmann is established in the plant rooms on the roof caring for the orchids, each comfortably doing his job and very particular about his personal status in the house. (Wolfe's schedule with the plants is another minor but critical-element aspect of the novels that appears full-blown in this book.) In addition, the three operatives who will assist in many of the future investigations also appear. Fred Durkin opens the book by bringing Maria Maffei to the brownstone in the opening chapter; Saul Panzer is quoted by Archie (especially by the typical 1930s phrase "lovin' babe") and we meet Fred and Saul when the whole group of operatives takes part in the investigation toward the end.

Another continuing element is the brownstone house itself. In many ways the building is as full-grown in this book as its inhabitants. The layout is embedded in the text, from the plant rooms on the roof down to the kitchen, including the placement of the bedrooms, and many of the smaller details are in place. It has already been noted that, in a seldom-repeated gesture of hospitality, the house even becomes a participant early in the book. The only missing piece of furniture is the famous Red Chair in the office, in which a long list of clients and villains are destined to sit. The chair would not appear until the fourth novel in the series, *The Red Box*, an important, if minor, addition to Wolfe's surroundings.

Despite the overwhelming assets Stout brought to his new profession in *Fer-de-Lance*, this is clearly the work of a man not yet entirely comfortable in the mystery genre. The concept is weak, the means of death is esoteric to the point of being bizarre (even by the weird standards of the early 1930s), and the solution becomes evident very early. Though in many ways, as we have seen, this is clearly the same man who would write such classics as *The Red Box, Too Many Cooks,* and *The Doorbell Rang,* he does not yet have all of his material cleanly arranged and at hand.

To recap the main plot, Wolfe is first introduced to the puzzle of a missing man, Carlo Maffei. Later Peter Oliver Barstow, the well-known President of Holland University, dies mysteriously in the midst of a round of golf, and no reason is found for his demise. Wolfe determines the cause of Barstow's death and ties it to the disappearance of Maffei. Not to destroy the somewhat meandering plot, he and Archie also connect the bizarre means of death to the killer, and resolve the problem to their satisfaction. Even the reader who does not care about finding the answer can't help figuring out what has happened here. The solution, unique in Wolfe novels, comes a full fifty pages before the end, and the key clue comes twenty pages before that. In later novels Stout would perfect the last-second clue and the last-chapter revelation by Wolfe that would make the investigator's genius status clear, but that is not the case here.

As has already been noted, all three of Wolfe's other regular operatives make cameo appearances here. The major missing piece, though, has not been mentioned. When this book leaves the brownstone, it does not stay in New York City but travels north to Westchester County. Wolfe's and Archie's nemesis here is the county District Attorney, Fletcher M. Anderson, who shows himself in his few appearances to be only somewhat brighter than the usual run of dumb opponents faced by the Great Detectives of the time. The only New York cop who comes to the Brownstone is one O'Grady, in a one-time cameo role. This eliminates the third most important character in the series, Inspector L.T. Cramer of the New York Police Department. Cramer, with his gruff facade and the perpetually unlit cigar in his jaw, never shows up in Wolfe's office until the fourth book in the series, *The Red Box,* published in 1937. (For symmetry, it should be noted that from the first Cramer takes the red chair as his personal domain, from which he challenges Wolfe in many of their cases.) However, on one of his trips to White Plains, Archie mentions his friend and nemesis on the force, Purley Stebbins. Purley will appear as Cramer's right-hand man in later novels, and some of the short fiction gives him an even bigger role.

Rex Stout's *Fer-de-Lance,* then, may be said to have heralded the beginning of several eras. It was, first and foremost, the opening of one of America's best detective series, introducing Nero Wolfe and

Archie Goodwin and their world to generations of readers. Second, Archie's presence raises serious questions about the possible roles that the detective's assistant could and should play in the investigative process, some of which remain open even today. Rather than merely admire the hero, as had been the lot of all earlier assistants such as Christie's silly Hastings, or following but never taking the lead, as did Dorothy L. Sayers' more serious Charles Parker and Margery Allingham's Oates and Luke, Stout's Archie realized the possibility for an active assistant with a mind of his own.

Third, Wolfe and Archie began to redefine the relationship between the two traditions of the Great Detective and the hard-boiled sleuth. In the classic story that emerged in the 1920s the investigator (Christie's Poirot most obviously) discusses his intuitions (Wolfe's "phenomena") throughout the tale, but reveals the truth only in his last-second revelation. In the new private eye tale the hard process of "finding clues" becomes predominant; the detective seeks "just the facts" and fits them together with difficulty and an occasional brawl. By identifying both of these strands and personifying them in Wolfe and Archie, Stout challenged the world of detection to analyze itself. The genre has never been the same since.

It was quite a start. In spite of its problems and questions, and the occasional misstep, *Fer-de-Lance* remains an impressive book, and its introduction of the two heroes is worth the time spent returning to them. Fine detectives, unlike the orchids they may cultivate, do not grow weak or wilt with time. Instead, like fine wine, they age well and should be enjoyed periodically.

Notes

1. Mason's first case was *The Case of the Velvet Claws*, followed the same year by *The Case of the Sulky Girl*. Dr. Fell arrived in two books as well: *Hag's Nook* and *The Mad Hatter Mystery* both appeared in 1933.

2. In the first novel, *A Man Lay Dying*, newspaperman Nigel Bathgate became Alleyn's chronicler and assistant, a role he would play in several novels. Alleyn's police colleague and confidant Inspector Fox (well-known as "Br'er Fox" and "Foxy" in later books) plays only a minor role in the books through the 1930s. And Alleyn's great love, Agatha Troy, showed up only in *Artists in Crime* (1938), the sixth novel in the series.

3. The first of these novels, *A Question of Proof*, is generally unmemorable. It was only with the creation of Georgia Cavendish,

Strangeways' first love, in the next novel, *Thou Shell of Death*, that Day Lewis really hit his own stride. Their adventures, particularly *The Corpse in the Snowman* and *The Smiler with the Knife*, raised the series to its highest level and made Strangeways one of the last great heroes of the British Golden Age.

4. Though Appleby never had a Watson-like assistant, his career is notable for its interest in the theater and in art. Like his fellows, Appleby also fell in love. His wife, Judith Raven, first appeared rather late; *Appleby's End*, a 1945 novel, provides a weird and wonderful adventure among the mists of the country.

5. There were three collections of these stories, issued between 1905 and 1925. It should be remembered, however, that the title character is not immovable, only unmoving, preferring a corner table in a tea-shop to the outside world.

6. An interesting and important side-note is the historical importance of the incident. Prohibition had just ended, and the recently re-legalized breweries and distilleries constantly fought for clientele. Another angle may be played on the question of liquor. In one of the most famous books of the year, Hammett's *The Thin Man*, several scenes (including the first) take place in speakeasies. The whole novel, in fact, is awash in alcohol, as is the quickly produced film version, which was also released that year.

7. The other major policeman of the age, Stanislaus Oakes, began as a buffoon for Margery Allingham's Albert Campion but became more serious over time. His successor, Charlie Luke, continued that development and occasionally served as an almost-equal to Campion. But that was later and may be considered a post-war phenomenon for the most part.

8. Dashiell Hammett published *The Thin Man* in 1934, and it is important to recall that the Continental Op, hero of most of the short stories, appeared in only the first two of the five novels, *Red Harvest* and *The Dain Curse*.

9. He may still be one of the brightest of his ilk and proved himself during Wolfe's absence in *In the Best Families* (1950).

Work Cited

Stout, Rex. *Fer-de-Lance*. 1934. New York: Bantam, 1992.

Ngaio Marsh's Roderick Alleyn

MaryKay Mahoney

Picture a detective who apologizes mendaciously—and unconvincingly—for his "filthy memory." A detective whose first utterance in print—in reply to the question, "Has someone found you a job?"—is the amazingly mawkish reply: "You've guessed my boyish secret. I've been given a murder to solve—aren't I a lucky little detective?"

Now imagine a Scotland Yard detective who spills his detecting secrets to a journalist because of his need for a sidekick: "Every sleuth ought to have a tame half-wit, to make him feel clever. I offer you the job." A detective whose less than competent "tame half-wit" ends up briefly undergoing torture because he's been told just a bit too much about a band of traitors for his own foolish good.

Next add a plot with an elaborately complex murder that occurs in under five minutes, a murder that requires that the unsuspecting victim remain in exactly the right place—back turned—to make the killing possible. Then mix in a secondary plot involving a Russian secret society, complete with the necessary accessories: a letter-seal with a dagger printed on it; a knife so associated with a secret brotherhood that to merely possess it is to court danger; secret meetings, passwords, and traitors forced to speak with pins shoved under their fingernails.

Given all of this—would Ngaio Marsh *really* be the author's name that springs to mind? Yet each of these elements occurs in the first of her Roderick Alleyn series, the 1934 novel *A Man Lay Dead*.

Marsh has described her decision to write this first novel both in her autobiography and elsewhere. After a rainy Sunday spent reading a detective novel—possibly an Agatha Christie—Marsh wondered "if I had it in me to write something in the genre" ("Birth" 23). Her starting point was a plot germ: a Murder Game disrupted by the appearance of a real corpse. Her central character would be an attempt to break away from the eccentricities and mannerisms of detectives like Wimsey, Vance, and Poirot; Marsh decided that instead "my best chance lay in comparative normality: in the invention of a man with a background resembling that of the friends I had made in England" ("Birth" 24). Thus she created Scotland Yard's Chief Inspector-Detective Roderick Alleyn: "a professional policeman but, in some ways, atypical: an attractive, civilized man with whom it would be pleasant to talk but much less pleasant to fall out" ("Birth" 24).

Despite Marsh's attempt at the "comparative normality" of a gentleman sleuth who was no gifted amateur but part of the official justice system, or perhaps because of her attempt to merge that more sober detective figure with the detective-fiction conventions of the day, there is throughout *A Man Lay Dead* a sense of imbalance between an awkwardly facetious level and a smoother and more sure substratum. This lack of equilibrium occurs not only in the contrasts built into Alleyn, but also in the process of narration and, more dramatically, in the overall plot.

One clear difficulty in the first in any series is defining the narrative voice. In *A Man Lay Dead*, the third-person narration is done through a variety of minds, but most notably through that of Nigel Bathgate, journalist, cousin to the dead man, and, eventually, Alleyn's Watson. Unlike Doyle's original Watson, who in his experienced middle-age not surprisingly had a solidly defined character, Nigel is somewhat of a chameleon. In his general bounciness and in his love affair with Angela North, he is a sterling example of a young juvenile lead. At the beginning of the novel, Nigel excitedly asks his cousin—"not for the first time" (10)—who else will be at Sir Hubert Handesley's weekend party; that "not for the first time" suggests clearly Nigel's endearing, if sometimes exhausting, enthusiasm. This Nigel enjoys life and trots happily through it, as his inward comments frequently illustrate: "'What with daggers, deaths, and eavesdroppings,' he pondered, 'there's an undercurrent of sensation in this house-party. All rather fun, but I wish old Charles [his cousin] wasn't cast for the first philanderer's part'" (28-29).

But other comments *about* Nigel emphasize his inherent sensitivity, in the tradition of characters like the early Wimsey, where a comical exterior conceals a complicated, introspective interior. The narrative points out that Nigel is "mentally on tenterhooks" during the house party because of "being particularly sensitive to the timbre of emotional relationships" (30), and the family lawyer speaks of how Nigel was "always an imaginative, sensitive sort of individual" (102).

This emphasis on Nigel's deeper self is useful for two purposes: first, it makes Nigel an appropriate confidant for the even more sensitive and imaginative Roderick Alleyn; and secondly, it allows Marsh to use Nigel's mind to make subtle observations about the other characters, such as Nigel's evaluation of Marjorie Wilde: "There are some women who, when they dance, express a depth of feeling and of temperament that actually they do not possess. He saw that Mrs. Wilde was one of these women" (34). Unfortunately, the effect of such observations is undercut by the basic unlikelihood of their arising from the mind of the rather ordinary and conventional Nigel.

The overall plot also shows an uncertain seesawing between the reasonably probable and the most melodramatic unlikelihoods. Marsh's murder plots often have a vividly melodramatic quality; Earl Bargainnier points out that "Marsh's penchant for such bizarre, even outlandish, methods of murder contrasts with her usual moderation in presenting the action of her novels" (98). In *A Man Lay Dead*, however, the grotesquely constructed killing of Charles Rankin is also amazingly improbable on a literal level, and its emergence from the relatively prosaic mind of Arthur Wilde makes it even less convincing.

The difficulty in probability is easy to identify. Charles Rankin is standing in the hallway by the drinks table when Arthur Wilde goes upstairs; a maid speaks briefly to Rankin. In under five minutes a gong sounds—Rankin, stabbed in the back, has fallen forward, with his head sounding the gong on the way down. The killer has entered the hall area, taken a knife off the wall by the stairs, killed Rankin, and exited. The blow has been driven into Rankin's back with great force and from slightly above.

When the murder is eventually explained by Alleyn, the sequence of events becomes thoroughly unbelievable. Arthur Wilde leaves the hall at ten to eight; he goes up to his room, turns on a bathtub, exchanges a few shouted comments with Nigel to establish an alibi, pulls off his clothes, slides back down the banister to the hall, pausing to snatch the dagger from the wall along the way, and then stabs Rankin in the back. All in less than five minutes. The reader's hoped-for suspension of disbelief is not at all helped by the mental picture that the explanation conjures up: the mousy Arthur Wilde, barefoot and clad either in underwear or a robe, sailing down the banister, knife firmly fixed in his gloved hand as he heads for the ever so conveniently placed back of Charles Rankin. One cause of the improbabilities in this scenario may be Marsh's belief that it is nearly impossible to treat the murderer and his actions with the same degree of seriousness as other elements of style and characterization; in her autobiography, Marsh comments that "the mechanics in a detective novel may be shamelessly contrived but the writing need not be so nor, with one exception, need the characterisation. About the guilty person, of course endless duplicity is practised" (*Black Beech* 228). And killer Arthur Wilde is indeed finally a less coherent and integrated character than his non-murderous companions.

As unlikely as it may seem, Wilde's murder of Rankin is not even the least probable event in *A Man Lay Dead*. That honor goes to the subplot about Russian secret societies, with treason, passwords, the superstition-surrounded ancient knife, and fake Russian accents abounding. The parodic tone of the subplot is set early on when Dr. Tokareff, whose language inexplicably gets more grammatical and coherent as the book develops, demonstrates a fractured English presumably intended as humorous: "Excuse me, please . . . I am still, how you say, unintelligible. I have not been so happy to gambol in susha funny sport heretobefore, so please make him for me more clearer" (19).

Such an opening bodes ill for the Russian element generally; and the subplot fulfills its early lack of promise when Nigel, in one of the most foolish moves ever committed by a Watson figure, over-enthusiastically exposes the identity of Alleyn's double agent within the conspiracy and is then himself taken prisoner and tortured—in Alleyn's own flat, no less. The element of absurdity is compounded when Alleyn ultimately rescues Nigel by coming down a chimney. Marsh herself said of this first Alleyn novel, "I don't think that before or since this weekend I have ever written with less trouble and certainly never with less distinction" (*Black Beech* 195). It is at moments like the Russian subplot that a reader may be tempted to agree.

The chief impression that the book gives to someone looking back at it as the first of a series is that sense of elements not quite yet under control. Marsh is relying more than she later will on established conventions like the Watson figure; she has difficulties reconciling the grotesqueness of some incidents with the rest of the book; and she has problems with the tone on a variety of levels.

This sense of a lack of control, of a voice not quite found, is even clearer in the language of the novel. LeRoy Panek points out that Alleyn's language when he erupts from his fireplace—"No funny business . . . You're covered all round, you know. Put 'em up, my poppets" (Marsh, *Man* 163)—is "straight out of the thriller" (Panek 186). But throughout the novel as a whole, there is an aura of artificiality, a sense in which much of the novel's language is presented in quotation marks. This attributing of the novel's language to sources other than the author and her characters appears immediately in the first lines of the novel: "Nigel Bathgate, in the language of his own gossip column, was 'definitely intrigued' about his week-end at Frantock" (9). This distancing convention continues to occur: Doctor Tokareff points out that it is "English shilling shockers"—and journalists—who tell melodramatic tales about Russian secret societies (23); Alleyn asks, "Mr. Wilde . . . in the words of the popular coloured engraving, when did you last see Mr. Rankin?" (57); and Alleyn tells Nigel and Angela that their fortunately alibied status could be subtitled "Saved by the Servants" (142). The Russian conspiracy sections carry out on the plot level a sense of something imported into the novel, something foreign to and unreconcilable with the more prosaic and familiar country house setting with its weekend house guests.

There are, however, also elements which very strikingly indicate where Marsh will go in future novels. A few references, like Alleyn discussing Arthur Wilde's bathroom as if it were a stage set, or the descriptions of the reenactment of the crime at the end of the novel, suggest the fascination with drama that is so memorable in Marsh's novels. And the novel's overall structure fits neatly into the pattern that Panek finds throughout the series: "The formula, then, is: introduction, murder, interviews, recapitulation, action, reenactment, and summary" (196). Even *A Man Lay Dead*'s Russian subplot fits into this formula in terms of the "action" stage, which Panek describes as usually containing either an adventure element or an additional murder (196).

What is perhaps most striking in *A Man Lay Dead* is how noticeably Marsh's Alleyn, in his first appearance, shows clear signs of his later incarnations. Except for an element of awkwardness in his mannerisms—perhaps due to shyness at his first appearance in print—Marsh's detective Roderick Alleyn is much the same in *A Man Lay Dead* as in later works—the tall man described by one character as having a "grand" voice and hands (45). He is carefully differentiated from the stereotyped popular image of the police detective—an image personified in later novels by Inspector Fox—by the comments of those who observe him at work. Nigel Bathgate notes that Alleyn "doesn't conform to my mental pictures of a sleuth-hound. I had an idea they lived privately amidst inlaid linoleums, aspidistras, and enlarged photographs of constabulary groups" (140), and concludes that Alleyn "must be a gent with private means who sleuths for sleuthing's sake" (140).

Angela North's mental description of Alleyn in this first novel echoes many later comments:

Angela had time for a good long stare at her first detective. Alleyn did not resemble a plain-clothes policeman she felt sure, nor was he in the romantic manner—white-faced and gimlet-eyed. He looked like one of her Uncle Hubert's friends, the sort that they knew would "do" for house-parties. He was very tall, and lean, his hair was dark, and his eyes grey with corners that turned down. They looked as if they would smile easily but his mouth didn't. (37)

Marsh herself, commenting on a description of Alleyn as a "nice chap" in a review, said "that was how I liked to think of him: a nice chap with more edge to him than met the eye—a good deal more" ("Birth" 24). That description—"a nice chap" with an "edge"— captures the two central elements of Alleyn's character: gentleman and policeman. And, as Panek points out, it is Alleyn's professional role that is essential to his identity: Alleyn "is an aristocrat, but he is, nevertheless, a policeman, and the glamor of his upper class background is subordinated to his police work" (189).

But the Alleyn of later novels is recognizable in *A Man Lay Dead* in more metaphysical ways. The sense of isolation that the detective's role often produces in Marsh's novels comes through clearly in Alleyn's need for anyone—even Nigel—as a listener when he expounds his theories on the case. Inspector Fox will eventually fulfill that role for Alleyn, but Alleyn will also need Troy in this capacity and even, in *Last Ditch*, his son Ricky. The detective's isolation is under-scored here, as it is countless times in later Alleyn novels, by the sense of betrayal involved in characters' reluctance to mentally confront what Alleyn does. Comforted by the "grand" hands and voice, witnesses and suspects find it pleasant, throughout Alleyn's career, to deal with him—until they are themselves forced by Alleyn to make ethical choices, to examine their own relationship to the forces of justice he represents. In *A Man Lay Dead*, when Nigel refuses to help Alleyn with his reconstruction of Rankin's death, Alleyn replies quite bitterly,

For you it's all over. Rankin was your cousin; you have had a shock. You have also, you must confess, enjoyed the part you have played up to date in helping to round up a bunch of mad Russians. But now, when a criminal who is prepared—even schemes—to let an innocent person hang, turns out to be someone you know, you become all fastidiousness and leave the dirt to the policeman. Quite understandable. In a couple of years you will be dining out on this murder. Pity you can't write it up. (175)

Nigel, like most of the later characters forced by Alleyn to re-examine their own motives and "fastidiousness," capitulates; but that picture of Alleyn as the isolated detective, regarded with distaste by those he helps protect, is a striking one that reoccurs through the series, complicating, among other things, Alleyn's later courtship of Troy. Alleyn, in fact, defensively describes in *Death in a White Tie* how he fears Troy pictures him:

If you painted a surrealist picture of me I would be made of Metropolitan Police notebooks, one eye would be set in a keyhole, my hands would be occupied with somebody's else's [sic] private correspondence. The background would be a morgue and the whole pretty conceit wreathed with festoons of blue tape and hangman's rope. (312)

At the end of *A Man Lay Dead*, Nigel takes temporary leave of Alleyn and bounds off in romantic pursuit of Angela, who will later become his wife. Yet while Nigel's refusing Alleyn's dinner invitation in favor of taking Angela to a show highlights Nigel's constitutional unfitness to take on the permanent role of Watson, Nigel's final comment on Alleyn shows that in this case at least, Nigel has both seen and observed: "You are an extraordinary creature. . . . You struck me as being as sensitive as any of us just before you made the arrest. Your nerves seemed to be all anyhow. I should have said you hated the whole game. And now, an hour later, you utter inhuman platitudes about types. You *are* a rum 'un" (188).

In Marsh's succeeding books, the murder plots are constructed with more skill and consistency, the detective's confidants are eventually better chosen, and the Russian secret societies have disappeared—perhaps back to their motherland. But Alleyn, as described in essence by Nigel, continues—the one essential thread, from the first to the last of the series.

Works Cited

Bargainnier, Earl F. "Ngaio Marsh." *Ten Women of Mystery.* Ed. Earl F. Bargainnier. Bowling Green, OH: Bowling Green State University Popular Press, 1981. 81-105.

Marsh, Ngaio. "Birth of a Sleuth." *The Writer* 90 (Apr. 1977): 23-25.

____. *Black Beech and Honeydew: An Autobiography.* Rev. and enlarged ed. London: Collins, 1981.

____. *Death in a White Tie.* New York: Jove, 1938.

____. *A Man Lay Dead.* New York: Jove, 1934.

Panek, LeRoy Lad. *Watteau's Shepherds: The Detective Novel in Britain, 1914-1940.* Bowling Green, OH: Bowling Green State University Popular Press, 1979.

The First Six in a Series:
Nicholas Blake

Mary P. Freier

In many ways, Nicholas Blake—pseudonym of Cecil Day-Lewis—had six first novels: *A Question of Proof* (1935), *Thou Shell of Death* (1936), *There's Trouble Brewing* (1937), *The Beast Must Die* (1938), *The Smiler with the Knife* (1939), and *The Corpse in the Snowman* (1941). These first six Nigel Strangeways novels are very different; the character of Nigel Strangeways develops so radically from novel to novel that it could be said that the detective and his role change completely from one novel to the next. In *The Smiler with the Knife*, Nigel Strangeways is not even the detective; his wife Georgia is. In *The Beast Must Die*, Nigel is nearly the antagonist. Blake also experiments with narration and point of view in his early novels. The result is that none of these novels is very much like the long string of Nigel Strangeways novels that followed them, and none of them is very like any of the others. The only constant is Blake's attempt to create a Freudian, anti-fascist detective, but after six tries, he seems to give up. He kills off Georgia, and Nigel becomes a fairly typical professional detective in the landscape of detective fiction.

Sean Day-Lewis has pointed out that, in *A Question of Proof*, Nigel Strangeways is a nearly exact replica of W.H. Auden, but that "as Cecil grew away from that powerful poetic influence, Nigel became increasingly like himself" (86). Nigel is certainly little more than a collection of quirks in the first novel, and even his quirks are not well-carried-out.

Evans, Nigel's old friend who brings him into the case, warns his lover, Hero, that Nigel will not be a typical house guest, and describes him as "like one of the less successful busts of T.E. Shaw. A nordic type. He's rather faddy, by the way; his protective mechanism developed them, I daresay. But you must have water perpetually on the boil; he drinks tea at all hours of the day. And he can't sleep unless he has an enormous weight on his bed. If you don't give him

77

enough blankets for three, you'll find that he has torn the carpets up or the curtains down" (93). While Nigel does keep asking for inordinate quantities of tea, the other peculiarities never seem to appear, although he is described as nearsighted and as moving awkwardly (94). He also feels the need to sing loudly during the novel's chase scene (95-96). However, he gets along almost miraculously well with both women and children, as well as men, which helps him solve the Sudeley murders.

By the second novel, *Thou Shell of Death*, Nigel's quirks have become less pronounced, and many of them have disappeared. Although he is posing as a guest at a country house in this novel, there is no reference to his need for weights and extra blankets. He drinks less tea, but has developed the annoying habit of setting his cup on the edges of furniture so that the china is in danger of falling. But even this quirk has disappeared by the end of chapter one. It seems that Blake thought that he must create a character out of eccentric mannerisms, but dropped the mannerisms as soon as Nigel actually had any work to do.

Thou Shell of Death is also the novel that introduces Georgia Cavendish, who is later to become Georgia Strangeways. In her early manifestation, Georgia is just as quirky as Nigel. He first sees her when she drives up to the house in her baggage-covered car, with her bloodhound and her parrot (who is later referred to as a cockatiel). Georgia is supposed to be an adventuress and world traveler; she first met daredevil pilot and soon-to-be murder victim Fergus O'Brien when he rescued her from a difficult situation in Africa. Like Nigel's eccentricities, Georgia's parrot and bloodhound disappear later in the novel when Blake finds a way to characterize her more genuinely as the frustrated lover of Fergus O'Brien and the doting sister of Edward Cavendish.

Georgia and Nigel are married in *There's Trouble Brewing*, but Georgia appears only in the first chapter. She spends the rest of the novel on one of her famous journeys (5). Nigel has, somewhat suddenly for readers of the series, become a literary critic. He is the author of a book on the Caroline poets, and he lectures on modern poetry (3, 14). He now sings loudly only while shaving, and contents himself with humming in public places (121-22, 18).

By *The Beast Must Die*, Georgia and Nigel are married, and Georgia seems to have dwindled into a wife. She is primarily concerned about Nigel's physical and mental health, although she is still capable of asserting herself, as she does when Nigel lies about her being exhausted from the trip: "So I'm 'done up,' am I? Coming from a gentleman on the verge of physical and mental collapse, that was good" (107). Her knowledge of the world, drawn from her travels, is useful in analyzing the characters whom she and Nigel encounter, but she says that she wants nothing to do with the case (108), and, as it progresses, she becomes little more than a solicitous sounding board for Nigel.

Nigel, on the other hand, has become less quirky and is more concerned with the morality of what he's doing; Georgia even comments that she doesn't like his methods (108). But by the end of the novel, Nigel and the local police detective, Inspector Blount, have a major falling out because Nigel has allowed the murderer to commit suicide, which Blount perceives as allowing him to escape. However, Nigel still provides some labored comic relief by singing loudly and badly (140-41).

Part of the reason for the confusion about the characters in the first four novels is that Blake can't seem to decide if he wants them to be comic or serious, and he doesn't handle the shifts between the two elements very well. In *The Smiler with the Knife*, a serious thriller, this tension has resolved somewhat, and the humor is confined to sarcastic remarks about the government's impotence in the face of the Fascist threat. By *The Corpse in the Snowman*, Nigel and Georgia's quirks have been transferred to their eccentric relatives.

In *The Smiler with the Knife*, Georgia is chosen to find out more about the insidious English Banner (or E.B.), a Fascist organization. Nigel is too well-known to undertake the task (one wonders what has happened to Georgia's reputation as an adventuress, not to mention the bloodhound and the bird). In this novel, Georgia is portrayed as the nervous amateur, and Nigel as the calm and seasoned professional. Nigel seems to have become more of a father-figure than a lover; at one point, Georgia even wishes that she were able to confide in him and ask for advice. In *The Corpse in the Snowman*, Georgia has earned the privilege of discussing the case and the psychology of the characters with Nigel on an equal footing. However, Blake felt the need to get rid of Georgia before the next novel; he had decided that she was a "bore" (Sean Day-Lewis 169). The elimination of Georgia may have helped Blake settle on a characterization for Nigel.

Blake also used these six novels as an opportunity to experiment with narrative strategies. *A Question of Proof* begins with a pseudo-dramatic scene setting, written in present tense. Like Nigel's peculiar habits, this rather annoying method of narration disappears as the novel gets under way. In *Thou Shell of Death*, Blake employs a more traditional narrative style. However, both novels seem to be trying to be novels by Dorothy L. Sayers, with their heavy use of irony, the eccentric characterization of the upper classes, and the stress on the education of the major characters. While the educational emphasis may be understandable in *A Question of Proof*, since it is set in a school, having an Oxford don as one of the houseguests in *Thou Shell of Death* is a bit farfetched. In *The Beast Must Die*, the first third of the novel is given over to Felix Lane's diary. The second part of the novel is done with a third-person narration, and when a character's point of view is used, it is Felix Lane's. The third section of the novel, where Nigel is called in to deal with the murder, is also done in third-person narration, and the point of view is clearly Nigel's, except when it shifts to another character to allow us to see Nigel through that character's eyes. One of the reasons for these shifts in point of view is to permit us to see Georgia's concern for her husband's health.

There's Trouble Brewing is seen primarily though Nigel's eyes, with occasional glimpses from the other characters' point of view. These shifts again allow us to see Nigel, but they also enable us to see the fear of the community of Maiden Astbury. *The Smiler with the Knife* uses Georgia's point of view to show her anxieties about her espionage and emphasize her position as inspired amateur. Her desire to get back to her country home and her joy upon reaching it are clearly designed to create reader empathy and to convince the reader that, without the efforts of average people, the Fascists would win the day.

Blake returns to a more traditional third-person narration in *The Corpse in the Snowman* and again uses Georgia as a part of the narration. However, in this novel, she is used primarily for Nigel to think out loud to, a narrative strategy that Blake returned to after he replaced Georgia with the artist Clare Massinger.

Other drastic changes between these novels are caused by Day-Lewis's own political confusion. While he was a strong anti-fascist and believed that Freudian psychology had replaced Puritan Christianity, he was never able to stop loving his country and much of what was considered "bourgeois" about it.

He believed that culture was making a great shift, a revolution, and that one of the major changes was its turning away from a disintegrating Christianity (*Revolution* 27). Puritanism had lost its "religious fervor and single-mindedness," leaving only what he called the "nonconformist Conscience," which has an "inveterate feud against everything that people mean by the word 'beauty.'" This feud has "led it to condemn poetry equally with sex as something at best flippant and at worst immoral" (*Hope* 33). As a poet, Day-Lewis found this attitude threatening, and his loathing of evangelical Protestants persisted well into the 1950s in the character of Daniel Durdle in *The Dreadful Hollow* (1953). Nicholas Blake was especially fond of the idea of the murderous Puritan in the late 1930s and early 1940s.

Although Day-Lewis believed that Christianity was losing its influence, he also believed that something would come to take its place. Day-Lewis thought that this "something" would be the theories of Sigmund Freud. Freud's theories, according to Day-Lewis, "altered all the values of the human equation. [They have] given us a new conception of character . . . above all [they challenge] us to reconstruct our morality on [their] new foundations." He believed that a new religion could be created through the study of Freud (*Revolution* 13-14). He also believed that a detective could use Freud's theories to track down murderers.

Nigel Strangeways "neglected Demosthenes in favor of Freud" during his brief stay at Oxford (*Shell* 8), and his study of psychology is quite obvious in *A Question of Proof*. As soon as he gets to the school where the murder has occurred, Nigel walks through the halls, listening to the masters while they teach. His summations of character are based not only on personal judgment but on his reading of Freud: he notes that one instructor "doesn't talk to the boys like a homosexual, repressed or otherwise," and he decides that Percival Vale would do nothing to hurt the school, since it is an extension of his own ego (101). He immediately diagnoses Sims as having "the slave mentality. Chock-full of inferiority feeling no doubt . . . Is there a point at which such slaves rebel?" (103). He later wonders how to ask Sims about a piece of evidence, since he suspects that he has "a first-class persecution mania" (134). Nigel also suspects that Wrench plays up his aesthetic interests and leftist politics in order to assert his character, "a common enough manifestation of inferiority feeling" (146). And when Nigel has discovered the murderer, he explains that

Sims's "religious mania" did not actually bring him to murder: "at the bottom of the heap we find that old chestnut, the inferiority complex" (224). Nigel's knowledge of Freud literally helps him discover the murderer.

A Question of Proof, in many ways, shows Day-Lewis's conviction that Freud's theories would replace Christianity; the murderer turns out to be the ineffectual Puritan, Sims, who attempts to throw the blame for his murders on the lovers, Hero and Michael. Nigel explains that Sims probably followed them when they had their trysts in the woods: "It was a kind of self-torture to him . . . but he kept whipping up his Puritan blood . . . till in the end he believed himself the instrument of God to punish the sinner . . . [In his diary] he's terribly outspoken on the subject, and there's nothing quite so nasty as the Puritan's fascinated horror of sex, when he finds words for it" (219).

Nigel is so pleased with this solution that he tries to use it in his next case. In *Thou Shell of Death*, when Fergus O'Brien's man-servant is severely wounded by someone wielding a poker, Nigel immediately suspects the judgmental Calvinist cook. However, he must give up his theory: "One expected a Calvinist to disapprove of everyone else on principle, but scarcely to carry this disapproval to the length of poker-work" (89). Besides, she has no motive. Nigel's perceptive capabilities, however, are still considered superior to those of the other characters because of his knowledge of Freud: when Fergus O'Brien suggests that the world will never be at peace because "it wants to die," he defers to Nigel: "y'know more than I do about Freud's death will" (27).

In *There's Trouble Brewing*, the psychology of the entire village is extensively discussed by Nigel and his host, Dr. Herbert Cammison. Maiden Astbury is rife with repression, persecution mania, neurosis, and dementia praecox, among other psychological illnesses (43, 27, 111, 112). While most villages in detective fiction seem to suffer from similar epidemics of dysfunction, clinical terms are not used nearly so often.

Blake's psychological religion is presented less clinically in *The Corpse in the Snowman*. The first corpse in this novel is that of the beautiful but licentious Elizabeth Restorick. Although Clarissa Cavendish wants Nigel to "save Elizabeth from damnation" (22), she does not judge her. In fact, she warns Nigel against judging Betty "too harshly" (17) because she has had an American education.

Clarissa has listened to Betty's confidences about her lovers, and she finds it impossible to despise her activities: "Glorying in wickedness, the world would call it, but I am a foolish old woman, I was so dazzled by the glory I could not see the wickedness" (55). We are also told that Betty is "good at heart." Will Dykes tells Nigel that "Betty was what the world made her," and insists that "in her heart she was innocent" (41).

The character in the novel who cannot accept Betty's true innocence is her loving brother, Andrew. Bogan, the psychiatrist, immediately classifies Andrew as "a puritan. Repressed" (140), which agrees with Georgia and Nigel's analysis of Andrew's history and character: "He admitted he behaved like a prig and a prude [when Betty became pregnant in high school]. He must have been wrapped up in a sexual idealism to have treated his beloved sister so harshly. . . . That tragedy perverted his idealism, left him with a hatred for sex. . . . The idealism, having nothing positive to build on, has turned bad" (121). And when Andrew responds somewhat violently to Eunice Ainsley's remarks about Betty's promiscuity, Nigel thinks that "Andrew has not lost the priggish, puritanical idealist. . . . streak" (103). Andrew's puritanism, like Sims's, drives him to murder and to attempting to incriminate someone else for the crime.

Day-Lewis's modern views also took in modern politics. He once summarized the attitude of the thirties liberals by claiming that they had believed that "the capitalist system was obsolescent, that mass unemployment and fascism were evil things . . . that the nationalization of the means of production would cure a lot of our troubles and that this would never be effectually done except under Communism . . . we believed that a second world war was on its way" (*Buried Day* 208). The first five Nicholas Blake novels were written in the 1930s, and they all are very much imbued with Day-Lewis's social philosophy. Earl F. Bargainnier has noted the political commentary in the first three novels (145), but Day-Lewis remained an anti-fascist until the end of World War II, and the Nicholas Blake novels clearly show this. However, the politics in the novels sometimes seems labored and even sophomoric, in part because of the author's own divided loyalties.

The major problem with Blake's use of politics in his detective novels is that it is essentially superficial. Most of Blake's "proletarian" characters could be the creations of any good "bourgeois" detective novelist. Justin Replogle has pointed out that Day-Lewis "was firmly rooted in the upper middle-class traditions of England. . . . he never shook himself free of the pleasant bonds of British middle-class convention. . . . The facts were . . . that he cherished many of the features of the old capitalist England" (141). Although Blake goes out of his way to create "proletarian" characters, he retains a strong sense of social position: Will Dykes in *The Corpse in the Snowman* may be a character of "upper-class" sensibilities in a "lower-class" body, but Rosa in *A Question of Proof* never rises above her station in any positive way. The country policemen in both *A Question of Proof* and *There's Trouble Brewing* are foolish yokels, and, although Blake wants us to sneer with him at Percival Vale's snobbery toward Wrench in *A Question of Proof*, we are never instructed to feel any other way about the character who is first termed an "incurable petty bourgeois" and reads books with "artistic" illustrations (16).

Another example of Day-Lewis's conflict is exhibited in his philosophy of the detective novel. Sean Day-Lewis tells us that one of his father's reasons for writing detective stories was to portray the "guilt motive": he believed that the detective novel appeals to the middle class because it is a "kind of substitute religious ritual" in which the detective portrays the "light" and the murderer the "dark" sides of "man's nature," so that the reader can identify with both of these characters, as can the author of the work. The detective solves the mystery "because he has more or less supernatural powers." However, Day-Lewis's bourgeois tendencies surface when he claims that this sort of detective novel would not appeal to workers, since they have "less time and incentive" to be concerned about the state of their consciences. Day-Lewis also believed that human life matters less to the workers, who read "bloods" in which life is cheap (86-87).

Blake became more interested in pure evil and less interested in guilt as he continued his series and Hitler continued his conquests. By 1941, in *The Corpse in the Snowman*, Andrew Restorick complains that "The trouble about detective novelists is that they shirk the real problem. . . . The problem of evil. That's the only really interesting thing about crime . . . the criminal in the average detective novel is [dull], a mere kingpin to hold together an intricate, artificial plot, the major premises of an argument that leads nowhere. But . . . what about the man who revels in evil? The man or woman whose very existence seems to depend upon the power to hurt or degrade others?" (27). Later, Dr. Bogan is described to us as a man motivated by "the horrible satisfaction of destroying people body and soul . . . with a dreadful relish for power, a genius so perverted that it could feel that relish only in corruption" (159). It is no accident that this description of the evil man was written in 1941, and that, when Andrew first brings up the subject of evil for evil's sake, the inane Eunice Ainsley immediately thinks of Hitler (27). It is also no accident that the fiendish E.B. leader, Chilton Canteloe, was created in 1939, when the Fascist powers were being conciliated.

In the early Blake novels, the political setting is frequently used to develop the characters and to make political statements. In *Thou Shell of Death*, Sir John Strangeways says of the Home Secretary: "fussy old hen, he's suddenly developed Communist-phobia; thinks they're going to put a bomb under his bed. Ought to know they don't allow acts of individual violence" (17). Blake shows Sir John as a confident, capable man with a sense of humor, but he does not ridicule the Communists; rather, he ridicules the Home Secretary's fearful ignorance.

There's Trouble Brewing deals with the supposed murder of a tyrannical brewery owner, who acts as virtual dictator of the village of Maiden Astbury. He also embodies the worst of capitalism. He refuses to modernize his brewery, which endangers his workers and actually costs him money. When Dr. Cammison tries to get him to improve working conditions, he is blackmailed for his efforts and his wife is sexually harassed (69-75).

In *The Beast Must Die*, Blake brings up the current events of 1938 when his not-so-dumb starlet, Lena Lawson, remarks, as part of her seemingly endless chatter, that "all these Jews are in league I must say we could do with a bit of Hitler here though I do rather bar rubber truncheons and sterilization" (36). We have been introduced to Lena as a possible accessory to Felix Lane's son's murder; her thoughtless, anti-Semitic remarks show her to be an accessory to murder on a large scale as well.

We are not supposed to sympathize with Lena or her remarks; we are, however, supposed to sympathize with Felix Lane, who remarks to his diary that "only generals, Harley Street specialists and mine-owners can get away with murder successfully" (8). In one sentence, Blake comments on the slaughter of war, the influence of wealth, and the poor working conditions in the collieries. Day-Lewis was to say later, in *The Buried Day*, that accidents are much more frequent in the mines than most people ever know; the public learns only about "major disasters" (145).

The Smiler with the Knife is an almost straightforward warning to the British about the forces of fascism, and is probably the most successful of the first six novels. When Nigel is explaining the probable conspiracy masked by the E.B., he warns Georgia that the leader may not be an ordinary politician and reminds her of the British love for the "inspired amateur." Georgia agrees: "it's part of our national romanticism to trust the amateur rather than the professional" (39). Georgia, of course, is an "inspired amateur" herself and saves England. However, when she succeeds in her mission, "Important Personages" want to give her "the thanks of a grateful nation," but she refuses their invitations: "she did not wish to be reminded of [her year-long ordeal] by the fulsome compliments of politicians whose own pusillanimity or self-interest were responsible for its having happened at all. She had performed her task and wanted no thanks for something which should never have been necessary" (241). Blake is saying that if the politicians continue to conciliate Hitler, someone may have to perform a task like Georgia's, and there is always the possibility that the inspired amateur may fail.

Despite his criticism of the government, Day-Lewis's loyalty to England comes through strongly in the early Nicholas Blake novels, particularly *The Smiler with the Knife* and *The Corpse in the Snowman*. D.E.S. Maxwell has summarized the conflict in *The Smiler with the Knife* as "the traditional English pleasures—cricket, country life—against the conspiracy of a Mosley-like organization to seize power in Britain" (60). Sir John Strangeways finally talks Georgia into taking on the E.B. by using this view of England. He asks her to look at the people:

It was the rush hour. A hundred yards away she could see the crowds hurrying home along the main thoroughfare. Typists, shop-assistants, business girls, tired yet moving with a gallant swing. She knew instinctively what Sir John wanted her to see there. His words only echoed what her own heart was telling her.

"Look at them," he said quietly . . . "They're not a bad lot, are they? Silly, vain, pert, ignorant, vulgar—some of them. But they've a grace of their own, haven't they? They've youth and independence and courage. They're England. And you know what the other side says—'Woman is for the recreation of the warrior'—'Woman's place is in the kitchen'—all the rest of the neanderthal tommyrot. That's what would happen, though. No young man to meet her outside the cinema tonight. He's got a date with a sadist storm trooper in a concentration camp. That'll spoil him for her." Sir John squeezed her shoulder, and his hand dropped to his side. "You can't let that happen," he said. (41-42)

When Georgia has completed her task, she exults, "We're all safe, all the decent, ordinary, hard-working people, the people who make England" (238). The England that Georgia saves is the same petty bourgeois populace that Blake portrayed as pretentious in A Question of Proof. Here, however, they are presented as heroic. These "decent, ordinary" people are the people who help Georgia escape from the E.B.: the adventurous department store manager and the clerk from accounting, the pantechnicon [furniture van] drivers, and the vicar's wife (206-08, 209, 219). None of these people is "political" in terms of spouting platitudes, although the pantechnicon drivers are "staunch Trade Unionists" (207). The England that Georgia saves is the England of the middle class, an England that would resist Day-Lewis's communism to the end.

The pantechnicon drivers who save Georgia do so while talking about soccer (209). This conversation is a nice, realistic touch that breaks up the tension of the pantechnicon's journey. It also betrays one of Day-Lewis's least intellectual diversions. Day-Lewis was the only one of the "Auden Group" who had indulged in "the so-called Philistine world of games" while in school (Stanford 38). The pantechnicon drivers' interest in sport implies an interest in fair play.

Day-Lewis employs the sporting metaphor more than once, and the game that he usually uses is cricket. In A Question of Proof, Nigel discovers himself mentally eliminating Tiverton from the list of suspects because he is "a born cricketer" (116). In There's Trouble Brewing, Inspector Tollworthy is deemed a "good sort" because Herbert Cammison has played cricket with him (60). The best example of good sportsmanship, however, is Peter Braithwaite, the Test cricketer in The Smiler with the Knife. One of the noblest of Sir John's agents, Peter plays the spy "game" in the same way that he plays cricket; he's usually good, but he tends to take risks (151). Peter also plays both games fairly; that is, he "plays cricket." His motivation for the risk that costs him his life is the guilt that he feels for the death of Rosa Alvarez, a woman he seduced in order to learn the secrets of the E.B. When Peter realizes that his only hope of doing any damage to the E.B. is to blow up the munitions dump, he makes a mental note of his location, thankful that he will not have to hurt any innocent people. He takes his death as calmly as if it were merely the end of the game: "He'd take it standing up, not like those quitters grovelling against the wall over there" (157). The true Englishman is cool and sportsmanlike to the end, unlike the "quitters" and poor sports who make up the fascist conspiracy.

In *The Corpse in the Snowman* we are never allowed to forget that the novel takes place during wartime. The blackout is mentioned several times (14, 23) and is the means of ascertaining the time of Betty's death (58). Hereward and Charlotte have a motive for murdering Betty because they lost money during the invasion of Poland (86, 132), as did Eunice Ainsley (105). Betty discusses making a will because of the war (109), and Charlotte has been considering donating Easterham Manor for a hospital (110). Many of the characters are employed in some sort of work on the war: Georgia works on a refugees committee, Nigel is working on a "war diary" (12), and Hereward Restorick "[fiddles] about on war agriculture committees" but is really "half-demented because they won't let him back in his old regiment yet" (49). The tension at Easterham is compared to that of the war in Europe (48), and Nigel and Blount assume that Andrew and Bogan are probably still in the country because the war has made leaving the country extremely difficult (192). All of these war references set us up perfectly for Andrew Restorick's act of contrition: he goes off to Germany to "do as much damage as I can before they find me out" (176). His desire to hurt the power-hungry Germans parallels his murder of the power-hungry Dr. Bogan.

The most strongly worded criticisms of the complacency of Great Britain come from the would-be dictator in *The Smiler with the Knife*, Chilton Canteloe. He explains to Georgia that the British people's character is going to be their downfall. "Chillie" is going to be named "First Guardian of Public Safety," since "the English like the idea of being looked after, without having to admit any filial piety." He also foresees no problem in getting rid of any who oppose him: "Our countrymen dislike purges; but, in a state of emergency, they're willing to bury their heads in the sand and let someone else do their dirty work for them—provided it's done with all the legal paraphernalia, a chaplain in attendance, and officials to sign the document in triplicate" (178-79). The coldness of a bureaucracy that can depersonalize murder is also seen in Chillie's Plan A: it is described as being like "the prospectus of a respectable company" in its dryness and in "its cold, impersonal setting-out of detail, its translation of flesh-and-blood hopes, greed, fears, idealism, into an inhuman document" (189). A militaristic Fascist regime would have no room for the warm, emotional vagaries of humanity.

The emotional coldness of the power-mad Chillie (and the name *is* significant) is recreated in the blackmailing, drug-dispensing Dr. Bogan in *The Corpse in the Snowman*. Andrew Restorick takes a peculiar pleasure in being able to hide Bogan in a snowman: "I can't help feeling a lively satisfaction that that devil, with his ice-cold heart and his 'snow,' should have ended up in a snowman" (176). Both of these early Blake villains are emotionally cold, cold-blooded, and cold-hearted like the fascist regimes that they represent.

Nicholas Blake actually wrote six first novels, because of his own indecision about the kind of detective he wanted to create, the type of novel he wanted to write, and his own internal political conflicts. After six "first" novels, he had settled down, both politically and artistically, and was able to create a consistent Nigel Strangeways series.

Works Cited

Bargainnier, Earl F. "Nicholas Blake." *Twelve Englishmen of Mystery*. Ed. Earl F. Bargainnier. Bowling Green, OH: Bowling Green State University Popular Press, 1984. 143-68.

Blake, Nicholas. *The Beast Must Die*. New York: Harper, 1978.

____. *The Corpse in the Snowman*. New York: Harper, 1977.

____. *A Question of Proof*. New York: Harper, 1979.

____. *The Smiler with the Knife*. New York: Harper, 1978.

____. *There's Trouble Brewing*. New York: Harper, 1982.

____. *Thou Shell of Death*. New York: Harper, 1977.

Day-Lewis, C. *The Buried Day*. New York: Harper, 1960.

____. *A Hope for Poetry*. Oxford: Blackwell, 1934.

____. *Revolution in Writing*. Day to Day Pamphlets, No. 29. London: Hogarth, 1935.

Day-Lewis, Sean. *C. Day-Lewis: An English Literary Life*. London: Weidenfeld & Nicolson, 1980.

Maxwell, D.E.S. "C. Day Lewis: Between Two Worlds." *Poets of the Thirties*. London: Routledge & Kegan Paul, 1969. 83-126.

Replogle, Justin. "The Auden Group." *Wisconsin Studies in Contemporary Literature* 5 (1964): 133-50.

Stanford, Derek. "Stephen Spender, Louis MacNeice, Cecil Day Lewis: A Critical Essay." Contemporary Writers in Christian Perspective. Gen. ed. Roderick Gellema. Grand Rapids, MI: Eerdmans, 1969.

Mike Shayne:
A Series Starts and Restarts

Sharon A. Russell

In many series an author's first mystery establishes a pattern of relationships that is developed in subsequent volumes. Characters may enter or leave the detective's life and locations may change, but change generally occurs gradually. Some authors improve their mastery of the genre with each successive addition to their series, and some add new series with new detectives to their work. Brett Halliday, one of several pseudonyms of Davis Dresser, does develop the character of the detective Mike Shayne throughout this hard-boiled private eye series, but the major shifts his detective experiences before the series settles into its final form are interesting not only in the career of the author but also because they have implications for the kinds of characters who can operate in the hard-boiled subgenre of the detective novel.

Dresser's first published novel, *Mum's the Word for Murder* (1938; one of two in this series) introduced Jerry Burke, a former cowboy who has been appointed "co-ordinator of all the law enforcement agencies in El Paso" (11). His activities are chronicled by Asa Baker, the pseudonymous author as well as narrator of the series, a western novelist. Baker becomes Burke's Watson because he is facing a deadline with no inspiration. Baker's ability to jump from genre to genre with ease indicates not only an individual author's view of how quickly this shift can be made but also some of the general qualities shared by two popular genres such as the concern for justice and the investigation of criminal activities in a western setting.

Dresser was born in Chicago and grew up in Texas. He wrote mystery, adventure, and western pulp fiction (Collins 489) and gained his greatest fame with Mike Shayne, a hard-boiled hero who still retains the mixture of big city detective and western hero found in the classic examples of this genre well into the fifties. While the Shayne novels are not first person narratives, they are, with rare exception, presented from Shayne's point of view. Michael Collins, in *Twentieth Century Crime & Mystery Writers*, describes those traits that Halliday and Shayne share:

He was one of the last of a generation that grew up on the closing of the frontier. . . . Both men stood for a simpler, more confident, less confused time in America. They are loners because they rely on no one but themselves in either action or thought. Wrong they may be, from time to time, but it will never be because of anyone but themselves, because of any code but their own. And that code is in essence the code of the old frontier, of a rugged individualist populism. (491)

Mike Shayne's code emerges slowly in the first book of the series, *Dividend on Death* (1939). However, Halliday's relaxed use of genre conventions is evident in the first line and suggests one of the reasons for the novel's twenty-two rejections before it was accepted for publication. "The girl who faced Michael Shayne in his downtown Miami apartment was beautiful, but too unblemished to interest Shayne particularly. She was young, certainly not more than twenty, with a slender niceness of figure that was curiously rigid as she sat in the chair leaning toward him" (5). Phyllis Brighton is too young to be the romantic interest, especially in a first novel in a series. If Phyllis is too young, Mike is too big. If Phyllis is a juvenile lead, Mike, physically, is a lanky cowboy.

Michael Shayne slowly unlimbered himself and stood up. He had a tall angular body that concealed a lot of solid weight, and his freckled cheeks were thin to gauntness. His rumpled hair was violently red, giving him a little-boy look curiously in contrast with the harshness of his features. When he smiled, the harshness went out of his face and he didn't look at all like a hard-boiled private detective who had come to the top the tough way. (8)

While Halliday's alteration of some of the descriptive elements of genre conventions is not radical, it does lead to some of the shifts the series takes. Genres are seldom pure. As Robin Wood suggests about film genres, "they represent different strategies for dealing with the same ideological tensions" (62). Wood lists the components of the classic Hollywood genre films, components shared by much American popular fiction. Wood's point in listing these components is to indicate their inherent contradictions. The first two components, capitalism and the work ethic, reinforce each other. The third, marriage, is to a certain extent dependent on the first two, since financial success is necessary for the lifestyle of a couple. The fourth component has a dual aspect—nature as agrarian Garden of Eden and nature as wilderness. In opposition to the fourth is the fifth— progress, technology, the city. The sixth, success and wealth, is a value that also produces its opposite, number seven, the "Rosebud Syndrome," which demonstrates the corrupting power of money. The eighth is the culmination of the others—the belief that in America everyone can be happy. The two final elements are, again, related—the images of the ideal man and the ideal woman. The ideal male as the independent individualist and the ideal woman as the married housewife are contradictory images which give rise to their shadows—the settled husband and the erotic woman. For Wood the friction caused by the shifting relationships among these components generates the real interest in genres. Individual artists focus these tensions (60-61).

Some of these components have greater impact for certain genres, but they are all applicable to popular American literature as well as to film. The conventions are observed by the Shayne books in the development of the crime story, but the series has to work hard to conventionalize those genre elements that are not essential to the mystery. Capitalism, for example, is such a strong element that those few times that Shayne works for no fee are significant. *Dividend on Death* is one such novel. Usually this detective is quite open in his manipulation of events to ensure not only justice but also his fee. But capitalism is an indication of character rather than the real motivation for action in the Shayne series and the hard-boiled genre in general, an indication of the professionalism of the detective. The private investigator wants to make money, wants success, but also knows through experience how money corrupts. The drive for financial success conflicts with the detective's ethics, forcing the detective to seek work from rich people, but the professional's code also necessitates the refusal of jobs from the evil client. Pure jobs usually come from poor but honest people who must be served on a *pro bono* basis. The questionable rich client, in essence, supports the poor one. Shayne novels often carry these contradictions to extremes. Mike is not above taking a fee and then proving the client guilty, as in *Counterfeit Wife* (1947). Shayne's strong ethical commitments may resolve the troubling contradictions created by his need for money, but the relationship between money and work remains a recurring, disturbing subtext in the series.

While concerns about wealth as success are central to the hard-boiled genre and the Shayne series in particular, they provide the motivation for the crime more often than the inspiration for the detective, who solves crimes because he is compelled to do so—the work ethic in action. However, the third item on Wood's list (marriage) and its interaction with nine and ten (ideal male and female) are far more troubling in the form. Much of a detective's work relates to male-female relationships and crimes dealing with conflicts generated in marriage, but the detective, like the priest, must deal with these problems without partaking of them. The detective's code of ethics is most lax and most complex when dealing with the opposite sex. Some detectives never sleep with their clients, some do whenever they can, and some would like to but don't. In all cases the possibility of illicit sex is one of the attractions of the hard-boiled genre. Halliday may have been drawn to the image of the lone male, an image shared with the western novel, but he had more difficulty reconciling the image of the ideal female with the hard-boiled genre.

In the Western the good woman is the civilizing influence; she is the inevitable result of the progressive closing of the frontier, and as such, is viewed as both positive and negative. There can be no future without her, but the future with her is quite different from the idealized past of the heroic loner. The erotic female is always disruptive but also attractive. She tests the hero's code of behavior but poses no threat for the future because she has none. She is as transient as the hero. These elements of the Western can also be found in the hard-boiled mystery. In this context the concern for the future is not as important as the maintenance of the values of the present, the prevention of any further erosion of what we already have. Dresser, in moving from one genre to another in his first Shayne novel, produced such conflicting elements that it took several novels to regain the usual direction of the series and several further novels to reconcile the effects of these necessary shifts.

The locus of all of these conflicts in the early Mike Shayne novels is the character of Phyllis Brighton—a woman who starts out as a young erotic female but is transformed into a wife. More than Phyllis Brighton's youth as a love interest is unusual in her first appearance in Halliday's first Shayne novel. Mike Shayne operates from his own apartment in Miami, a location which is not typical for the genre and one which undergoes significant alterations as the series progresses. Miss Brighton has come to hire Shayne because she is afraid she will kill her mother. She has been convinced of the possibility of this action by a doctor. "They say I've got an Electra complex and it's driving me insane with jealousy because Mother married Mr. Brighton and I'll kill her before I'll let him have her" (*Dividend* 9-10). She engages Shayne's sympathy because she is so young, and he becomes more fully involved when she tries to kill herself. Shayne also comments on a "feel of beneath-the-surface stuff that set his nerves tingling in a way that hadn't happened to him for a long time" (12). He accepts Miss Brighton's pearl necklace as a retainer.

The novel's plot follows a rather conventional genre pattern. Additional elements are established and become part of Halliday's style. The entire case takes only four days, a time span which can be even shorter in the majority of Shayne cases. Mike Shayne is shot and beaten and still manages to keep going. He also drinks large amounts of Martell cognac with a side glass of ice water and never gets drunk. He claims the brandy helps his thinking process. By the end of the novel Shayne manages to trick several guilty parties into paying him for his services and collects an additional reward from Peter Painter. The latter is the chief of the Miami Beach detective bureau, the bad cop to Will Gentry, the head of the Miami detectives, as the good cop. This first novel establishes Shayne's relationship to these two detectives, a relationship which intensifies as the series continues. Gentry becomes a more positive character, and the antagonism between Painter and Shayne grows. Only Painter is present for the end of this first case because the murder has taken place on the Beach. Often both are present when Shayne, in traditional mystery style, gathers together everyone for the final solution. In *Dividend on Death*, Halliday breaks this rule before he even establishes it. Shayne sets up the situation so the bad guys kill each other off, and all he does is explain the how of it to Painter so the police can take credit for the solution.

The few individualizing touches that can be found in Halliday's first novel are not as significant as the major problems raised by the interaction on the level of both plot and characterization of Mike Shayne and Phyllis Brighton. As has already been suggested, Phyllis does not appear as an ordinary client, and Mike's interest in her is mitigated by his perception of their age differences. Mike decides to take the case because it interests him. "Hadn't he started passing up routine stuff a long time ago? That's why he had no downtown office and no regular staff. That sort of phony front he left to the punks with whom Miami is infested during the season" (12). After he has taken Phyllis as a client, the doctor treating her also hires Mike. This time Mike is happy to take the money. The doctor makes claims about her mental state that seem exaggerated. When Mike next sees her the doctor's assertions seem more possible, but Mike still trusts his instinct and protects her.

She looked ghastly in the dim light. The lashes were drawn back from her eyeballs as though by some mechanical device, and the pupils were so contracted that the entire eyeball seemed to consist only of smoky iris. Shayne saw that she was wearing a flimsy chiffon nightgown and that her feet were bare. Streaks of blood showed darkly red down the front of her nightgown. (20)

Mike, with a delicacy not customary in his profession, looks away as he tells her to remove the stained gown. "This was a hell of a time to be thinking about—anything except earning that string of pearls Phyllis had given him" (24). Of course, the string of pearls is not his motivation but a screen. Concern, not greed, is often the real reason for the hard-boiled detective's actions. He manages to smuggle the bloody items connected with Phyllis out of the house.

His next encounter with Phyllis is the most interesting in the novel and, perhaps, his most unusual meeting with a woman in the entire series. Phyllis appears at his apartment/office to seek reassurance that she did not commit matricide. Shayne has already changed into pajamas and a dressing gown even though he tells her he has been expecting her when she arrives. "She was wearing a two-piece knitted dress which clung tightly to her firm young body. Hatless, her black hair was wind-blown and very curly; without make-up, her complexion seemed engagingly fresh, though she was unnaturally pale" (33). She rejects Shayne's suggestion that she fix up a good story; she wants the truth. Together they try to reconstruct the night of the murder, but Phyllis has a hard time distinguishing dreams from reality. She seems to remember removing her nightgown in front of Mike who denies it with an assertion of his masculinity. "I'm not the kind of guy to watch a girl take off her nightgown in a bedroom—and not do anything about it" (39). He thinks Phyllis is concerned about what might have happened between them. But her actual problem is more unusual. Dr. Pedique, who has been treating her for this "Electra" complex has suggested that her unnatural love for her mother has deeper roots. "His books are full of case histories of people with curious sexual complexes. I didn't realize—I didn't know there *were* that sort of people in the world" (40). She then enters into a discussion with Mike of the possibility of her having those feelings, of her being, in the word that cannot be spoken in the text, lesbian.

Mike suggests she is a victim of autosuggestion, but Phyllis wants further proof; she wants Mike to help her, not as a doctor, but as a man. She needs proof of her heterosexuality and wants it from Mike, who is a "grown man," unlike the men she has dated. He protests he is old enough to be her father. "I'm nineteen. And you're only thirty-five. You said so this afternoon" (41). Shayne resists, afraid of what a kiss will lead to, and the force of his resistance is so strong it is transferred to Phyllis. "Shayne forgot that he had been thinking of her as just a kid who was trusting herself with him alone in his apartment. He was drawing her closer, hurting her cruelly, but she did not flinch. Exaltation shone in her eyes. She lifted her head offering him her lips" (41). Mike's response to this invitation is also intense. "God have pity on us both if I kiss you, Phyllis" (41). She presses even closer, igniting a "blaze." When he warns her that he cannot control his feelings, "You can't turn things like this on and off, you know—like an electric switch" (42), she asks where the bedroom is. "There wasn't a trace of coquetry in her smile. It was a smile of sincere and honest gladness" (42). She undresses and calls to him. "His mind was racing, trying to puzzle something through in spite of the clamor in his blood. Nothing quite like this had ever happened to him before" (42). As he knocks and enters the bedroom, another knock is heard on the door to his apartment. He tells Phyllis to lie quietly since the police must have followed her. He tries to remove obvious evidence of her presence before he opens the door to both Gentry and Painter.

"This is a hell of a time to come visiting" (43), he tells them in the first of series of double entendres. When asked where Phyllis is, he responds, "I must have mislaid her" (45). Painter believes Mike is involved in her disappearance. Mike continues a verbal battle with Painter, careful not to lie as he avoids telling what he knows. By the time the police leave, Phyllis has fallen asleep. Mike settles down on the studio couch in the living room. "For all his profession, Mike Shayne had something domestic in him. Years of hotel rooms had made him fond of his own brand of comfort" (53). Mike makes Phyllis breakfast the next morning, leaves her in the apartment, and sets out to solve the case.

Once he has cleared her of the crime, they return to the situation halted by the arrival of the police. Mike claims the only thing he regrets is being interrupted that night. Phyllis offers to continue, and he responds with familiar words. "God help me, I almost weakened once before" (191). Just as they are about to kiss, he returns her pearls and tells her, "Go out and grow up. *Then* come back, and we'll do something constructive about it—if you still feel the same way"(191). She protests his returning the pearls, stating he can't afford to take cases without money or credit. She is not aware of the tally of $24,200 Mike has just made of money received in this case. Mike does decide to collect a slight fee. They kiss. "Shayne leaned down and collected more than a slight fee, then sent her away with a little push, closing the door behind her" (192). Mike is aware his life has changed. "Something new had come into his life—and gone out of it" (192). He is no longer interested in the receipts for the case. While he reads the items on his tally the sound of the traffic comes up through his window: "The sound was not unlike the rumble of a distant drum, but Shayne's mind was occupied with other things, and he paid no heed to it" (192).

Obviously, it is not just Mike's refusal to have a sexual relationship with Phyllis that troubles this narrative. Halliday sets in motion certain concerns that bring into direct confrontation conventions of the genre at the same time as he gives voices to conflicts which are generally avoided in this genre. The ideal male faces image and shadow in both genders. Before the series has really started the independent male must deal with the possibility of marriage, having rejected the illicit affair, but the same woman offers both marriage and erotic love. Phyllis cannot be relegated to the role of the blonde babe who passes through the pages of so many hard-boiled novels, but she uses the techniques associated with this image. Mike, unlike his "love'm and leave'm" counterparts, resists. But Phyllis approaches Mike because she feels the need to prove her femininity, which has been challenged by the evil Dr. Pedique. Phyllis is caught. If she does not attempt sexual activity with Mike, she will retain her fear of being a lesbian.

Mike has no doubts about Phyllis's sexuality, first, because his instincts do not suggest revulsion (11) and second, because the source of this information, Dr. Pedique (with the hint of pedophile in his name) does revolt Mike with his obviously homosexual characteristics. Both Pedique and Phyllis appear in the first chapter, but Pedique is successful in his suicide attempt, unlike the one Mike prevents in Phyllis's case. The solution of the case restores sexual normalcy to the story. Phyllis is cleared of the taint of possible matricide. The feelings she rouses in Mike eliminate lesbianism as a threat to the sexual roles of the genre. The symbolic incest has already been prevented by the intervention of the "law of the patriarchy" when the two police officers interrupt Mike, who is older than Phyllis, perhaps old enough to be her father. Mike now will be able to wait, with God on his side, for Phyllis to become a woman, a process that is already beginning by the end of the novel when he no longer calls her a kid. He can abandon his role of fatherhood and move on to his role as lover.

Mike is successful in solving the case, making money and at the same time working without the usual fee from Phyllis, the love-interest client uniting some of the conflicts between greed and service inherent in the genre. But the fee he collects from her, the kiss, generates further conflict in the interaction of male and female genre types. While the "unnatural" sexuality that troubles *Dividend on Death* can be subsumed by the triumph of patriarchal order by the end of the novel, certain problems for the genre continue in the series.

The second novel in the series, *The Private Practice of Michael Shayne* (1940), describes their "courtship" in the context of a complex case which deals directly with money and ethics. Larry Kincaid, a friend of Mike's and a new lawyer in town, asks Mike to help him deal with an extortionist. The detective refuses because he thinks it's a bad way for Larry to get started with his career, no matter how much the lawyer may need money. Mike is even more concerned when he learns Larry has been approached for this job by Harry Grange. "He and hundreds like him flock to Miami and Miami Beach in the winter and put up a swell front, dragging down a percentage from the gambling houses by bringing suckers in to lose their money" (11). Larry informs Mike that Grange has been escorting Phyllis around: "The pretty heiress you took to your paternal bosom when she was accused on murdering her mother last month. Lots of people think . . ." (11). Larry's suggests that Mike's interest in Phyllis is doubly ironic. Mike could be her father, and Larry also believes Mike is after his wife. Larry reveals he doesn't understand Mike's concern just as he doesn't understand the general relationship between work and money. But Larry is driven to his pursuit of money and eventual death by his wife's desire for material things, a union of women and money which is opposite to Mike's lack of interest in Phyllis's inherited wealth.

In this conversation Mike reveals his opinion of his own life and the choices he has made:

Keep clear of it, Larry. God knows, I know what I'm saying. I was once just where you are. I didn't have the guts to wait for success. Like you, I thought it was a hell of a lot more important to make a gob of money at once. Well—look at me now. (12)

Larry, of course, is not convinced by Mike's arguments and disappears after Grange is found dead. Mike tries to rescue Phyllis from Grange's influence, but she is trying to prove to Mike that she is old enough to be a romantic force in his life. An indication of Mike's attitude toward her is his rare appreciation of the beauty of Miami Beach after seeing her. The novel follows the pattern Halliday has established as Mike investigates Grange's death. He is drawn into the investigation both because of Larry's involvement and because of his concern about Phyllis. She arrives at Mike's apartment at various points in the novel. In chapter 7, titled "The Girl Who Was Growing Up" (59), Phyllis has once again appeared at Mike's apartment. This time she makes the coffee, a sign of her incorporation into his life. She passes the coffee test: "You're actually making coffee a man can drink. You'll make some man a swell wife when you grow up" (61).

The most complex moments at the apartment occur during Phyllis's next visit. Mike is convinced that Larry is dead, and, as a kind of punishment, he asks Helen to come to his apartment and pretend to seduce a suspect. When the man arrives, Helen hides in Mike's bedroom waiting for him to give her the signal to appear. Before he can get to the appropriate moment, Phyllis arrives. When Helen does emerge from Mike's bedroom, Phyllis, of course, suspects the worst of Mike. He tries to send her signals indicating what is happening, but she does not catch on. In a bizarre approach to romance, Helen works on her assigned man, while Mike attempts to make Phyllis understand what is happening. She is the first to confess her love. Mike explains his plans for Helen, and Phyllis responds, "I wish I could believe you. If you'd only stop treating me like a child" (138). Mike responds by admitting his love for her, finally moving from father to lover. Phyllis enters the ranks of "good women" as he tells her she will have to figure things out if she is going to be his wife. She does not need to solve mysteries, but she is going to "have to learn to keep your mouth shut and your eyes open" (138). He is really asking her to understand the difference between fake and real emotion, but he is also telling her to learn the difference between the two types of women if she is going to become a wife, a good wife as opposed to the gold digger represented by Helen. After Mike and Phyllis kiss, sealing their relationship, Helen finally leaves with the other man. When she reports back to Mike, Helen has learned nothing from her encounter with the man who actually did kill her husband, but she feels dirty—her punishment.

As the series continues, Mike does marry Phyllis. They move to a new apartment above his old one, which is retained for work. The novels that include Phyllis as wife seem to have difficulty in assigning her an adequate role. She has to be good enough to be Mike's wife but not so good that she is a better detective than he is. As a result she often starts out forcing herself into a position where she works with him. When he leaves her behind she strikes out on her own and is then often captured or controlled by the criminals while Mike solves the crime. Sometimes her capture involves danger for both of them. Once a case interrupts them as they are about to leave on vacation. Mike sends Phyllis on to New York while he rushes to solve it and join her, in *Bodies Are Where You Find Them* (1941).

At the end of this novel Halliday includes a strange narrative, "Michael Shayne As I Know Him," which purports to be the story of his relationship with "a red-headed, fighting Irishman whom I call Michael Shayne" (183). Even though this narrative is published at the end of a novel dated 1941, it seems to be an addition to a reprint because it refers to later novels and events that have yet to occur. According to this account, Halliday first sees Shayne (not his real name, as this pseudo-biography indicates) in a fight in a waterfront bar in Tampico and encounters him again four years later in New Orleans. Halliday later broadcasts a request for information about him over the radio on a show that attempts to unite people who have lost contact. He finds one incorrect version of Mike Shayne and is finally contacted by Mike while working in a cabin at "Desolation Bend" in Colorado (185). They form a friendship, and Halliday joins Shayne in Miami where he begins the job of chronicling Shayne's life. He is even best man at the wedding of Phyllis and Mike. "The next few years, I am positive, were the happiest Mike has ever known. Phyllis worried him sometimes by insisting on acting as his secretary and getting herself mixed up in some of his cases, but there was perfect companionship and understanding between them" (186).

Perfect companionship and understanding may be fine in this "life story," but they don't seem to work well in genre fiction. Domestic life is usually antithetical to the character of the hard-boiled private investigator. Just as the good woman brings the promise and threat of civilization to the Western, Phyllis as both civilizing and erotic female disrupts the detective genre. With the new apartment—decorated by Phyllis and associated with marriage and control of male sexuality—above him, Mike cannot conduct business as usual in the working apartment below. It's hard to get on top of a sexy client or suspect with your wife living above you. At times he is put in the position of pretending not to care about Phyllis or acting as though he is unfaithful, in order to lie to Gentry so he can solve a case. When Gentry or Tim Rourke, his best friend, defends Phyllis, the male bonding between them and Mike is strained.

As Halliday recounts in his story of Shayne's life, Phyllis dies in childbirth. While Phyllis's death is referred to in the next novel, *Heads You Lose* (1943), the cause of her death is not directly confronted until later in the series, in *Blood on Biscayne Bay* (1946). Mike solves the case in this novel with no fee and actually asks for public credit at its conclusion, an indication of the importance of Phyllis's death and the way her loss disrupts his usual pattern. After Phyllis's death Mike moves to New Orleans for a while and forms a relationship with Lucy Hamilton, his secretary there. He returns to Miami to solve the attempted murder of his best friend, Tim Rourke, who has a near fatal attraction for blondes, in *Marked for Murder* (1945). But he does not remain in Miami, despite Will Gentry's request, until he solves a case involving Phyllis's best friend and another string of pearls, in *Blood on Biscayne Bay*. When Mike refuses the fee after saving the marriage of Phyllis's friend he states, "For once in my life let me do something for nothing. Let's say— Phyllis would want it that way" (192). He does accept a false set of pearls, copies of the real set that had been his retainer for the case.

As he takes them, Christine, Phyllis's friend, tells him they would fool an expert. "Shayne thought of Lucy Hamilton. Maybe a gift like this would persuade her to forgive him for all the trouble and anxiety he had caused her" (192).

Lucy Hamilton does move back to Miami with Mike. They retain separate apartments, with an implied sexual relationship but no marriage. In addition to this arrangement, which normalizes the sexual tensions of the genre, Lucy also persuades Mike to rent a regular office. "He had forgotten momentarily, that in order to persuade her to resume her job as his secretary he had rented office space in a six-story building downtown after more than fifteen years of doing business in his apartment" (*This Is It, Michael Shayne* [1950] 5). With the addition of Lucy, the series finally takes on the standard characteristics of the genre. The first novel, which took so long to sell, is finally transformed into a series that continues even after Dresser stops writing it. The wife, Phyllis Brighton-Shayne, could not be accommodated in a hard-boiled series. The domestic problems, the conflicts between husbands and wives, the damsels in distress because of problems with lovers—the standard plot devices of the genre—run counter to the image of marital bliss generated by Mike and Phyllis. The excessive violence associated with the genre also poses problems for the married detective. Phyllis could not continue to be exposed to the same threats as Mike, especially those threats that often occurred at his office/apartment, the intrusion of violence into home and family. The presence of a wife also disrupts the male camaraderie of Mike and his friends. For example, Phyllis generated a set of expectations about family and wife in Gentry. When Mike is forced to ignore these conventions their friendship is affected.

Lucy Hamilton may be Mike's lover, but more importantly, she is his secretary. She works for him and is not expected to work with him. Just as the independent woman of the World War II era gives way to the contained images of the fifties in genre films, Lucy replaces Phyllis and the series restarts itself. Once Shayne finally deals with Phyllis's memory and accepts the pearls he had returned to her in the first novel, the series settles into accepted genre patterns. But the pearls he gives Lucy are false. Phyllis keeps her real pearls, her independence, but loses her life in childbirth when she takes on her role as legitimate wife. Lucy gets paid, but she will not be an equal. Mike will do as she asks, not for love but because he needs her. He likes her, but she will have to be happy without the commitment of marriage. She will not make a home or family for Mike. She will not threaten the rules of the genre, and she will not be destroyed by them. Phyllis's sexuality is troubling from the moment she enters the first novel. She brings suggestions of alternatives beyond the law of the father. The aspects of her sexuality, the threats of lesbianism and of incest, are contained by her marriage. But marriage is also a disruption of the genre and its enduring image of the tough, lone male. All of these threats are purged with Phyllis's death in childbirth. Mike Shayne leaves Miami so the series may restart with the threat of the female contained within the confines of the genre.

Works Cited

Collins, Michael. "Halliday, Brett." *Twentieth Century Crime & Mystery Writers*. 3rd ed. Ed. Lesley Henderson. Chicago: St. James, 1991. 489-91.

Halliday, Brett [Davis Dresser]. *Blood on Biscayne Bay*. New York: Dell, 1966.

____. *Bodies Are Where You Find Them*. New York: Dell, 1971.

____. *Dividend on Death*. New York: Dell, 1959.

____. *Mum's the Word for Murder*." Originally pub. by Asa Baker. New York: Dell, n.d.

____. *The Private Practice of Michael Shayne*. New York: Dell, 1965.

____. *This Is It, Michael Shayne*. New York: Dell, 1962.

Wood, Robin. "Ideology, Genre, Auteur." *Film Genre Reader*. Ed. Barry Keith Grant. Austin: U of Texas P, 1986. 59-73.

Cop Hater:
Gateway to the 87th Precinct

George N. Dove

It would be hard to imagine a more unpretentious beginning to a series of detective novels than the drab little volume that appeared on the paperback shelves in 1956. With a cover in muted red, yellow, and gray, and pictures of plainclothes policemen, uniformed policemen, skyscrapers, and terrified heroines not discernible from more than a few feet away, it sold for twenty-five cents and seemed almost apologetic of its own presence. This, however, was *Cop Hater*, the first of Ed McBain's series that has grown to some forty-five volumes, the longest and, by almost complete consensus of fans and critics, the strongest series of police novels ever written. *Cop Hater* was planned from the beginning as the first of a series of at least three books (McBain, "87th" 95), and before the end of the year two others, *The Mugger* and *The Pusher* (in somewhat brighter covers, by the way), had appeared.

Whatever *Cop Hater* lacked in external visual appeal, however, it more than made up in internal literary merit, a fact quickly recognized by Anthony Boucher, mystery critic of *The New York Times* and one of the most influential book reviewers in the country. Boucher not only wrote a rave review of *Cop Hater* but selected it and *The Mugger* for listing in his Best Suspense Novels of 1956. When Simon and Schuster collected the first three into a hardbound volume in 1959, Boucher wrote an insightful introduction in which he recognized that McBain had done exceptionally well what the public had been hungering for.

At the conclusion, he identified McBain as Evan Hunter, already known as the author of two bestsellers, *The Blackboard Jungle* and *Strangers When We Meet* (Dove 2).

Cop Hater is the story of a series of murders of plainclothes detectives, all of whom are attached to the 87th Squad. Only after an intense investigation that consumes more than three weeks of a

105

blistering July and August and after the deaths of three plainclothes police detectives are the members of the Eight-Seven able to bring the cop-hater to justice.

Read after some of the more mature accomplishments of the series, *Cop Hater* may seem a little sparse and stiff, but it does prefigure some of the elements of the 87th Precinct saga that have occasioned so much praise, not the least of which is its accurate handling of police methods. In this novel, McBain follows the pattern established by Lawrence Treat in *V as in Victim* (1945), the first classic police procedural. Treat portrayed two aspects of police methodology, one represented by Mitch Taylor, the old-style foot-slogging cop, who depends more heavily on the questioning (and intimidation) of suspects, the interviewing of witnesses, and the ringing of doorbells than upon the findings of the police laboratory, and who is inclined to goof off and to take short cuts when he deems them necessary. The other approach is represented by Jub Freeman, a forensic scientist who capably operates the police laboratory and who is constantly on the lookout for means of applying the most recent science to police detection.

The older style of detection in *Cop Hater* is represented by Hank Bush, who hates difficult cases, and who believes that physical effort in police work takes priority over brilliance: "Legwork and stubbornness, that was all it amounted to." Bush is also not averse to slipping off to his apartment during duty hours for a little unauthorized leave, especially when the weather is unbearable, as it is in the summer of *Cop Hater* (78-79). Not all the old methods are wasteful and inefficient, however. One of the most valuable weapons is the police lineup, in which the chief object is to give the cops a chance to familiarize themselves with the criminals of the neighborhood; occasionally, though, the lineup gives them a real lead in a current case, as it does for Carella and Bush when they chance upon a choice suspect in their search for the serial killer in the 87th Precinct (90 ff). An invaluable (and unscientific) aid to crime-detection is the informer, without whom any police detective is almost non-competitive; Steve Carella's "stoolie" is Danny Gimp, who goes everywhere and hears everything and knows how to keep his ears open and his profile low (57).

The practice of forensic science in the 87th Precinct is personified in Lieutenant (later Captain) Sam Grossman, who heads the police laboratory, and who will subsequently become one of the second-magnitude stars of the series (115). After the first murder it is discovered that the gunman had stepped in some dog droppings, and the forensic boys go to work immediately taking advantage of what may become an aid to his apprehension, first photographing the heel-print, then making a cast that will give the cops some idea of the general appearance of the man they are looking for (52-54). The data are not sufficient to apply the formula for estimating the length of the man's stride, but the equation is reproduced anyhow, an awesome mathematical statement that requires half a line of print (54). This is just one of a long string of formulas and tables that will be offered to the readers of the series: in *Cop Hater* we are also introduced to the table for judging a person's age by the diameter of the hair (118) and a discussion of sweat pores in the fingertips (140). The information is always highly exact (like the fact that human perspiration is 98.5 percent water), but always presented in such a way that instead of boring the reader it serves to reinforce the general atmosphere of the exactness of police science.

One point we must not miss: in spite of all the accumulated police experience and in spite of all the highly developed forensic science available to the police in the 87th Precinct, the apprehension of the cop hater is the result of pure dumb luck. This feature is important for more than one reason: it introduces a precedent that will appear repeatedly in the 87th Precinct stories, but even more significantly it sets the tone of heavy irony that pervades the entire series.

We should not leave the subject of McBain's faithful handling of police methods without at least mentioning his portrayal of the police subculture. One of the themes of *Cop Hater* is that the police detective (unlike the glamorous private eye of fiction) is a family man with all kinds of problems, including overwork, insufficient pay, and constant danger. Usually the personal problems relate to the policeman's family, as is the case with Lieutenant Byrnes, commander of the 87th Detective Squad, who is caught in the cross-fire between his wife and their rebellious seventeen-year-old son (161-62). These family problems will intensify, by the way, as the series moves into the 1970s and 1980s, with the constant threats of drugs, promiscuous sex, disease, and gang violence. McBain's police detectives talk the way we would expect cops to talk, their conversation heavily laced with rough, good-natured banter and almost inexhaustible griping (9). Unlike the energetic geniuses of the classic tradition of literary detection, some policemen are inclined to avoid work, as we have already seen in the case of Hank Bush; when the case of the serial killer turns out to be a tough one, Bush's suggestion is, "We ought to leave it to Homicide. We're in over our heads" (16).

Unlike those writers who hit upon a successful formula and repeat the same story until the reading public tires of the pattern, McBain has refused to allow himself to become attached to one kind of plot, motive, situation, or character but has varied his strategies with each new book, an accomplishment especially remarkable in the light of his prolific output. As we will see, *Cop Hater* sets the tone of the later 87th Precinct stories, but not the tight mold. Much of that tone is effected by the remarkably off-axis, slightly tilted geography and chronology of the series, both of which are more than hinted in *Cop Hater.*

Where is the 87th Precinct located? The reader who misses the disclaimer statement at the beginning of the story will undoubtedly answer, New York, and with considerable justification. It has the feel of New York, except that the perceptive reader may notice a slightly skewed orientation upon confronting in the first sentence a reference to "the river bounding the city on the North," or finding that in this city the numbered streets run north and south, the avenues east and west (136). The population of the 87th Precinct, we are told, is 90,000 (10), which sounds very much like a crowded urban area such as Manhattan, and the city is divided into five boroughs, although they have unusual names: Isola, Riverhead, Majesta, Calm's Point, and Bethtown, instead of Manhattan, the Bronx, Queens, Brooklyn, and Staten Island. Outside the precinct there are locations that seem familiar, like Grover Park, which sounds very much like Central Park, Mott's Island that has all the earmarks of Coney Island, and the River Dix, which in New York would be the East River (126-27).

At the beginning of *Cop Hater* this disclaimer appears:

The city in these pages is imaginary. The people, the places, are all fictitious. Only the police routine is based on established techniques.

This statement, with exactly the same wording, has introduced every one of the novels in the series and, if taken literally, would seem to settle the question once and for all. It would, except for the fact that if the Imaginary City is *not* New York, it is so close that the two merge right into each other. In *Cop Hater* for example we learn that one of the suspects in the lineup had served two years at Sing Sing (103), and in subsequent stories that people can work in the City and live in Connecticut and that the City once had an airport named Idlewild (Dove 23). The resultant ambiguity substantially defines the off-axis orientation that colors the atmosphere of the whole series.

As more stories appeared, and as the outlines of the City began to emerge, it became apparent that this was indeed New York, but with a difference. What had happened was that the real city, maintaining its original shape and spatial relationships, had been rolled over one quarter-turn clockwise, so the directions were changed: the New York east became south in the City, north became east, and so on. All geographical names had been changed, in addition to those of the five boroughs. Thus the Hudson became the River Harb, Long Island became Sand's Spit, Broadway became the Stem, and so on. The whole place continued to feel like New York, however; the people of the City talked like New Yorkers and had the New York attitude, and occasionally the real city would simply usurp the place of the imaginary one, as it had in *Cop Hater* when the hoodlum served his time at Sing Sing instead of Castleview, the state penitentiary in the stories.

In *The Great Detectives* McBain explains the reason for the imaginary geography in terms of practical necessity. Granting that his stories needed a recognizable location, he did not want to confine himself to the police routines of any specific city: "I recognized at once that I could not change *my* police working procedure each time the cops in New York City changed *theirs.* Keeping up with the departmental or interdepartmental memos or directives would have been a full-time job that left me no time for writing" (McBain, "87th" 95). Although the explanation is beyond question, we must also recognize that the Imaginary City is a part of the special sense of reality that gives the series its unique tone and flavor.

Another one is what we will call the Imaginary Year. *Cop Hater* sets a precedent that will be followed throughout the series, of precise dating of events, or rather *apparently* precise dating: after our experience with what looked like so much exactness in the geography of the City, we must not expect too much in the way of literal reality. Thus, "Thursday, July 27" seems as real as any date can be. If, however, we consult the calendar to confirm the *year* of *Cop Hater*, just as we consulted the map of New York City to confirm exactness of location, we make a highly meaningful discovery. The year cannot be 1956, the date of publication, because in that year July 27 fell on a Friday; 1955 gives no better results, because then the 27th was a Wednesday. Incidentally, this scheme of dating is continued in the other two novels published in 1956, the days of the week being a day too late for one year and a day too early for the other. McBain has invented an Imaginary Year, situated between 1955 and 1956, just as he invented an Imaginary City that was not New York but shared its geography. We should not overlook the fact that for most of the rest of the novels in the series, the calendar has been on track, with the day of the week corresponding to the day of the month for the year of publication, but McBain had by no means exhausted the number of variations he could work with the flow of time.

Most readers will never even notice the incongruity of the calendar for these early stories, any more than they will be conscious of the slightly off-base geography of the 87th Precinct and its environs. Neither will they be bothered by the tricks played on the chronology of the later books of the series, in which time stands still for Meyer Meyer, who is always thirty-seven years of age, moves at varying rates for several of the characters, and in the case of the Carella twins, stays with the calendar up to a point and then stops. There is no special importance in any of this except for the fact that we must not look for anything like a naturalistic approach in the 87th Precinct stories; the original concept of the series was a much closer parallel with the real world, but the direction was altered, as we shall see shortly in the death and resurrection of Steve Carella (for a more detailed discussion of the chronology of the 87th Precinct, see Dove 30-40).

Besides the faithful representation of police methods and the police subculture and the special reality of place and time, *Cop Hater* set a number of precedents for the rest of the series, one of which is the overpowering sense of spreading urban blight. It makes its appearance on the first page of the novel, where it begins to show itself amidst the glitter and glamour of the City:

[The buildings] faced the river, and they glowed with a man-made brilliance, and you stared up at them in awe, and you caught your breath.
   Behind the buildings, behind the lights, were the streets.
   There was garbage in the streets,

and a few pages later we discover that Grover Park, which borders the 87th Precinct, is overrun by muggers and rapists (10). The blight continues to spread, gaining momentum from the added problems of poverty, the drug scene, crime, and disease, until it becomes a major theme of the later novels, to the extent that Teddy Carella in *Vespers* prays that her husband will get out of police work before it kills him (124).

In this connection we must note that the 87th Precinct novels, although they are governed by a strong sense of society, especially of urban decay and its effect upon people, have almost nothing to offer the critic seeking evidences of ideology in detective fiction (Winston 198-99). In the 87th Precinct series, McBain demonstrates some definite feelings about what society is and should be, but he offers no ideological platform.

The plot of *Cop Hater* becomes a precedent for several of the later books in the series, like *Lady Killer* and *Calypso*, but as we have already seen, McBain refused to succumb to the temptation of hitting upon a good plan and staying with it throughout the series. The plan of *Cop Hater* is that of the single plot, but the author was to use several others as the series developed: two major plots related by subject (*The Pusher*), two major plots related by theme (*Killer's Wedge*), major-minor plots related by subject (*The Con Man*), major-minor plots related by coincidence (*Killer's Choice*), major (plus minor) plots related by spinoff (*Killer's Payoff*), and the apparent single plot that becomes two actual plots (*The Mugger*) (Dove 132-33). We should not miss the fact here that McBain did not even stay with the plan of *Cop Hater* through the first three novels of the series: the simple single plot gives way to the concealed plot structure of *The Mugger* and then to the two related major plots of *The Pusher*.

One neat piece of irony that became a precedent for the series was the ambiguous title of *Cop Hater*. In this story there are two conceptions of the cop hater, the maniac killer who hates policemen and is trying to eliminate them all, and the murderer who hates only one cop and is out to kill him. A few later examples are *Killer's Wedge*, in which there are two wedges, the wooden one that holds the door shut in the case Carella is investigating and the figurative one Virginia Dodge has driven between Lieutenant Byrnes and his squad; *He Who Hesitates*, in which the irony arises from the old saying, but in this case the perpetrator who hesitates saves himself from apprehension; and *Long Time No See*, in which there are two kinds of seeing. McBain has all kinds of fun with his titles, varying them in length from the terse *Ax* to the half-line *Let's Hear It for the Deaf Man*, and there are times when he seems determined to run through the alphabet with his titles (*Fuzz, Ghosts, Heat, Ice, Jigsaw*), an additional reminder of the danger of trying to read the stories in anything like a realistic mode.

The style of *Cop Hater*, superior as it is to that of most writers in the genre, seems a little anemic in comparison to the crackling prose of the later novels. The statement that May Reardon has "an Irish nose with a clicheful of freckles" (49) is a nice try, but it may strike today's reader as a little self-conscious. Other stylistic devices, such as the abundant irony we have already mentioned, enjoy a slightly higher level of maturity. McBain had already mastered the art of dialogue, and the repartee of the first novel shows up well in comparison. McBain has always been good at carrying along dialogue for page after page with the characters so carefully differentiated as to make "Savage said" and "Rip replied" unnecessary in the extended passage on pages 73 to 75. Repartee is skillfully handled also, as in this passage in which the cops are trying to find out why a suspect was sitting alone in his car late at night:

> "Well?" Carella said.
> "I was checkin' up on my dame," Kelly said.
> "Yeah?" Bush said.
> "Truth," Kelly said. . . .
> "What's there to check up on?" Bush asked.
> "Well, you know."
> "No, I don't know. Tell me."
> "I figured she was maybe slippin' around." (35)

It is not as good as some of that delivered after Cotton Hawes enters the series, but still not at all bad.

One thing the reader must be prepared for (and fans will love) is the author's tendency to stop the story at a convenient point and deliver himself of a little homily on a subject that happens to be of interest at the moment. There are several in *Cop Hater*. Thus very early (during the guided tour of the precinct station house) there is one beginning, "Now there was something very disgusting about policemen in general, and bulls in particular" (19), one on the smells of a tenement (23), and an especially meaningful one beginning,

"Homicide, if it doesn't happen too close to home, is a fairly interesting thing" around the middle (88). The discourses are never annoying because they are always well written, and they serve the technical purpose of delaying the action and prolonging the suspense for a few moments without getting on the reader's nerves.

One device that has occasioned some admiration is the use of real-looking visuals in the 87th Precinct stories. There are three in *Cop Hater*, an application for a pistol license (30), a ballistics report on the bullet that killed Mike Reardon (38), and a file card on the arrest record of Luis Ordiz (56), all on genuine-looking police forms and typed in with the kind of nondescript typewriter that might be expected at police headquarters. These filled-in official forms will continue through the series and will be supplemented in the later novels by copies of the pictures the Deaf Man sent to annoy the boys of the 87th, a cut-up photo of the stretch of the River Dix, dental charts, personal appointment memos, and a variety of others.

There are few stock characters in the 87th Precinct stories, but we meet one in *Cop Hater* who will serve the same function for years to come. The role will be filled later by an assortment of people, but they will all play a standard part, the Nut. She makes her appearance in this story as Miss Oretha Bailey, who comes to Carella with some inside information on what is killing the cops: they are being eliminated by the Cockroach Men, who are out to take over the planet (123-25). Carella listens politely and then ushers her out, but she will assume other forms, including one who is being annoyed by a gorilla in a top hat or one who knows the murders were committed by Superman, wearing blue underwear and a red cape, until the reader is inclined to agree with Sergeant Dave Murchison when he says, "More of them outside than in" (Dove 55). All of this confirms the absence of standard "realism" from the series.

Most of the people who will be the familiar fixtures in the 87th Precinct saga are in place by the end of *Cop Hater*, including especially Detective Steve Carella, who will become, in violation of McBain's original concept, the hero of the series. It is not hard to recognize, upon Carella's first appearance, that he is not just another crude, insensitive city bull. As he leans over the body of the first victim his face remains expressionless "except for a faint, passing film of pain which covered his eyes for a moment." Carella has been in police work for twelve years but knows he will never get used to violent death (9). He is, as we have seen, courteous to Oretha Bailey, and when she expresses surprise at his ability to speak English, Carella smilingly replies, "I picked up the language from the natives" (123). There is just a hint of it here, but increasingly through the series Carella will come to speak for McBain (McBain, "87th" 97).

Throughout *Cop Hater*, Carella is deeply in love with Teddy Franklin, and they are married at the end of the book. They are on their honeymoon through most of *The Mugger*, with the result that Carella is missing from that novel until the next to last page. Back in action in *The Pusher*, he pursues a drug dealer named Gonzo, who shoots and kills him. Carella's death lasted just long enough for the manuscript to reach the desk of the editor, who called to tell McBain he could not kill off Carella because he had become the hero of the series. The story of the conversation with his editor as told by McBain in *The Great Detectives* (91) is a significant account because of what it reveals about the nature of police fiction and because of its explanation of the reason so few writers of police procedurals have been able to achieve what McBain calls a "conglomerate protagonist," a team of policemen working together on a mystery without stars or heroes. The conglomerate protagonist is much closer to the real world of police work, but the reading public doesn't want reality; it wants heroes. The detection formula lays a heavy hand on the procedural, which, as a tale of detection, tends to conform to the pattern laid down by Poe in the Dupin stories.

Another member of the *Cop Hater* cast destined to be a series regular is Teddy Franklin, who at the end of this first novel becomes Teddy Carella. It is important that when she is introduced, Teddy's physical handicap is not mentioned until several paragraphs have been devoted to her physical beauty and sensitivity and her strong sexuality (39-40). The reader of the series may tend to remember Teddy only in terms of her total deafness, but her role is that of sex goddess, who is wholly bound up in her husband; when the children arrive later she also becomes a faithful mother, but chiefly Teddy is the lover of Steve Carella.

Several of the members of the 87th Precinct force are introduced, including especially Lieutenant Peter Byrnes, who commands the detective squad of the precinct. At his first appearance Byrnes is laying down the law to his squad about the necessity for finding the killer of Mike Reardon as quickly as possible. Byrnes is succinct and direct; handle it however you want, he tells his squad, but find him (13-14). Byrnes will be one of the admirable characters in future stories, always strict and strongly professional, but also compassionate and understanding when the occasion requires.

Bert Kling is a green young patrolman in *Cop Hater* (65), but in the next novel, after some foolhardy risks that almost get him killed, Kling will be promoted to detective. He is destined to play a tragic role, finding his fiancée murdered in one story, then later making an unfortunate marriage that almost wrecks his spirit. Destined for a somewhat lesser role is Hal Willis, who will always be typed as the short member of the squad. Willis barely made the minimum height requirement of 5'8", but his appearance is deceiving; he is a judo expert capable of breaking the back of a man much larger than himself (135-36). Like Kling, however, Willis suffers his own emotional crisis later when he falls desperately in love with a woman who, unknown to him, has a criminal past that finally catches up with her.

Among the minors is Captain Frick, the elderly bumbling commander of the 87th Precinct, whose judgment is at least still good enough to let Lieutenant Byrnes run the detective squad without interference. Frick is getting old in *Cop Hater* and gives the impression of needing to retire (108-10). He seems, however, to be stuck on one of those unmoving time-tracks that serve some of the other characters, because in books published decades later he is still around and still incompetent.

In *The Great Detectives* McBain compares his detective squad to a family, with Lieutenant Byrnes the father, Steve Carella the elder brother, Bert Kling the younger brother (92-93), and so on. Naturally, every family has its black sheep, and *Cop Hater* introduces one of the blackest, Roger Haviland (83 ff). Haviland does not rise in this first novel to anything like the heights of pure nastiness of which he is capable, but later we learn that he once had his arms broken by a gang of teenagers, underwent a long and painful recovery, and has been carrying on a war of revenge against the world in general and teenagers in particular ever since. When McBain killed him off in one of the early novels he saw his mistake at once and was forced to replace Haviland with Andy Parker, who is still operating as family black sheep. The myth apparently works two ways; just as the public demands heroes, it must also have villains. McBain does not extend his family metaphor to include Sam Grossman, whom we have already mentioned as the director of the police laboratory, but he might be considered the brilliant first cousin, the pride of the clan, to whom members of the family turn when they need information (115-20). Like Haviland, Grossman will receive fuller development later, and he and his lab boys have considerably strengthened the series with accounts of unusually well informed police science.

Sergeant Alf Miscolo makes so brief an appearance in *Cop Hater* as to leave almost no impression on the reader (122), but he provides a good example of one of McBain's excellences as a writer of fiction. Although Miscolo never rises above the level of back-up among the dramatis personae of the series (except for the time in *Killer's Wedge* when he almost dies of a gunshot wound), he is not allowed to remain two-dimensional. Miscolo is in charge of the clerical office of the precinct, and he maintains those files with a severity that would make the fussiest file clerk seem slovenly by comparison. He also makes the world's worst coffee, but McBain is not content to leave him with even this much character; we learn that, when Miscolo is at the point of death after being shot in the back, he calls for "Mary," whereas his wife's name is Katherine, and we are given a brief account of how he loved and lost Mary. Unlike many writers of detective fiction, McBain is not satisfied with cardboard characters, even when they are little more than walk-ons.

We have already mentioned Danny Gimp, the informer, who will become a periodic regular of the series. Danny is joined later by several other stool pigeons who will also be regular fixtures.

Two other luminaries who will play leading roles in the series have not appeared at the end of *Cop Hater*. One of these is Meyer Meyer, the Jewish detective whose father thought it would be a great joke to give him the same first and last names and who is perpetually thirty-seven years of age. Meyer comes on in the second novel, *The Mugger*, while Steve Carella is away, and he has hardly been absent from a single book ever since. Cotton Hawes, the brainy detective with the dramatic streak of white in his red hair, joins the 87th Squad in *Killer's Choice*. Cotton, like Meyer, was the victim of a father with his own ideas about names, who in this case was such an admirer of the colonial Mathers that he felt obligated to name his son for the most notable among them. In course of time, Cotton will join Carella, Meyer, and Kling as series mainstays.

Cop Hater, finally, serves as an introduction to the 87th Precinct only to the extent that it sets the reading mode for the rest of the series. The representation of the world of the Eight-Seven is not a faithful copy of reality in the ordinary sense but is, rather, off-axis and ironic, and any reading that fails to take this idiosyncrasy into account is likely to result in misinterpretation. In its accurate depiction of police methods and its faithful portrayal of the police subculture, *Cop Hater* sets the literary standard for the other novels, but McBain would need more time to achieve all he was capable of doing in terms of character depiction, ironic tone, command of dialogue, and exploitation of the full possibilities of time and space. The best was yet to come.

Works Cited

Dove, George N. *The Boys from Grover Avenue: Ed McBain's 87th Precinct Novels.* Bowling Green: Bowling Green State University Popular Press, 1985.

McBain, Ed. *Cop Hater.* New York: Permabooks, 1956.

___. "The 87th Precinct." *The Great Detectives.* Ed. Otto Penzler. New York: Little, Brown, 1978.

___. *Vespers.* New York: Morrow, 1990.

Winston, Robert P., and Nancy C. Millerski. *The Public Eye: Ideology and the Police Procedural.* New York: St. Martin's, 1992.

Elizabeth Linington—a.k.a. Dell Shannon:
Creation of a Formula

Mary Jean DeMarr

No glamour, no excitement, no big names. Nothing to go in the books, the clever whimsy on Classic Cases or the clever fiction, ten wisecracks guaranteed to the page, a surprise ending to every chapter, where fifteen people had fifteen motives for the murder and fifteen faked alibis for the crucial minute, conveniently fixed by a prearranged long-distance phone call. (Shannon, *Case Pending* 101)

Often referred to as the "queen of the police procedurals," Elizabeth Linington (1921-88), who also wrote under the pseudonyms of Dell Shannon and Lesley Egan, developed a clearly defined and recognizable formula that constitutes a large part of her appeal for her many faithful fans. Her novels are both extremely predictable and, occasionally, startlingly unpredictable. They are predictable because the interlocking of plots (crimes and their investigations, on the one hand, and the personal lives of the detectives who carry out those investigations, on the other) follows a regular pattern. But unpredictably, her police officers are expendable: occasionally one of the characters whom readers have comfortably followed through several novels will be killed, and other officers, previously little more than names, will "[evolve] . . . into three-dimensional characters" ("Foreword" x), as the author put it. The blend of the grim world of the streets, of sordid crime realistically described, with the sane and healthy private lives of police officers, is central to the structure and the appeal of these novels.

Linington is best known for the Luis Mendoza books written under the name of Dell Shannon; this series opened in 1960 with *Case Pending*. Following almost identical formulaic elements, except for its employment of Ivor Maddox and Sue Carstairs (later Maddox) as a kind of double protagonist, is the series written under the author's own name and beginning with the publication in 1964 of

119

Greenmask! Slightly more complex is the group of novels written under the pseudonym of Lesley Egan, which commenced with *A Case for Appeal* in 1961. These novels contain two separate protagonists, attorney Jesse Falkenstein and police officer Vic Varallo. Both lawmen appear in some of the novels of this series, while other novels center around one or the other of them. Thus these books differ in that they are not all, strictly speaking, police procedurals and that they lack both the series-unifying focus on a single character (or even two characters, as in the Linington stories) and the interest in a large group of continuing characters. Both Falkenstein and Varallo appear in *A Case for Appeal,* but because of the important differences between these novels and those published under the Linington and Shannon names, it will not be considered here.

Case Pending and *Greenmask!* are generally superior in a number of ways to the novels that succeed them. Their author apparently wrote more thoughtfully, certainly more perceptively and originally, in these opening novels than she was to do later. They contain precisely observed descriptions of a sort less frequent in later books, for instance, and the treatment of criminal minds is much more interesting. As the writer's career advanced, she fell more and more into easy patterns; some devices that seem fresh in the early novels become clichés, and the pot-boiling nature of the novels becomes more and more evident. This does not mean that the novels lose their appeal: the depictions of continuing characters that made them attractive in the first place become increasingly central to the books, and the result is a kind of novelistic soap opera, carrying the private lives of a number of likable characters from book to book.

A brief consideration of what the formula developed into is helpful here. George N. Dove aptly describes it as being "characterized by the remarkable number of story-lines, representing the number of cases (twenty-four in *Spring of Violence*) on which her policemen are employed, and by an often-stated conception of police work as the never-ending struggle between good and evil" (17). (For a fuller examination, describing especially the evolution of the formula, see DeMarr 75-78.) The formula includes generally one main case followed throughout a novel along with several other cases, most often unrelated to the main case. The cases are in various stages of investigation; occasionally a story line is carried from one novel to another, generally when a book ends with the announcement of a crime that will be investigated in the next novel.

Personal and crime plots are developed concurrently, with the relative emphasis on personal plots generally increasing as the series proceeds. The crime plots stress the sordid lives, characters, behaviors, and motivations of perpetrators, while the personal lives are presented idealistically (the police officers have or acquire happy marriages and loving children—divorce and depression or other serious psychological problems are nonexistent). In the solutions of the crimes, coincidence—or chance—plays an important role; thematically this is represented as being typical of the randomness of human life. In both series, the central character or characters serve as protagonist, detective, central consciousness, and illustration of a sane social order battling unthinking forces of chaos and cruelty.

The author was very conscious of the way in which her protagonists control the nature of their series. Describing the writing of *Case Pending*, Shannon comments that Mendoza unexpectedly appeared, almost full blown, and that he then surprised her by taking over the novel, turning it in a direction that she had not intended:

Mendoza . . . existed, and he refused to be ignored; he insisted on appearing on more printed pages, and more . . . The immediate consequence of that was *The Ace of Spades*. By the end of that one I had discovered that it was a good deal more fun, and a good deal easier, to write such books than long-winded tomes of historical novels; and I had settled down with Mendoza in a kind of temporary truce. With scarcely a pause I proceeded on to *Extra Kill*. But it was with *Knave of Hearts* that it dawned on me that I had, willy-nilly, entered into an involuntary partnership, probably for life; I was stuck with Mendoza and his emerging cohorts, and there was nothing in this world I could do about it. ("Foreword" viii-ix; the second ellipses are Shannon's.)

Perhaps Shannon was not aware that another way of describing this process would be to say that as she wrote these first four novels, she discovered along with a group of interesting characters a rather simple formula that made regularly producing novels about them relatively easy. Certainly as this series—and the Linington series, as well—proceeds, individual novels become less distinctive. In most cases what distinguishes them from each other—what makes any one of them memorable—is not the crime or the detection but rather some event in the personal life of one of the police officers: a marriage, the birth of a child, the acquisition of a pet dog or cat or bird, for example. Plot construction is generally quite linear, as the detective work and the home lives of the police are followed, and many of the novels could be concluded (or the crimes could be solved) at just about any time the author chose. In fact, one can trace construction patterns that are quite mechanical: by the end of her career, after working with a gradually declining number of chapters in her novels, she settled into a ten-chapter form, with each book having approximately 220 to 230 pages.

Case Pending clearly presages much of what follows in later novels. The central detective and some of his surrounding characters are introduced; their depictions are completely consistent with later novels. Mendoza changes, but those changes are gradual and are developed over the course of many books. When first met, he is a bachelor, no longer young, but happy in his single life-style. He meets Alison Weir in *Case Pending* and is immediately attracted to her; they enter upon a kind of joking semi-courtship, which has strong overtones of sexual attraction, but Mendoza seems at this point not to see his incipient relationship with Alison as being more important than any number of other relationships he enjoys indulging in. In the last line of the novel, for instance, he is smiling to himself as he thinks of her; "he expected to enjoy Alison" (156). Only gradually, through several more novels, does their connection deepen, forcing this fiercely independent man to capitulate to emotions that have unexpectedly overtaken him. The reader, of course, is not as surprised by this course of events as is Mendoza himself, for the reader like Mendoza has seen and enjoyed Alison's wit, charm, and humor.

Biographical details are also established early, including Mendoza's ethnic and family background as well as some of the indulgences he is able to allow himself because of the wealth inherited from his disreputable grandfather. He carefully explains to Alison:

My grandfather was shrewd enough to buy up quite a lot of land. . . . And fortunately I was his only grandson. It was a great shock to everybody, there he was for years in a thirty-dollar-a-month apartment, saying we couldn't afford this and that, damning the gas company if the bill was over two dollars, and buying secondhand clothes—my God, he once got a hundred dollars out of me on the grounds of family duty, to pay a hospital bill—and me still in the rookie training school and in debt for my uniforms! And then when he died it all came out. . . . My grandmother hasn't recovered from the shock yet—she's still furious at him, and that was nearly fifteen years ago. . . . For fifty-eight years she'd been nagging at him to stop his gambling—she'd been telling him for fifty-eight years that gamblers are all wastrels, stealing the food out of their families' mouths. . . . And that's where he got his capital—his winnings . . . Frankly, I think myself it wasn't all luck, the old boy wasn't above keeping a few high cards up his sleeve, but you know the one about the gift horse. (71)

This same information is repeated in various ways in later novels. What Mendoza does not mention here is that he, too, has been something of a card shark: for relaxation, in later novels he will often pull out a deck of cards and practice dealing crooked hands. Imagery associated with him and with the theme of chance so prominent in the novels often focuses on cards; a number of his novels are titled with references either to cards or to the randomness symbolized by games of chance (for example, *Ace of Spades, Knave of Hearts* [1963], *Chance to Kill* [1967], *Deuces Wild* [1975], *Felony at Random* [1979], and *Chaos of Crime* [1985]). Mendoza's liking for expensive cars, his natty dress, his penchant for neatness (in the world at large as well as in his personal appearance), the intense curiosity that is the motive for his detecting, his habit of sprinkling his speech with Spanish phrases—all these are already present at his first appearance.

Perhaps most unexpected of all these indications of continuity is one brief, almost off-hand, remark by a character who appears for only a moment: an Irish priest, on being told by Mendoza that the policeman has drifted away from his Roman Catholic roots in the church, says, "Ah, . . . but not forever, my son, will you say that to God. One day you will return the full circle" (28). Shannon explored that return only fifteen years later, in *Deuces Wild*, motivating it by a crisis in Mendoza's personal life.

The often grim city setting depicted in the crime plots of the entire series is carefully established in *Case Pending*; in fact, more attention is given here to details of scene than generally in later books. A striking example occurs early in the novel; as Mendoza drives through city streets on his way to interrogate some witnesses, a full page traces his route through gradually deteriorating neighborhoods. The description is detailed and evocative. A few snippets will convey the flavor:

Once off the main streets here, away from the blinding gleam of the used-car lots, the screamer ads plastered along store-fronts, these were quiet residential streets, middle-class, unremarkable. Most of the houses neatly maintained, if shabby. . . . This was all Oriental along here, largely Japanese. When he stopped at an intersection a pair of high-school-age girls crossed in front of him—"But honestly it isn't fair, ten whole pages of English Lit, even if it is the weekend! She's a real fiend for homework—"

Past rows of frame and stucco houses, lower-middle-class respectable houses. . . . Past bigger, older, shabbier houses with Board-and-Room signs, rank brown grass in patches, and broken sidewalks: dreary courts of semi-detached single-story rental units, stucco boxes scabrous for need of paint: black and brown kids in shabbier, even ragged clothes, more raucous in street play. . . . Then a corner which marked some long-ago termination of the street: where it continued, across, there were no longer tall old camphorwoods lining it; the parking was bare. . . .

At the next intersection. . . a faded admonition to Rely on J. Atwood and Son, Morticians, for a Dignified Funeral. . . . (62-63)

Similarly careful descriptive passages occur several times in this opening novel and depict a variety of settings within the city, revealing an interest in scene setting that is less obvious in later novels.

A thematic concern prominent throughout the series is a self-conscious tolerance for ethnic groups—or rather an insistence on judging members of all ethnic groups by unvarying middle-class values, an insistence based on the assumption that anyone can hold to and live by those values. Unlike the descriptions of the cityscape, that theme becomes more obvious in some of the later books, but it is present in *Case Pending*, most notably in the treatment of Mendoza's Mexican background and his frequent use of Spanish phrases; it might be noted, however, that here as elsewhere his Spanish rather than Indian appearance is emphasized.

This theme of ethnic tolerance also appears interestingly in a brief characterization. Agnes Browne, who discovers a body and thus is subject to police examination, is obviously and deeply frightened by this experience; a sense of guilt clearly lies at the root of her fright and of the untruths she tells as a result. Her fear communicates itself to Mendoza and the other investigators. Since she accepts middle-class values of honesty, she finally confesses to the source of her guilt: she is black and has been passing as white, and the boyfriend who has been defending her against what he sees as the harassment of the police does not know her terrible secret. Convinced that her actions were illegal, she has given the police a false address in her attempts to hide the truth. But when her conscience leads her to confess—believing that she will go to jail and that she will certainly lose the boyfriend whom she loves—both the police and boyfriend laugh at her. Joe, the boyfriend, says, "You mean *that's* why you'd never go out with me, always acted so— Well I'll be damned . . . I—I been in kind of a sweat about it because I figured it was on account I'm Catholic and you wouldn't have nothing to do—[.]" Her reply states in different terms the moral that the police teasingly try to point to her: "Why Joe! However could you think such a thing of me, I'd never—why, that's *un-American*, go judging people by what church—" (128). Joe and the police officers, who are stunned by this manifestation of her concern about her race, forcefully express the firmly color-blind attitude that is typical for these books.

Generally missing from this earliest entry in the Mendoza series are some questionable aspects of later books, principal among them the clichés and the obtrusive politics. In later novels both the characters and the narrative voice often fall into a number of phrases that become peculiarly hackneyed: "the thankless job" or "the dirty thankless job," for example, or the description of families as "hostages to fortune" are among those locutions that become most wearisome and that are absent here. The author's personal politics were extremely conservative (she was a strong supporter of the John Birch Society), and in later novels her characters regularly express opinions with which she may be assumed to have been in agreement: they complain about the leniency of liberal judges, about members of minorities being given special treatment, and so on. And several groups are singled out for special condemnation: young criminals and homosexuals are particularly scorned. In fact, her novels now seem an oddity—fortunately!—in that the terms "fag," "faggot," and "queer" are used frequently by her police officers, with no indication from the narrative voice that there is anything wrong with them. Young toughs and homosexuals as soon as they appear may be guessed by the reader—always correctly—to be perpetrators. These political and social beliefs and assumptions, so marked in the later novels—and defensible there only because they are put into the mouths of police officers and their families, who might realistically be expected to hold such opinions—are not yet significant in the series' first novel.

This opening novel is stronger than many that were to follow because of its more thoughtful construction and more varied writing techniques. In *Case Pending*, unlike many of the later books, careful use is made of timing, and the misdirection of the reader is skillfully managed. The climactic scene occurs as the result of a number of people having separate reasons to be at a particular apartment building at the same time, and suspense is gradually built toward that moment as the reader sees the various strands converging. Here violence resolving several plot lines occurs when it must, not just when the writer has created the requisite number of pages and chapters. Hackett states it neatly, at the conclusion of the novel:

The way things dovetail, sometimes—Morgan just happening to be there, and with a gun on him—because if he hadn't had, you know, I don't think he could have handled that one alone, I don't think any two men—Without the gun, maybe Morgan dead too. And maybe it was all *for* something, Luis—that we don't know about, never will. To save the boy—maybe he's got something to do here, part of some plan. You know? Maybe . . . so Agnes Browne could get all straightened out with her Joe. (155)

The importance of chance, of the randomness of human life, usually so strongly emphasized by this author is here explicitly—and paradoxically—denied.

Plotting, especially of the crimes and investigations, in general is more interesting and original here than it was later to become. Balanced against that is a lesser concentration on the private lives of the police officers: that story line consists simply of the meeting of Mendoza and Alison Weir, his future wife, and the beginning of their association—little more than a flirtation at this point. Pets, which are to loom so importantly in later novels, are represented only by brief mentions of Mendoza's Abyssinian cat, Bast, and the arrangements he has made for her care while he works his long hours. Other officers, who would be developed later in varying degrees, are with the exception of Arthur Hackett little more than names (Higgins, Dwyer, Lake, Galeano).

The crime plot is somewhat more complex than often in the later books, and it is supported by a skillful use of varied points of view. Here there are two primary strands: two murders, which Mendoza is convinced are the work of the same killer, about whose perpetrator the reader is skillfully misled, and one potential crime, a planned killing. They seem unrelated but soon lead to two families' living in the same apartment building. One apparent criminal is a fourteen-year-old boy, a driven, suffering, confused youngster divided within himself—as we know because we are repeatedly taken into his point of view. The other, the potential murderer, is an investigator in the DA's office, cornered by a blackmailer who knows of the irregularity of his and his wife's adoption of the baby they dote upon and about which their lives revolve; his point of view is also frequently employed.

One interesting chapter early in the novel may be used to demonstrate the skill with which Shannon creates sympathy for these characters and thus some of the freshness of her approach in this early novel. In chapter 5, a shifting point of view is employed, as often elsewhere in the novel. Here we are first taken into the confused and pain-filled mind of Martin Lindstrom, the above-mentioned fourteen-year-old. Then his friend, Danny Smith, another adolescent, a tough boy who is being led into criminal activity by his father, becomes the focus. Last to be presented is the perspective of Dick Morgan, the investigator for the DA's office whose job consists of locating fathers who have deserted their families and identifying families who are colluding to defraud the welfare system. All three are clearly troubled, in quite different ways, and for all three parent-child relationships are crucial. Marty Lindstrom and his mother have been deserted by their father and husband; Marty's thoughts indicate clearly that at least a part of his perturbation relates to the absence of that dearly loved and greatly admired parent. Danny is in a mood of elation because his father is trusting him for the first time to participate in his activities. The two boys, one apparently the tormented and divided perpetrator of horrible crimes who has been deserted by his father and the other just at the outset of a cynical life of crime into which he is being led by his father, are contrasted sharply and ironically in motivation, mood, and moral scruples. And Morgan is desperately concerned to protect Sue and Janny, his beloved wife and their twenty-six-month-old child. The facts of their situations are not yet clear, but their respective obsessions are, along with the ways in which each is being impelled to some particular course of action.

As the first of the author's mystery novels, Case Pending reveals her formula in its most incipient form. Most of the characteristics that were to become so recognizable in later books are either already present here or are hinted at. What makes this novel superior to many of its successor books is the fact that those characteristics have not yet hardened into a mold and that the novel contains some freshness of plotting, scene, and characterization. *Greenmask!*, her first book in the Maddox-Carstairs series, was published four years later, the year of the appearance of the seventh Mendoza novel. Thus *Greenmask!* shows early development of the formula while it introduces a new group of characters. But it is distinctive in some ways that make it stand out above the general run of its creator's work.

Paralleling the change in Shannon's conception of the earlier series when Mendoza took over, so the Linington series changes as Sue Carstairs achieves prominence. In *Greenmask!* "good old reliable Carstairs" plays a relatively unimportant role, and Ivor Maddox is the sole protagonist. The novel opens and closes with him, and it follows his point of view throughout the investigation of a series of killings. A running motif which constitutes the main personal plot line here is that of Maddox, who has just moved into a new little house, unpacking and shelving his extensive library (in fact, his move had been inspired by the need for more space for that collection). His wide interests are indicated by the subdivisions within his collection, but for a major portion of the novel he is alphabetizing by author his large collection of mystery and detective fiction, which seems to have a particular focus on traditional novels of the puzzle type.

The other principal characteristic of Maddox stressed here, and continuing into later novels, is his unexplainable attraction for women; they cluster around him despite his lack of obvious physical appeal. While clearly not unattractive, he is not particularly handsome, not especially tall or muscular, not physically striking in any way. He finds their pestering him a nuisance and sometimes a professional hindrance, as his superior officers occasionally assume he has invited the attentions that he actually strives to discourage. His general attitude toward this situation is one of somewhat frustrated and amused tolerance; good-natured about it, he nevertheless finds it a constant irritation. Linington most nearly explains it by calling him an "utter male," a phrase also used for Mendoza, and continues to use this thread in succeeding novels, until his marriage to Sue Carstairs gives him some protection from the marauding females.

Like Mendoza in his early books, Maddox serves as detective, protagonist, and central consciousness; like Mendoza, Maddox is surrounded by other detectives who will be more fully developed in later novels. However, three of these secondary police characters are portrayed more fully here than even Hackett, the most rounded of the subordinate police characters in *Case Pending*, and reveal the author's movement toward the depiction of a group of officers working together rather than a single protagonist. D'Arcy is already given his identifying characteristics: his susceptibility to pretty women and the unspeakably awful first name, which he goes to great lengths to conceal (it turns out to be "Drogo," only a little worse than Maddox's own middle name of "Goronwy"—but at least Maddox has an acceptable first name!). Rodriguez in the course of this novel discovers the existence and fascination of detective fiction, an obsession that he will carry through a number of succeeding books.

More important is Sue Carstairs, who enters relatively late. Even the fact that she is just as attracted to Maddox as the many other women who swarm around him is not clarified here; it will be developed in later novels. Her restraint and professionalism in relating to Maddox is her tactic, since she recognizes that to try overtly to attract him would simply put her in the same category as all the other women whom he generally seeks to avoid: but even this is not made clear here, though her behavior is certainly consistent with that understanding. In an off-hand remark, Sue's mother suggests her awareness of something special in Maddox that Sue must have told her about: on first meeting Maddox, "Mrs. Carstairs said to [Sue] cryptically, 'I do see what you mean, dear'" (128), a line not explained in this novel but quite clear in the context of later books. Sue is repeatedly referred to as an absolutely reliable policewoman, one whom Maddox calls upon when he needs a female officer of professionalism and sensitivity. He appears to think of her largely as a fixture of the job, until he first sees her in off-duty shorts and halter and is startled to observe that she is in fact an attractive woman.

The story of their growing relationship and Sue's care in nurturing it—her fear of making any sudden moves that would frighten him—is followed through several novels, until finally they marry. Sue continues to work after their marriage. They then detect in tandem, and the series is gradually transformed into a doubly centered presentation with two protagonists. Sue develops from a functionary generally called upon when a woman is needed for nurturing purposes into a fully participating member of the detective squad. The characterization of Sue as a fully competent professional is surprisingly sympathetic for this anti-feminist author.

Along with Sue, other continuing characters are introduced: one is Sue's mother, Mrs. Carstairs, with whom she lives and with whom Ivor and Sue will live after their marriage. She is a level-headed, thoroughly nice and understanding widow, never developed with any real depth but always a pleasant presence in the protagonists' lives. Additionally, as always in this author's work—and growing more important as the years and novels pass—there is the presence of animals. Just as Bast, Mendoza's cat, is introduced in *Case Pending*, so is the Carstairs' Welsh Cardigan dog, Goronwy. By an odd coincidence, which Maddox finds rousingly funny, the dog has his own middle name, and it is only because of the dog that he learns the Welsh meaning of that name—"fierce protector" (128).

One evidence of the development of the author's formula by 1964 is the general absence here of specific and detailed description of settings. The city, with its variety of grim backgrounds is assumed rather than directly depicted. Since the Maddox-Carstairs series is placed in Hollywood, the reader might be surprised to note the absence of the world of film. Instead, what is revealed might be any large city. In *Greenmask!* the victims, witnesses, and perpetrators are apparently ordinary middle- and working- or criminal-class people, and the glamor associated with this enclave within Los Angeles is simply missing. The actual settings are consistent with the descriptions given in *Case Pending*, almost as if Linington assumes that readers will carry over their familiarity with her scenes from the Shannon series. And doubtless many do exactly that.

Also handled in a manner consistent with what had been introduced in the earlier Shannon novels is the theme of ethnicity. Here again the police and other good people are almost insistently tolerant, quite consciously refusing to apply any different standards of judgment to people of other backgrounds than those they apply to themselves. Again a Mexican-American is one of the investigators, though this time he is not the protagonist. Like Mendoza, Rodriguez shows more evidences of Spanish than Indian background, this pattern perhaps being a subtle—and paradoxical—indication of ethnic classism in the author's assumptions. When a witness refers to Rodriguez as a "Goddam dirty Mex cop," Rodriguez meets this prejudice mildly:

Rodriguez smiled at Stover amiably and said, "And I assure you, sir, I had a bath last night and intend to have another when I get home—unless you delay us too late." And his tone was, like his whole person, suave and sophisticated. (58)

Linington adds her own comment through Maddox's point of view:

Considering that his great-grandfather had been at one time personal aide to the Crown Prince of Spain, Maddox considered his tone remarkably polite. (58)

Another brief scene later in the novel, in which a black doctor and nurse are involved, illustrates again this obtrusive color-blindness. A victim, severely injured when he is stabbed, is taken to a hospital where his bigoted middle-class family is appalled to discover a multi-racial staff. The physician tells Maddox, "We had to produce one of our few nice superior-white-Protestant doctors to back us up he couldn't be moved" (169), and Maddox of course is sympathetic.

Prejudice against undisciplined young people, and—especially—against homosexuals, is open and strong in this novel, much more so than in the earlier *Case Pending*. As usual, critical, even defamatory, remarks are put into the mouths of the police and other admirable characters and thus made to seem acceptable. And here, interestingly, the two shibboleths are combined with each other and with the conservative political observations that become increasingly frequent as the various series proceed. Interviewing the son of the man who had just called Rodriguez a "Goddamn dirty Mex cop," Maddox mentally sums up the boy:

They were getting this kind in quite a lot lately: the ones from moneyed homes, the spoiled ones, the privileged ones. As well as the more usual types, the slum kids. Insolent, contemptuous: very well aware that as they were under-eighteen the cops couldn't do much more than slap their wrists and say naughty-naughty. These Goddamn lenient juvenile judges. And let any cop so much as talk back a little, the perennial yell going up, Brutal police. In Maddox's opinion, they could be reached better by being treated as the children they were: that annoyed them. (58-59)

The prejudice against homosexuals is introduced later but is even more blatant. A victim who survives an attack remembers only the scent of Tweed after-shave lotion. Maddox and his colleagues are bemused by this, observing that such products are mainly sold to women to be given as gifts and then left unopened on cabinet shelves. Maddox observes:

"I've run into a few witnesses—and of course a lot of the fags." Rodriguez dismissed the fags with a gesture. (170)

This comment, made in passing, seems an irrelevancy until, at the climax of the novel, it is revealed that the murders have been committed by two high school students, both from comfortable homes, who are involved in a homosexual relationship. The motivation for the crimes was the concealment of their affair and thus of their sexuality. When the revelation is made, Maddox engages in some amateur psychological analysis, commenting to a loving and now grieving father that his wife's puritanical treatment of their son was perhaps responsible in part for his being seduced by his lover:

"I don't know whether the head doctors are right," said Maddox quietly. "I wonder if they do. You can make some deductions here, sure. You knew your wife was—wrong—in the way she treated Allan. Trying to keep him too close, you said. He'd naturally resent that. And a couple of other things you mentioned. But maybe that wouldn't have been enough in itself, if he hadn't met Rudy Warren. . . . A lot of people think the fags can be spotted at a glance. It's not so. Quite a few of them look just as masculine as Rudy Warren." (208)

Noteworthy here are the tone of reasoned objectivity, the reliance on the popularly received psychological ideas of the day, and the brutal and unthinking use of an offensive slur, all by a character who is generally admirable and is the central consciousness of the novel. Not only is the motivation for some complex crimes explained in this way but concurrently some popular prejudices are supported.

Linington, however, insofar as she takes conscious note of the contradictory tendencies both to attack and to assume stereotypes, explains them as dangerous but grounded in truth. In an exchange early in the novel, Maddox and Rodriguez discuss stereotyping:

"You are a Celt," said Rodriguez. "They are not a tolerant people."
"I'm an American," said Maddox irritably. "You can't classify people, damn it, under labels."
"That's a fallacy," said Rodriguez intellectually. "What you mean is, we shouldn't judge people by labels. No. But certain people have certain

qualities, foregone conclusion. As a Celt, you can't help being ruled by your emotions. Now, the Latin race is logical—"

"I do *not*—"

"You can't help it, said Rodriguez. "It's a fascinating thing, comparing the racial qualities, I've always thought. The Celts, they're the race of salesmen. What's called canny, oh, sure—but the primary quality in them, it's their ability to get the nuances from other people, emotionally speaking. So they always know the right approach. Whereas the Latins—"

Maddox opened his mouth to say damn nonsense, and shut it again. Suddenly remembering those Beaker people . . . pretty certainly the remotest ancestors of the Celts. Moving in on the territory of those much bigger, stronger tribes, and not only persuading them to dig the clay for their funny-looking beakers, but turning around and selling the beakers to them afterward. (59-60)

It is crucial to note here that Linington picks for her example of a group characterized by a particular trait one not currently subject to discrimination based on that trait. In this way she makes innocuous the prejudice that is so obvious here and so much in apparent conflict with her insistence that individuals be judged as individuals without reference to group characteristics. She resolves the conflict by concluding that group traits may be used as guidelines but not as rules for judgment.

Greenmask! also reveals its similarities to the later books in which the formula is fully established by the presence of some of the cliches that eventually become so characteristic of the writer. They are less obtrusive than later on, but at least one, the very familiar reference to the "thankless job" (214), occurs. Similarly, use of point of view here is simplified, more like the general practice of later novels. The author does, through the years, sometimes experiment with point of view, in several notable cases even using the point of view of animals, but by and large the later novels rely on the narrative perspective of the protagonists. *Greenmask!* is told completely from the point of view of Ivor Maddox.

It is in plotting and construction that this novel is most interesting in its own right and for which it has been most praised. In this regard, it is rather different from the evolving pattern. One primary case, what we would now call serial murder, is followed throughout, with only passing references to other crimes. And that case is unusual, in that the killings are copied from a well-known mystery novel, not from actuality. In fact it is Maddox's realization of the connection between his killer, who signs his work with the name "Greenmask," and the plot of Agatha Christie's *ABC Murders* that gives him the clue needed to solve the case. This book, however, is not as tightly constructed as *Case Pending*, its linear plot coming to conclusion as a result of chance and Maddox's intuition, with none of the suspense so skillfully set up in the earlier novel. In these latter respects, it is typical of the evolved formula.

Linington uses her plot device, essentially copy-cat killings with a twist, not only to construct this plot but also to comment on detective fiction. As happens so often in her crime fiction, police officers remark on the unreality of mysteries and their contrast with the harsh and sordid truth of the actual crime they see every day on their city streets. And this contrast, dramatically rendered here, is played against Rodriguez's discovery of and fascination with the fiction of writers like Christie and Carr. But it is pointed up in several ways.

First there is the fact that Maddox is throughout the novel spending his spare time arranging and shelving his books, primarily his collection of mystery fiction, mostly traditional British detective novels. The book opens and closes on this note and returns to it regularly. A witness interviewed in connection with one of the killings is also a mystery fan, thrilled by his connection to a real-life murder, particularly one with the embellishments of a signature and clues left at the scene. The witness contrasts this case with the usual fare:

"So many real-life murders are most uninteresting, aren't they—quite sordid really, just low-class people losing their tempers or getting frightened. I've been following this one with a *great* deal of interest, and to think of one of the murders actually being done in *my* theater—" He took a deep breath; his eyes shone happily. "Really, I haven't been so fascinated with a murderer since the Case of the Screaming Spinster." (98)

Emphasizing the crime fiction motif, from this effusion, Maddox "deduc[es] absently that Mr. Wolfe was an avid reader of *True Detective Stories, True Police Cases*, et cetera" (98).

In fact, it is Maddox's persistent and quite reasonable sense that these crimes are more like fiction than fact that keeps teasing at him until, as he is shelving Christie's novels, he suddenly realizes that his weird case bears many uncanny resemblances to the tricky plot of *The ABC Murders*. At this point he knows that he is not after all confronted with a lunatic striking at random but with someone having a particular motive to kill one of the four victims. The criminal, he realizes, is a person of intelligence, familiar with at least one Christie novel but lacking the creativity to come up with an original scheme to mislead and mystify. From this moment, it is simply a matter of time and following normal police procedures (plus a healthy admixture of Maddox's intuition, including his suspicion that any man wearing Tweed must be sexually abnormal!) until he solves the crimes.

As a result of using this device, Linington is able to have it two ways. She can on the one hand use a rather intricate plot with clues carefully dropped and with a sudden reversal near the end of the book; in short, she can essay a crime novel in some ways like a traditional puzzle story. But on the other hand, she is able to emphasize repeatedly her usual contention about the sordidness and ugliness of crime in real life, so different from the artificial and ultimately ordered world of much crime fiction. In the novel's last pages, Maddox and Rodriguez discuss the appeal of crime fiction of precisely the sort their pair of murderers had been inspired by. Maddox says to Rodriguez:

"You've found it's fun to read about it. Murder in print. Because it's all a lot tidier that way—hell of a lot more interesting than the crude real-life stuff. The characters and the problems, the nice complex interesting problems. . . . As cops we know the real thing is a lot cruder. We run into the raw ones quite a lot, but even so we can get shocked. Now and then. It's a lot prettier between book covers, isn't it, Cesar?" (202; ellipsis Linington's)

And a bit later, thinking it all over in the perhaps inescapable aftermath of concluding a difficult case, Maddox muses,

So much more fun, on paper. The complex problem posed and solved, jigsaw piece by jigsaw piece. And you closed the book and thought, a good story.

You closed the book on all the pain and self-blame and human tragedy. All the aftermath. The astute detective explained away the last mystery, and the book ended. You weren't shown the long-drawn-out trial, the howl of publicity on innocent, honest witnesses and relations, the long terrible time between the sentence and the appeal and the postponed execution dates and the denials of clemency. (203)

So despite her flirtation here with the conventional puzzle, Linington finally uses that familiar and artificial motif to re-emphasize the sordidness and ugliness of real violence and crime. Maddox in his new home shelving his books under the watchful eyes of his landlady's young daughter, Sue Carstairs living simply with her mother and their dog, D'Arcy falling in love with a pretty young woman and fearing she will learn the awful secret of his name, Rodriguez carrying about the mystery novels of his new obsession—all these bear the marks of normality and sanity. They represent the world of the middle-class reader, appalled at cruelty and greed and selfishness. As Linington puts it, from Maddox's point of view, their lives as fighters of crime are simply a part of a universal struggle: "Nobody realized clearer or harder than a cop that there were the two forces operating, eternally contending with each other. Call them whatever you liked, good and evil, God and Satan" (204). This statement introduces a note of melodrama not usually present in this author, but it does express overtly the attitude underlying her depictions of her officers and their contrasts with the criminals against whom they battle, the "never-ending struggle between good and evil" (Dove 17).

Simpler in plotting and point of view though more complex in its central plot device, *Greenmask!* begins its series at a slightly later stage in the evolution of the author's formula than did *Case Pending*, her first mystery novel. Nevertheless, both books bear the clear stamp of their creator—in characters, in theme, in method, in plotting, in politics. Where they are distinguished from their successor novels, they are generally better, simply because they are fresher. The heavy hand of formulaic writing has not descended on them, as it is to do on later books. While her fiction is always readable and has an intense appeal to readers who become caught up in the continuing life stories of her very likable police officers, the books soon settle into a predictable rut. Plots as well as tone vary from novel to novel. Occasional flashes of originality occur from time to time. But in general the crime plots become less important, less interesting, more subordinated to the personal plots, while the personal stories, continuing from book to book, constitute the main appeal of the series.

After beginning as a reasonably insightful and original writer about realistic crime and criminals, the author became an interesting if unoriginal portrayer of the private lives of some unrealistically and idealistically depicted police officers. Nevertheless, her novels do present a readable delineation of the struggle between antisocial criminal forces and the law officers employed by the community to battle them. And the books' representation of those lawmen and their lives, while idealized, is both interesting and sometimes even compelling. Linington with all her weaknesses as a writer could always tell a good story and involve readers in the daily lives of her characters; she deserved the title of "queen of the police procedurals."

Works Cited

DeMarr, Mary Jean. "Dell Shannon's Luis Mendoza." *Cops and Constables: American and British Fictional Policemen.* Ed. Earl F. Bargainnier and George N. Dove. Bowling Green, OH: Bowling Green State University Popular Press, 1986. 69-85.

Dove, George N. *The Police Procedural.* Bowling Green, OH: Bowling Green State University Popular Press, 1982.

Linington, Elizabeth. *Greenmask!* New York: Harper, 1964.

Shannon, Dell. *Case Pending* (1960). Rptd. in *First Four by Shannon.* Garden City, NY: Nelson Doubleday, 1980.

____. Foreword. *First Four by Shannon.* Garden City, NY: Doubleday, 1980.

P.D. James's Adam Dalgliesh Series

Joan G. Kotker

In her third novel, *Unnatural Causes* (1967), P.D. James has an editor describe one of his mystery writers as someone who "kept to familiar characters and settings." He goes on to elaborate,

You know the kind of thing. Cosy English village or small town scene. Local characters moving on the chess board strictly according to rank and station. The comforting illusion that violence is exceptional, that all policemen are honest, that the English class system hasn't changed in the last twenty years and that murderers aren't gentlemen. (159)

In this passage James could well be describing her first novel, *Cover Her Face* (1962), a traditional Golden Age type of mystery that is far simpler in its world view and characters than her most recent Adam Dalgliesh mystery as of this writing, *Devices and Desires* (1989). In comparing the first and last of her Adam Dalgliesh works, one can find surface similarities in setting, characters and crime, but significant differences in the underlying world view of each novel make it apparent that James's work has gained far more in depth and realism than her first, formulaic novel might lead one to anticipate. She has also altered her central character, detective Adam Dalgliesh, who has gone from being a two-dimensional character with no existence outside of his professional life to being a fully realized person.

Cover was first published in 1962 and in terms of genre, it is a traditional cozy. It is set in the Essex village of Chadfleet and opens at a dinner party at Martingale, for 300 years the home of the Maxies. The reader is alerted to the fact that the dinner is "a ritual gathering under one roof of victim and suspects, a staged preliminary to murder" (5). The guests at the dinner—the vicar, the doctor, the director of a refuge for girls—are here because they belong here; they are integral parts of the community and there is a timelessness about them, as though they or their counterparts have been sitting at this same table, making perhaps this same conversation, for generations.

The Maxie family is represented by Mrs. Eleanor Maxie and her two adult children, beautiful, widowed daughter, Deborah Riscoe, and handsome son, Stephen, who is studying medicine. Catherine Bowers, daughter of an old friend of Mrs. Maxie, is visiting the family and has hopes of becoming Stephen's fiancée. Mr. Maxie, an invalid who has been ill for a long time and who is expected to die quietly and decorously in his bed at any moment now, is not at the table and no longer takes any active role in the family, although his expiring presence hovers over the novel and is an important plot element.

The family and their guests are waited on by Sally Jupp, an unwed mother from the refuge for girls who has been hired by Mrs. Maxie as a house-parlor maid. Sally, the victim of the novel, is the only outsider; she has come to Chadfleet from another village and has no ties here other than those formed during the brief time she has spent at the refuge. There are two other significant characters, Martha, the family cook, and Felix Hearne, partner in a publishing firm and rumored lover of Deborah Riscoe. Although Hearne is not from the village, his background as a school chum of Deborah's husband serves to make him, too, a long-standing member of this small community. Sally Jupp's death brings about a disruption of the community but we are led to believe that its solution will return Chadfleet and Martingale to their customary peaceful, bucolic state.

Like *Cover, Devices* is also set in an English village, in this case Larksoken on the northwest coast of Norfolk in East Anglia. Nearly all the events of the novel take place on Larksoken headland, a contained area that serves as a closed world in the same way as does Martingale House. However, the inhabitants of this headland are all newcomers with no long-term ties to either the place or, with one exception, each other. As with most of us in the contemporary world, they live where they live because of their jobs rather than because they have roots and tradition to maintain, and the jobs themselves are new and non-traditional: the headland is the site of Larksoken Nuclear Power Station.

As she did in *Cover* James introduces *Devices'* major characters at a dinner party, although without the helpful signposting that herein can be found both victim and murderer. This dinner party is given by Alice Mair, a well-known writer of cookbooks who has prepared the dinner herself, with only a teenage neighbor girl to help her. So much for the pleasant English world of resident cooks and parlor maids. Also at the table are Alice Mair's brother, Alex Mair, director of the nuclear station; Hilary Robarts, its administrative officer; Meg Dennison, housekeeper for a retired vicar and his wife; Adam Dalgliesh, the Scotland Yard detective first introduced in *Cover*, and late arrival Miles Lessingham, an engineer at the station. None of these is native to the community: the Mairs, Robarts, and Lessingham are here because of the station, Dennison is a recent arrival, having come to escape persecution by the politically correct faculty of the London school where she taught, and Dalgliesh is here to settle the estate of his Aunt Jane, who herself had lived in the area for only the last five years. Like the contemporary world, the world of Larksoken is one of transients.

Another difference between the two works is in the function of the characters themselves. People and events appear in *Devices* because they are essential to the plot; in *Cover*, they sometimes seem to be there because novice writer P.D. James is seeking to create the look and feel of the traditional British cozy. A case in point is *Cover*'s vicar, Mr. Hinks. He performs no plot function but just acts in the benign, rather ineffectual way that we have come to associate with vicars in British cozies, whose minds, we are to understand, are on subtle matters of theology rather than on the practicalities of daily living. This is in marked contrast to *Devices*, whose vicar is the retired clergyman, Mr. Copley. He and his wife have come, in their eighties, to spend their last years in the rectory where he had once been curate. The church itself has been demolished, having been "a building of absolutely no architectural merit serving a congregation at the major festivals of six at the most" (107). Unlike *Cover*'s ornamental vicar, Copley is tightly woven into the action of the novel, since the temporary absence of him and his wife is a key element in the denouement.

Another example of James's growing ability to integrate events and action is her handling of the amateur detecting done by characters in each of the two novels. Each book has a scene in which a boyfriend takes it upon himself to do some investigating in the hopes of learning more about his beloved. *Cover*'s Stephen Maxie decides that the answer to Sally Jupp's death must lie in her life before she came to Martingale. Over his lunch hour he goes to the Select Book Club, where Sally once worked. Everyone at the club cooperates in giving him information, despite the fact that the police have already been there and for all the informants know, they may well be talking to Jupp's murderer. And when Maxie is dismayed to learn that the police have preceded him to the club there is a suggestion in Jupp's supervisor's comment to Maxie that all of this is only a game anyway: "Cheer up! You may beat them to it yet!" (197). Although we do get more information about both Jupp and Maxie from this scene, it is not information that leads to the denouement and overall, the scene is not very credible: would Maxie really have time over his lunch hour to take on this sort of investigation? And would these people really be so open with him? Finally, would one really use the game analogy when talking about the murder of someone he or she knew and had worked with?

A similar scene appears in *Devices*. Jonathan Reeves, a technician at the power station, is in love with Alex Mair's personal assistant, Caroline Amphlett. She asks him to provide her with an alibi for the night of the murder, saying that she was near the spot where the body was found and has no protection other than him. She creates a story about her poor mother that Reeves at first accepts but then begins to question. He decides that Amphlett must be in trouble of some kind and that, because he loves her, it is his duty to discover what this trouble is. He intends to begin by tracing her family to learn the truth of the situation with the mother. However, before going off detecting on his own he does what anyone might do in similar circumstances: he calls a detective agency. He finds, though, that it isn't quite as simple as he thought to have an agency undertake a formal investigation. The agency wants a letter with a formal request giving the information he has and specifying exactly what it is he wants the agency to do, accompanied by a down payment of one hundred pounds. Jonathan "had imagined that they would take the information down over the telephone, tell him what the cost would be, promise him a quick result. [This] was all too formal, too expensive, too slow" (266).

He attempts to trace the family himself, and feels silly when he looks them up in the London telephone directory and immediately finds the address. His subsequent plan to approach them is both competent and plausible. He creates a story of having met Caroline when they were both in Paris and of looking her up now because he happens to be in London, and he carefully rehearses his lines before going to the apartment. Unlike Stephen Maxie, Reeves plans the time well, too: he does his investigating on a Saturday, when he will have a free day and there will be no need to explain his absence from Larksoken. The scene in which he puts his plan into action gives us a fascinating character, the Amphlett's housekeeper, Miss Beasley, but rather than presenting us with an interesting if not particularly relevant interlude, as was the case with Stephen Maxie's private detecting in *Cover*, this scene becomes crucial to the novel's ending. As soon as Reeves leaves the apartment Beasley calls Caroline and tells her that someone is making inquiries about her—surely something that any of us would do under the circumstances—and this in turn sets in motion a series of events that lead to the novel's ambiguous resolution. Such careful integration of each scene with the plot as a whole gives *Devices* a much more controlled feel than *Cover*.

Another area of surface similarity in the first and last of the Dalgliesh novels is in the crime that is central to each novel. In both works, a young woman is murdered because she threatens the future of a man, in one case a son and in the other, a brother. The two women are similar in terms of character: both are forceful, assertive women, both are very attractive, and both are self-centered. Neither is sexually inexperienced: Sally Jupp, *Cover*'s victim, is an unwed mother (or so it would appear) whereas Hilary Robarts, *Devices*' victim, has had an abortion. Both are manipulative and very much disliked by many of the characters who surround them. Jupp is murdered because Stephen Maxie has proposed to her and it looks as though she will accept the proposal, threatening his place in the solid community for which Martingale is the center. After all, it wouldn't do for the heir of Martingale to be married to a parlor maid with an illegitimate child. There is also the suggestion that Jupp has no genuine feeling for Maxie and has led him on out of general mischievousness. She is killed by Maxie's mother, Eleanor Maxie, but lest we shudder at the idea of the upper classes committing murder, it is made very clear to the reader that the killing is really accidental: Mrs. Maxie had only wanted to talk with Jupp, sound out her feelings about Stephen, and when Jupp laughed at her and told her that she was again pregnant, this time with Stephen's child, Mrs. Maxie suddenly found Sally dead in her hands. We are left to imagine the intervening action, one that clearly was not premeditated.

Devices' crime is, on the surface, similar. Hilary Robarts is insistent on marrying her ex-lover Alex Mair, who is in line for an important government position, one that he has worked long and hard for and that will be the crown to his career. Robarts is much in love with Mair and has information that she can and will use to blackmail him into the marriage. Mair's sister, Alice, who has been taken into his confidence, is convinced that Robarts will always be a danger to him, that the marriage will be only the first of many demands that will eventually destroy Mair, professionally as well as personally. Just as Eleanor Maxie has killed the person who threatens her beloved son, Alice Mair kills the person who threatens her beloved brother. However, the similarity ends here. Where Eleanor Maxie, who is presented to us as a good person, kills almost by accident, Alice Mair, also presented to us as a good person, kills deliberately, carrying out an intricate, masterfully planned copy-cat murder that mimics those of a serial killer who is terrorizing the area. The two women's justifications reflect their manner of killing: Mrs. Maxie tells us, "I went to [Jupp's] room to talk to her. It seemed that the marriage might not be so bad a thing if she were really fond of my son" (247). In other words, Mrs. Maxie was trying to make things better, to resolve the issue in such a way that no one suffered, and somehow, the death just sort of happened. Alice Mair has also gone to confront her victim. She says,

I went to see her on that Sunday afternoon. You could say that I went to give her a chance of life. I couldn't murder her without making sure that it was necessary. That meant . . . talking to her about Alex, trying to persuade her that the marriage wouldn't be in either of their interests, to let him go. I could have saved myself the humiliation. There was no argument, she was beyond that. She was no longer even rational. Part of the time she railed at me like a woman possessed. (416)

The result is that Hilary Robarts, like Jupp, ends up dead. In each case the murderers first confront their victims with the hope of peacefully resolving the conflict, but in the case of Alice Mair, murder as an option is already in her mind when she goes to see Robarts and when it happens, there is nothing accidental about it. The simplistic characters of *Cover*—characters who if they are "good" can commit a crime only by accident—give way in *Devices* to complex characters whose actions cannot be predicted on the basis of Sunday school morals. Of the two murderers, Alice Mair is both the more terrifying and the more convincing. We believe her when she says of her brother, "I owed Alex a death" (416), because we know that Alice is a victim of incest, having been abused by her father when she was a child. We also know that as teenagers, she and her brother witnessed an accident involving their father and chose to let him die rather than seek help. It is the brother who instigated this, saying to Alice, "Whatever he's been doing to you, he won't do it again. Ever" (97). The incest motif is in itself indicative of how far P.D. James has come in *Devices* from the traditional cozy. In the pastoral village of Chadfleet, incest and deliberate patricide would be unthinkable; in the contemporary world of Larksoken Nuclear Power Station, they provide a convincing motive.

Differences in the early and later James are also apparent in the way in which the death of the victim is described in each novel. We are told that Sally Jupp's "death was due to vagal inhibition and was very sudden. It may well have taken place even if the strangler had used considerably less force. The picture on the face of it was of a single unpremeditated attack" (222). The description of her body, while certainly not pretty, is understated and will give no reader nightmares. She is lying in bed, and "over the pillow Sally's hair was spread like a web of gold. Her eyes were closed but she was not asleep. From the clenched corner of her mouth a thin trickle of blood had dried like a black slash. On each side of her neck was a bruise where her killer's hands had choked the life from her" (57). In retrospect one can comment on the baldness of the language: "a thin trickle of blood . . . like a black slash" and "choked the life from her," but overall, this is well within the cozy tradition of presenting death in cleaned-up, sanitized versions. It is in marked contrast to the description of the body in *Devices* where Adam Dalgliesh, taking an evening walk along the shore, sees something white in the light from his flashlight and steps off the path to investigate:

And then he saw her. Her distorted face seemed to leap up at him and hang suspended in the bright glare of the torchlight like a vision from a nightmare. Staring down, and for a moment transfixed, he felt a shock in which incredulity, recognition and horror fused into a second which made his heart leap. . . . She lay on her back, the head towards him, the dead eyes upturned as if they had been fixed on him in a last, mute appeal. The small bush of [pubic] hair had been pushed under the upper lip, exposing the teeth, and giving the impression of a snarling rabbit. . . . She was wearing only the bottom half of a black bikini, and that had been pulled down over her thighs. He could clearly see where the hair had been sliced away. The letter L precisely in the centre of the forehead looked as if it had been cut with deliberation, the two thin lines precisely at right angles. (155)

This exact, almost ghoulish description of the body of the victim is typical of James's later work (see, for example, the death of a student nurse who has been fed carbolic acid instead of warm milk during a demonstration of esophagal feeding in James's fourth novel, *Shroud for a Nightingale* [1971]). Based on her first novel, though, readers would be hard-pressed to predict that such graphic descriptions of violence would become a hallmark of James's mysteries.

Along these same lines, the disposition of the criminal is also much harsher in *Devices* than in the first novel. *Cover*'s Eleanor Maxie will of course be punished, as she would in any cozy, but true to the form, the punishment is handled in a most civilized manner. She will go to prison for an unspecified length of time on a charge of manslaughter, and her family reacts by taking the attitude that

going to prison must be rather like going to hospital, except that it was even more involuntary. Both were abnormal and rather frightening experiences to which the victim reacted with a clinical detachment and the onlookers with a determined cheerfulness which was intended to create confidence without giving the suspicion of callousness. (248)

There is every suggestion that Maxie will atone for her crime and return to her family and friends, who will think no less of her than they did before the unfortunate incident of Sally Jupp occurred.[1]

In contrast to Eleanor Maxie, there will be no such atoning for Alice Mair. Confronted by her friend Meg Dennison, Alice confesses to the murder of Hilary Robarts and then apparently commits suicide by setting fire to her kitchen. Again, it is Dalgliesh who finds her,

lying between the stove and the table, the long body rigid as an effigy. Her hair and clothes were alight and she lay there staring upwards, bathed in tongues of fire. But her face was as yet untouched, and the open eyes seemed to gaze at him with . . . an intensity of half-crazed endurance . . . and he smelled above the acrid smoke the dreadful stink of burning flesh. (424)

Dalgliesh is badly burned in his attempts to drag her out of the flames. "Then," James writes, "he made the last effort and felt himself falling into the softness of her body. He rolled away from her. She was no longer burning. Her clothes had been burnt away and now clung like blackened rags to what was left of the flesh" (425).

Ironically, had she not died Mair might very well have gotten away with her crime. Dalgliesh says that she probably wouldn't even have been arrested. He tells Dennison, "there still isn't a single piece of concrete evidence to connect Miss Mair with Hilary Robarts's death, and certainly not enough circumstantial evidence posthumously to brand her as the killer" (431). There were three possible suspects for this crime, and all three are now dead, allowing the police to close the case knowing that the murderer is no longer alive, even if they are not sure who that murderer was. The reader, of course, knows that it was Mair, but such ambiguity of record would not be predictable based on *Cover*, where again there was no hard evidence but the murderer did the right thing and confessed to the police, only waiting to do so until her invalid husband had died so that she could be with him until the end, as she had promised him she would. Thus, both Eleanor Maxie and Alice Mair are driven by love of family but the consequences of their acts are very different. In Maxie's case there is a rather peaceful making of amends; in Alice Mair's, James gives us a horrifying death that not only makes no amends but does not even establish the truth. The first disposition of the criminal is wholly consistent with the world of the cozy while the second shows once again how far James has come from her beginnings.

The most surprising discovery that comes about as a result of comparing James's first and last Dalgliesh novels is the change that has occurred over the course of the series in her central character, Adam Dalgliesh. The Dalgliesh of *Cover* is much more simplistic than the Dalgliesh of *Devices*, so much so as to create the impression that in *Cover* James doesn't really have a fix on Dalgliesh yet and is still working out the possibilities. He is brought in midway through the story, and very little of it is told from his point of view. He exists for the reader only as a Scotland Yard detective, and his profession is his sole reason for being in the novel: without the murder, there would be no Dalgliesh at Martingale. James gives the reader a fair amount of information on Dalgliesh the professional, but almost none on his personal life. In *Cover* he has the rank of Detective Chief Inspector, and we learn that his first big case was the murder of a Soho prostitute. When he looks at Sally Jupp's body he is reminded of seeing the prostitute's body and thinking, "This is it. This is my job" (61). There is a sense of exaltation here and certainly no questioning of what he does or why he does it. He is quite well known, since Felix Hearne's response to him when he appears at Martingale is, "Adam

Dalgliesh, I've heard of him. Ruthless, unorthodox, working always against time. . . . At least they've brought us adversaries worthy of the best" (72).

Like all good detectives Dalgliesh is exceedingly perceptive, seeing much more than we do. He is an infinitely patient interrogator and one witness says of him, "The man has an uncanny facility for extracting uncomfortable truths" (122), while another thinks that he has the ability to be all things to all people. This last observation is echoed by Dalgliesh's subordinate Sergeant Martin, who is watching Dalgliesh question a suspect and thinking, "In the end he'd crack. Before long he would see in Dalgliesh, patient, uncensorious and omnipotent, the father confessor whom his conscience craved. . . . It was a man's own mind which betrayed him in the end and Dalgliesh knew that better than most" (171). It is also Martin who comments, on observing Dalgliesh with another witness, "The old man can be pretty brutal" (76). Nonetheless, we are told that Dalgliesh has never been known to lose his temper with a witness, and it is apparent that he cares about the people in his cases, that they have a life for him beyond that of figures in an investigation. At the end of *Cover*, one month after Eleanor Maxie's trial, he returns to Chadfleet, where he conveniently meets Deborah Riscoe as she is coming out of a village store. He gives her a ride home and during the ride, we are informed through their conversation of what has happened to the main characters in the interval since the case was closed. The function of this conversation is to reassure us, in true cozy fashion, that everyone's all right and that things are working out for the best. With the conviction of Eleanor Maxie a debt has been paid to society, which will now return to its usual benign state. And while Dalgliesh doesn't know quite what to say to Riscoe about his role in her mother's imprisonment, we leave the book with the message that "they would meet again. And when that happened the right words would be found" (254).

Up to this point, all the information on Dalgliesh is consistent with what we learn of him in *Devices*, even including his returning weeks later to the scene of the crime. However, readers looking forward to a further development in this novel of his relationship with Riscoe will be disappointed. There is no mention of her in *Devices* and those who backtrack through James's work will discover that in the third Dalgliesh novel, *Unnatural Causes*, Riscoe breaks off the love affair that had developed between her and Dalgliesh, saying that she can "no longer bear to loiter about on the periphery of his life waiting for him to make up his mind" (256). A new love affair may be looming on the horizon, though. In *Devices'* final scene Dalgliesh once again returns to Larksoken headland and the home he has inherited from his aunt. As with *Cover*, he meets a woman from the case here, Meg Dennison, and the meeting is again used to update the reader on what has happened to the major characters in the novel, giving a formal sense of closure to the work as a whole. When they part, Dennison realizes "with a smile of happy surprise that she was a little in love with him" (433). Since Dennison and Dalgliesh both now own homes here, it is not inconceivable that they will continue to meet and that something will come of the relationship. Thus, if readers were to predict an ending to *Devices* based on that of *Cover*, it would be wholly consonant to predict a closing scene that promises—or at least hints at—a future romantic liaison for the detective.[2]

In addition to Dalgliesh's relationship with Deborah Riscoe there is another relationship strongly suggested in *Cover* that has also disappeared in *Devices*. One of the most interesting characters in the first novel is Felix Hearne, family friend and would-be fiancée of Deborah Riscoe. Hearne is a hero of the Second World War Resistance. During his service he killed at least two people, he was captured and tortured by the Gestapo, and he was been decorated by both the British and French governments. Obviously, he is the stuff that heroes are made of, and it is clear from Dalgliesh's comments and attitude toward him that Dalgliesh has high regard for Hearne. When Hearne and Deborah Riscoe undertake some detecting of their own, it seems that this may well be the prelude to a partnership with Dalgliesh of the type so dear to the cozy, the union of the gifted upper-class amateur with the professional policeman. This impression is given weight in the novel's closing pages, when Riscoe is updating Dalgliesh on what has happened to the major characters, among them Hearne and her brother Stephen, and he thinks that while he has little interest in Stephen, he has "too much interest in Felix Hearne" (253). Whatever the nature of this interest, it has ceased to exist in *Devices*, and readers who go back through the earlier novels to find out exactly what has happened to Hearne will receive no enlightenment. We know from *Cover* that he was transferred to his firm's Canadian office and there is one mention of him in the second novel, *A Mind to Murder* (1963), when we are told that he has found a job for Riscoe with his family's publishing house, but then he disappears. He is potentially a most interesting character, one who would seem ideally suited to the genre, and it would be interesting to know what James had in mind when she created him and why she did not develop him further in subsequent novels.

Nevertheless, although Hearne is gone from James's cast of characters, his name lives on, and in a most suggestive way. The Dalgliesh who holds center stage in *Devices* has been advanced in the police to the rank of Commander, as we might well expect of someone with his intelligence and skills. He is also now a famous poet, something we could surely never have predicted on the evidence in *Cover*, where there is no indication that he has any interest in writing or in poetry. However, somewhere in the 27 years between the publication of *Cover* and *Devices*, Dalgliesh the acclaimed poet has emerged. His publisher's publicity director says to him, "There's tremendous public interest in you," to which Dalgliesh responds, "They're interested in a poet who catches murderers, or a policeman who writes poetry, not in the verse" (13). He does a rundown of the questions he's always asked: "'Why does a sensitive poet like you spend his time catching murderers?' 'Which is the more important to you, the poetry or the policing?' 'Does it hinder or help, being a detective?' 'Why does a successful detective write poetry?' 'What was your most interesting case, Commander? Do you ever feel like writing a poem about it?'" (14).

It is clear that James is having fun with these questions and when it comes to the poem about the most interesting case, the reader may be forgiven for imagining one that begins, "It was a dark and stormy night. . . ." As to Dalgliesh, he is much pleased by the fact that he is published and that people read his poetry. At one point, he thinks that there is one person in particular that he would like to have read his work and "having read the poems he wanted her to approve" (14). Hmmm. Shades of Deborah Riscoe? James doesn't say. Nonetheless, the role of poet has become so closely associated with Dalgliesh in the minds of James's readers that most will be surprised to learn that the original character had no such interest. They may be intrigued, though, at his choice of publisher. In *Cover*, when Sergeant Martin is filling Dalgliesh in on the background of Felix Hearne, we learn that Felix "is a partner in Hearne and Illingworth the publishers. His great-grandfather was old Mortimer Hearne who founded the firm" (186). In *Devices*, one chapter takes place at a party at Dalgliesh's publishers, who, lo and behold, are Herne and Illingworth, and once more, backtracking through the novels establishes that this is the very same publishing house as that mentioned in *Cover*, despite the slight change in spelling. Can it be that the Dalgliesh of *Cover* was a closet poet, and that his interest in Felix Hearne was based on the fact that Hearne was a publisher? Each reader will have to answer this for him or herself; James gives us no further enlightenment here.

She does, though, give a great deal more information on Dalgliesh the person in *Devices*. In *Cover*, the only significant personal information we are given on Dalgliesh is that his wife and son died three hours after the baby was born and that he grieves for them. In *Devices*, much of the story is from Dalgliesh's point of view and although he is still a professional detective he is no longer an outsider but instead a central character, here not because of his job but because of his personal life. In fact, the murder, once it is committed, isn't even his case, nor does he solve it. He is simply one of the characters caught up in the killing and our interest in him lies not in the answers he can give us but in the sort of person he is and the answers he will find for himself, in his own life. He has come to Larksoken to the home his aunt has left him to spread her ashes on the headland she loved. Going through her books and papers he becomes very introspective, as any person might who has come to bury his or her last remaining relative. We learn that he grew up in a rectory, and that his passion for privacy has its roots in his having been "the much-wanted only child of elderly parents, burdened by their almost obsessive parental concern and overconscientiousness, living in a village where little the rector's son did was safe from scrutiny" (69), and that even as an adolescent he wanted to be a poet. He still thinks of his wife and baby but although he can vividly see the child, he can no longer recall his wife's face and his memory of her has softened so that she is part of "a boyish, romantic dream of gentleness and beauty now fixed forever beyond the depredation of time" (63).

Temperamentally Dalgliesh is still the loner in *Devices*, the essential observer. A colleague asks him why he has stayed in the Metropolitan Police despite the corruption and politics rampant there, and then answers his own question: "You were detached about it all, weren't you? It interested you." Dalgliesh agrees, saying, "It's always interesting when men you thought you knew behave out of character" (68). Later, when he is considering that with the inheritance from his aunt he now has enough money to leave his job, he examines its appeal for him, thinking that part of the attraction is

that the process of detection dignified the individual death, even the death of the least attractive, the most unworthy, mirroring in its excessive interest in clues and motives man's perennial fascination with the mystery of his mortality, providing, too, a comforting illusion of a moral universe in which innocence could be avenged, right vindicated, order restored.

This vision is a strong affirmation of the world view of the British cozy, with its straightforward solutions that set everything to rights, but Dalgliesh immediately negates its promise when he says, "But nothing was restored, certainly not life, and the only justice vindicated was the uncertain justice of men" (161). The question of whether or not he will remain a policeman is, at novel's end, still an open one.

P.D. James's writing career has now spanned more than a quarter of a century, with some 27 years between the publication of *Cover Her Face* and *Devices and Desires*. Focusing on these two novels, the first and (so far) last of the Dalgliesh series, emphasizes that James has gone from being a writer of formulaic cozies to a writer of the modern novel, from a developer of plots to a developer of characters. Where her early world is one of parlor maids, cooks, the upper classes, the settled village community, a world where amends are made for wrongs committed, her later world is the one we live in today, one where few people have the luxury of servants, where position is more likely to be based on one's place in the business or technical community than on one's birth, where most of us are rootless and where justice is often only an abstract notion and no amends can be made. This shift in the kind of novel she is writing is accompanied by a shift in Adam Dalgliesh, her central character, who develops from a simplistic character defined by his work into a complex character defined by his poetry at least as much as by his profession. In this way, Dalgliesh demonstrates James's move from the genre mystery to what Julian Symons calls the crime novel, a novel whose focus is on character rather than on puzzle (191). James has said in numerous articles and interviews that she always wanted to be a writer and that with her first novel, written when she was forty, she chose to write a mystery because she felt that the restrictions imposed by the form would provide her with a structure that would enable her to learn the craft of writing.[3] In this statement, she foreshadows her own achievement: she has indeed learned the craft and in doing so has taken the mystery far beyond its usual genre boundaries.

Notes

1. In A Mind to Murder, which takes place three years after Cover, we learn that Riscoe's mother died about six months earlier, and that Dalgliesh considers himself partly responsible for her death. He does not explain why he considers himself responsible, and we are not told what the circumstances of the death were. However, there is no hint of this particular resolution to the story in Cover, whose opening suggests that Eleanor Maxie lived for many years after the events described in the novel.

2. It is unlikely, though, that this will occur. When interviewer Lynn Barber tells James that she would not be surprised if, in the next Dalgliesh novel, James were to have her detective fall in love, James responds: "It would be so difficult, my dear! I know everybody would like it, and I'm not sure that he oughtn't. I think the splinter of ice in the heart had really better melt. But I'm not quite sure if I'm competent to melt it!" (94).

3. See, for example, her introduction to Crime Times Three, an omnibus edition of three early James novels.

Works Consulted

Barber, Lynn. "The Cautious Heart of P.D. James." Vanity Fair Mar. 1993: 80+.

James, P.D. Cover Her Face. New York: Warner, 1992.

____. Crime Times Three. New York: Scribner's, 1979.

____. Devices and Desires. New York: Knopf, 1990.

____. A Mind to Murder. New York: Warner, 1992.

____. Shroud for a Nightingale. New York: Warner, 1992.

____. Unnatural Causes. New York: Warner, 1992.

Symons, Julian. Bloody Murder. New York: Mysterious, 1993.

The Professor Tells a Story:
Kate Fansler

Lois A. Marchino

And because everything is a story; one only has to discover what story one is in. (*No Word From Winifred* 172)

The brilliant and innovative Carolyn Heilbrun ("Amanda Cross") in her series featuring English professor Kate Fansler breaks the boundaries of the detective fiction genre more self-consciously than other mystery series, moving from conventional murder plots to novels that question the premises of detective fiction and literature itself. Readers watch Kate Fansler change from her introduction in *In the Last Analysis* (1964) through the tenth novel in the series, *The Players Come Again* (1990), most obviously in her attitude toward women and women's issues—women's struggles in a patriarchal culture, friendships between women, women confronting aging, women writers. As Maureen T. Reddy points out in "The Feminist Counter-Tradition in Crime," Heilbrun "began the revival of the feminist crime novel, a literary form that had been moribund since the publication in 1935 of Dorothy Sayers's *Gaudy Night*" (174). But beyond this resolutely feminist stance is Kate's (and Heilbrun's) increasing examination of the uneasy boundaries between detection and scholarly research, fact and truth, biography and fiction, literature and life. As the series develops, Kate more and more understands that it is necessary to arrange information into a "story," creating what is necessary for a "truth," deciding the story's outcome. In short, the series increasingly asks metaphysical questions and becomes more and more metafiction, writing about the nature of writing.

Carolyn Gold Heilbrun, distinguished professor of literature at Columbia University in New York City throughout the twenty-six-year span of the first ten books in the series (she retired in 1992), was aware of choosing an unconventional protagonist (because intellectual, female, and committed feminist) when she started the

155

series. One of the reasons she chose to use a *nom de plume* was that she did not yet have tenure, and she suspected her colleagues (males) would be less than enthusiastic about her witty critique of the academy. Heilbrun produced scholarly works in her field as well, and as part of the growing women's liberation movement of the 1960s and 1970s steadily wrote about women. Studies such as *Toward a Recognition of Androgyny* (1973), *Reinventing Womanhood* (1979), *Writing a Woman's Life* (1988), and her collected essays in *Hamlet's Mother and Other Women* (1990) demonstrate her developing theories and emphasis on questions of gender in life and literature, particularly in regard to biography.

Kate Fansler is in many ways an idealized, fantasized alter ego who follows similar stages of development. In the first book of the series, Kate's interests are literary but with no particular focus on women's literature. As the series develops, so does Kate's interest in writing by women and in a wide variety of feminist issues. She becomes especially interested in the methodologies of writing about women's lives.

What kind of life has the character Kate Fansler had in the years we have known her? Of her childhood we know little except that she had a nurse and then a governess. Her father is never mentioned. Her nameless mother settled for a traditional role as wife which Kate rejects; her most typical reference is that because her mother always drank sherry Kate never does. Only once, and in the first book of the series, does Kate do what she remembers her mother doing— cleaning closets as a remedy for stress (*In the Last Analysis* 38). Kate's inheritance from her prosperous family provides her an independent income; she can "afford" to critique the establishment and can take leaves from teaching as she chooses. In the first book and the other early earlier books she willingly finances the costs of sleuthing, but later she is more often involved with others interested in the case and expects them to contribute. She is the considerably younger sister of three stuffy older brothers, all lawyers out of Harvard who regard Kate as *outre*, and she resists socializing with them. She does, however, get along well with selected offspring, namely nephew Leo, niece Leighton, and a fiancé of another niece, each of whom she pays for sleuthing assistance in the early books.

From the beginning, Kate is perpetually slim and *soignee*, elegant and attractive. Although she takes this for granted, as the series continues and she gets older, she is more likely to acknowledge that slimness is either in the genes or achieved at great cost. In the first book and throughout the series, Heilbrun quite successfully manages to make readers feel that we know Kate, though in fact we are given no further details about her appearance. Once she pulls her hair back in a French twist, but what color hair is it? Her eyes? Her clothes? She is a walker, though with no regime, and she eschews exercise. She likes plain food but would never admit it, avoids airline food even on transatlantic flights, and chooses restaurants less for the cuisine than for an ambience that allows for conversation. Foods she eats are occasionally mentioned, but they seem to have no connection to changing or eccentric tastes, age, social fads, or her sleuthing.

Health concerns are never mentioned. She smokes cigarettes, though over the years with changing social attitudes she avoids smoking around those who object, and by the tenth novel the subject is not raised. By far the most used delineation of personal characteristics is her frequent relaxation with alcoholic beverages. Kate is certainly no hard-boiled hard-drinking private eye, but she regularly enjoys vodka martinis and variously enjoys beer, brandy, gin, single-malt whiskey (starting with the Laphroaig in *Sweet Death, Kind Death* [1984]), expensive wine, and imported champagne. She occasionally discusses the amount of her drinking with her husband Reed and is aware that others suggest she over-indulges, but she always concludes—apparently correctly—that there is no problem.

As to love and marriage, Kate's primary concern in the first three books is that she not be trapped into a wedded twosome. She cherishes her independence and wants neither to have someone take care of her nor to have to take care of someone, and she finds it difficult to believe the protestations of her old friend Reed Amhearst that he does not thus view marriage. She has had lovers; two who are named are Emanuel Bauer in *In the Last Analysis* and Moon Mandelbaum in *Death in a Tenured Position*. She remains on friendly terms with them despite changes in marital status, and indeed she and Moon have a brief and cheerful renewal of intimacy when circumstances bring them together while Reed is on one of his extended trips abroad.

Kate had rescued Reed from some unspecified disaster in the past, we are told early in the first book of the series, and they are comfortable friends. In the first book Kate calls on him for legal assistance; in the second (*The James Joyce Murder*, 1967) he proposes twice and is turned down twice; by the third (*Poetic Justice*, 1970) Kate decides she would like to live with him and agrees to marriage. She seems to enjoy repeatedly telling colleagues and acquaintances the interesting news, and the book ends with a brief epilogue saying they were married on Thanksgiving Day and spent their honeymoon in Reed's apartment "cooking all their meals in the electric fry pan, which required very little attention" (*Poetic Justice* 169). In an article on Kate Fansler's character development Eugene Schleh notes that "overall Reed becomes a perfect partner. He appreciates that Kate needs room, and has his own career to carry on (at first as a Deputy District Attorney and later as a well traveled Professor of Criminal Procedure at Columbia). . . . Kate, in turn[,] feels quite comfortable and secure with Reed. She does not wear a ring and retains her maiden name, but as she puts it, 'for all that I'm married'" (78).

Kate and Reed throughout the next seven books in the series settle in as dear close friends. Reed is no longer needed as the rescuer he was in the early books, but he still loves to listen to Kate talk and faithfully serves as sounding board, dispenser of advice, and convenient contact with legal authorities. He tells her he misses her when she is gone, welcomes her back home, and lets her know she is cherished. There are (happily, I think) no sex scenes; intimacy is now and again implied in a wry sentence or two, though less frequently as the series continues. Both Kate and Reed acknowledge their good fortune in having such a happy marriage. Reed laughs that he sounds like Kate, and "maybe a good marriage is a contagion of observations and sentence structure" (*No Word from Winifred* 133-34). Kate had noticed this similarity in speech even before she agreed to marry him; in *The James Joyce Murder* she comments, "Do you know, you're beginning to talk like me, full of subordinate clauses, and penultimate climaxes, interspersed with periodic sentences" (86). But, in all fairness, Reed is hardly the only one who sounds like Kate. Throughout the series nearly everyone, like Kate, quotes authors right and left and is prone to charming digression and learned allusion. This makes for a very doubtful verisimilitude but provides a sustained cleverness in the prose, both in the witty dialogue and in the narrative voice.

It is worth reviewing the Kate-Reed partnership at some length (and mentioning such issues as the fact that so many of the characters sound like Kate) because it raises some of the criticisms and limitations of the author's conception of her central character and, for that matter, of the partial failure of the plots to support the themes and stated or presumed intentions.

Reed is left almost totally undescribed except for mention of his long legs. As with Kate, we seem to know him much better than is warranted by the sparse evidence. He is presumably a sort of calmer Kate, a steady and stabilizing presence. In this sense he can be seen as part of an androgynous gemini figure, an aspect of Kate herself. Cross's technique here may suggest that as women enter what were formerly male professions and achieve equality of rights, and as men become more alert to their own capacities for caring and are willing to listen to women, the two genders can come together in considerably greater harmony. But the texts give contradictory signals and raise other questions. What, for example, are we to make of Kate's telling Reed she wants to live with him because "being a woman alone doesn't seem as easy as it has been" and that she needs "the confidence of having a man"? (*Poetic Justice* 50). How is this to be reconciled with the premise of an autonomous, independent, feminist sleuth? Surely this is more than merely a reminder that we must understand that there are feminisms, not a monolithic feminism?

A major point here is that while given information can be interpreted in a variety of ways (as Kate herself often mentions), the text can also reflect confusion and contradiction. Maureen T. Reddy identifies such a problem in regard to female friendships in the Amanda Cross books: "Although Cross asserts through Kate that women's friendships are of the greatest importance . . . she fails to portray these friendships with any degree of complexity or intensity. . . . the only ongoing intimate relationship Cross invents for Kate is with Reed Amhearst" (184). Reddy points out that in the recent novels we are told Kate has a close friendship with a woman but none of these women are continuing characters; they have "no history and no future," so the claim of the centrality of women's friendships has "a hollow sound" (184). Often the stated closeness and community is the result of only a single meeting with another woman rather than of any on-going friendship.

Reddy, in the same essay, cites an analogous failure to match plot to theme in *A Trap for Fools*. Cross depicts Kate as "concerned about the distance between black and white women," but "Outrageously, Kate blames black women as a group for making her uncomfortable" (185). Edna Hoskins, the white woman Kate says is her friend, turns out to be involved in the illegal activities, and since she is Kate's only woman friend in the novel her betrayal makes Kate rely only on men. The novel, Reddy says, "suggests that *all* women's friendships are ephemeral at best, sometimes even dangerous, in any case not to be relied upon, an impression I assume Cross did not set out to create and one that undercuts the explicit assertions about friendship in the novel" (185). Another disturbing point that Reddy cites is the ending of the novel when Kate blackmails the university administration into establishing large scholarships in return for her silence about their embezzling: "Kate ceases to speak and act with feminist authority, abandoning a feminist standpoint and operating instead within the system of power the novel has shown to be corrupt" (186). Kate has "succeeded" only marginally. Kate's thoughts and actions here imply that all change must take place within existing institutions, and in increments—a slow evolution, not revolution—and Kate has accomplished this small change only by using underhanded tactics similar to those she opposes.

Every fiction writer faces the difficulty of trying to establish a sense of realism in characterization and plot vs. trying to create a more utopian vision of what could be. Jeanne Addison Roberts refers to this difficulty in a study of the relationship between the Amanda Cross novels and Heilbrun's works on feminist theory. Roberts quotes Heilbrun's statement in *Writing a Woman's Life* that Virginia Woolf, who specifically called for a "new plot" for women's lives, was never able to conceive such a plot: "She wrote one with her life, but never with her fiction: nor did George Eliot, or Beatrice Webb—nor has anyone." As Roberts concludes, "The problems of imagining a positive view of an autonomous woman remain evident and incompletely solved" ("Amanda Cross Revisited" 2).

With this caveat in mind about the creation of female characters and Amanda Cross's version(s) of feminism(s), we can list several other themes and motifs that are presaged in the beginning novel, *In the Last Analysis*, and then continue throughout the series:

1) the continuing critique of the academy—individual and institutional greed, jealousy, corruption—in conjunction with the predominant university settings;

2) the constant quoting and references to authors and literary works— including fictional detectives—and what Elaine Budd calls the

"leitmotif" of "works of one of the major writers that are Cross-Heilbrun's speciality: James Joyce, or Auden, or T.S. Eliot" (15);

3) the *roman a clef* flavor of several major characters, for example, Professor Frederick Clemance (who turns out to be the murderer in *Poetic Justice*) as "Heilbrun's revenge on Lionel Trilling, who was her favorite professor at Columbia despite his callous treatment of women" ("Feminist Murder" 10); the solitary woman writer (Cecily Hutchins) along the rocky coast of Maine in *The Question of Max* who is clearly derivative of May Sarton, with whom Heilbrun had become friends; in the same novel the history of Cecily Hutchins's youthful Oxford friendship with Dorothy Whitmore is reminiscent of the friendship between Vera Brittain and Winifred Holtby; and the English writer Charlotte Stanton in *No Word from Winifred* is modeled on Heilbrun's much admired Dorothy L. Sayers;

4) parallels between the plot selections and current events, e.g., the relating of death in *Poetic Justice* to the student protests of the 1960s, in *The Theban Mysteries* to the Vietnam war, and in *The Question of Max* to the era of Richard Nixon and the Watergate scandal ("Feminist Murder" 4).

In addition to these on-going themes and techniques, another way to examine the connection between the first in the series and the novels that follow is to look at the individual novels chronologically in terms of what Kate "detects" and what she does once she has "solved" the case. What we see is an increasingly questioning Kate, and one who is more and more interested in "story," both form and function.

Kate becomes involved in criminal detection for what Patricia Craig and Mary Cadogan call "that most usual, most benign of reasons: to clear a friend" (243). The friend is psychoanalyst Emanuel Bauer, a former lover, now married. A young woman has been found stabbed to death on the couch in his office. Kate herself is questioned by the police since the victim, Janet Harrison, was one of her students in the previous semester. Janet had asked Kate to recommend a psychiatrist, and Kate referred her to Emanuel. The police seem to think Kate must be somehow involved or even the guilty party. Kate's methodology in trying to clear Emanuel Bauer and herself differs from the methods of the police. The police detectives see only the core facts; Kate follows her intuition and makes good use of her literary skills as well. Kate makes up a "Once upon a time" fairy tale that she says is the only story line that explains the events: the murderer must have been an imposter who killed

Janet to secure his secret. Since we are told Kate is "an avid reader of detective stories" (*In the Last Analysis* 8) it is not surprising she is familiar with this classic gimmick, the imposter. One of her major clues is that the murderer has not read a D.H. Lawrence novel that the other evidence suggests he should have known. Reed and the police get involved in the final confirmation of Kate's story, and the guilty party ends in police custody, where Kate apparently thinks justice will be served. The novel follows traditional crime fiction conventions in that it is a whodunit rather than emphasizing character and idea as the later Kate Fansler mysteries do.

Already by the second in the series, *The James Joyce Murder* (1967), the murder of Mary Bradford seems a secondary issue, almost an afterthought. This is the only one of the novels to include much description of the setting. City-loving Kate is spending a few weeks in the country to write and reflect, and she seems thoroughly confounded by farm machinery and cows. Literature again plays an important role, not only because Heilbrun uses the short story titles from Joyce's *Dubliners* as chapter titles and actually manages to work them into the text of each chapter but because Mary Bradford is shot because she knew the murderer had found an unknown manuscript by James Joyce, which he wanted to claim. In this novel it is a graduate student working for Kate and Reed who solves the murder; he says he is "beginning to think like a professor of English" (169). And it is Reed who sets up the trap that exposes the guilty party. Reed does this without even letting Kate in on the plan; she stands by as a spectator. However, when Reed is ready to tell what happened, Kate does make up a sentence for him to use as the beginning of the story of how he arrived at the proper solution. As she did in the first book in the series, Kate sees the "case" as a story with a beginning, middle, and end, even if here it is Reed who gets to tell the middle of the story. The ending here is that no one likes Mary Bradford, not even her husband, and everyone hopes the Joyce enthusiast does not spend too long incarcerated.

In *Poetic Justice* (1970), it is a senior professor in Kate's department who turns out to have killed a colleague, but there are extenuating circumstances and Kate feels residual admiration toward him and current sympathy for his action. Reed is again much involved in the action, and at the end he and Kate call Professor Clemance to Kate's apartment, confront him with their knowledge, and agree that "there need not be a prosecuting lawyer" (161).

Clearly they agree that there is more involved in "justice" than legal action. Much of the book is built around a visit to campus by poet W.H. Auden and around quotations from his works. Kate says that what we learn from literature can be used in life: "Our greater awareness, if nothing else" (157).

A study of the many dramatic versions of the Greek story of Antigone and the story's contemporary relevance highlight the literary focus in *The Theban Mysteries* (1971), since Kate is called on to teach a seminar on Antigone in her old school, the Theban. The murder victim is a neurotic and manipulating mother of one of the girl students, and students are very much involved in the murder and the plot. After Kate has determined those guilty (partly through their resemblances to various roles in *Antigone*) she confronts them and again dispenses her own justice, calling it "minor blackmail" (184), to get them to do as she decides.

The Question of Max (1976) has another academic killer, this time because he wants to write a biography of a woman writer and a student has learned the subject had forbidden him to do so. Clearly Kate is becoming more and more embroiled in questions of literary identity, journals, and biographies. Reed rescues Kate from the mad murderer, who presumably is carted off to a mental ward.

The sixth Amanda Cross mystery, *Death in a Tenured Position* (1981), quickly became her most famous, and it is still the most read and critiqued. It is a major break in the direction of the series because of its overtly feminist context, complete with hostile males confronted with their first female colleague in the English department at Harvard, a cadre of lesbian separatists and other feminists who resent the fact that the female professor is anti-woman, and the male-identified professor who cannot understand why no one likes her. It is this book that most clearly begins to raise questions of gender, including even the relationship between gender and literary studies. This is the first case in which Kate is specifically called upon to help with a difficult academic situation. When Kate eventually determines that Professor Janet Mandelbaum's death was suicide, the problematic and theoretical boundaries of guilt are forced to a wider arena; everyone is guilty, including those who see people in terms of labels. To what extent is or should gender be of relevance in any given context? How can the particular strengths of any individual or group be integrated into the larger culture? Toward what goals should feminist theory and practice be directed? Such questions continue in subsequent novels, particularly in context of "writing a woman's life." The emphasis shifts away from crime detection to the solving of larger problems.

Sweet Death, Kind Death (1984) has Kate called to Clare College where she is officially to serve on a gender studies committee and unofficially to investigate the death of Professor Patrice Umphelby. This time an apparent suicide turns out to be murder by a jealous colleague and his wife. The foul play is less highlighted than a journal Patrice was writing about aging, the interests of two men who plan to write her biography, and questions of what constitutes a life or a satisfactory conclusion to life. With considerable understatement, sleuth Kate says, "I have a habit of being inspired by literature" (170).

No Word from Winifred (1986) and *A Trap for Fools* (1989) probe questions of literature and identity even further. In the first, a woman who wants to write a biography of writer Charlotte Stanton asks for Kate's help in gathering information. Complications abound. Thirty-three pages are devoted to a journal written by Winifred, an "honorary niece" of the famous writer. Winifred is now missing. Kate has never known her, but the journal intrigues her and eventually she feels, "I had to put it [tracing Winifred] together in a story, because I love Winifred, it's that simple" (186). She admits that her theorizing about what happened to Winifred is a story whose truth may never be proved but cites the example of a Sylvia Plath critic: "Let me tell you a story," Kate says. A critic who studied Plath's poems said she was influenced by Woolf's *The Waves*. Later the critic examined Plath's papers at Smith College and found Plath's copy of *The Waves* "underlined at exactly those points the critic had mentioned" (189). Kate Fansler's point is that one can know things before having actual proof. In *No Word from Winifred*, Kate decides she knows what is going on even if she does not want to prove it. The cast of characters and plot are convoluted, but there is no dead body and when Kate determines Winifred's whereabouts she leaves her there. Kate is thus making up her own ending to her "story" about the "case." This is also the novel that includes Heilbrun's insider jokes about the Modern Language Association (of which she is past president). It is husband Reed who has to explain to Kate that the physical clue she found is a clear plastic nametag holder, and a colleague has to tell her she can check the *PMLA* November issue which lists papers presented at the annual convention. Professor Fansler seems unfamiliar with this fact, yet later at MLA headquarters says she is a member in good standing, a point the woman who assists her has already checked.

A Trap for Fools is the shortest and darkest of the novels. The lines of Kipling's poem "If" are quoted, in order, for chapter epigraphs for no discernible reason; a professor is found dead on the ground beneath his office window; an African-American activist student is similarly killed; a woman Kate calls her friend embezzles university funds; other top administrators are guilty of bribery, cover-ups, and other criminal and immoral deeds. When the top administrators ask Kate to investigate the death of the professor, Kate keeps feeling she is being set up, and she is. Early on she concludes that "We are all guilty" and that there is no innocence in the university community; she suggests that rather than investigate the death they should all "let it go unsolved" (10). But "since literature was her life" (121) Kate puts together a story about what happened. "I've never thought of working out problems, detection, as only the gathering of clues, or even facts, important as these are. Whatever happened is a story; it's a narrative, and my job is to try to find out what that story is" (109). Even Reed says, "Every good investigator in the world, criminal or scholarly, has to take a sudden leap. . . . Without it, all you've got is a fact-grubber. . . . But in the end, it comes together in your mind or not at all. That's true of detective work, biography, history, and even science, I think" (139). Kate later comments that an administrator's mistake in asking her to investigate "was not to realize I look for narratives, that's my profession, not being a detective. He thought to provide a diversion, but lit crit teaches you to be on the watchout for exactly that. We deal in subtexts, in the hidden story" (152).

With *The Players Come Again* (the title is from Virginia Woolf's *The Waves*, quoted in the epigraph), Cross creates more layered fictions within fictions, and the emphasis shifts entirely away from current murder and mayhem. Instead, the novel poses central questions familiar to many readers, especially feminist scholars: What is the relationship between text and writer and reader? How does revisionist study of authors and works contribute to social change? What is the conceptual interplay between/among fact and invention, fiction and biography, detective fiction and literature? What are the parallels between detecting and researching and reading? How do we construct and deconstruct our own lives?

In this novel Kate is self-examining as she interviews others about the woman whose biography she plans to write, and the novel becomes self-reflective, raising questions of meaning and specifically asking the extent to which biography is a fiction, a story. To use a convenient term, the novel is metafiction.

As the first chapter of this tenth book in the series opens, Kate has recently finished an academic study on Henry James and Thomas Hardy, "published to general approbation and the usual snappy remarks about American scholarship that passed for a review in the *Times Literary Supplement*" (3). (Readers may be rather surprised that Professor Fansler is writing about these male authors; one wonders if perhaps it is a subconscious reaction to her deep disappointment at the betrayal of her friend Edna Hoskins in the previous *A Trap for Fools*.) Kate feels at loose ends. She wants a project other than another academic study but not memoirs. Fortuitously, an editor from a major publishing company proposes she write a biography of Gabrielle Foxx, enigmatic wife of Emmanuel Foxx, a famous novelist of the modernist period. His masterpiece *Ariadne* is purportedly the inner thoughts of its central woman character. Probably that woman was Gabrielle; perhaps she helped write the book? A surviving granddaughter, Nellie, her cousin Dorinda, and their close friend Anne are the three women Kate deals with most in her search for the truth about Gabrielle. She first meets these three women in the pages of the unpublished memoirs Anne has written about growing up with Nellie and Dorinda. The entire memoir is given in the novel (53 pages). It ends with the information that near her death Gabrielle gave Anne various papers; these unread papers are still stored in a London vault.

As Kate becomes more intrigued with her subject, she meets the three women and talks with others who have an interest in Gabrielle. There are enough plot twists right through the final pages of the novel to create suspense and reader interest, but clearly Kate's (and Cross's) mind is more centered on other questions than on following a conventional detective formula. The narrative voice and Kate herself repeatedly comment on the congruence of detection and biographical research and between scholar and sleuth.

Even more, Kate consciously affirms these worlds of literature and sleuthing as telling a story. "I'm going to invent the story of Gabrielle's life. But, like a good biographer, I shall search for the evidence to substantiate my interpretations," says Kate (82). Later

Reed says to her, "But what I can't decide is whether you are engaged as a detective or as a scholar and writer." "I haven't a clue," Kate replies. "If you want a definition of our time, there it is: there are no longer any clues to the labyrinth, not for love, and not for power. . . . One must find the thread for oneself, now that Ariadne has given us the clue" (127). Kate reiterates this when Dorinda speaks about what happened to Gabrielle; Dorinda admits there is no evidence for her account but asks, "I think it has a certain air of verisimilitude, don't you?" Kate answers, "I haven't a clue. . . . But I do like your story. It's both appropriate to the facts and creative. Perhaps that's the best that can be said for any biography" (169). At the point at which Kate agrees to consider editing Gabrielle's papers, she thinks, "What had begun as biography was, before her eyes, transforming itself into something else, as yet vague and troubling. Her literary self had become a detective, not, as always before, the other way around" (147).

Gabrielle's papers turn out to be Gabrielle's own novel in challenge to her husband's famous *Ariadne*. Hers is a powerful woman-centered re-interpretation of the myth of Ariadne in ancient Crete. *The Players Come Again* elaborately summarizes this novel-within-the-novel and its argument that the Greeks violently destroyed the matriarchal Minoan culture and deliberately rewrote its history to suit male-dominated Greece. Since it further argues that a return to feminist power is essential in the modern world, Kate knows Gabrielle's novel will be controversial not only for its radical message but because it subverts Emmanuel Foxx's masterpiece and questions the whole masculine bias of high modernism. Kate anticipates that she herself will be attacked by many of her peers for publishing the novel. She accepts this challenge, and she also agrees not to reveal certain facts about the family history that Nellie, Dorinda, and Anne insist should not be used. Kate does this in part because of her admiration for the three women who have chosen to trust her with their stories. Or, as Anne says of her own memoir, written before even she knew all the family secrets, she sees no need to alter it: "I think it's a lesson in biography; perhaps facts don't matter all that much" (160).

Cross/Heilbrun seems to prove this frequent irrelevance of "facts" within her novel as a whole. *The Players Come Again*, more than other books in the series, contains minor inconsistencies as well as the misleading stories by the "players." Kate posits a fiction/truth continuum rather than seeing fiction and truth as opposites or dualities. Kate feels a variety of confusions, "like someone who had learned the lines for one play and found herself in another for which, mysteriously, she was supposed to know her part" (146). Everything illustrates the difficulty of knowing the truth(s) or even its relevance.

A good example here of "inconsistencies" and "irrelevance" is the question of Kate's age. The narrative voice gives us facts: Nellie was born in 1926 (17), and her two friends Dorinda and Anne "almost at the same moment" (158). Kate repeatedly refers to these women as in their sixties, and age 63 would fit the time stated at the opening of the novel, "late that year as the eighties were beginning to run out" (3) as well as the publication date of 1990. Kate describes how these women look in terms of their age and how they approach their present and future. She repeatedly implies a gap between their sixties and her age, referring to Dorinda having lived a generation earlier than herself (220) and she specifically says, "Dorinda's probably twenty years older than I am" (101). Yet Kate as 43 or thereabouts does not fit the implications of her age in other books in the series when she generally seems about the age of her creator, Heilbrun, born in 1926 (the hardcover *Sweet Death, Kind Death* also lists "Cross, Amanda, 1926- "). That would logically place Kate in her late thirties in the 1964 opening of the series, and indeed the internal textual evidence suggests this, e.g., she is an Associate Professor who has taught for several years, and she first turns down Reed's proposal because she feels rather old for marriage and is used to her independence. In *The Theban Mysteries*, "Kate had been in the lower school of the Theban at the end of the depression, the middle school during World War II, the upper school during the Cold War. . . . Kate had left the Theban before the fifties" (20). By 1989, then, Full Professor Fansler, long married, long sought out as a sleuth and a writer, should according to the "facts" be in her sixties, the age of the three women in whom she is so interested. But the "story" of *The Players Come Again* is of optimism for "second chances" for those three women, for Gabrielle (through her book), and for Kate herself. For purposes of the novel, it "fits" that a younger Kate looks to the older women as models. The final page of the novel reads:

Kate felt as though a rare chance had come to her, one of those moments when all of the missed opportunities, the less than perfect literary accomplishments, the administrative defeats and the triumphs of small-minded men devoted to the past, might be redeemed. The moment would not last, but she let it have its force. She had told Dorinda that all English literature was the story of second chances. This, then, was her second chance, and Gabrielle's, and Ariadne's. (229)

Heilbrun here presents a Kate who consciously strives to make available a novel that will encourage contemporary readers to reclaim our history and seek empowerment in our present and future. Heilbrun's theme is this sense of discovering the past to create the reality of the present and envision a more satisfactory future. The "facts" of Kate's age are less relevant than the story. Kate Fansler is "timeless" in the way only literature can create. Set in a particular time and place, those settings are endlessly recreated just as Kate is recreated with each reader/reading. Kate's age varies from late thirties to mid-forties over the twenty-six-year course of the series, but her interests and accomplishments change from discovering who murdered a student to discussing the problematic nature of self and reality.

And Kate remains marvelously consistent in good-humored repartee, slick literary quotations, and wit in its broadest sense of combined intelligence and intuition. Throughout the series she is loved and respected. She takes teaching seriously even though university administrators have other agenda. She believes crimes of greed and violence must be identified and acknowledged, though the guilty need not necessarily be punished in conventional ways such as imprisonment. Sometimes getting scholarships established in memory of a murdered African-American woman student may be the most appropriate ending to the story of greedy administrators. Throughout the series Heilbrun tells the story of a Kate Fansler who understands that some things cannot be changed, but who maintains a self-honesty and human decency that delights and inspires. Ultimately, Heilbrun helps us see the value of good stories.

Works Cited

Budd, Elaine. *13 Mistresses of Murder*. New York: Unger, 1986.

Craig, Patricia, and Mary Cadogan. *The Lady Investigates*. New York: St. Martin's, 1981.

Cross, Amanda. *In the Last Analysis*. New York: Avon, 1966.

____. *The James Joyce Murder*. New York: Ballantine, 1982.

____. *No Word from Winifred*. New York: Dutton, 1986.

____. *The Players Come Again*. New York: Ballantine, 1991.

____. *Poetic Justice*. New York: Avon, 1972.

____. *Sweet Death, Kind Death*. New York: Dutton, 1984.

____. *The Theban Mysteries*. New York: Warner, 1973.

____. *A Trap for Fools*. New York: Dutton, 1989.

Reddy, Maureen T. "The Feminist Counter-Tradition in Crime: Cross, Grafton, Paretsky, and Wilson." *The Cunning Craft: Original Essays on Detective Fiction and Contemporary Literary Theory*. Ed. Ronald G. Walker, June M. Frazer, and David R. Anderson. Macomb: Western Illinois UP, 1970. 174-87.

Roberts, Jeanne Addison. "Amanda Cross Revisited (1992)." Unpublished paper presented at the Popular Culture Association meeting in New Orleans, Spring 1993.

____. "Feminist Murder: Amanda Cross Reinvents Womanhood." *Clues: A Journal of Detection* 6 (Spring/Summer 1985): 47-51.

Schleh, Eugene. "Character Development of Kate Fansler in the Amanda Cross Novels." *Clues: A Journal of Detection* 13 (Spring/Summer 1992): 73-79.

Fadeout:
Dave Brandstetter's First Case

Landon Burns

When *Fadeout* was published in 1970, it was a first in several ways. Not only was it the first of Joseph Hansen's Dave Brandstetter novels, it was the first mystery novel to feature a gay protagonist that found an enthusiastic mainstream audience. And the fact that it was everywhere critically well-received awarded it another first:

Unusual in two respects. One is that the investigator, though ruggedly masculine, is thoroughly and contentedly homosexual and that his homosexuality (and that of several others) is an integral part of the plot. The other is that Mr. Hansen is an excellent craftsman, a compelling writer, and a social observer (the scene is California) with something of the quality of Ross Macdonald. ("Briefly Noted" 192)

While in the 1990s there are many sympathetic gay and lesbian characters in mysteries, until *Fadeout* was published homosexuals were, as Hansen says:

treated shabbily in detective fiction—vilified, pitied, at best patronized. This was neither fair nor honest. When I sat down to write *Fadeout* in 1967 I wanted to write a good, compelling whodunit, but I also wanted to right some wrongs. Almost all the folksay about homosexuals is false. So I had some fun turning cliches and stereotypes on their heads in that book. It was easy. I gather from the reviews that it worked. But before there were reviews there had to be a published book. And that took some doing. It also took three years. Publishers were leery of my matter-of-fact, non-apologetic approach to a subject that the rule book said had to be treated sensationally or not at all. At last a brave lady named Joan Kahn, mystery editor at Harper and Row, took a chance on me. (Baird 498)

Furthermore, *Fadeout* is the first of an unusual series in that Dave Brandstetter is forty-four when the series begins. Most hard-

171

boiled detectives begin when they are much younger, and remain, more or less, the same age throughout the series. Not only is Brandstetter middle-aged at the beginning, he ages at about the same rate as the novels were written so that by 1991, when the elegiac, twelfth and final novel, *A Country of Old Men*, was published, he is in his mid-sixties. He has grown old and weary in spirit as well as in body; he has also grown in character, building upon the remarkable knowledge of human relationships and self he demonstrated as early as *Fadeout*.

In part because he has recently lost his lover of twenty-two years, Dave is in a melancholy mood in *Fadeout*. Rod's death has led him to near suicidal depression and to rumination about the nature of love and regret:

> In twenty years you could say and do a lot you wish you hadn't. In twenty years you could store up a lot of regrets. And then, when it was too late, when there was no one left to say "I'm sorry" to, "I didn't mean it" to, you could stop sleeping for regret, stop eating, talking, working, for regret. You could stop wanting to live. You could want to die for regret. (45)

Yet anyone as sensitive, as committed to helping the weak and abused, as kind and gentle as he is shown to be, is going to be pained almost constantly by the harsh, self-serving cruelty of the "real" world. Dave is by nature acutely aware of how ephemeral are the very things one wants most to be enduring, of how experience inevitably leads to disappointment, the reduction of expectations, and ultimately to a kind of *Weltschmerz*, though in his case certainly not a maudlin one.

This is why in *Fadeout* Dave goes out of his way to play chess with the retarded teenager, Buddy Mundy, and has taken pains to notice the lonely boy whose mother worked for Rod Fleming. It also explains why in *A Country of Old Men* the plight of an abused child can bring him out of retirement for what turns out to be his last case. In the later novels, such as *The Boy Who Was Buried This Morning* (1990), the retirement of colleagues he has known for up to forty years, the deaths of his father and the restaurateur, Max Romano, make him feel that his world is slipping away:

> "Goodbye, Mr. Brandstetter," Alex said, and steered the car toward the driveway. "Goodbye, Mr. Harris."

And he was gone. Another one gone.

Dave was so tired when they reached the canyon house that he didn't give another thought to eating. All the energy he had left went into taking a shower and dragging himself up the raw pine stairs to the sleeping loft. (131)

Thus, from the very beginning and clearly at the end, Dave is a man who is deeply aware of mortality and loss, the fragility of love and friendship, the need to appreciate those whom one cherishes.

While Dave's grief for Rod is pervasive in *Fadeout*, he never allows self-pity to cloud his clear mind, his sound judgment, or his sense of self-irony. For example, Anselmo, the boy who has had a crush on Dave since childhood, begs to try being Rod's replacement:

Dave drew a deep breath. "How old are you, Anselmo?"

Pride. "I'll be eighteen my next birthday."

"And I'll be forty-five. Look . . . you're very beautiful. You must know that. I want you. You must also know that. But I am not going to bed with you. Because there's something that I know that you don't. . . ."

"Why? You mean because I'm a dumb kid? You'd get tired of me?"

"You'd get tired of me first. My books, my music. And I'm a morose bastard. . . . Find somebody young, Anselmo. If you'll forget me, that won't be so hard. Somebody to keep you laughing and happy, the way you should be at eighteen." (116)

When, later in the novel, Anselmo tricks Dave into a sexual encounter, Dave good-naturedly forgives the ruse, enjoys the romp, but still firmly sends the boy on his way:

"Let's do it some more."

Dave laughed. . . . "We not only can't do it some more. I'm going to ask you to split. . . ."

"It . . . wasn't good for you too?" Anselmo worried.

"It was very good. . . ."

He gave the hard little butt a pat. And Anselmo went, small and silent and not looking back. For a bleak moment Dave stared after him. (186)

At one point Madge Dunstan, one of Dave's closest friends, who has just been jilted by her lover, suggests that, since they are both lonely, perhaps they should share her large beach house. Dave immediately senses that, dear friends though they may be, this is not a good idea:

She meant this. In dead earnest. And he was sorry. Because she was wrong. About herself for openers. Cuff had left scars but they would heal. About him, because somebody would take Rod's place. Who he couldn't say. But he would find somebody. Until this minute he hadn't known that. He knew it now. He half rose, leaned across the table and kissed her forehead. Solemn and brotherly. Then he sat down again and took hold of her skinny hands. (87)

With this kind of wisdom at forty-four, it is hardly surprising that, as he grows older, his human understanding increases. He also remains firm in his ethical values and self-discipline. He reacts with controlled anger whenever sneering references are made about sexual or ethnic differences. He refuses ever to take shortcuts or to give up even when every line of inquiry seems dead-ended. Thus, he knows that it is time to quit when in *Obedience* (1988) he is tempted to compromise his principles:

The aim of his work had never changed, to get at the truth no matter who got hurt. That would maintain, if he kept at it into the next century. But he wouldn't. He hadn't the stomach for it anymore. Let somebody else do the wrecking after this—of lives, of hopes, of fortunes. The wrong-doers he didn't give a damn for. It was the blameless ones. (178)

If sensitivity and introspection constitute one side of Dave Brandstetter's character, strength and stoic courage constitute another. Although there is only one incident in *Fadeout* in which he is forced to rely on his physical power and agility to avoid a potential killer, in the ensuing novels he is frequently placed in situations where alertness, muscle, and stamina are vital for his survival. Indeed, it is the weakening of these qualities in the late novels that is one of the major things that depress him and make him realize it is time to retire. Hansen does not emphasize this physical prowess in the early novels, but, almost as if he is preparing the reader for the end, he emphasizes its loss repeatedly in the last three. Early in the series Dave gets beaten about but seems to recover very quickly; later the physical damage is greater and the recovery time longer. But, early or late, he never whines or even complains very much. He is the stoic who accepts physical risk and damage as part of the territory.

Less obviously a part of the territory are his tastes in music, art, and literature, clearly outlined in *Fadeout* and constant throughout the series. A love of Beethoven or Tchaikovsky, Shakespeare and Robert Frost, would only confirm the other aspects of his sensitivity, but Dave's musical and intellectual interests are much more esoteric:

In record shops, while Dave sweated out a choice between Messiaen's new *Chronochromie* and an E. Power Biggs Buxtehude organ recital . . . Rod with cries of glee, would gather armloads of glittering original-cast albums. . . . He [Rod] had, after all, sat cheerfully through chamber music recitals Dave knew bored him, trudged amiably at Dave's heels through long galleries of paintings and sculptures that meant nothing to him, listened while Dave read aloud articles on science and war and politics. (48-49)

And it is not only the accepted classics that Dave knows and reveres. He makes brilliant use of Allen Ginsberg's "Song" as he is trying to console Madge Dunstan: "The weight of the world is love. Under the burden of solitude, under the burden of dissatisfaction, the weight, the weight we carry is love" (87). These refined tastes come up again and again in the series. Dave Brandstetter savors the fine cuisine at Max Romano's restaurant, the headiness of single malt Scotch, and the elegance of a chocolate brown Jaguar. It is not so much that he is a "morose bastard" that sets him apart as it is that his interests are more specialized than most.

Finally, there is the matter of Dave's homosexuality, which Hansen intentionally fails to introduce until page 44 of *Fadeout*. On rereading, one recognizes hints and foreshadowing, but Hansen's obvious and successful intent was to establish Dave Brandstetter as a capable, masculine, psychologically solid man, and only as a kind of afterthought to reveal that he is gay. This is one of the basic premises of the series: Dave Brandstetter is a first-rate, nationally known claims investigator (in the later novels he will have had TV appearances with Donahue and been featured in *Newsweek*) who happens to be gay, not a gay man who happens to be involved in a mystery plot. This distinction bears out what Hansen claims as the falsity of stereo-typing, and it is critical in establishing the tone of the novels.

In all of them Dave's private life figures as an important element, often intersecting the mystery plot, sometimes simply as a factor that readers of the series have come to expect as part of the books' appeal. Therefore, his sexual orientation, his relationships with friends and lovers, and his interaction with the straight world are always in clear focus. Neither in *Fadeout* nor in any of the subsequent novels are there explicit sexual descriptions though we are certainly aware that Dave is sexually active. In spite of several casual encounters in the first few novels, he is essentially monogamous. He had been with Rod Fleming for more than twenty years before *Fadeout* begins. After a brief but psychologically interesting relationship with Doug Sawyer, one of the major characters in *Fadeout*, Dave settles with Cecil Harris in *Gravedigger* (1982), and they are together (with one short hiatus) through the rest of the series.

In *Fadeout* Dave bristles at being identified as "one of us" by an effeminate old man and acknowledges that he felt slightly uncomfortable at first with Rod's giddiness. Later in the series he would shrug off such things, for both he and, to some extent, society have become less uptight about superficial mannerisms. But never, from the beginning, is Dave apologetic or guilty about his sexual orientation. In a potentially difficult conversation with his father in *Fadeout*, he calls himself "a middle-aged auntie" (99). While it is clear that Carl Brandstetter wishes his son were straight and were to provide him with grandchildren, it is equally clear that he respects Dave as a person of ability and integrity:

"Now let me ask my brutal question. Why be a middle-aged auntie if you don't want to?"

"Did I say I didn't want to?"

His father blinked at him for a moment, then, with a resigned shrug, turned and walked out. (100-01)

In addition to establishing the character, Dave Brandstetter, *Fadeout* is an effective introduction to the series in a number of other ways. Several continuing characters and the subplots concerning them also make first appearances: Madge Dunstan (who as late as *A Country of Old Men* is still searching for a young lover); Carl Brandstetter and his uxoriousness (he will ultimately have nine wives before he dies); Max Romano, at whose restaurant Dave has a permanently reserved table. As the series goes on, there will be many more continuing characters added, and they come to form a network of friends and colleagues that gives the novels continuity. Moreover, in *The Boy Who Was Buried This Morning* and *A Country of Old Men* it seems as if Hansen is deliberately creating ways for these characters to make cameo appearances, or at least be referred to, in order to add to the sense of closure.

More important than the introduction of several continuing figures is *Fadeout*'s introduction to Hansen's methods of characterization. While it would be stretching to say that many of Hansen's characters are fully three dimensional, they are, nevertheless, colorful and believable human beings. *Fadeout*'s presentation of the two major characters on the mystery level is daring and unusual in that one does not appear at all and the other only sporadically in the last forty pages. Fox Olson, dead before the novel begins, was a confused, flawed, unfulfilled man whose literary ambitions had been thwarted. As his daughter says, "He was a . . . good writer. But something was missing" (39). That "something" was his repressed homosexuality. Fox had married and had a relatively positive relationship with his wife, at least until just before the novel begins. (This is the kind of detail that Hansen uses constantly to make the characters realistic: just because the marriage has soured and there has been something missing, this is not to deny that there were good aspects of it.) For such a man, though enormously popular as a Garrison Keillor type of radio entertainer but one with little self-knowledge, to be presented indirectly through the eyes of wife, daughter, manager, lover, and others seems exactly right. This indirection also serves to romanticize him; we hear about his weaknesses and naivete, but we don't actually see them.

Much the same is true of Doug Sawyer whose twenty-five years in France we hear about only in rough outline. When he reappears and goes off with Fox to the seaside resort that was the scene of their youthful affair, he too seems a romantic figure, capable, at least briefly, of thinking he and Fox can pick up where they left off so many years before:

"Forty-four years old and like a couple of moonstruck adolescents. Wonderful! He was going to write. Did write. Honestly, at last. I . . . was going to paint again. Most of all, we were going to love each other, that went without saying." (155)

In spite of, perhaps because of, the indirect presentation, both men are made believable and likable. Hansen achieves this, not with omniscient description, but with deft, small touches such as the observation of Doug's mother, who, without comprehending at all what she is revealing, says:

"Do you know . . . I never knew two people as close as those two boys. Not in my whole life." She gave a little thoughtful headshake. "And when Doug came home from Europe and saw that story in the *Times* [about Fox's running for Mayor] . . . he yelled. Really. Right out loud. Jumped out of his chair and came running into the kitchen, flapping the paper, and threw his arms around me, and I swear I don't know whether he was laughing or crying." (90-91)

Mrs. Sawyer may not realize what her words imply, but they have gone a long way in conveying the spontaneity of Doug's nature and the depth of his feeling for Fox. In the case of Fox's ill-fated attempts to write a novel and the demoralization that this has caused him, Dave comments, as Fox's wife opens file cabinets:

Lined up inside, like the sheeted dead after some disaster, he saw thick manuscripts in binders. She slid one out, stood and turned over the pages. They were, he saw, neatly typed, but the paper had been cheap. It was turning brown at the edges. (16)

Thorne, the unfaithful wife, speaks of his warmth and sense of humor; we learn that, like Dave, he has been kind to Buddy Mundy. Thus, with incisive, indirect strokes, a recognizable character emerges.

Although this technique is used for the creation of characters who are essentially "off stage" in *Fadeout*, it is the same one used for many characters, both major and minor, who populate each of Hansen's books. When the characters are "on stage," he reveals them, for the most part, externally—through their actions, dialogue, and the comments of others. Hansen can and does go into the minds of the primary characters—a notable example is Leonard Church of *Early Graves* (1987)—but psychological depth is not his major interest. He gives us enough to make the characters interesting and individual, but not so much as to slow the pace of the action.

In *Fadeout* the secondary characters are credible people, who, if not fully rounded, are not stereotypes either. In one page of description and dialogue Hansen captures memorably the pathetic degradation of a drunken old woman (42) and in another the awkward attempts at communication of her retarded son (40-41). Even so minor a character as the landlady of the boarding house to which Fox and Doug flee is given a vivid personality:

Mrs. Kincaid looked like a line backer. Not one who had scrimmaged lately, but still muscular. She wore a one piece knit swimsuit that looked as if she'd always worn it. The sun had faded it and tanned her until they were the same color. The effect was arresting. She was about sixty-five. . . . "Listen, I been trying to get my swim for hours now. I realize there's been a death, and nobody feels worse about it than I do. He was a sweet boy and just as sweet a man. Sweeter. Cuts me up he had to come here and die. . . . But . . . life goes on. Has to. I need my swim, I'm used to it." (134, 141-42)

Hansen almost always creates interesting characters, even if they have walk-on roles, but there are some notable failures—especially several of the villains who are cardboard caricatures. This is not true in *Fadeout*, but it is the case in two or three of the later novels: the homophobic police chief in *The Man Everybody Was Afraid Of* (1978); Colonel Zorn, the maniacal anticommunist of *The Little Dog Laughed* (1986); Gerald Dawson, the hypocritical religious zealot of *Skinflick* (1979). Fortunately these are exceptions. More typical are the fascinating misfits who appear in almost all the novels: Chrissie Streeter, the blind girl in *The Little Dog Laughed*; the eccentric novelist, Jack Helmers, of *A Country of Old Men*; the reclusive old homosexual, Witt Gifford, of *Nightwork* (1984). These, and many more like them, are remarkable characters who really could not have been predicted on the basis of those who appear in *Fadeout*, but who are created by the same technique. On the whole, then, whether villain or victim, major or minor, Hansen's characters and his ways of presenting them continue through the series as one of his strengths.

Fadeout also provides a fine example of Hansen's plotting skills. The basic suspicious event/murder is relatively simple: an apparent death by accident or suicide draws Dave as insurance investigator to the case because no body has been recovered from the "accident." In the first third of the novel, at least five theories about what actually happened are advanced (often by characters who have a self-serving interest in having their theories accepted). This naturally leads to multiple suspects and multiple lines of inquiry. Like any good mystery writer, Hansen carefully makes one of these theories seem about to be certified when another of them casts doubt on the previous one. *Fadeout* does this superbly well, and, in some more successfully than others, so do the remaining novels in the series. What is particularly effective in *Fadeout* and what is one of the things that mark Hansen as a superior craftsman is the way in which those characters who turn out not to be the chief villain(s) have, nevertheless, been at the scene of the murder and are guilty of some lesser crime or misdeed.

The mystery plot of *Fadeout* involves a gay relationship, and, in one way or another, gay characters and gay themes figure in all the novels. In *Early Graves* a serial killer seeks out men with AIDS; in *Troublemaker* (1975) Dave is investigating the death of a gay bar owner; in *Death Claims* (1973) gays in the theater and television are suspects; in *Gravedigger* one of the major characters is a closet homosexual. Although this element is always present, it is treated simply as a given, never sensationally or pruriently.

Fadeout's version of this plot-theme is a particularly moving one in that two men who had been teenage best friends are reunited after many years and totally different experiences. Their naive attempt to "fade out" is doomed for a variety of reasons, but the romantic reunion and its inevitable destruction are a touching, if violent, parallel to the theme of loss in Dave's private life. As is true in all the novels of the series, this gay element is merely one aspect of the plot, and although in *Fadeout* it is a prominent one, it is smoothly integrated into the larger whole.

If Fox Olson and Doug Sawyer want to fade out to recapture the relationship of their youth, this is only one of a number of ways in which the title reverberates through the novel so that it becomes a powerful theme. From the beginning Dave thinks Fox has faded out rather than been killed in the extremely suspicious automobile accident. Two murders fade out characters on the mystery level while death has faded out both Dave's and Doug's young lovers. In the comic conclusion of the novel Madge Dunstan and her new girlfriend, the very proper Miss Levy, fade out when Anselmo makes a nude appearance just before Dave makes him fade out to search for a more suitable lover. Fox Olson is a radio personality, and "fadeout" is a term from that medium. This careful handling of title-theme in *Fadeout*—and also in the second novel of the series, *Death Claims*—is one of the elements that make them integrated, memorable novels of theme as well as mystery. Although some of the later novels in the series do not follow this pattern so thoroughly, the use of the quotation from Yeats's "Sailing to Byzantium" as the title and motif in *A Country of Old Men* sets up an equally powerful resonance and foreshadowing.

This use of the title as theme is not only an example of Hansen's concern with more than bare-bones mystery plot, it is also an example of his nuanced handling of language. In the reviews of *Fadeout*, nearly every commentator praised Hansen's style: "Writing well above average" (Richardson 34); "Joseph Hansen is a writer of taste and maturity" (Frankel 39). In other novels of the series, even when plotting and character seem less than vintage Hansen, the style retains its power: "Hansen writes crisply with a lean, spare prose" (White 16); "sophistication and verbal elegance" (Callendar 18). Especially in passages involving action, it is clean and direct; he has frequently been cited as the successor to the Hammett-Chandler-Macdonald tradition. Hansen has said, "The task of a fiction writer is to be a faithful observer of things as they are" (Baird 499). And in *Fadeout* one can find many passages that do a splendid job of "things-as-they-are" observing. The very first paragraph is a fine example:

Fog shrouded the canyon, a box canyon above a California ranch town called Pima. It rained. Not hard but steady and gray and dismal. Shaggy pines loomed through the mist like threats. Sycamores made white, twisted gestures above the arroyo. Down the arroyo water pounded, ugly, angry and deep. The road shouldered the arroyo. It was a bad road. The rains had chewed its edges. There were holes. Mud and rock half buried it in places. It was steep and winding and there were no guard rails. (1)

"It rained. Not hard but steady and gray and dismal" comes close to a parody of Hemingway, but Hansen is too good a writer to be imitative or derivative: "Hansen may write in the manner of the California private eye genre, but in his best efforts he is a unique individual with a style you can't wait to find again" (Baird 499). This observation-of-things-as-they-are is the basic style of the novels, but what makes Hansen's writing special is the way in which he modulates seamlessly into metaphor, humor, sprightly dialogue, an occasional interior monologue, or a poetic evocation of mood:

Bell Beach was lost miles from the freeway. Sand lay in the empty, sun-baked streets. Wiry brown grass thrust through the sand. In the grass, gulls and pelicans stood like moth-eaten museum pieces. The buildings were cheap stucco with mad carnival turrets. Gaudy paint had faded and scabbed off. Shingles had curled and turned black. Windows were broken. Where not broken they were boarded up, had been for years: the rust from nailheads had written long, sad farewells down the salt-silvered planks. The corrugated iron roof of a hot-dog stand had slumped in. A metal filling station turned to black lace in the sun. Beyond padlocked grillwork in a crimson-and-gilt barn shadowy carousel horses kicked through gray curtains of cobweb. (125)

And this is the world of prison and decay in which Fox and Doug seek to recapture the freedom and joy of their youth!

Other elements of style and structure in this earliest novel include a frequent paragraph of description—either of person or place—without an anteceding identification: "She was rolling a wheel" (25), when we don't know who "she" is. This is a device obviously used to create interest and suspense, but when it is overused, as Hansen occasionally does, it can be annoying. Another and effective Hansen hallmark is the use of very short chapters. In the twelve novels there are very few chapters of more than ten pages and none with as many as twenty. In *Fadeout,* and to some extent in the novels that follow, these chapters often end with a surprise, a question, or a portentous event. This, of course, creates a fast pace and another element of suspense. Like any good writer, Hansen builds to a climax, with subclimaxes along the way, and then ends with a chapter of anticlimax and closure. In *Fadeout* that chapter is a wonderful blend of humor (nude Anselmo scaring off Miss Levy), resolution (the mystery solved and Anselmo sent away), and hope (Doug Sawyer arriving to thank Dave for having cleared him of Fox's murder and with the suggestion that Dave and Doug may be able to establish a rapport).

Fadeout is then an excellent introduction to what was to become a unique series. *Death Claims* and *Troublemaker,* the second and third novels, are worthy successors, and many of the others meet the high standards set by the first three. In the middle and late novels of the series Hansen frequently centers the plot on a social or political theme of current interest. In *Nightwork* it is toxic waste and the environment; in *The Little Dog Laughed* and *The Boy Who Was Buried This Morning* it is anticommunist paranoia and training camps for mercenaries and skinheads; in *Obedience* it is the Vietnamese subculture in Southern California. This focus on "occasional" issues gives the novels an added dimension and reinforces Dave Brandstetter's caring nature, but it can interfere a bit with the kind of careful plotting and structuring that were the strengths of the earliest novels. Yet Hansen never loses control. Indeed, *Early Graves*, the ninth novel in the series, may be one of the very best. Here the focus is on a serial killer, himself dying of AIDS, who sends other young men with AIDS to early graves by the knife as he gradually succumbs to dementia. Hansen weaves plot and subplot into an intricate pattern while he conveys a vivid picture of the disintegrating mind of the killer through his own words. Like at least four or five of the other novels in the series, it will stand up to that severe test on any mystery story: rereading for character, style, and theme even though the who- and whydunit be known.

This literary achievement is one of the major things that make the Dave Brandstetter series a memorable one; another is its pioneering use of homosexual characters and themes: "By means of the mystery and detective problems in his best work, Hansen universalized the fact of homosexuality, a commendable achievement" (Baird 499). But, and this is really why Hansen is so successful on this score, neither in *Fadeout* nor in any of the other novels in the series is there a hint of special pleading or polemics. By making Dave Brandstetter an investigator of strength, rectitude, and sensitivity, Hansen created a character who stands with Lew Archer, Travis Magee, and Parker's Spenser. That he happens to be gay is, as Baird says, a way of universalizing the subject.

Because Dave ages as the novels progress, and because there is a definite conclusion, they form a kind of biography of Dave Brandstetter as well as being twelve individual mystery novels. Or, to put it another way, they are twelve "chapters" in one long novel. Surely in 1967 Hansen did not conceive the direction the series would take nor the conclusion it would reach. Nevertheless, there is a valid sense in which the series has a beginning, middle, and end. It would be overly programmatic to break the novels into three tightly limited groups of four, but it is certainly true that *Fadeout*, *Death Claims*, *Troublemaker*, and *The Man Everybody Was Afraid Of* form a kind of unit. Dave is still at the height of his physical power and feels that what he is doing is important and salutary. In *Early Graves*, *Obedience*, *The Boy Who Was Buried This Morning*, and *A Country of Old Men*, he speaks repeatedly of retirement, his physical and emotional weariness, and his disillusionment with society and the ability of any individual to make an impact on its ills. If this puts *Skinflick*, *Gravedigger*, *Nightwork*, and *The Little Dog Laughed* into a somewhat miscellaneous middle, they nonetheless share neither the forward-looking tone of the first four nor the weariness of the last four. It is also in this group that Hansen's concern with social issues becomes a major component of plot and theme.

Fadeout is a special novel in its own right even if there had not been eleven more Dave Brandstetter episodes to come. Since there were, it provides a solid foundation and a high standard for the subsequent installments. It sets up character, of course, but it also sets up the linked symbols and themes which will continue to the end, an important factor in the unity the series achieves. Hansen could not have known that, some twenty years after the beginning, he would decide to bring the series to an end. It is, however, a testimony to the integrity of his vision that he decided to do so. For practical reasons, he could not have gone on much longer in the same pattern with Dave approaching seventy. There might have been ways around that problem, but Hansen chose an ending of finality and dignity that is exactly the way Dave Brandstetter would have chosen to go. With its theme of ephemerality and loss, Fadeout, in the beginning, foreshadows the poignant fade-out at the end in A Country of Old Men: "and then he couldn't breathe, and the pain was fierce, and it was morning, so it wasn't supposed to be dark, but it was dark as night" (177).

Works Cited

Baird, Newton. "Hansen, Joseph." Twentieth Century Crime and Mystery Writers. 3rd ed. Chicago and London: St. James, 1991.

"Briefly Noted." Rev. of Fadeout. The New Yorker 17 Oct. 1970: 192.

Callendar, Newgate. Rev. of Nightwork. New York Times Book Review 8 Apr. 1984: 18.

Frankel, Haskel. Rev. of Fadeout. Saturday Review 26 Sept. 1970: 39.

Hansen, Joseph. The Boy Who Was Buried This Morning. New York: Viking, 1990.

____. A Country of Old Men. New York: Viking, 1991.

____. Fadeout. New York: Harper, 1970.

____. Obedience. New York: Mysterious, 1988.

Richardson, Maurice. Rev. of Fadeout. The Observer Review 7 Jan. 1973: 34.

White, Jean M. "Extortionists and Exhibitionists." Rev. of Skinflick. Washington Post 21 Oct. 1979: 16.

"And the First Shall Be Last": James McClure's Kramer and Zondi Series

Don Wall

The writer who manages to captivate readers with the first novel in a series has set him- or herself a difficult task. On the one hand, readers form certain expectations, which the writer must meet in order to sustain interest in subsequent novels. On the other, too much sameness will kill interest: within the parameters of the series, there must be new developments, surprises, unexpected twists, and ongoing, vital relationships among characters.

In James McClure's eight novels featuring South African Police Lieutenant Trompie Kramer, "Trekkersburg" Murder and Robbery Squad, and his Zulu assistant, Bantu Detective Sergeant Mickey Zondi, the author has managed this creative balancing act with great skill. The first-published novel in this series, *The Steam Pig* (1971), establishes a number of conventions and features that subsequent novels maintain and often expand upon.

The opening scene of this novel plunges us into the middle of a situation that is both funny and grimly serious. We are introduced to George Henry Abbott who "for an undertaker was a very sad man" (1). Unhappily married, he fantasizes about his comelier clients, with the result that he makes mistakes. He makes one this time when, distracted by the corpse's beauty, he sends the wrong body off to be cremated. This turns out to be fortuitous, because an autopsy is performed, revealing that the young woman had been murdered by a sharpened bicycle spoke thrust through her armpit into the heart. An apparent mixup over the woman's eye color foreshadows a hidden identity, the revealing of which is crucial to solving the case. Thus McClure includes a clue to solving the mystery as well as introducing Abbott, who is developed during the course of the novel and who appears incidentally in later books.

This kind of dramatic beginning, either the discovery of a murder or the commission of one, is a hallmark of the series: the McClure fan expects to be thrust into the middle of a situation, and is not disappointed.

The second novel, *The Caterpillar Cop* (1972), has an even more striking opening scene, an attempted seduction which goes horribly wrong. Jonathan Rogers, a young tennis star on tour, goes off into the underbrush with a groupie, the smitten but virginal Penny Jones. There is a hint of the ominous in the proceedings when we are told Jonathan regretted not having glanced over his shoulder to look into the underbrush; he would not then be regretting "Poor Penny Jones, spinster of the parish. Forevermore" (9). But the seduction goes on, humorously enough so that we are inclined to overlook this jarring note. The first kisses had been most unsatisfactory: "her lips were soft enough but they parted wrongly so their teeth clinked together and she had pretty hard teeth" (8). Finally, she responds fully, and

For one terrifying moment he thought he would have to learn to talk with his hands. And then she abandoned herself to her first adult sensation and took his breath away. Literally. Using every muscle in his athlete's torso to subdue a coughing fit, he went straight into the next stage. (11)

At the last minute, as he is about to achieve his goal, he glances over his shoulder and sees a face watching them from the crotch of a tree. Enraged, he rushes the watcher, pushing the person to the ground and simultaneously realizing that it is a corpse. Meanwhile, the thoroughly aroused—and terribly nearsighted—Penny, glasses off, rushes after him. Thinking it is Jonathan on the ground, she throws herself down by the recumbent form and takes the initiative. "Then she felt the rigor of the flesh. And blood where manhood should be" (13). Thus is the body of young Boetie Swanepoel discovered, and the case begins.

Unlike *The Steam Pig*, there are no clues present here that figure in the solving of the case, nor do either Jonathan or Penny play any further roles beyond being the hapless discoverers of the crime.

The third book in the series, *The Gooseberry Fool* (1974), opens with a startling sentence: "Hugo Swart entered purgatory just after nine o'clock on the hottest night of the year" (1). There follows a matter-of-fact account of Swart, a pious bachelor, coming home, pouring himself a drink, turning on the radio—and entertaining newly acquired but unspecified expectations of a successful future. As he sips a drink and listens to the radio, waiting for an interlude of chamber music, he is viciously attacked by a knife-wielding assailant. "On the cello's introductory note came the punched stab to the chest. . . . Then, in the two beats of silence that followed, artfully contrived by the composer to key listeners for a bright gush of vital sound, Hugo Swart had his Adam's apple cored, and bled swiftly to death" (4). The chapter ends with a mention that Swart's hearing aid had been crushed—an important clue to unraveling the mystery.

As in the case of Theresa le Roux, the murdered young woman in *The Steam Pig*, the knowledge of who and what Hugo Swart was is at the center of this mystery. As Kramer (and the reader) learns more and more, the murderer and his motive emerge little by little.

Snake (1976), the next novel, begins with an equally dramatic first sentence (as well as first chapter): "Eve defied death twice nightly, except on Sundays" (7). Eve, an exotic dancer who uses a five-foot python in her strip-tease act, admits a gentleman admirer to her dressing room. Experienced and cynical, she taunts the man, leading him on with her nudity and provocative movements but keeping him away with the threat of the huge snake. She finally goes too far, and ends up being strangled to death.

More than any of the previous novels, this book provides a number of clues throughout this scene that direct the reader to both the murderer and his motive. Eve thinks of men as "babies" and taunts her caller by asking him if she reminds him of his mother. These Oedipal clues are all clearly and logically explained by book's end, justifying McClure's comment that "this is a love story," and making his observation that "not many people seem to have realised this," a sad commentary on the perspicacity of too many reviewers and critics (Letter).

The dramatic situation that opens *The Sunday Hangman* (1977) is written from the point of view of a career criminal about to be hanged and in a terrible state of confusion: he doesn't know where he is, how he got there, or quite why he is being executed. Part of his confusion is because, as a former prisoner, he was aware of the sights and sounds of an official state execution, and there are enough similarities here to make the differences in circumstances very puzzling. As it happens, the semi-official nature of the proceedings is a clue to understanding the motives of the murderer.

This ex-convict, Tollie Erasmus, is not at the center of the mystery as were Hugo Swart and Theresa le Roux, but learning of his past and his former associates is essential to solving the mystery.

The next in the series, *The Blood of an Englishman* (1980), opens with a character who has just acquired a reputation as "a dirty old man." Droopy Stephenson, a humble garage mechanic apparently no more suave or dashing than his nickname suggests, is being kidded about his new status by a number of malicious shop girls in the neighborhood who seem to be vastly enjoying his discomfiture. Called upon to open a car's trunk car that had a matchstick jammed in it and being teased unmercifully by Glenda, his chief tormentor and the originator of his new reputation, he smashes the lock in a towering fury. The trunk lid springs open to reveal "what was undoubtedly the dirtiest old man either of them had seen. He was covered in mud, excrement, and blood" (15). He is also dead.

As with *The Steam Pig* and *The Caterpillar Cop*, we begin with a dramatic situation that starts as humorous and ends as horrible. Here again, the section serves to provide shock value, but there are no clues hidden here for later development, nor does Droopy figure in the case.

The Artful Egg (1984), the last in the Kramer and Zondi sequence (but not the last published; there is a "prequel," which will be discussed last), is quite different in degree from any of the earlier books. The protagonist of McClure's opening mini-drama, the Indian postman Ramjut Pillay, plays a major part in the book and is the most developed (and one of the most engaging) of all of McClure's secondary characters. Pillay, a lecher who rationalizes his lusts by imagining that all he seeks is to emulate his hero Ghandi's "brahmacharya" experiments in self-control with naked young women, discovers the nude body of Naomi Stride, a world-famous South African novelist, as he seeks her out to deliver the mail.

Shaken by the discovery, Pillay abandons his postbag and post office boots and is fired as a result. He is even more shaken when he realizes later that he has taken off with some undelivered mail— including a death threat to Stride. Terrified at the prospect of being accused of stealing evidence, Pillay, a Sherlock Holmes fan, decides to solve the case himself, and his various misadventures provide a hilarious but also very touching subplot.

Thus we see that McClure maintains the familiar and expected in each of his Kramer and Zondi novels: all begin with a dramatic (or traumatic) opening scene that gets us quickly into the initiating circumstance of the mystery. The reader who has come to expect and look forward to this feature is not disappointed.

Neither is the reader bored, for there are variations within this pattern. Some novels provide clues, others do not; some introduce characters who will be developed, others do not; some ongoing characters serve important purposes in the book, others do not.

This same variety in the midst of the familiar applies to the plots of the novels as well. A critical view of apartheid and its ramifications, often subtly rendered, pervades all the novels in many different ways and is often the mainspring of the novels' plots (for a fuller discussion of the social criticism, see Wall).

This is true of *The Steam Pig*, which depends upon apartheid as the root cause of the crime. As Kramer pokes about in Theresa le Roux's life, he uncovers the tortuous concatenation of events that culminated in her death. He discovers that the family was originally classified as white, until the father's hospital stay. Some sort of physiological discovery was apparently made there, and the family was reclassified as colored.[1]

The effect of this was to ruin life as they knew it. The father commits suicide. The family, whose friends and neighbors no longer spoke to them, had to give up their home and move to a non-white area. The son, Lenny, wanted to be a pilot, but this is a job reserved for whites; in his bitterness and frustration, he turns to a life of crime. Theresa, a very talented pianist, wanted still to pursue a career as a concert pianist, so she changed her name from Johnson to le Roux and attempted to pass for white, an option not available to Lenny, whose looks are not as Caucasian as his sister's and who therefore grows to hate her.

After the reclassification, the Belgian who teaches Theresa offers to continue giving her lessons, presumably because he esteems her talent. Soon, however, he insists upon her granting him sexual favors, which increases her bitterness. It is shortly after this that she assumes her new identity. She knows she must leave the country if she is to have a concert career, but she needs a forged passport to do so. She turns to her brother for help, knowing of his underworld connections (but unaware of his jealous hatred); he says he will help her, but such forgeries are very expensive. To acquire the money, Lenny sets her up as a prostitute with a limited and important clientele: some Trekkersburg businessmen and city officials.

The gangster Lenny works for is behind this. After setting Theresa up with the local bigwigs, he informs the men that he has tapes of all the goings-on and will expose them as having violated the Immorality Act by having intercourse with a nonwhite unless they see to it that various contracts are given to companies he recommends. Faced with imprisonment, fines, divorce, and loss of status, the men cave in after they are assured the tapes will be destroyed—along with Theresa.

It is apartheid that brings all this about, and the novel can thus be seen as a mordacious indictment of a system that blights the lives of several prominent citizens, ruins the life of a family, and brings about several deaths.

Apartheid also plays a part in bringing about the death of young Boetie Swanepoel, the unwitting interrupter of the seduction scene that opens *The Caterpillar Cop*. Boetie, it turns out, was a member of the Detective Club, an organization rather like the Hitler Youth and sponsored by the police. Boetie had gotten a number of blacks arrested for not carrying the hated passbooks; his success in these cases caused him to meddle in another—the one that gets him murdered.

Ironically, it is apartheid that prevents this case from being solved as rapidly as it might have. A young Indian boy who, like Boetie, fancies himself a detective, is involved in investigating the same case and acquires some information that would lead Kramer to the murderer. Danny is arrested on suspicion of housebreaking: he was carrying a "burglar tool"—a garden spade!—in a nonwhite area. Danny is being questioned in the police station right next to Kramer, who pays the boy, a mere coolie, no heed. When Danny is killed in a needless accident while in custody, that information is lost forever.

Apartheid leads Hugo Swart into fatal temptation in *The Gooseberry Fool*. Swart, an agent for a super-secret government agency, has been sent to Trekkersburg to pose as an ardent Catholic; his job is to amass evidence to be used against a liberal (and thus probably treasonous) priest. Swart bugs the confessional, and what he hears gives him the idea of blackmail.

The role of apartheid in this novel is complex. Apartheid sets up the basic situation, but when Swart dies, apartheid is responsible for impeding Kramer's investigation: government officials don't want him (or anyone else) to learn of this secret agency. To distract him, the government gets Kramer's superior to shunt him off investigating a traffic death. Kramer is furious, but the final irony is that the seemingly unrelated traffic death is integrally connected to the Swart case, and if Kramer had *not* investigated it, Swart's death would never have been solved.

Eve's death at the beginning of *Snake* also owes its genesis to the racial separation that apartheid enshrines. This is the story of a tortured young white man; rejected by his unloving mother, he attempts to find anew the love he had experienced with his black nanny but which his society inhibits him from either comprehending or admitting. Eve can know nothing of all this, of course, nor would she be capable of responding properly if she did. She says all the wrong things, with tragic consequences.

A system as restrictive as apartheid seems to need the protection of censorship, and it is censorship that shapes the course of the plot of *The Sunday Hangman*. A father whose criminal son was hanged by the state becomes obsessed with two things. First, he wants to hang his son's accomplice, who got off by turning state's evidence. Also, he is tortured by not knowing whether his son's death was quick and painless, and he cannot find out because the government severely restricted all information about prisons and what goes on inside them. Thus the father must learn the hangman's trade by himself, and learn by doing. . . .

In *The Artful Egg* there are two unrelated plots side by side. One centers around a retired high-ranking police officer who had been notorious for his brutality toward prisoners, behavior that was long tolerated under apartheid. The past comes back to haunt him, resulting in terrible consequences for him and his family. The other, the murder of the novelist Naomi Stride, is motivated by greed, but the racist murderer had learned to kill in Rhodesia fighting black terrorists as a member of the Selous Scouts, "a homicidal bunch of psychopaths" (261). He kills Stride, whose liberal books had been banned, in a spirit of righteous hatred, referring to her as a "terr-loving [sic] bitch" (269).

While many of the plots are thus driven by the customs and practices of apartheid, the social criticism in these books is far broader and more pervasive than just this. Each novel, often very subtly, presents dozens of situations and incidents that stand as indictments of this society's mores and actions. In *The Steam Pig*, as Kramer is trying to type a report, "A suspect in the next room screamed. Not continuously, but at irregular intervals which made concentration difficult" (7). The implication is that had the screaming been more rhythmical, it would have been no more bothersome than Muzak. On the same page we read about the murderer of a Bantu woman, "one Bantu male Johannes Nkosi, [who] had resisted arrest before dawn and was *mostly* in the intensive care unit" (emphasis added).

The Steam Pig also introduces us to the complex conflicts that were—and to some extent still are—so much a part of South Africa. It is not simply a matter of whites *versus* nonwhites: this novel includes situations where we find black *versus* black, black *versus* Asian, black *versus* coloured, Asian *versus* coloured, and even white *versus* white—Afrikaners and English South Africans are often at odds. And this same smorgasbord of ethnic skirmishes infuses every book in the series. The reader who becomes aware of these antagonisms will find them repeated in hundreds of variations, and the cumulative effect of this amounts to a wholesale and scathing indictment of the system.

The Steam Pig also establishes another one of the hallmarks of the series: humor. This feature of the series sets it apart from much other South African fiction (for example, the books of Alan Paton and Nadine Gordimer, and the crime fiction of Wessel Ebersohn). The humor, often cynical (or realistic), pervades all the books—a number of examples have already been given. Most of it centers around the protagonists, Kramer and Zondi, and it is one of the indications of the depth of their relationship.

These characters and their relationship constitute one of the strongest reasons for the success of the series—or of any series. The reader who becomes a fan looks eagerly forward to the next book, and often the plot is of almost secondary importance, for what is really happening here is that the reader is being reunited with old friends and acquaintances, so the major characters must be likeable to some extent and certainly interesting and vital. In some series the characters are unchanging, and there are readers who find that reassuring and happily anticipate encountering the stability of that fictional world once more. Other series have characters who grow and develop, who enjoy good fortune and suffer adversity, who interact with each other in not always predictable ways.

The Kramer and Zondi series is primarily of the latter type. There is the stability of their friendship, which endures, but in the midst of constant change and danger.

Our introduction to Kramer in *The Steam Pig* gives us a genuinely tough guy who is a thoroughgoing professional, a man obsessed with his job. When he learns that Theresa le Roux was murdered, a death that would have gone undetected except for the undertaker's mixup of bodies and the resulting post mortem, it "was like being love-struck; he felt lighter than air, eager and ready for action. All he wanted was to go charging out and get his man. Sick. It was altogether a condition to be profoundly distrusted" (23). He is even more pleased to learn that as he begins the case, no other policemen are around, including the Colonel, so "this meant no pressure to delegate. The case was all his—and Zondi's" (25).

As this last indicates, Kramer is very independent, a loner— except for Zondi. He has little respect for most of the other policemen, including his immediate superior, Colonel Du Plessis (whom Kramer refers to as "Colonel Dupe"). Our first meeting with Kramer finds him unenthusiastically trying to finish a report on a Bantu murder by an arbitrary deadline. Kramer sees no need for hurry. He knows the Colonel won't read the report, his attitude being, "if you've read one Bantu murder you've read the lot" (8). Kramer reflects cynically that the Colonel simply wanted to add the case "to his Crimes Solved graph and get back to arse-creeping the Brigadier —yet another triumph for law and order reduced to a colonic toehold" (8).

Our first glimpse of Kramer and Zondi together comes when Kramer goes to Theresa's flat to investigate and falls asleep, then awakens suddenly:

The face above him was black. His right fist heaved up, missed, and flopped back. Somebody laughed. He knew that laugh; he had heard it where children played, where women wept, where men died, always with the same depth of detached amusement. Kramer closed his eyes without troubling to focus them and felt curiously content. (36)

This passage becomes something of a leitmotif; it is found in various forms in every book in the series. Its importance underscores the depth of mutual trust, a trust that transcends even the rigid rules of apartheid. Still lying on the couch, Kramer watches Zondi pick up the autopsy photos and calls him a "cheeky black bastard," but Zondi "went on with his illicit scrutiny of Miss le Roux's bromide image. Even dead a white woman had laws to prevent her from primitive lust." Kramer says, "You want to get me into trouble, hey?" but Zondi continues to examine the pictures, finally commenting that she was "a good woman. . . . She could have given many sons." Kramer says, "Is that all you think about?" and then "they both laughed. Zondi was an incorrigible pelvis man" (37).

They often laugh together, and sometimes at the expense of Kramer's Afrikaner colleagues. Later in the book, Kramer and Zondi have discovered the ripe corpse of a paralyzed Bantu informer, Shoe Shoe, in a cornfield. The two watch Sergeant Van Rensburg arrive to pick up the body:

The mortuary sergeant came coughing and hawking out of his dust cloud, trying to find a handkerchief. He was a colossal man. The combination of banana fingers and thighs that stretched trousers tight made the search quite something.

Kramer cuffed the grin off Zondi's face and then the pair of them got out [of the car], averting their eyes. (81)

Kramer sympathizes with Van Rensburg about the nasty state of the corpse, but Van Rensburg doesn't mind—he'll have Zondi put the body on a tray. Kramer tries to spare his friend, saying, "Sergeant Zondi's not a big man" (81), but Van Rensburg has him do the job anyway. Afterwards, "Zondi came over smelling his hands gingerly." Kramer asks the police surgeon, Dr. Strydom, for some tissues so Zondi can wipe his hands. Strydom is surprised at this, but accedes to the request promptly when Kramer explains, "He's driving my car, you see" (84).

Finding a way around the culture's restrictions and stereotypes is something that both Kramer and Zondi do well, and they do it almost automatically. On occasion, they even use the system to their advantage. Later in the book, when Kramer wants another policeman, Van Niekirk, to take over some tedious investigative work, the man demurs:

"But haven't you got someone working on that already, sir?"
Kramer smelled tact.
"I've got a coon. He's no bloody good for what I want done."
"Which is?"
"Statements, phone inquiries, paper work." (113)

Van Niekirk agrees, and Kramer is free to keep Zondi on more important work. Van Niekirk would certainly resent knowing how he had been used, but he should be grateful, for on another situation Zondi unwittingly protects him. Kramer criticizes Van Niekirk, and then, realizing he had done this in front of Zondi, next speaks to him in a very friendly manner. This lasts only a few minutes, when Kramer learns Van Niekirk had neglected to pass on some vital information: "Only Zondi's presence saved Van Niekirk from castration. Anything less drastic had no interest for Kramer" (127).

Throughout the series, the two friends laugh and joke together —including racial jokes—whenever they are alone. When someone else is around, however, they revert outwardly to the superior/inferior roles society expects, but they often do it tongue-in-cheek. It is part of the fun, for them and for the reader, to triumph over the less intelligent bigots with whom they associate.

In *The Artful Egg*, McClure creates another black/white police pair, Lieutenant Jacob Jones and Gagonk Mbopa, who serve as foils to Kramer and Zondi and who are very jealous of them. Jones, not very bright, always insists nevertheless that his orders be carried out; he never listens to Gagonk who, though nobody's idea of a genius, several times has much better courses of action to suggest. The relationship of this duo is marked by antagonism, open on Jones's part, covert on Mbopa's, which helps ensure their ineffectuality. This is in sharp contrast to the open and flexible give-and-take of Kramer and Zondi, who thus make the best use of their combined and superior intelligence.

This is not to imply that Kramer is some sort of paragon; in many ways, he is a typical brutal South African cop: he never hesitates to use physical force on a suspect, and Zondi joins right in. But, while he is no liberal, he has a strain of sensitivity. Mrs. Johnson, Theresa's mother, comes to see her daughter's body and is apprehended and questioned. While she is officially a "coloured," and hence by definition inferior, Kramer is very gentle in questioning her, for she is unmistakably a lady. When she asks if Theresa was "*marked* in any way" (138), "'She was not marked, Mrs. Johnson,' Kramer said softly" (139). Later he provides her something to eat and, instead of keeping her in a cell as Van Niekirk suggests, Kramer simply says he knows a place and takes her out to a neat bungalow in the country, owned by a coloured family with whom he is obviously friendly. Greeted enthusiastically by the family and conscious of Zondi's gaze, at first "Kramer affected a bluff manner but gave in to the children's teasing. One of their little friends edged his way into the circle to see what manner of white man could cause such excitement" (166).

This sensitivity, or perhaps sense of fairness, is one of the things that makes Kramer an appealing character throughout the series. This sense of justice that transcends apartheid often appears in incidental incidents. For example, when he sees a white man drive off without paying a young Indian paperboy, Kramer pulls the man over and arrests him (*Artful* 43-45).

Toward the end of the book, Kramer phones Van Niekirk and learns that he has sent Zondi alone into a potentially very dangerous situation. "Kramer's next seven words whipped off two pairs of headphones [worn by women at the telephone exchange] and spilled the tea. But the eavesdroppers made miraculous recoveries" (224). Kramer rushes off to help his friend, and saves his life.

Previous books had carefully detailed the development of their deep friendship and absolute mutual trust—and their inter-dependency. Thus when in *The Sunday Hangman* (1977) Zondi's recovery from a bullet wound in the leg is in doubt, Kramer worries during the entire case about whether his friend will be able to continue as a policeman or be mustered out. A professional life without Zondi is unthinkable, and Kramer goes to great lengths to prevent him from being examined by Dr. Strydom, risking a charge of insubordination by doing so.

The other important relationship in Kramer's life that *The Steam Pig* introduces us to is his continuing—and growing—attachment to the widow Fourie, and to a lesser extent, to her children. Kramer lives alone in a rented room; his life-style is nomadic and spartan. He finds time for occasional overnight visits and brief talks and seems to value her thoughts on his cases. As the series continues, his relationship with her deepens, surviving some stormy periods and intermittent affairs. He buys a house for her in the suburbs, ostensibly only as a good investment for retirement purposes, but it also reflects a growing attachment. In *Snake*, Kramer helps her son Piet through a troublesome adolescent period. One of the things many readers look for is just what their situation will be in the next book, and the next.

The reader gets to know and care about Zondi, too, in this first book. As the series progresses, we meet his wife, we see his impover-ished living conditions, we share his frustrations about his intelligent children's poor schooling and lack of prospects, we respect his extraordinary abilities as a policeman, and above all, we come to admire him as a man of superior intellect, loyalty, and determination—and a genius for survival.

When readers get involved in a series, inevitably they want to know more about their favorite characters, and McClure parcels out bits of information that fill in their backgrounds. We learn that Kramer was brought up on a small, very poor farm; his father was a stern religious fanatic who caused his wife to die in childbirth because he wanted to prevent Kramer's being born on Christmas, so Kramer grew up without a mother. This history explains some of Kramer's harshness and also his animosity toward people as unyielding and self-righteous as his father. Along with his job, it may also explain his unwillingness to trust very many people.

Zondi was educated in a mission school, where the kindly, well-meaning nuns told him that hard work and study would enable him to achieve any goal. He knows better but is not bitter toward the nuns' idealism. He worries a great deal about his children, for he sees them already becoming frustrated with the quality of their education and their lack of opportunity, but, as a part of this powerful system, he knows they will probably be crushed if they rebel against it.

Many readers have wanted to know even more about these characters. How did Kramer and Zondi meet? How did their friendship and mutual respect develop? How did Kramer come to meet the widow Fourie, and what were her circumstances?

A writer could conceivably thread all this information into subsequent books, but it would be difficult to integrate it naturally into the story line. Thus the prequel is the logical way to deal with these issues, and McClure does so with *The Song Dog*. The book also hews to the conventions that readers have come to expect and value in the preceding books. Thus, although this is the last Kramer and Zondi novel written, it is really the first in the series. Here the problem is to invent the beginnings without contradicting anything that the later books portray.

As in all the other novels, *The Song Dog* opens with a bang—in this case, literally. A torrid love-making session turns unintentionally fatal; this is followed by a dynamite blast under the dwelling where the tryst is taking place, an event that contributes spectacularly to the confused evidence at the scene. Subsequently, we learn that human interference afterward is instrumental in adding to this confusion, but there are no clues in this opening drama to indicate this, or to reveal who the characters are and why they are together (apart from the obvious).

The mystery is slow to unfold, and in the course of it enough red herrings are strewn across Kramer's (and the reader's) path to misdirect him time and again, until nearly the end of the book. As in the preceding novels, the villain here generates a certain amount of sympathy because we get to know his warped circumstances.

A secondary mystery here is the ubiquitous presence of a cocky, zoot-suited African, who Kramer suspects is involved in the double murders the book opened with. Eventually we learn that this elusive person is Zondi, who has been sent to this northern territory to capture his cousin, Matthew Mslope, a Zulu who has been raping and murdering nuns and was responsible for burning a mission—crimes unrelated to Kramer's case. Zondi must avoid being exposed as a policeman in order to gather information, hence his need to avoid Kramer and the other cops.

At Kramer's first meeting with Zondi, the Zulu saves his life—an action calculated to get any relationship off on the right footing. But it is Zondi's intelligence and cockiness—two qualities for which Kramer himself is known—that cement that relationship.

The instant where they connect, one man to another, is worth noting. Kramer is questioning Zondi about the latter's giving him the slip at an Indian store after Kramer suspects he is being spied upon.

"So getting a close look at me within minutes of my arrival in Jafini was just a coincidence, hey?"

"Indubitably, Lieutenant."

"Don't you bloody try lying to me, hey?"

"*Hau*, would your most humble servant ever do such a thing, my master?"

"Damn right you would, kaffir!"

And they both laughed, as though they had just invented a new kind of joke together. (164)

In a sense, they had—certainly for themselves, in this society. The joke is a complicated one: the deepening mutual admiration, affection, and respect that an African and an Afrikaner can nourish together while hiding this from a culture in which such a growth is nearly unthinkable. In a sense, they are putting one over on South Africa.

This is a kind of idealism that, existing in the midst of the country's harsh realities, is an enduring and appealing feature of the series and of Kramer himself. Usually he keeps this side well hidden, but in the case of his friendship with Zondi, we see it fairly often (and often in humorous guise), for as a co-protagonist, Zondi enjoys center stage a good deal of the time.

Kramer's relationship with the widow Fourie, however, is a more erratic one; sometimes the reader wonders how lasting it will remain. Thus it is illuminating to learn that Kramer was attracted to her beauty, stability, and common sense early on, that he liked her children, especially Piet, from the beginning, and that he hid the truth behind her husband's death from her and from officialdom, both to spare her feelings and to prevent her from becoming bitter about life—and any subsequent man in her life. With this kind of beginning, the relationship has a good chance of permanence.

Zondi first meets his future wife, Miriam, when she is a servant girl in the household of an irascible, alcoholic Afrikaner woman. Zondi questions Miriam and is immediately impressed by her beauty, intelligence, and spirit. She is obviously a fit mate for him.

The case Zondi is pursuing gives us an additional glimpse into his character and perhaps into the fate of the country. Zondi had been a classmate of his cousin, Mslope, at a mission school. It was there, for Zondi,

the best dreams of his life had been dreamt; all you had to do, the white nuns had said, was to learn your lessons well and then, when you grew up, you would be the equal of any man and could do whatever you wanted to do. They had been wrong, those stupid, kind women, who believed all men were brothers, totally wrong, but Zondi still could not feel bitter. Unlike his classmate, his cousin Matthew Mslope, who had gone back with a mob to burn, pillage, rape, and wreak his revenge. Which had also been wrong, and meant that he, too, had to die now. (180)

Interestingly, this same passage appears nearly *verbatim* in *The Gooseberry Fool*, but with a difference. There, we are told that Zondi had arrested Mslope and had him hanged; here, it is intimated that Zondi will shoot him—an execution. Either McClure forgot the earlier statement or he changed it for some reason. As we are never actually told what Zondi does in *The Song Dog*, and as McClure is a meticulous craftsman, the latter seems the likelier guess. Certainly this later version casts Zondi in a more humane light.

Mslope assumes more importance here, both as a character and as a symbol. His motivation is better developed and his character is made more complex by having him experience increasing and ultimately debilitating guilt. As a symbol, his bitterness is doubtless far more typical than Zondi's larger comprehension and forgiveness. Mslope's course of action is unfortunately a better indicator of the country's future than is Zondi's.

Mslope's revenge therefore stems from the frustration of apartheid, a theme we have seen throughout the series. The subtler social criticism that careful readers have learned to discern is also present here, delightfully so in one instance.

Kramer asks about an old Zulu, and Terblanche, the Jafini station commander, tells him the man is crazy, offering this anecdote as proof:

He used to do some odd-job garden work for me, until the day he decided he was going to take out all my roses and return them to this tribal homeland he had set up for them. Can you imagine? Holes left all over the place, and my poor roses struggling to grow, stuck in a pile of broken bricks I had? (121)

What Terblanche takes for humor here can be seen as a pointed and poignant parable about the relocation of millions of Africans to the barren homelands and about the holes left in the lives of the families whose members had been uprooted and transplanted to that inhospitable soil.

Thus this prequel does indeed invent the beginnings readers have come to be curious about in the course of following the series. All the themes and many of the characters of the later books appear here, often with a depth of exploration that makes our apprehension of the later novels fuller and clearer. *The Steam Pig*, first in the series, is a thorough introduction to everything that follows, but *The Song Dog*, which comes before the beginning, does it even better.

There is one very disturbing note in this prequel. There are a few references to the government's being after a rising troublemaker, one Nelson Mandela. And at the end, Zondi tells Kramer that the *songoma*, the witch he had consulted, had warned that Mandela's wife would be the cause "that one far-off night . . . you and me would stand alone together, arm in arm in a black township, wearing red necklaces as bright as petrol flame" (296).

When asked about this, McClure acknowledged that the passage did in fact foretell the demise of Kramer and Zondi, but that it meant something else as well: "the death of the whole country." Then he added, "But I can always write other Kramer and Zondis that fit in between" (Telephone call).

One can only hope he will, for while *The Song Dog* is the last in the series, the paradoxical fact that it is also the first may remind us that it is possible for there to be any number of others. The realization of this possibility would gladden the minds of McClure's many fans, who would like him to fill more of the spaces between the inception and the end.

And given Nelson Mandela's promising and statesman-like beginning as President, perhaps the prediction of the country's death is premature, if he is allowed to effect the broad reforms he has espoused. Should the country's future prove brighter than seemed likely to McClure at the time of his writing *The Song Dog* and should he choose to revive the Kramer and Zondi series, perhaps he could conceive of a logically happier continuation of the relationship between the two than their sharing a death by a burning tire. This would gladden the hearts of fans of this pair even more, for we part with such old friends reluctantly indeed.

Notes

1. Under apartheid, South Africans were officially classified by race: Caucasian or white; Asian, primarily Indian; African, or black, and (Cape) coloured, of mixed European and African background.

2. It is ironic that the only one of these books banned in South Africa was *The Sunday Hangman*, because it contains information about hanging, which was forbidden. As for the others, South African readers did not see them as subversive; readers, including policemen, simply accepted descriptions as being accurate portrayals of everyday life under apartheid— which indeed they are.

202 In the Beginning

Works Cited

McClure, James. *The Artful Egg*. London: Macmillan, 1984.

———. *The Blood of an Englishman*. New York: Harper, 1980.

———. *The Caterpillar Cop*. New York: Avon, 1974.

———. *The Gooseberry Fool*. New York: Pantheon, 1974.

———. Letter to the author, 2 Feb. 1976.

———. *The Song Dog*. New York: Mysterious, 1992.

———. *Snake*. New York: Avon, 1976.

———. *The Steam Pig*. New York: Avon, 1974.

———. *The Sunday Hangman*. New York: Harper, 1977.

———. Telephone call to the author, 8 Jan. 1993.

Wall, Don. "The Achievement of James McClure." *Clues: A Journal of Detection* 10.1 (Spring/Summer 1989): 1-29.

Paradigm Established, Paradigm Surpassed: Colin Dexter's *Last Bus to Woodstock*

William Reynolds

Despite the popularity of Colin Dexter's novels about Chief Inspector Morse and Sergeant Lewis and the enthusiasm generated by the television movies adapted from Dexter's novels, ideas, and characters, it has until recently been difficult to fault Bernard Benstock's assessment that, on the basis of the seven novels published between 1975 and 1986, "Dexter is . . . the best of the second rank" (55). But in *The Wench Is Dead* (1989), *The Jewel That Was Ours* (1991), and *The Way Through the Woods* (1992) Dexter has written at a higher level; and the Crime Writers Association Golden Daggers for best novel of the year awarded to *Wench* and *Way* support anyone wishing to admit Dexter to the first rank.[1] In looking at Dexter's first novel, *Last Bus to Woodstock*, it is, then, important both to consider the pattern it set (especially for the next six novels—characterized by Benstock as "consistent in style, tone, atmosphere, and intellectual level" [55]) and to describe how the most recent novels have maintained and improved upon its pattern while surpassing it in characterization and narrative technique.

A summary of *Last Bus* will prove a useful prologue to further discussion. On Wednesday, September 29 of an unnamed year, two women are waiting for a bus to Woodstock; incorrectly informed that the day's last bus goes only to Yarnton, they leave the bus stop to look for a lift. At 10:30 p.m. one of them, Sylvia Kaye, is found murdered in the courtyard of a Woodstock pub; nothing is known of her companion, and she does not come forward to present evidence. Morse searches for two people: Kaye's companion and the driver who gave the women a ride. The first (Sue Widdowson) proves more difficult to find than the second (Bernard Crowther), and Morse's job is made more complicated because almost everyone refuses to tell the truth. Eventually, Morse sorts through the lies; determines means, motive, and opportunity by assigning killer and victim their proper

203

places in a complicated series of extramarital affairs; and arrests the murderer—a woman who tells him in their last interview, "I loved you" (214).

Trained in the classics at Cambridge University, Dexter did not publish his first novel until he was forty-five. In making the transition from earlier non-fiction books (*Liberal Studies: An Outline Course* and *Guide to Contemporary Politics*) to detective novels, Dexter made some very conventional decisions: he paired a brilliant yet eccentric detective (Morse) with a long-suffering but admiring assistant (Lewis), and—to ground his creations in real life—made them policemen, not amateurs or private investigators. But even as early as *Last Bus*, Dexter set his own stamp upon this material and gave it a life uniquely its own.

One key decision on Dexter's part was to make Morse and Lewis members of the Thames Valley Constabulary headquartered at Kidlington near Oxford (Dexter's home since 1966), allowing him to center the plot in Oxford and its environs. The first result of this choice is, simply, verisimilitude. Readers who secure the appropriate map can trace Crowther's path as he drives to the roundabout at the north end of the Banbury Road, turns left and continues to the roundabout at the northern end of the Woodstock Road, turns off the A40, follows the road north, and comes upon Kaye and Widdowson standing "alongside the self-service filling station" (95). But Oxford offers far more than this. As Dexter says, Oxford is a "place that many know, or at least would like to know" (qtd. in Spurrier 319); it is the city's image that has led such writers as Edmund Crispin and Dorothy L. Sayers to use it as the setting for novels. And it is this image that Dexter manipulates in *Last Bus* and its successors.

Much of *Last Bus* is designed to reveal a reality that coexists with, and perhaps is deliberately concealed by, the Oxford tourists visit. The first page, with its description of Blenheim Palace and its picture of the pleasing village of Yarnton, conjures up an image the remaining chapters replace with visions of evil, most frequently evil pretending to be something else. Kaye is the victim of what appears to be a brutal sex murder, struck across the back of the head with a tyre-spanner and left to die half-naked in a dark corner behind an upmarket pub. Lewis stakes out Studio 2 in Walton Street and observes a suspect entering the theater to view its "double sexploitation bill" (101); John Sanders, the first to discover Kaye's body, later bypasses "a bewildering variety of gaudy, glossy girlie magazines" (72) to make his weekly purchase of hard-core pornography. The murderer is a staff nurse at the Radcliffe Infirmary. And, while most of the action is centered in North Oxford, Dexter uses his academic background to take readers within the walls of Lonsdale College and reveal that the dons of Oxford University can be every bit as unprincipled and evil as commercial and working-class Oxford.

Although television takes Morse to Australia (*Promised Land*), Dexter's later novels are remarkably faithful to Oxford. Morse travels to such places as Bath (*The Jewel That Was Ours*) and Wales (*Last Seen Wearing*); but rarely is the police budget asked to cover an overnight stay, and most of the important action in all ten novels takes place within an hour's drive of Oxford. In the five novels immediately following *Last Bus*, Dexter also continues the pattern of using Oxford to contrast respectable externals with rotten cores— secondary schools in *Last Seen Wearing*, higher education in *The Silent World of Nicholas Quinn* and *The Riddle of the Third Mile*, the Church of England in *Service of All the Dead*, and business in *The Dead of Jericho*—before abandoning it in the most recent novels. Moreover, so often do readers follow Morse and Lewis to and from real places that the effect of the process begun in *Last Bus* is that fictional locations like Lonsdale College and Morse's flat seem just as authentic as Carfax or the Ashmolean Museum.

However, only rarely has Dexter constructed plots which establish an integral connection between plot and setting. The extramarital affairs and sexual perversions of *Last Bus* have no special connection with Oxford. And the same lack of correlation between crime and setting also characterizes most of the later novels, particularly *The Secret of Annexe 3* (a locked-room mystery which could take place anywhere) and *The Wench Is Dead* in which Morse investigates a murder which took place in 1859. And even though Dexter adds a new street to the section of Oxford known as Jericho and devotes several pages to the history of Jericho and its intriguing name, *The Dead of Jericho* revolves around events which happened many years before to people whom fate or chance brings together in Oxford.

Only in *The Silent World of Nicholas Quinn* and *The Riddle of the Third Mile* has Dexter moved beyond *Last Bus* and produced plots intimately linked with settings. *Silent World* involves the death of Nicholas Quinn, a member of the Foreign Examinations Syndicate headquartered in North Oxford near the Oxford Delegacy of Local Examinations, Dexter's own place of work. The mystery soon turns into Morse's constructing a list of suspects' whereabouts at key times, but the plot is closely linked to the work of the Foreign Examinations Syndicate, an imaginary organization which still fits perfectly into academic Oxford. Quinn is murdered because he discovered that two of his colleagues are selling advance copies of the O- and A-level exams (vital, among other things, for admission to Oxford), which the Syndicate administers. The mystery of *Riddle* is grounded even more deeply in academic Oxford. While Morse spends an unusual amount of time in London and two of the principal characters are concerned with what they think took place during the Battle of El Alamein (November 2, 1942), the novel centers on the hatred two fellows of Lonsdale College feel for one another (because each believes the other kept him from being elected Master of Lonsdale) and on the complex process of awarding University degrees. Because of Dexter's preoccupation with plot, neither novel fully evokes a sense of place; but *Riddle* succeeds well enough to justify Newgate Callendar's opinion that nothing in "Dexter's previous five books has prepared the reader for such a *jeu d'esprit.*"

In addition to establishing a sense of place, Dexter makes his major and minor protagonists well defined and memorable, if not truly rounded. Even in *Last Bus* Morse and Lewis display the basic temperaments and modes of action that characterize them throughout the series.[2] But readers of *Last Bus* learn little about the internal lives of Morse and Lewis; Dexter shows only how they think and act, not why. Such flatness, perhaps not surprising in a first novel so clearly designed to feature a complex plot and a surprise ending, is particularly observable in Dexter's account of Lewis. Lewis is first and foremost a good policeman. Morse is impressed by his "level-headed competence" (11); though Lewis has never been an "ideas man" (114), he is "nobody's fool and . . . a man of some honesty and integrity" (12). He respects the law and comes across as a genuinely good man, repelled by the monstrous evil of Kaye's murder. He is married, has children (including a thirteen-year-old daughter), takes the *Mirror*, and rarely does even the coffee-time crossword. His fondness for eggs-and-chips and fast-driving—major traits in later novels—are unmentioned.

The Morse of *Last Bus* is also clearly defined, and anyone who reads one of the later novels before *Last Bus* will find few major surprises. The early Morse is very much the "conceited, civilized, ruthless, gentle, boozy, sensitive man" (*Way* 40) Claire Osborne describes and very much the loner who "though never wholly happy when alone . . . [is] usually slightly more miserable when with other people" (*Wench* 150). Several of Morse's characteristics—among them his passion for crossword puzzles, the music of Wagner, and the poetry of A. E. Housman—are modeled on those of his creator (Spurrier 319). Dexter, a multiple winner of the *Observer*'s Ximenes clue-writing competition, has given Morse a similar passion. Only hours after the start of their investigation of Kaye's death, Lewis finds Morse working *The Times* crossword and leering over the connection between a clue and the state of Kaye's clothing; throughout the later novels Morse continues to pride himself on his cruciverbalist skills (*Way* 35, for example). Later in *Last Bus* Morse combines his first avocation with a second, working on *The Listener's* puzzle while listening to *Das Rhinegold*; while he does listen to the music of other composers (like Bruckner [*Jewel* 10]), Wagner dominates Morse's listening hours in later novels as well (*Way* 273, for example). In addition, Morse is a man of letters. Though Housman is not quoted in *Last Bus*, Morse does allude to Coleridge, Wordsworth, and Hardy, and he keeps a copy of Fowler's *Modern English Usage* in his Kidlington office. Both Morse's concern for proper English and his familiarity with literature continue throughout the series; the first shows itself in his castigating *every* error in grammar or spelling he encounters, while the latter—handled more skillfully as the series progresses—develops into a tool which Dexter uses to flesh out Morse's character and to develop thematic issues.

The Morse of *Last Bus* also displays characteristics which are his own, not Dexter's, and which likewise continue in the later novels. Several of Morse's traits are considerably muted from what they will become later. While Morse enjoys drinking beer, he has not yet taken up his crusade for cask-conditioned "real" ale and is willing to buy drinks rather than expecting Lewis to pick up the tab. He can look at Kaye's mutilated body for "a few minutes" (11) whereas a brief glimpse of Philip Ogleby's body makes Morse feel "nausea rising in his gorge" (*World* 141), a reaction which becomes the norm in later novels. Other features are fully developed. One of the series's deliberate eccentricities is that Morse's first name is never given. While the same is true of Lewis's, it is Morse's forename that receives the most attention. In *Last Bus* Sue Widdowson's final words to

Morse are, "Inspector, you never did tell me your Christian name" (214); in *Service of All the Dead* his initial is revealed as E. (73); in *The Riddle of the Third Mile* Morse's friend Max guesses Eric or Ernie, but Morse refuses to be drawn (56-57). Second, in addition to his fondness for literature and music, Morse has a coarser side; his language is often vulgar, and he displays an appetite for pornography. In *Last Bus* he is disappointed when a search of Kaye's room turns up "not even a paragraph of pornography" (17); and at the end of *The Silent World of Nicholas Quinn*, he rewards Lewis with a trip to Studio 2 to view *The Nymphomaniac* (225). Third, Morse is irascible, impatient, and self-centered. His first official action in *Last Bus* is to bellow, "How the hell do I know" (12) at a hapless constable to whom he has given a vague order. Later he all but takes Lewis off the case for saying that Morse's solution is wrong; by the next day, Morse has forgotten about the damage he did and never thinks to apologize to Lewis (157-58, 164-68). The pattern repeats, sometimes more than once, in the other novels—usually with Lewis absorbing Morse's anger.

Key to Morse are two defining characteristics: what Dexter calls his "alpha-plus acumen" (Spurrier 319) and a loneliness so deep that Morse finds it almost impossible to establish significant relationships. Morse's intellect, which sees possibilities others never consider, makes him a brilliant detective. In *Last Bus* he has not yet acquired the almost mythic reputation he enjoys in, for example, *The Dead of Jericho* where he is called "a towering, if somewhat eccentric, genius" (126). But even in *Last Bus* Lewis—who has never worked with Morse before—knows him by reputation, as does Constable Dickson with whom he discusses Morse. And it is a rare reader who will solve a mystery before Morse. But this same brilliance contributes to Morse's isolation and, in *Last Bus*, seems its sole cause.

Throughout the series, Morse's besetting flaw is pride; in *Last Bus* this weakness is presented in a most uncompromising light. Morse seems a victim of the common Oxford disease of confusing expertise in one field with omniscience, finding it difficult to deal with those who do not think as he does or to modify his position. Morse's reconstruction of Kaye's murder is referred to as a "Grand Design"; and while the narrator uses playful imagery (referring to the tide of facts licking at the "sand-castles of Morse's Grand Design" [116]), there is nothing playful about Morse's anger when he is wrong or about his triumph when he reassembles the pieces in the correct order.

Even Morse's attempt to remedy his loneliness by establishing a relationship with Sue Widdowson fails to present him favorably. Much of the novel's punch comes from a single line—"Hello, Sue" (204)—from which readers learn the identity of Kaye's murderer. But the inexperienced Dexter has not given readers sufficient preparation for this grand climax. While Morse and Sue's relationship is not love at first sight, it belongs in the next closest category, lasting less than three weeks from beginning to end and encompassing no more than five meetings between Morse and Widdowson. In addition, the alleged depth of the relationship cannot be verified from the text; the most serious thing that Morse tells Sue is, "I find you so very beautiful and I wanted to be with you" (128), hardly enough for what Dexter is trying to erect upon its foundation. If readers were shown the love the two have for one another, or if Dexter had waited until a later novel when readers have learned more about Morse and developed greater empathy for him (and when Dexter's own story-telling ability had matured), this *coup de théâtre* might have succeeded. But despite repeated allusions to how much Morse has been affected by his discovery that Sue is the killer, Morse's account of how he reconstructed what had happened on the night of Kaye's death leaves readers wondering how much of his pain comes from his awareness of the mistakes he made in handling the investigation.

If in *Last Bus* Dexter placed too heavy an emotional burden on Morse, he did not make the same mistake with the most important part of his novels: the puzzle and its solution. Dexter readily voices his admiration for the plots of Agatha Christie, John Dickson Carr, and Ellery Queen (Interview), and has written, "I can't see [that my novels have] any useful function at all" (Campbell). His goal is simply "that people read one page and . . . turn to the next" (Campbell), and throughout all ten novels he has sought to achieve this goal through stories "with many a twist and many a turn, as well as . . . one almighty wallop of a surprise at the end" (quoted in Spurrier 319). No novel demonstrates this aspect of Dexter's art better than *Last Bus*; in addition, *Last Bus* provides a model of the process by which Morse solves the puzzle presented to him.

Even in his first novel Dexter commands the usual stock in trade of the mystery writer: innocent parties lie or suppress the truth in order to protect others from imagined danger; circumstances make separate crimes appear the work of one person; a seemingly innocent letter contains a coded message. Dexter even toys with the reader by including a subplot which is not simply a red herring but something akin to a red whale. It has no relevance to the case being investigated; but before the reader realizes this, Morse has solved the case, never needing to learn anything about the subplot. But what sets Dexter apart is his willingness to pile one trick upon another, upon a third, upon still more until, shortly before everything deconstructs, Morse makes the right connections and identifies the murderer. In addition, the word "unlikely" has no place in a Dexter novel; the one quality which, beyond all others, typifies his novels is coincidence.

Even in its basic premise *Last Bus* exemplifies both complexity and coincidence so fully that it is difficult to determine where one ends and the other begins. Kaye's death seems a textbook example of a rape-murder: she is wearing nothing but shoes, a brief miniskirt, and the torn remnants of a blouse; and a postmortem investigation reveals that she had engaged in sexual intercourse shortly before her death. In fact, Kaye was murdered after consensual sex; her clothing was removed and torn by John Sanders, who tells Morse that he "often had a dream about undressing the body of a dead girl" (197). The reasonable assumption that Kaye was the victim of a sex-killer complicates matters by sending the police down a deadend trail. But this result would be impossible were it not for at least four coincidences: Sanders is at the pub for a prearranged meeting with Kaye; he is attracted by necrophilia; he is the person to find her body; and he is able to undress Kaye's corpse without being observed.

Not *every* subsequent novel is as byzantine as *Last Bus*, but complexity and coincidence are the essence of all Dexter's plots: murder takes place in one location, the corpse is moved to another, and appearances are manipulated to give the appearance of suicide (*The Silent World of Nicholas Quinn*); a group of people conspire to commit a murder and agree on a story that provides each with an alibi (*Service of All the Dead*); twins take advantage of their physical resemblance to switch places (*The Riddle of the Third Mile*). Within each wheel are other wheels—a second murder in an attempt to prevent the solution of the earlier killing (*World*); the murder of a conspirator rather than of the pretended victim (*Service*); the discovery of a body successively identified as that of men who are then found dead (*Riddle*).

To solve the puzzles he creates, Dexter has given Morse a distinctive approach to problem-solving: an instinctive method, the opposite of anything in textbooks or in most mystery novels. As Dexter puts it, "logic sometimes . . . [holds] less sway in Morse's mind than feeling and impulse" (*Way* 170); and just as he solves crossword puzzles by "starting at the end—never the beginning" (*Jewel* 180), Morse approaches mystery-solving not by working inductively from clues but by formulating a theory and then locating evidence to support it. Inevitably this leads to a wrong turn or, in Lewis's words, to Morse's being "six or so furlongs ahead of the field only later to find himself running on the wrong racecourse" (*Way* 189). But, just as inevitably, Morse—with Lewis as innocent catalyst —is "able to extricate himself from the straitjacketing circumstances of any crime and to look at that crime from some exterior vantage point" (*Way* 183) from which the picture clicks into focus.

In *Last Bus* Morse's solution process is fully developed; and through Dexter's comments and access to Morse's thoughts, readers receive a commentary upon what Morse is doing, at least in the earliest stages of his investigation. Four days after Kaye's murder, Morse realizes how little progress has been made on the case. Yet, at the same time, he senses "in some intuitive way . . . that he was vaguely on the right track" (62). Morse had missed the track because he had "made the mistake of concentrating upon individual mistakes and not even bothering to see the . . . whole" (52-3). Later, he sells himself on a new initiative:

I am formulating a hypothesis, that is, a supposition, a proposition, however wild, assumed for the sake of argument; a theory to be proved . . . by reference to facts, and it is with facts and with airy-fairy fancies that I shall endeavour to bolster my hypothesis. *Im Anfang war die Hypothese* [in the beginning was the hypothesis], as Goethe might have put it. (83)

Morse holds to his method throughout, and the breakthrough comes when Lewis points out the blindingly obvious—that people other than garage mechanics can change a flat tire—and Morse exclaims, "You're a genius, sergeant" (138). Even when his "Grand Design" collapses, apparently for good, Morse's response is to keep its broad outline and rearrange its parts until—aided by a coincidence which in any other context would be called "outrageous"—the last piece falls into place.

Dexter is too good a craftsman to lock himself into a formula; so even though this method of solution has become a signature of the series, Dexter has created many variations. For example, in *The Silent World of Nicholas Quinn*, Morse has the wrong man arrested, and only after a second illumination leaves his body tingling (a sure sign of success) does he see things as they truly are; in *The Secret of Annexe 3* Morse arrests, releases, then rearrests the same man. But the basic pattern is present even in the most recent novels. In *The Wench Is Dead*, Lewis's reminiscing about his mother's measuring his height by placing marks on the wall of their kitchen triggers things for Morse; and in *The Jewel That Was Ours*, Lewis's reading aloud a story from the *Oxford Times* about a traffic accident having no relationship to the case at hand sends "the old tingle of high excitement thrilling strangely across . . . [Morse's] shoulders" (224).

Some of Dexter's recent success can be attributed to more skillful handling of formulas, like the one just described, whose key elements are present as early as *Last Bus*. However, *The Wench is Dead* and *The Way Through the Woods*—and to a lesser degree *The Jewel That Was Ours*—display qualities absent from Dexter's first novel and present only occasionally in its six immediate successors. For one thing, Dexter has progressively increased the humor in the novels. *Last Bus* is almost unrelievedly serious, reminiscent of the many Golden Age novels which treat their puzzles with the awe usually reserved for real-life matters of life and death. It is possible to produce a cruel laugh at Dexter's description of Morse's falling from a ladder like "Hephaestus, thrown o'er the crystal battlements" (79) and injuring his right foot. But less sardonic laughter occurs only once: when Lewis mimics the overly cautious speech of a pompous physician and—in "an isolated moment of levity in the grim last days of the case"—asks Morse, "Did he er did he er er" (173), never completing his thought.

In later novels the mood is lighter, in part because of what has become a characteristic device, beginning each chapter with a headnote—usually a quotation, taken from sources ranging from Shakespeare to "Directions for applying a beauty mask" (*Last Seen* 25).[3] Sometimes Dexter uses these epigraphs seriously, prefacing the "Epilogue" of *Last Seen* with, "There are tears of things and mortal matters touch the heart" (*Aeneid* I). But far more often, even in this early novel, he laughs at himself, selecting a quotation from *The Mikado* as the epigraph of Chapter 26, "Merely corroborative detail, to add artistic verisimilitude to an otherwise bald and unconvincing narrative," or at a character, using "An ill-favoured thing, sir, but mine own" (*As You Like It*) to begin chapter 28 in which Lewis presents his solution.

In addition, Dexter has moved away from the tight format of *Last Bus*, in which virtually every part of every episode develops either the mystery plot or the relationship between Morse and Sue. It is impossible to draw a smooth curve tracing these changes or even to say that a particular novel marks the turning point. (The decision would be easier had Dexter written *The Secret of Annexe 3* before rather than after *The Riddle of the Third Mile*.) Scenes set in The Penthouse, a Soho strip club, devote more attention to the performance than is necessary to advance the plot of *Last Seen*, in which Dexter includes three paragraphs of his own musings about gambling (137-38). But except for the brief scene at the end when Morse takes Lewis to see a blue movie (225), the next novel, *The Silent World of Nicholas Quinn*, reverts to the style of *Last Bus*. Nonetheless, particularly in the three most recent novels, Dexter has told his stories in a more relaxed manner, including sections not germane to either the crime or the romance plots and giving himself the opportunity to reserve a serious tone for serious topics and to use a contrast in style to emphasize a change of content. For example, in *The Way Through the Woods*, Morse is not put in charge of the search for Karin Eriksson until one-third of the way through the novel; and a large share of what takes place earlier is good story-telling for its own sake. Similarly, the account of Max's death and its effect on Morse (most of chapters 31 to 33) adds a note of seriousness and reveals a new side of the Chief Inspector's character.

While even the most recent of Dexter's novels place primary emphasis upon plot,[4] fuller characterization of his protagonists is another distinctive feature of his recent novels. Though Lewis is far from a Nigel Bruce type of second banana, he is a simple man, perhaps even "stolid," as Morse once categorizes him (*Riddle* 61). Dexter has wisely not tampered with the integrity of his creation; Lewis's still waters run no deeper in the most recent novels than in *Last Bus*. But Dexter has explored more fully the Lewis half of the Morse-Lewis partnership. As early as *The Secret of Annexe 3* Lewis's wife marvels "at the way in which Chief Inspector Morse could . . . have such a beneficent effect upon the man she'd married" (*Secret* 98). Lewis is slower to come to terms with the issue. Even in *The Wench Is Dead* he can assure a constable, "Nobody knows him

[Morse] all *that* well" (107); and in *The Jewel That Was Ours* he finds himself wondering if he really does enjoy working with Morse. But in the course of *Jewel* Lewis recognizes that he is "never happier than when watching Morse come face to face with a mystery" (113), in part because of his admiration for Morse's artistry but to a greater degree because he knows that he has become an irreplaceable part of a team and, as he tells his wife later, Morse "sort of—*lifts* me a bit" (*Way* 199).

While no one will confuse Dexter's characterization of Morse with the work of P. D. James or Ruth Rendell, Dexter has fleshed out Morse's portrait as well. The largest infusion of information comes in *The Riddle of the Third Mile*, where readers are told of a failed love affair that led to Morse's leaving Oxford without a degree. More recent novels have added nothing major to Morse's biography, but have portrayed a Morse somewhat more aware of other people and their needs than in *Last Bus* and other early novels. Following a serious illness, the Morse of *The Wench Is Dead* acknowledges—albeit only to himself—that Superintendent Strange acted with kindness by phoning Morse after his release from the hospital (150); and he can say "simply and quietly" to Lewis, "I shall feel a jolly sight better once I've had the chance of apologising to you—for being so bloody ungrateful. . . . I'm just sorry, that's all" (90).

In *The Way Through the Woods* Morse becomes involved in his most serious relationship with a woman. In the first nine novels, Morse's self-centered reserve allows him only a handful of opportunities to move beyond unsatisfied lust and only one encounter (with Ruth Rawlinson in *Service of All the Dead*) based on anything like mutual trust, respect, and openness. Morse's relationship with Claire Osborne in *The Way Through the Woods* is far from perfect. His attempt to take Laura Hobson to bed fails only because she insists that if "there *ever is* going to be anything between us, Chief Inspector, it'll have to be when we're borth [sic] a bit more sorber [sic]," giving Morse more than the benefit of the doubt by adding, "I think *you*'d prefer it that way too" (274). Morse is almost as inept in dealing with Claire. While she and Morse are strongly attracted to one another, she finds herself forced to tell him: "You write to me as if you think I'm an ignorant little schoolgirl. . . . You quote these poets as if you think you're connected on some direct personal line with them all. Well you're wrong. There's hundreds of extensions. . . ." before concluding, "Dare I send you a little of my love?" (110).

Claire's advice does little good; the next time she and Morse talk, he moves from bad to worse by mixing police business with something she has told him privately. Claire responds, "Don't you realize I'd have swapped all the lecherous sods I've ever had for you—and instead of trying to understand all you ask me—Christ!—is who fathered [my daughter]—" (149). Claire does not let Morse reply directly; but later in a note accompanying a cassette of *Tuba Mirum Spargens Sonum*, he tells her, "I enjoyed so much our foreshortened time together, you and the music. . . . The *Recordare* is my favourite bit—if I'm pushed to a choice. 'Recordare' by the way is the 2nd person singular of the present imperative of the verb 'recordor': it means 'Remember!'" (255). Morse has never opened himself up more than this, and at present is probably unable to be more honest. But he and Claire have connected at some non-hormonal level; and near the end of the novel, his plan to resume his holiday by traveling to Salisbury (Claire's home) is preempted when Claire appears at his flat and replies to his question, "What time will you have to go, my love?" with "Who said anything about going, Chief Inspector?" (294).[5]

Dexter has also given the criminals of his two most recent novels more humanity than their earlier counterparts, using them to allow readers to see more deeply into Morse and through him explore serious issues. Sue Widdowson of *Last Bus* is a pleasant person and murdered Kaye out of passion, not premeditation. But she seems unaffected by her action while, amazingly, worrying about whether/how to break off her engagement in order to further her relationship with Morse. Dexter's other murderers are little more than monsters. They kill for the basest of motives; plan their crimes carefully, sometimes waiting months or years until conditions are right; and carry them out in ways calculated to cast suspicion upon others. Thus, it is impossible not to believe that society will be safer with individuals like Harry Jacobs (*Service of All the Dead*) and Charles Richards (*The Dead of Jericho*) dead or in prison.

The Jewel That Was Ours and *The Way Through the Woods* suggest the emergence of a new pattern. In *Jewel* Theodore Kemp's death results from a blow struck in anger by Janet or Phil Aldrich, whose only child died in a car accident for which Kemp was responsible. No attempt is made to whitewash the Aldriches' "implacable hatred, and . . . lust for . . . retribution" (268). But both Morse and Strange are struck by the enormity of the Aldriches' loss and comment on their courage and resourcefulness, not their orchestrating the confrontation which led to Kemp's death or their concealing the truth from the police. Morse and Strange are united as well in their respect for the courage of Kemp's wife, Marion; deprived of her unborn child and crippled in the automobile accident in which the Aldriches' daughter was killed, she had witnessed her husband's death and then waited alone for Eddie Stratton to come to her house hours later and carry away his corpse. Again, no excuses are provided for Marion's complicity, and her suicide represents a harsher retribution than what society would have exacted; but the two men's empathy is undeniable. Moreover, Morse—who most unusually blames himself for not having talked with her after her husband's death—penetrates further, seeing into "the abyss of Marion's despair" (270) and recognizing that her suicide resulted not from remorse but from the emptiness of knowing that her constant suffering could no longer be offset by her hatred for her husband.

The Way Through the Woods probes deeper. The novel opens with an account of an unnamed penitent's confession to a priest in which the person expresses a desire to be reported to the police and a fear of "repeat[ing] . . . [the] sin" (3-5). As soon becomes clear, the penitent is the murderer whom Morse is seeking; and though the killer's identity eludes Morse until late in the novel, her actions are consistent with her confession and take on added meaning (at least in retrospect, for few readers will identify her before Morse) when viewed in terms of what she says to the priest.

In addition, *Way* gives the reader Dexter's most thorough examination yet of Good and Evil. Morse feels "almost a bond" (265) between himself and Karin Eriksson and is near tears when she is placed under arrest. Later, from the statement she gives the police, he learns of "her fear that her lack of contrition at having killed . . . was almost a greater sin than the killing itself had been; [and] her fear that she might kill again, kill wildly and regardlessly if anyone came to threaten her own and David's [her husband's] happiness" (272). Morse is, in fact, so affected by his understanding of Karin that he asks himself questions about how abstractions like Law and Justice relate to particular people, serious questions he has asked himself only once before: when he arrested the Aldriches. This time, Morse's understanding of the criminal's mind takes him still further: to the solution of a second murder in which Karin was involved and to a discussion with Strange that is unlike anything else in the series.

[Morse:] She's a complex woman, as I say, sir. . . .

[Strange:] Perhaps she's a bit of a mystery even to herself. . . .

[Morse:] Same thing in most cases, isn't it? We never really understand people's motives. In all these things it's as if there's a manifestation—but there's always a bit of a mystery too.

[Strange:] Now don't you start going all religious on *me*, Morse!

[Morse:] No chance of that. (290)

Once again, no one will mistake this for a passage from P. D. James or Ruth Rendell, but it is difficult to see how Dexter could do more without making a fundamental change in the type of novel he writes—something he affirms he is not going to do (Interview).

One final feature accounts for the gap between Dexter's two Gold Dagger winners and his other novels: a shift in narrative strategy. In all ten novels Dexter uses an omniscient third-person narrator. In *Last Bus*, he tells his story in strict chronological order; in fact, in all the novels before *The Wench Is Dead* the narrator does nothing more exciting than provide an occasional flashback (like the one which begins *Last Seen Wearing*) and make wry comments about upcoming events. Dexter supplements the narrator with little more than a map (*The Dead of Jericho*), the left half of a typewritten document whose right half Morse reconstructs (*The Riddle of the Third Mile*), and the chapter headings already mentioned. While this narrator continues to do the bulk of the work in the most recent novels, Dexter enriches his story-telling through masterful use of an interpolated narrative (*The Wench Is Dead*) and documents ostensibly written by a variety of people (*The Jewel That Was Ours* and, more importantly, *The Way Through the Woods*).

Before *The Wench Is Dead* Dexter's only significant experiment with a second narrator had come in *The Riddle of the Third Mile* when Dr. O. M. A. Browne-Smith writes Morse a chapter-long letter claiming responsibility for the murder Morse is investigating and pitting his own cleverness against the Chief Inspector's (124-29). The letter is brilliant, capturing in its style everything the rest of the novel tells us about the personality of Morse's former tutor and providing Morse most of the material he uses later in a psychological analysis of Browne-Smith—the first to appear in the series.

The Wench Is Dead goes much farther. In the dedication, Dexter writes, "For Harry Judge, lover of canals, who introduced me to *The Murder of Christine* [sic] *Collins*, a fascinating account of an early

Victorian murder, by John Godwin." Using Godwin's real book as his basis, Dexter invents *Murder on the Oxford Canal* by Wilfrid M. Deniston and gets the book into Morse's hands while he convalesces following a stomach hemorrhage. Morse finds Deniston's style "pretentious . . . a bit too high-flown" (42); but his story is riveting, and he tells it skillfully. After he reads the first chapter, Morse is so filled with questions and speculations that when he next has the chance to read he sets aside *The Blue Ticket* (a pornographic novel) and, not surprisingly, *Scales of Injustice*, a study of crime in Shropshire from 1842 until 1852, and turns to *Murder on the Oxford Canal*.

As Morse reads the rest of Deniston's book, he questions more of the details Deniston supplies about the murder of canal-boat passenger Joanna Franks in 1859 and the arrest, trial, and conviction of three of the boat's crew. Unable to leave the hospital, Morse drafts Lewis and Christine Greenway (whose father is recuperating in the same ward as Morse) to gather information. As he learns more, Morse—in typical fashion—develops a hypothesis which turns the accepted version upside down, reconstructing events based on the premise that the crewmen were telling the truth when they maintained that they had not done anything to Franks. Once Morse is released from the hospital, he amazes even Lewis by "galloping ahead of the Hunt, chasing (as Lewis was fairly certain) after some imaginary fox of his own" (151). Morse eventually becomes as certain as circumstantial evidence permits him to be that his reconstruction is correct: Joanna Franks and her husband, F.T. Donavan, faked both his and her deaths to collect on life insurance policies and allowed the innocent crewmen to be convicted.

Though the reader knows that this puzzle can be of nothing more than academic interest, its mystery is no less absorbing than the ones Morse addresses professionally. Dexter also tells the story exceedingly well, furnishing what seems the final proof of Morse's theory only to provide still more definite evidence in the last sentence of the novel. Nonetheless, Deniston's narrative plays a major role. First, since Morse is not on duty, the narrative has to interest him and the reader; Deniston's first chapter succeeds, for example, in part because Dexter has filled it with echoes of Gray's "Elegy Written in a Country Churchyard." In addition, Deniston's familiarity with his topic leads him to omit information which Morse and the reader demand and wait impatiently for. Finally, Deniston serves as a foil for Morse in a way that Lewis cannot. Despite Deniston's developing sympathy for the boatmen, he is more upset by the way the citizens of Oxford treat the condemned men than suspicious of the process which led to their condemnation. He is not the sort to question British justice and, as a layman suffering "from a lack of imagination" (83), misses things which attract Morse's attention as they would any competent policeman's. And it is Deniston's inability to supply anything except the authorized version that turns what could have been the equivalent of another crossword puzzle into an attempt to protect "a fundamental principle, not only of substantive law, but of natural justice" (126).

The Way Through the Woods is Dexter's most innovative narrative. Morse does not take up the search for the missing Karin Eriksson until the twenty-third chapter. During the previous chapters (many devoted not to the mystery but to Morse's vacation in Lyme Regis, his exploration of the local area, and his encounters with Claire Osborne) Dexter alternates accounts of Morse with sections devoted to Osborne, excerpts from the diary of an unnamed don, three stories in and four letters to *The Times*, reports of several episodes of police activity in Oxford, a summary of the facts relating to Eriksson's disappearance and the early stages of the investigation in which Morse played a minor role, two letters to the Oxford police, and a postcard from Morse to Lewis. The structure of the rest of the novel is less spectacular. Except when more than one investigation is taking place at the same time, the story is told in chronological order; however, articles and letters from *The Times*, along with some in *The Oxford Mail*, continue to play important roles.[6]

In fact, a letter to *The Times* triggers the action of *Way*. On July 9, 1991, Eriksson was classified a "missing person." Morse had not figured in the investigation except for spending a few hours with the officer in charge, raising a few questions, and suggesting that the search for Karin's body be moved to Wytham Woods. No sign of Karin—living or dead—was found; and by late June 1992 the police are no longer actively looking for her. Then a mysterious poem about a "Swedish maiden" arrives on the desk of the Chief Constable (41), followed by a brief note, *"Why are you doing nothing about my letter? Karin Eriksson"* (42). With Morse on vacation, Strange suggests that the poem and a request for help be sent to *The Times*, which on July 3 prints the poem and assigns its literary correspondent, Howard Phillipson, the task of solving the riddles set by the poem and determining its connection with Karin.

Phillipson's analysis—very much in its own idiom—appears in the July 6 issue of *The Times*. On July 9, *The Times* prints an independent analysis by Professor (Emeritus) René Gray, and on July 11 publishes two more commentaries on the poem. Even the briefest of these has its own voice, and each represents a type of person one can imagine writing *The Times*; their explanations vary widely but prepare readers for the breakthrough furnished in a July 13 letter from Lionel Regis of Salisbury, pointing out that the word *wytham* appears in anagrammatized form in each of the poem's five stanzas. Since Morse's postcard to Lewis states, "I reckon *I* know what the poem means!" (65), it comes as no surprise that Morse has used a pen name to provide what is by far the most convincing explanation of the poem and to affirm, in as obliquely offensive a way as possible, that he has been right all along. "Regis's (Morse's) cracking of the Swedish Maiden verses . . . [sparks] off a whole series of letters about the Great Wood at Wytham" (101); some of them have little to offer, but Dexter gives each writer an individual voice. The fun reaches its peak when the reader figures out (or is told) that Morse wrote the poem in order to reopen the investigation and be placed in charge of it. But once this final rabbit is out of the hat, careful readers will recognize that Dexter has also been playing with the whole process of literary criticism.

Morse composed his poem to be mysterious enough to convince readers that it is intended to solve a mystery and to accommodate the five anagrams of *wytham*. Some of the readings provided by others are patently ridiculous, and Dexter must have chuckled as he worked them up. But the letter which relates the poem's "Find the woodman's daughter" (31) to John Everett Millais's painting *The Woodman's Daughter* and reminds readers that Millais painted "the background of his picture from nature in *Wytham Wood*" (101) explores an allusion which Morse probably did not intend but which is still plausible.

A study of *Last Bus to Woodstock* does much to clarify the nature of Dexter's achievement between 1975 and 1986. Even if one adds considerable salt to Dexter's claim that he used to do his writing after listening to The Archers and before going out for a pint of beer (Sanderson 13), *Last Bus* sounds the theme on which the next six novels are variations: ingenious plots and a basic formula which entertains brilliantly but stops short of real complexity. But in 1975 only the most optimistic readers would have extrapolated from *Last*

Bus to The Wench Is Dead and The Way Through the Woods. Since he retired from full-time employment in 1988, Dexter has perfected his art—sacrificing nothing on the mystery side while providing fuller pictures of his characters, introducing themes of real import, and devising narrative strategies which enhance his plots' hold upon readers. Speculation about the future direction of a series as dynamic as Dexter's is unlikely to produce good results, but this very dynamism suggests that Dexter will not be content with the status quo, not even the status quo of The Wench Is Dead and The Way Through the Woods. Browning, rather than Morse's favorites Hardy and Housman, sounds the right note: "The best is yet to be."

Notes

1. Dexter has also received Silver Daggers (given to the second best novel of the year) for Service of All the Dead and The Dead of Jericho.

2. Those who encounter Morse and Lewis on television before reading Last Bus will be surprised that Morse and Lewis do not resemble John Thaw and Kevin Whatley, who portray them in the television films. When Morse first appears in Last Bus, he is described as a "lightly-built, dark-haired man" (10) conscious that his hair is thinning (24); Lewis is several years older (63) and more rugged than Morse—the latter characteristic made explicit in later novels, which reveal that Lewis was light middleweight boxing champion while in the army. The contrast with the heavy-set, white-haired Thaw and the slender Whatley, clearly Thaw's junior by a number of years, could hardly be starker. Television viewers will also be surprised that Morse drives a Lancia, not a Jaguar, and continues to do so until The Jewel That Was Ours. However, in the omnibus editions—in which several novels are reprinted in one volume—Dexter has followed the films' lead and replaced the Lancia with a Jaguar (Interview).

3. Dexter first used headnotes in his second novel, Last Seen Wearing; he did not include headnotes in his third and fourth novels (The Silent World of Nicholas Quinn and Service of All the Dead), instead dividing these novels into sections with titles like "Why?" and "Who?" (Silent World) and "The First Book of Chronicles" (Service). Headnotes appear in all the later novels, but in The Riddle of the Third Mile Dexter draws on a technique familiar to readers of 18th- and 19th-century novels by supplying his own commentary on each chapter (e.g., "A brief interlude in which Sergeant Lewis takes his first steps into the Examination Schools, the Moloch of Oxford's testing apparatus" [72]).

4. In *The Way Through the Woods* Dexter plants a major clue on the second page. (Never has he placed one earlier.) So polished is his technique that I noticed this clue—one which now seems to beat me over the head every time I look at it—only after Dexter gleefully pointed it out to me as "something no one seems to have cottoned to" (Interview).

5. The woman's name is not given. If Laura Hobson, not Claire Osborne, is Morse's visitor, my argument collapses. Dexter deliberately omitted the woman's name, but the fact that Morse is listening to Mozart is meant as a clue that it is Claire who has come to see Morse (Interview).

6. Dexter also uses documents, some of them handwritten, by a variety of people in *The Jewel That Was Ours*, but his main goal in this novel appears to have been to develop a new solution for the "original storyline" which serves as the basis for *The Wolvercote Tongue*, the first television film not adapted from a novel, which was shown in Britain four years before the publication of the novel. Dexter obviously had a great deal of fun with some of these texts—particularly a letter containing nothing whatsoever of importance to the plot from "Miss Ginger Bonnetti (not 'Ginger,' but christened Ginger) . . . to her married sister living in Los Angeles, one Mrs. Georgie (as christened!) Bonnetti, who had married a man named Angelo Bonnetti" (72). Their main purpose, however, is plot-oriented. Morse obtains important information from crossed out words and phrases in one message; the others accustom readers to the presence of handwritten passages and help to divert their attention from the one that matters.

Works Cited

Benstock, Bernard. "Colin Dexter." *British Mystery and Thriller Writers Since 1940, First Series.* Ed. Bernard Benstock and Thomas F. Staley. Detroit: Gale, 1989. 55-64.

Callendar, Newgate. Rev. of *The Riddle of the Third Mile. New York Times Book Review* 25 Sept. 1988: 50.

Campbell, Mary. "Mystery Writer: Actor Helping Sales of Novels." *The Holland Sentinel* [Holland, MI] 22 May 1993: C6.

Dexter, Colin. *The Dead of Jericho.* New York: Bantam, 1988.

____. *The Jewel That Was Ours.* London: Pan, 1992.

____. *Last Bus to Woodstock.* New York: Bantam, 1989.

____. *Last Seen Wearing.* New York: Bantam, 1989.

____. Personal interview, 11 Mar. 1994.

____. *The Riddle of the Third Mile.* New York: Bantam, 1988.

____. *The Secret of Annexe 3*. New York: Bantam, 1988.

____. *Service of All the Dead*. New York: Bantam, 1988.

____. *The Silent World of Nicholas Quinn*. New York: Bantam, 1988.

____. *The Way Through the Woods*. New York: Crown, 1992.

____. *The Wench Is Dead*. New York: Bantam, 1991.

Dexter, Colin, and Geoffrey Rayner. *Guide to Contemporary Politics*. Oxford: Pergamon, 1966.

____. *Liberal Studies: An Outline Course*. 2 vols. Oxford: Pergamon, 1964.

Godwin, John. *The Murder of Christina Collins on the Trent and Mersey Canal at Rugeley in 1839*. Stafford: Staffordshire County Library, 1981.

Last Bus to Woodstock. Writ. Michael Wilcox. Dir. Peter Duffell. Prod. Kenny McBain. *MYSTERY!* PBS. WGBH, Boston. 15, 22 Dec. 1988.

Promised Land. Writ. Julian Mitchell. Dir. John Madden. Prod. David Lascelles. *MYSTERY!* PBS. WGBH, Boston. 22, 29 Apr. 1993.

Sanderson, Mark. *The Making of Inspector Morse*. London: Macmillan, 1991.

Spurrier, Ralph. "Colin Dexter." *Twentieth-Century Crime and Mystery Writers*. 3rd ed. Ed. Lesley Henderson. Chicago: St. James, 1991.

The Wolvercote Tongue. Writ. Julian Mitchell. Dir. Alastair Reid. Prod. Kenny McBain. *MYSTERY!* PBS. WGBH, Boston. 15, 22 Dec. 1988.

Contributors

Landon Burns is Emeritus Professor of English at Pennsylvania State University and an active member of the Mystery and Detective Fiction Caucus of the Popular Culture Association. He publishes an annual cross-referenced index of short-fiction anthologies in *Studies in Short Fiction* and continues to have an interest in the short story as well as in historical and mystery fiction.

Mary Jean DeMarr is Professor of English at Indiana State University, where she teaches American literature, composition, and women's studies. A former American editor of the Modern Humanities Research Association's *Annual Bibliography of English Language and Literature*, she has published two books on contemporary American fiction about adolescents with her co-author Jane S. Bakerman. She publishes regularly on mystery and detective fiction in *Clues: A Journal of Detection* and on midwest American literature in *MidAmerica*.

George N. Dove is Emeritus Professor and Dean, East Tennessee State University. Former President of the Popular Culture Association, he is an active member of its Mystery and Detective Fiction Caucus and the namesake of its Dove Award, given for distinguished contributions to criticism of crime fiction. In addition to editing essays on mystery fiction, he has written three books: *The Police Procedural* (1982), *The Boys from Grover Avenue* (1985), and *Suspense in the Formula Story* (1989).

Mary P. Freier received her Ph.D. from the University of Illinois at Urbana-Champaign in 1984. Since then, she has taught at Indiana University East and is currently a tenured Associate Professor of English at Dakota State University in Madison, SD. She teaches American literature, composition, and interdisciplinary honors courses, as well as courses in two- and three-dimensional computer graphics. She has conducted research on American literature, in particular on the popular writings of women, especially Mary Jane

225

Holmes and Mary Roberts Rinehart. She has also presented papers on detective fiction.

Frederick Isaac is Head Librarian at the Jewish Community Library of San Francisco. A long-time member of the Popular Culture Association and its Mystery and Detective Fiction Caucus, he has written papers on numerous aspects of detective fiction, including immorality, railroads in mysteries, and such authors as Nicholas Freeling and Richard Lockridge. He has also contributed to many other Popular Press collections and has published articles on several Bay Area writers, including Bill Pronzini and Julie Smith.

Kathleen Gregory Klein is Professor of English at Southern Connecticut State University and the author of *The Woman Detective: Gender and Genre* (1988). An active participant in the Mystery and Detective Fiction Caucus of the Popular Culture Association, she has published widely in the field of crime fiction.

Marty S. Knepper is Professor and Chair of English at Morningside College in Sioux City, IA, where she teaches detective fiction, American popular culture, and British literature. She has written articles on Dick Francis, Dorothy L. Sayers, Amanda Cross, and Agatha Christie. In 1991-93 she served as President of the national Popular Culture Association.

Joan G. Kotker teaches English and crime fiction at Bellevue Community College in Bellevue, WA. She is an active member of the Popular Culture Association's Mystery and Detective Fiction Caucus and has had essays, articles, and reviews published in *The Armchair Detective*. She is currently working on a project that focuses on P.D. James' other detective, Cordelia Gray.

MaryKay Mahoney is Associate Professor at Merrimack College in North Andover, MA. She has contributed articles on detective fiction to *The Baker Street Journal* and *Kansas English* and has articles forthcoming on Nicholas Blake's novels and on the film adaptation of Patricia Highsmith's *Strangers on a Train*. She has also regularly presented papers on detective fiction at the national conferences of the Popular Culture Association.

Lois A. Marchino is Associate Professor of English and Director of Literature at the University of Texas at El Paso. She has published numerous articles and reviews of works by women authors, including several on women mystery writers and their female protagonists. "The Female Sleuth in Academe," with references to the Amanda Cross series featuring Professor Kate Fansler, appeared in the *Journal of Popular Culture*.

William Reynolds is Professor of English at Hope College in Holland, MI. In addition to articles on *Beowulf*, Chaucer, and other topics connected with Old English and Middle English literature, he has published numerous essays on detective fiction. While he has written on such recent and contemporary figures as Anthony Price, Marian Mainwaring, and Raymond Postgate, his principal interest is Golden Age British detective fiction, in particular Dorothy L. Sayers.

Sharon A. Russell is Professor of Communication at Indiana State University. She has published many articles on mystery fiction and on horror film and fiction and is currently editing a collection of essays on animals in mysteries.

Don Wall is Professor of English at Eastern Washington University; his specialties are 17th- and 18th-century British literature, crime fiction, true crime, and sports literature. He is past President of the Northern Pacific PCA and Vice President of PCA. He has published articles on crime fiction in various books and journals and presented papers at regional and national PCA meetings. His published fiction includes mystery stories and a young adult soccer novel.

Paula M. Woods received the B.A. from Illinois Wesleyan University, M.A. from the University of Illinois, and Ph.D. from the University of North Texas. Assistant Professor of English at Baylor University, Woods has presented conference papers on mystery/detective fiction and has published criticism in *Explorations in Renaissance Culture*.

,